## IS IT ANY WONDER

"[A] pleasing tale of lost love, forgiveness, and rekindled romance. . . . Walsh's wholesome plot weaves faith elements nicely as Louisa relies on her faith to make sure all is finally made well. Walsh will please her fans and surely gain new ones with this excellent inspirational."

**PUBLISHERS WEEKLY**

"A story of forgiveness, hope, and enduring ties that proves it's never too late for a second chance. . . . Courtney Walsh once again shines as a master storyteller."

**KRISTY WOODSON HARVEY,** *USA TODAY* **BESTSELLING AUTHOR OF** *FEELS LIKE FALLING*

"Courtney Walsh's books always capture my heart! I love her poignant plotlines, quaint, small-town settings, and the romance she skillfully weaves through the pages."

**BECKY WADE, AUTHOR OF** *STAY WITH ME*

## IF FOR ANY REASON

"Second chances and new discoveries abound in this lovely tale from Walsh, featuring a nostalgic romance set against the backdrop of Nantucket. . . . Readers of Irene Hannon will love this."

**PUBLISHERS WEEKLY**

"*If for Any Reason* is a 'double romance' novel, beautifully written, poignantly sad in parts, but full of hope throughout. It is altogether a lovely book, with a strong Christian message and a really good story, and I cannot recommend it highly enough."

**CHRISTIAN NOVEL REVIEW**

"Warm and inviting, *If for Any Reason* is a delightful read. I fell in love with these characters and with my time in Nantucket. Don't miss this one."

ROBIN LEE HATCHER, AWARD-WINNING AUTHOR OF *WHO I AM WITH YOU*

"*If for Any Reason* took me and my romance-loving heart on a poignant journey of hurt, hope, and second chances. . . . From tender moments to family drama to plenty of sparks, this is a story to be savored. Plus, that Nantucket setting—I need to plan a trip pronto!"

MELISSA TAGG, AWARD-WINNING AUTHOR OF *NOW AND THEN AND ALWAYS*

# JUST LET GO

"Walsh's charming narrative is an enjoyable blend of slice-of-life and small-town Americana that will please Christian readers looking for a sweet story of forgiveness."

*PUBLISHERS WEEKLY*

"Original, romantic, and emotional. Walsh doesn't just write the typical romance novel. . . . She makes you feel for all the characters, sometimes laughing and sometimes crying along with them."

*ROMANTIC TIMES*

"A charming story about discovering joy amid life's disappointments, *Just Let Go* is a delightful treat for Courtney Walsh's growing audience."

RACHEL HAUCK, *NEW YORK TIMES* BESTSELLING AUTHOR

"*Just Let Go* matches a winsome heroine with an unlikely hero in a romantic tale where opposites attract. . . . This is a page-turning, charming story about learning when to love and when to let go."

DENISE HUNTER, BESTSELLING AUTHOR OF *HONEYSUCKLE DREAMS*

"Just the kind of story I love! Small town, hunky skier, a woman with a dream, and love that triumphs through hardship. A sweet story of reconciliation and romance by a talented writer."

SUSAN MAY WARREN, *USA TODAY* BESTSELLING AUTHOR

# JUST LOOK UP

"[A] sweet, well-paced story. . . . Likable characters and the strong message of discovering what truly matters carry the story to a satisfying conclusion."

*PUBLISHERS WEEKLY*

"*Just Look Up* by Courtney Walsh is a compelling and consistently entertaining romance novel by a master of the genre."

MIDWEST BOOK REVIEW

"This novel features a deeply emotional journey, packaged in a sweet romance with a gentle faith thread that adds an organic richness to the story and its characters."

SERENA CHASE, *USA TODAY* HAPPY EVER AFTER BLOG

"In this beautiful story of disillusionment turned to healing, Walsh brings about a true transformation of restored friendships and love."

*CHRISTIAN MARKET* MAGAZINE

# CHANGE OF HEART

"Walsh has penned another endearing novel set in Loves Park, Colo. The emotions are occasionally raw but always truly real."

*ROMANTIC TIMES*

"*Change of Heart* is a beautifully written, enlightening, and tragic story. . . . This novel is a must-read for lovers of contemporary romance."

RADIANT LIT

# PAPER HEARTS

"Walsh pens a quaint, small-town love story . . . [with] enough plot twists to make this enjoyable to the end."
**PUBLISHERS WEEKLY**

"Be prepared to be swept away by this delightful romance about healing the heart, forgiveness, [and] following your dreams."
**FRESH FICTION**

"Courtney Walsh's . . . stories have never failed to delight me, with characters who become friends and charming settings that beckon as if you've lived there all your life."
**DEBORAH RANEY, AUTHOR OF THE CHICORY INN NOVELS SERIES**

"Delightfully romantic with a lovable cast of quirky characters, *Paper Hearts* will have readers smiling from ear to ear! Courtney Walsh has penned a winner!"
**KATIE GANSHERT, AWARD-WINNING AUTHOR OF *A BROKEN KIND OF BEAUTIFUL***

"*Paper Hearts* is as much a treat as the delicious coffee the heroine serves in her bookshop. . . . A poignant, wry, sweet, and utterly charming read."
**BECKY WADE, AUTHOR OF *MEANT TO BE MINE***

# WHAT MATTERS MOST

# ALSO BY COURTNEY WALSH

IS IT ANY WONDER

IF FOR ANY REASON

A MATCH MADE AT CHRISTMAS

JUST LOOK UP

JUST LET GO

JUST ONE KISS

JUST LIKE HOME

PAPER HEARTS

CHANGE OF HEART

THINGS LEFT UNSAID

HOMETOWN GIRL

A SWEETHAVEN SUMMER

A SWEETHAVEN HOMECOMING

A SWEETHAVEN CHRISTMAS

Courtney Walsh

*A Nantucket love story*

# What
# Matters
# Most

Tyndale House Publishers
Carol Stream, Illinois

Visit Tyndale online at tyndale.com.

Visit Courtney Walsh's website at courtneywalshwrites.com.

*Tyndale* and Tyndale's quill logo are registered trademarks of Tyndale House Ministries.

*What Matters Most*

Designed by Faceout Studio, Amanda Hudson

Edited by Kathryn S. Olson

Published in association with the literary agency of Natasha Kern Literary Agency, Inc., P.O. Box 1069, White Salmon, WA 98672.

*What Matters Most* is a work of fiction. Where real people, events, establishments, organizations, or locales appear, they are used fictitiously. All other elements of the novel are drawn from the author's imagination.

For information about special discounts for bulk purchases, please contact Tyndale House Publishers at csresponse@tyndale.com, or call 1-855-277-9400.

**Library of Congress Cataloging-in-Publication Data**

Names: Walsh, Courtney, date- author. | Olson, Kathryn S., editor.
Title: What matters most : a Nantucket love story / Courtney Walsh ; edited by Kathryn S. Olson.
Description: Carol Stream, Illinois : Tyndale House Publishers, [2022]
Identifiers: LCCN 2021021564 (print) | LCCN 2021021565 (ebook) | ISBN 9781496455086 (trade paperback) | ISBN 9781496455093 (kindle edition) | ISBN 9781496455109 (epub) | ISBN 9781496455116 (epub)
Subjects: GSAFD: Love stories.
Classification: LCC PS3623.A4455 W48 2022 (print) | LCC PS3623.A4455 (ebook) | DDC 813/.6—dc23
LC record available at https://lccn.loc.gov/2021021564
LC ebook record available at https://lccn.loc.gov/2021021565

Printed in the United States of America

28  27  26  25  24  23  22
7   6   5   4   3   2   1

For you, dear readers

# CHAPTER ONE

~ ~ ~

THE LIST STUCK TO THE REFRIGERATOR was meant to motivate Emma Woodson, but in that moment, it seemed only to taunt. She stared at the words she'd scribbled in a rare moment of bravery and struggled not to roll her eyes at her own naiveté.

*The Year of Emma.*

The idea had come to her one night two months ago when her best friend, Elise, had shown up uninvited to force her to celebrate a birthday she very much did not feel like celebrating.

Turning thirty wasn't something to celebrate, after all. Not for Emma.

But try telling that to Elise. She was not the kind of person who would let a milestone birthday go unnoticed, which was why she dragged Emma out to a Mexican restaurant and forced her to wear a giant sombrero all the way through to dessert.

"What are you doing, Em?" she'd asked her in a tone that suggested a loaded question.

"You mean besides trying to find a way to set this hat on fire without burning the restaurant down?"

"I mean with your life," Elise said.

Emma picked up her Coke and took a drink. "I'm surviving."

Barely.

"Don't you think it's time you stopped surviving?"

"And what, die?" Emma set her drink down. She knew what was coming, and she wasn't interested. She didn't want to hear about how she was wasting her life. Not today. She already knew—she didn't need the reminder.

"No," Elise said. "You're practically coding and you're calling that a life. Enough's enough already."

It was easy for Elise to say. Her life was nearly perfect. She'd married Teddy, the love of her life, at twenty-three, had a baby at twenty-five on her first try, another baby at twenty-seven, also on her first try, and now she stayed home with her kids in the big, beautiful home funded by her husband's new job in private security.

Elise didn't understand Emma's circumstances, no matter how empathetic she was.

Elise pulled a notebook out of her purse and wrote in block letters: *THE YEAR OF EMMA*. She turned it around and slid it across the table.

"What's this?"

"Tonight we declare that this is the year everything changes for you," Elise said. "And we're putting it in writing."

Emma frowned. "My life is fine."

But Elise's sardonic laugh told the truth. "Em, when was the last time you did something for yourself? Or something just for fun? You work in a job you hate. You hardly sleep. Most days I don't even think you eat. And you never smile anymore."

The waiter returned with fried ice cream, and Emma's memory drifted back to the last birthday she'd spent with Cam. He'd made her a three-layer strawberry cake from scratch. As he presented it to her, the top tier slid right off the plate and onto the floor. He'd been disappointed at first, but the whole adorable scene struck Emma as so funny it took her a solid three minutes to stop laughing.

Was that the last time she'd smiled?

Elise took a bite of ice cream. "So here's the deal. You make a list of all the things you want to do to remind yourself you're still alive. You've been avoiding living—you know that, right?"

Emma jabbed her spoon into the ice cream, crunching through the outside layer. "So you've said."

"Sorry," Elise said. "It's worth repeating."

"I'm doing the best I can." She took a bite and avoided Elise's gaze. Because they both knew it was a lie, and Elise wouldn't let it slide.

Now, as she stood in the kitchen of the small Nantucket cottage, surrounded by unpacked boxes, she scanned the list one last time before heading out the door.

*Find a job I actually like* was number five on the list, and today was the day she hoped to cross it off. She glanced at the clock, and a sudden wave of nausea rolled through her stomach. She'd been working as a waitress the last few years, but this job—in an actual art gallery, a reputable, high-end gallery—would give her a chance to work in the field she'd always wanted to work in. Before she let her dreams become a distant memory.

First, she had to make it to the interview on time.

"CJ?" she called out. "You ready?"

She walked into the living room, where her five-year-old son stood, looking out the window. "There's a man out there."

Emma came up behind CJ and followed his gaze to the sidewalk, where a man approached the house. He had a duffel slung over his shoulder. "Oh! Probably answering the ad." Bad timing. She'd have to give him a rush tour of the apartment if she was going to drop CJ at day care and make it to the interview on time.

"You ready?" She took her son's hand and pulled him toward the front door. She opened it and waved at the man on the sidewalk. "Hey there!"

He met her eyes and stopped moving.

"You must be here about the ad." She pulled CJ down the stairs and toward the sidewalk. "I'm actually relieved. I was starting to think nobody was going to respond to it." She gave him a once-over. He was probably a year or two older than she was and rugged-looking, like Bear Grylls but with disobedient hair, the kind of disheveled that said, *I'm not trying very hard.*

It suited him. Emma had no interest in dating, but if she did, he would've probably been the kind of guy that would've captured her attention.

His bright hazel eyes alone seemed worth exploring.

"I'm kind of in a hurry." She forced herself to maintain her composure. "But I can run you up there quick to take a look?"

He almost appeared confused for a second. He glanced at CJ, who was staring at him—this stranger—and then back at Emma. "Okay."

"CJ, go sit on the porch, okay? We'll leave in just a minute."

Her son did as he was told. Emma took her keys from her bag and motioned for the man to follow her.

"The apartment is above the garage," she said. "It's nothing fancy, and it needs some work, but I suppose that's where you'd come in." She didn't look at him, but she knew he was following close behind as they walked up the steps to the apartment. Cam's apartment. He'd spent his summers in the cottage with his grandparents when he was a kid, and when he got older, they converted it into his space.

He'd always talked about turning it into a rental. It had been a dream, really. He said it would be a good extra income, but Emma had always suspected it was more than that. Cam wanted to share Nantucket with as many people as he could.

When she opened that door, the memory of her late husband would be waiting for her.

She'd had most of Cam's things shipped here after he died—it had always been her plan to move here once she was back on her feet. She just didn't expect that it would take five years, which was how long Cam's belongings had been sitting here.

Still in boxes. She couldn't bear to face it then, and she was pretty sure she wouldn't be able to face it now.

"I hope you have a good imagination." She stuck the key in the lock and glanced over her shoulder at the man. "It's a work in progress."

She pushed open the door, struck by the musty smell of an abandoned space that had been locked up and forgotten about, which was exactly what it was.

She really should've assessed the state of the apartment before placing that ad, but she hadn't found the courage. Now she took a step inside. A label on the box in the corner drew her attention. *Cam's stuff* was written in bold black marker in his handwriting. She hadn't seen his handwriting in so long.

The sight of it sent her pulse racing. She flipped the light on and looked at the man. "You can look around. I'll just wait outside."

She stepped out onto the deck and forced herself to breathe.

*Calm down, Emma.* She spotted CJ rolling a truck down the length of the porch. "I know it looks bad," she called through the doorway. "But that's why the rent is included. I figured I can't really pay much for someone to clean it out and get it ready for renters, but I can offer a free place to stay. It just might take a day or two to make it livable."

The man reappeared in the doorway. "So the rent's included?"

She frowned. Hadn't he read the ad? "Yes. In exchange for cleaning out the apartment and getting it ready to rent. I've got a list of things that need to be done—painting, cleaning, repairs. It's mostly cosmetic, but who knows what you'll find once you start?"

Truthfully, she'd made that list based on assumptions. She had no idea the condition of Cam's apartment.

"Okay," he said.

"Okay, you'll do it?"

He shoved his hands in the pockets of his jeans and studied her for a beat longer than she expected. She looked away.

"Yeah, I'll do it."

She turned to him and smiled. "Oh, good. Honestly, I was getting worried. I placed the ad two weeks ago, and nobody's even been by to look at it." Did she sound as desperate as she felt?

"Don't you need some references?" he asked. "Or at least my name?"

He was almost smiling. He was handsome. Maybe a little too handsome, with sandy-colored hair on the dark side of blond. A few days of growth on his face—he wore it well. Cam's face was always clean-shaven, and his hair was always military short.

"Ma'am?"

She realized she hadn't answered his question. That he was still considering taking this job was something of a miracle. "Sorry. Yes, I should probably get both. Your name and your references."

"Jameson Shaw." He extended his hand toward her, and she took it. "But most people call me Jamie."

She looked down at his hand, wrapped around her own. It was nothing, just a handshake, and yet she was so keenly aware of his touch it felt like something more. "Emma Woodson." She pulled her hand from his and pressed her palm against her leg.

"Can I drop my references off to you later? I don't have them on me."

"Of course," she said, though it was slightly irresponsible of him to apply for a job with no references. The thought reminded her that she had a job interview of her own, and if she didn't hurry, she'd be the irresponsible one. "I'm sorry. I really should get going. You can stop back later this evening with your references if that works for you?"

He started to say something but seemed to change his mind as the words were coming out of his mouth. "I'll be sure to do that."

# CHAPTER TWO

~~~

WELL, THAT DIDN'T GO THE WAY HE'D PLANNED.

Jamie watched as Emma drove off, her son strapped safely in the back seat of her Nissan. He hadn't counted on the boy. Or rather, he hadn't counted on how seeing the boy would affect him.

He'd determined how this would go before he ever boarded the ferry for Nantucket. He'd show up, leave the letter, and go. He wouldn't have to actually *talk* to her.

But then the door to her cottage opened and she appeared on the porch, and he froze. He'd underestimated the way it would feel to see her in real life. He'd overestimated his ability to stay detached.

He also hadn't accounted for *her*. Long, dark, wavy hair. Tall, but not as tall as him. Blue eyes that locked on and held you there. Her beauty wasn't flashy, but it was undeniable.

Then she started talking, and she was in a hurry—late for something—and while he should've cut her off and explained that he had no idea about an ad or an apartment or anything else she was saying, he couldn't bring himself to do it. Because she wasn't just a name anymore—she was a real-life person.

And seeing her stunned him silent. He hadn't counted on that either.

She was nothing like he'd imagined. She was a beautiful, young, vibrant woman who talked fast and didn't let him get a word in edgewise. Pain welled up inside him the moment he saw her. He had so much to say, and yet there were no words.

*Coward.*

He reached into his back pocket for the envelope he'd intended to leave in Emma's mailbox. Still safe. Not going anywhere. He'd find the right time to give it to her. After he helped her out—she'd seemed a little desperate. Didn't he owe her at least that much?

The room above her two-car garage was stacked full of unpacked boxes. It looked like a storage unit or a staging area for a big garage sale.

Emma seemed spooked by it. She wanted it cleared out, and he could help. He could do that. Finally something he could *do*. No more talking about it—a tangible way to help. It was what he needed.

His phone buzzed. He set his bag down and pulled it from his pocket. Hillary's photo lit up his screen. His older sister had practically forbidden him from taking this trip—he could only imagine the earful he'd get if he answered. Still, it would be nothing compared to the earful he'd get if he didn't.

"Hey, Hill."

"Jameson." She only called him Jameson when she was irritated with him.

He could practically see her standing in her kitchen, toddler on her hip, making lunches for her other kids.

"Tell me you're on the way back home."

Home wasn't calling his name. After five years in a studio apartment in an upscale Chicago suburb, Jamie was due for a change of scenery. He used to travel every week for work, but after that last assignment, he'd settled in for a different kind of life.

Hillary said if that was his way of punishing himself—forbidding creative expression—it was stupid. But Hillary didn't know everything.

At least that's what he told himself.

"I'm still here," he said, aware of what was coming next.

"Jamie."

"Hillary."

"You need to get home. You know Dr. McDonald didn't mean for you to go there in person."

"I'm fine," he said. "I think this is exactly what I needed to do." Besides, it wasn't the first time he'd delivered a letter. It had gone well the last time. Never mind that the last time didn't involve a beautiful young widow he was desperate to help.

He'd keep that to himself—no sense giving his sister the chance to point out he was a fool to try to be her knight in shining armor.

He heard Hillary sigh over the line. "This is a mistake," she said.

"I don't think so." The truth was, he didn't know. It might be. It might be a giant disaster of a mistake.

"You should've mailed the letter," Hillary said. "You didn't have to take a trip all the way out there. You're just dredging up the past—what if she's moved on?"

"Then I'll know," he said. *Then maybe I'll be able to sleep at night.*

"Henry, do not put your sister's hand in the toilet!" Hillary yelled into the phone.

"It sounds like you're busy," Jamie said. "We'll catch up later."

"Jamie, no—"

But he hung up. He knew Hillary's thoughts on his being in Nantucket. They didn't need to rehash it. He was here, and he was going to stay and help Emma.

And once he'd helped her, he'd tell her the truth.

It was the least he could do.

~

Gallery 316 was nestled in the Nantucket historical district, one of many storefronts that attracted visitors from all over the world. Emma understood why Cam loved it here. For him, it was a place of respite and nostalgia. She hoped that's what it would be for her and CJ too.

Their second chance. *Her* second chance.

Not that she thought she deserved it. She didn't. But CJ did, so all of this was for him. She didn't want her son to grow up with a mom who couldn't get out of bed some days, who relied on everyone else for every little thing.

After Cam died, his parents had been eager to help, to lighten her load, and she loved them for it.

But she'd been living in a daze. And Elise was right. It was time to pick herself up and move on. *The Year of Emma.* More like *The Year Emma Woke Up. The Year Emma Stopped Feeling Sorry for Herself. The Year Emma Reentered the Land of the Living.*

How hard could it be?

Very, it turned out.

The confident young woman she'd been once upon a time seemed to have gotten away from her. On a vacation or maybe hiding herself away. In her place was this imposter, a woman who doubted every decision, who would struggle to conjure a single bit of strength in this job interview.

She didn't even recognize this version of herself. When had she become so afraid?

Gallery 316 wasn't her first job interview since moving to Nantucket two weeks prior. She'd also submitted résumés to be an office assistant at a law office, a receptionist at a doctor's office, and a waitress at a bar. She hadn't even gotten a call about that last one. Could be because she'd made it clear on her application that nights would be hard for her because she had a little boy, and he was her first priority.

Now she hurried down the sidewalk, trying to mentally prepare for a job interview that had her stomach in knots. This was the first job she'd applied for that she actually wanted—she'd be perfect for it.

She'd forgotten how it felt to want something.

But she remembered how it felt to need something. That feeling was all too familiar and most unwelcome. Yes, she'd inherited Cam's cottage, but she still needed an income.

That's why she'd decided to tackle the garage apartment. The vacation rental market was good here, and she needed the extra income. She was determined to make it on her own.

And maybe she'd been foolish taking a perfect stranger up to the apartment and practically hiring him on the spot, but beggars couldn't choose. Jameson Shaw seemed to be her only choice.

*Please don't let him be a pervert, murderer, or delinquent.*

She needed him to be normal and helpful. She couldn't clean out the apartment by herself. As this morning had proven, she couldn't even stand to walk inside.

Emma knew very little about Gallery 316, but when the owner called to schedule her interview, she'd done a deep dive on the Internet. She'd learned that Travis Butler was a one-man show, and he was looking to hire a gallery assistant. Travis was eccentric but also highly renowned and had an excellent reputation. His taste was second to none, and because of that, he'd launched a number of artists' careers.

Working with him would be good for her. Maybe it would reawaken something inside her—something that had been lying dormant since she got the call about Cam.

After she made her *Year of Emma* list, she told Elise she felt selfish. She didn't elaborate, but it felt wrong, taking any time for herself after what she'd done.

Elise insisted this wasn't for her. "Your son deserves a happy mom," she'd said. "You're not just doing this for you; you're doing it for him. You both need it."

She understood what her best friend didn't say—that living but not really living was going to have adverse effects on her son—that it was time to pick herself up and move forward. Past time, really.

It had started with her move to the island, out of Cam's parents' house on Cape Cod. After Cam died, it made the most sense to move in with them. With her own parents out of the picture, she didn't have many other options. She was pregnant, brokenhearted, and full of regrets.

Jerry and Nadine Woodson took her in, gave her everything she needed and loved her like a daughter. Best of all, they loved CJ. Emma had only planned to stay a little while, until she could get back on her feet, but one year had turned into five, and she still wasn't convinced she could make it on her own.

She stopped on the sidewalk outside the gallery and peered through the front windows. The dark wood floors and white walls were every bit as elegant in person as they had been in the photos online. She glanced down at her green cotton dress, picked up from the clearance rack at Old Navy. She did not belong here.

Still, she had to try. She'd promised herself. She'd promised CJ.

With one minute to spare, she pulled open the front door and walked inside. The crisp gallery boasted delicious natural light. She was instantly drawn in by its clean lines and the perfect amount of white space. Travis Butler had certainly created the ideal setting for showing off artwork.

Along the walls, beach-themed oil paintings hung boldly, the pops of color jumping off each canvas, practically daring onlookers to ignore them.

"Miss Woodson?" A rail-thin man with slicked-back blond hair and round glasses emerged from the back of the gallery. His once-over of her Old Navy sundress nearly went unnoticed, but not quite.

Emma pushed aside her insecurity and forced a smile. "Mr. Butler, hello."

"Please, call me Travis."

"Travis." She nodded. "I'm Emma."

"Good to meet you." He waved a hand in the air. "What do you think of our gallery?"

"I think it's beautiful." Her eyes scanned the paintings hung underneath individual lights. Sculptures stood proudly on white, wooden stands throughout the space, and while the building was on the historical registry, the interior managed a modern feel.

"We feature local artists mostly, but we've had a number of other artists in throughout the years. Behind our building, there's a sculpture garden, and at the back is our staging area, where we work on new exhibits. We also have a classroom on the second floor." He led her around the gallery, stopping in front of a sleek white bench. "Let's sit."

She set her oversize brown leather bag down on the floor and took a seat at one end of the bench. Travis sat on the other end and seemed to be studying her.

"You're an artist," he said definitively.

A blush rose to her cheeks. "I used to be."

His brow furrowed. "Once an artist, dear, always an artist."

It was strange that this man who was likely only a decade older than her thought to call her "dear." It was a sweet term of endearment, but it reminded Emma that she wasn't presenting herself as a competent adult. She was presenting herself as a person who needed to be taken care of. She mentally referred back to her list.

*7. Become independent. I can take care of myself.*

"I suppose that's true," she said in response to his comment. "I'm still an artist at heart. I just haven't done much work in recent years."

"Years?" Travis practically gasped. "How is that possible?" Then he frowned. "Actually, I think it's been over a year since I worked on anything of my own. We should both remedy that. An artist who isn't creating is just a shell of himself."

She looked away. She'd been a shell of herself for a very long time, though she suspected that had more to do with losing Cam than not painting.

"So why do you want this job?"

Emma cleared her throat. She could give him the sales pitch she'd practiced in the mirror that morning while she curled her hair, or she could be honest with him. But that would mean talking about what had happened, and was she really ready to do that?

"Well," she said quietly, "I love art. I have a degree in fine art from the University of Colorado." Thinking of college always made her remember the day she first saw Cam. He was stationed at the base in Colorado Springs, and he came to the UCCS campus with a recruiter to give a talk about what the military could offer students. Her lecture in Columbine Hall had just ended, and she passed Cam on the way out the door. At the sight of him, she took a step outside, then turned around and went right back in.

She sat in the back, listening to the presentation with no interest in the Army other than the man in front of the classroom. She wasn't even embarrassed when he called on her to answer a question, and she had no idea what the answer was.

"I'm only here to see if I could buy you a cup of coffee," she'd said. The small audience laughed, and Cam flashed her a grin that she felt all the way to her toes.

Afterward, he'd come straight up to her. "So about that coffee . . ."

She'd been so much bolder back then, so much more confident. Was that girl still in there somewhere?

"What's your primary medium?" Travis asked.

"Watercolors," she said, as if it were still as common to her as oxygen. "But I'm also familiar with acrylics and oils, and I've done quite a bit of work with found objects. My entire senior project was a melding of high-end fine art and miscellaneous things I found in the trash."

He grimaced. Travis was a tiny bit prissy.

"Nothing gross," she said. "No hot dog wrappers or used tissues or anything."

"Well, that's a relief."

She reached into her bag and pulled out the portfolio she'd put together. "These are photos of some of my pieces."

He flipped through them quickly, and she was certain she'd lost him. He wasn't impressed. And why would he be? He worked with professionals, and she was showing him photos of a college project. Besides, she wasn't here to sell her art. She was here to sell herself.

"I'm going to be honest with you, Mr. Butler—"

"Travis," he cut in, not looking up from the book.

"Travis. Right." She drew in a slow breath. "I really need this job. I've only been on the island for two weeks. My husband had a house here."

"Did you get it in the divorce?"

"I got it in the will."

His eyes shot to hers. "I'm sorry."

"It's okay. He was killed in combat overseas. I have a son, and I'm really tired of working in food service. I'd like to do something in the realm of my education."

"Understandable. But what I need is someone who would be great in food service."

"Oh, I am. I'm a really good waitress. But I'd love to be surrounded by art again. I'd love to start painting again." It wasn't until that moment that she realized how true it was.

"This job is less about art and more about people," he said, "which is why I need help. It's time I get back to my own work. This gallery is my dream, but I haven't shown a single piece of my own since I opened it six years ago."

"I'd love to help you do that."

He crossed one leg over the other and regarded her for a long moment. She took the opportunity to admire his checkered bow tie and neatly tailored dark-blue suit. Safe bet he didn't shop at Old Navy.

"I'm looking for someone to handle most of the day-to-day operations around here," he said. "Customer service, answering phones, coordinating teachers and classes as well as events—we have a fair number lined up for the summer."

"That all sounds great."

"You'll also be working with the artists, and that isn't always easy. Since you speak their language, though, I feel like you might have an advantage."

"I think so, sir."

"And if you're up for it, I could use a second pair of eyes scouting new talent. Our gallery has found some significant new voices, and I don't want to stop because I'm taking a little sabbatical to remember how it feels to create something of my own."

"Of course not." Wow. She hadn't counted on that. Helping discover new talent would be a dream. A deep sense of longing invaded her chest. She wanted this job.

He inhaled a deep breath and nodded. "Very good."

"Very good. I'm hired?"

He smiled warmly. "Yes, Emma, you've got the job. After the last person I interviewed, you sound too good to be true, and I've got a good feeling about you."

She threw her arms around him. "Thank you, Mr.—Travis." She pulled back. "You won't regret it."

He extracted himself from her embrace and stood. "I'm not really a hugger."

"Right, sorry." Were her cheeks as red as they felt? "I got carried away. It's just—I really needed a win."

"Well, rah-rah." He half-heartedly waved a fist in the air. "You start today."

"Today?" She pulled out her phone and looked at the time. She'd arranged for CJ to stay at a local day care for an hour.

"Is that a problem?"

"Can I just make a quick phone call?" she asked. "I need to make sure my son can stay longer at the day care center."

"Sure," he said, then grimaced. "Just don't bring him to work with you. Kids are messy. And loud."

"Of course." She took a few steps away and dialed the day care. While she waited for someone to pick up the phone, she spotted Jamie walking across the street. He still carried the duffel, and he didn't appear to have a car. That wasn't unusual though—lots of people didn't bring their cars to the island. It occurred to her she probably should've gotten more information from him, but she was just so excited to have help with the apartment she would've let him move in then and there.

"Hello?"

"Delia?"

"Speaking."

Jamie stopped in front of a hotel, pulled out his phone, tapped a few buttons, then went inside. Was he staying in a hotel? Had he just arrived on the island that day?

"Speaking?"

"Sorry, Delia, it's Emma Woodson."

"CJ is doing just fine, Emma." Emma could hear the smile in the woman's voice.

"Great. Can he stay a little longer?" Emma turned back and looked at Travis, who was speaking in hushed tones to an older couple who had walked in. "I just got a job."

# CHAPTER THREE

~~~

JAMIE ARRIVED AT EMMA'S HOUSE later that evening after several unsuccessful attempts to find a hotel room for the night. Who knew Nantucket was so busy in late May?

Probably every other human on the planet besides him.

He stood out on the sidewalk and caught a glimpse of her through the window. He could leave the letter, get on the ferry, and go back to Chicago—no harm done.

He reached into his pocket and took out the envelope. On the front, he'd written *Emma Woodson* in his hurried scrawl. When he'd written her name, that's all she was—a name. A name he'd familiarized himself with over the years.

He'd searched for her online and discovered that she didn't have any active social media accounts. Her name was mentioned in two articles and her husband's obituary. And he'd asked a cop friend to help obtain her address, which had recently changed. The past five years she'd lived on Cape Cod, but recently she'd moved here, into a house that had been in her name since her husband's death.

He wondered what had prompted the move, but he knew it wasn't his place to ask. He didn't have the right to know anything about her other than the facts. And if you wanted to get technical, he really didn't even have the right to know those.

So why did he find himself wondering how she'd survived the past five years?

And why did he feel that he needed to know the answer to that before he left this island? After all, if he learned that she'd moved on—if he discovered she was happy—then maybe it would ease his guilt.

And maybe he could move on too.

He watched as her son sat at the table, ramming one toy car into another. She walked over, mussed his hair, and kissed the top of his head.

His thoughts turned to the apartment over the garage. No way she was going to be able to get that ready for a renter anytime soon. Did she even realize how much work it needed?

But he'd given his word. That still meant something, didn't it?

He strode up the walk to the front door and knocked, stuffing the envelope back into his pocket.

Hillary's voice rang like a warning bell in his mind, but he silenced it the second the door opened and Emma appeared on the other side.

"Hey. You're back." Her smile might've been out of politeness, but it stirred something in him that had been long dead. Affection.

Mostly Jamie didn't enjoy people these days. He knew how to fake it enough to make a living and run a successful business, but that genuine enjoyment of another person's company? He hadn't felt that in years.

"I brought my references," he said.

The memory registered on her face. "Oh, right." She opened the door. "Come on in. I've got a key for you, and we should probably discuss the job in a little more detail."

He walked inside and noted the unpacked boxes stacked in the living room. To his right, CJ continued to slam toy cars into each other, driving them across the dining room table, down onto a chair, and then underneath, where it seemed he'd built a whole city out of random objects.

The smell of food cooking—garlic and onion—filled the air. "Smells good." He said it without thinking, realizing too late it sounded like he was angling for an invitation to dinner, which he most definitely was not.

She glanced at the bag still hanging from his shoulder. "Set that down," she said firmly. "You can join us for dinner. I'll interview you while we eat spaghetti, and if I determine you're an awful person, I'll send you on your way."

He liked her instantly. She had a spunk that made him feel alive. Not to mention a pair of blue eyes that he feared could see straight through him.

A spark of attraction simmered at his core. He quickly extinguished it. He knew better than that. This woman, more than any other, was off-limits to him.

"So? What do you say?" She watched him now with a gaze so sharp it sliced straight through him, and yet he saw kindness behind her eyes. She thought she was helping him—and he absolutely did not want her to feel burdened by his presence. He should've stashed the bag before he knocked. It was a dead giveaway he had nowhere to stay.

"Look," she said. "I made a ton of food. You'd be doing me a favor. Plus, we're celebrating." Her face brightened with a wide smile. "I got a job today."

"That's great," he said.

"Yeah." She glanced at CJ. "It's really great."

A ding rang out from the kitchen.

"That's the bread," she said. "Come in, make yourself at home." She dashed off in what he assumed was the direction of the kitchen. A tiny neon-green car shot out of the dining room and smacked him in the foot.

He bent and picked it up as CJ emerged from under the table.

"Sorry, mister," the boy said.

Jamie marveled at the boy's big brown eyes and olive complexion. He looked a lot like his mom, but his face was familiar for another reason altogether.

"No problem." He handed the car back to CJ.

Emma's face appeared in the doorway. "Set your bag down," she repeated. "Make yourself comfortable. Do you want a drink?"

He did as he was told, as if taking orders from her came naturally. As if he owed it to her to do whatever she said.

"Water with dinner will be fine."

Her face brightened. "So you *are* staying. Good. I can't wait to be the one interviewing someone instead of the other way around."

He couldn't imagine she had a bit of trouble convincing a potential employer that she would be perfect for any job.

"I'll grab you a bottle of water." She vanished back into the kitchen, and CJ had disappeared under the table, leaving Jamie standing alone in the entryway.

On the wall, a photo of Emma and her husband caught his attention. They stood on the beach, arms wrapped around each other, and they were both smiling.

"That's my dad." CJ had come up behind him.

"Yeah?" Regret twisted in his belly.

"He was a hero," CJ said. "I'm gonna be a hero someday."

Emma breezed out of the kitchen and shooed her son back into the dining room. "Sorry about that."

"Do you need any help with dinner?" Jamie asked. *Or with life?*

"I think I've got it," she said. "Have a seat in the dining room, and it'll be ready in just a minute."

Again he did as he was told.

And the irony of that nearly took his breath away.

If he made a habit of doing as he was told, everything—everything— would be different right now.

～

Emma hadn't planned on a dinner guest, but truth be told, she wasn't sure she could host a celebratory dinner for just her and CJ. Her son was the light of her life and all that, but he was a terrible conversationalist, and after the day she'd had, she didn't want to be alone.

Even though she knew all too well that you could be surrounded by people and still be alone.

She'd called Cam's parents on the way home from the gallery to tell them the good news, and she was fairly certain they felt the same sadness she did in not being able to celebrate with her immediately.

"We'll make a plan to come visit soon," Cam's mom, Nadine, had said. "We sure do miss you both."

"We miss you too," she'd said. She hung up before the lump in her throat grew any bigger.

Now, as she put the garlic bread in a basket, she told herself she needed to find out more about this man if he was going to have access to her apartment. He could be the second step in working on *7. Become independent. I can take care of myself.*

Maybe she was naive to invite a perfect stranger in for dinner and offer him a job without talking to a single professional reference, but it wasn't only her desperation that had spurred her forward. There was something kind behind Jamie's eyes. Something in the way he carried himself, the way he studied her, his quiet demeanor. It endeared her to him instantly. She found herself wanting to nurture him, to feed him, to make sure he was okay.

Elise would have a field day dissecting that, which was why Emma planned to keep Jamie's presence in her house to herself, at least for now.

She picked up the basket of bread and carried it into the dining room, where Jamie sat, across from CJ, who was still playing with those blasted Hot Wheels.

The sound of the metal cars slamming into each other wrecked her nerves, but they made her son happy, and she was hard-pressed to take away anything that did that.

"Dinner is served." She sat down at the head of the table, between

CJ and Jamie, and felt suddenly awkward at the intimacy of the situation. She hadn't thought this through. She stood and brightened the chandelier over the table, then returned to her seat to find Jamie watching her.

Intently.

It set something off inside her. She hadn't been on a single date since Cam died, though not because she hadn't been asked out. Men at the restaurant where she'd worked made a point to hit on her. (Why did they all think she'd be so lucky to go home with them?) But she wasn't interested. Not only because she wasn't attracted to those men, but because she wasn't looking for romance.

That hadn't changed.

So why were her palms clammy?

"Uh, dig in," she said, motioning toward the large bowl of spaghetti on the table between them.

Jamie picked it up and served himself a hearty portion of pasta.

At her side, CJ made a motoring noise, winding a tiny red sports car across his plate. She clapped a hand over his. "No Hot Wheels at the table, buddy."

His face crumpled into a dark frown. "I'm not hungry."

She served some spaghetti onto his plate. "Sorry, bud, you've got to eat some dinner."

He dropped the car on the floor with a thud.

*Please don't throw a tantrum right now.*

CJ's eyes scanned the table, like a homing device locking onto a target. He was a really good kid, but he was a handful. And he hadn't wanted to leave his grandparents' house—why would he? There, the sun rose and set on that little boy. Had she made a mistake uprooting him and moving here? Had she been foolish to think she alone could give him a good life?

At her side, Jamie twisted pasta onto his fork while CJ watched with interest. He picked up his own fork and plunked it into the noodles, spinning it in circles with little success. Jamie seemed not to notice he was now the subject of her son's fascination.

Emma took the opportunity to dish up her own plate of food, then passed the garlic bread around the table.

"So tell me about yourself." She turned her attention to Jamie.

He swallowed the bite in his mouth and took a drink of water. "What do you want to know?"

"Where'd you come from?"

Jamie's almost laugh caught her off guard.

"I suppose that is an odd way to phrase that question."

"Kind of makes it sound like I'm from outer space."

"Are you?" CJ asked.

Jamie smiled warmly. "Sadly no. Nothing as cool as that."

She took a bite. Spaghetti had been a staple in the early days of her marriage to Cam. It had been the only thing she knew how to cook. She'd added a few more dishes to her repertoire over the years, but this meal always reminded her of him. Maybe that's why she chose it for her celebration, as if in doing so, he was here with them.

Even though she knew he absolutely was not.

Jamie kept his eyes on the plate in front of him. Elise would point out that inability to make eye contact was a red flag.

CJ finally gave up on the twisting and picked up a noodle with his fingers. He dangled it over his open mouth and coiled it inside. She decided now was not the time to discuss table manners with her son.

"I grew up in a suburb of Chicago called Evergreen Park." The low timbre of Jamie's voice drew her attention away from CJ. She glanced to her left and found this man—this stranger—looking right at her.

So much for the lack of eye contact. It occurred to her that speaking to the side of his face was a heck of a lot easier than looking him square in the eye.

"I moved to a different suburb called Naperville a few years ago," he said. "I own a business there."

She busied herself with her pasta, more so than any normal person would've. "What kind of business?"

"It's a production house—cinematography and photography. I mostly work with businesses to tell their brand story."

"Wow," she said. "That's amazing. Any companies I would know?"

He rattled off the names of a few big businesses, then a handful of others she didn't recognize.

"So you're an artist too."

He glanced away. Took a drink. "Not really. I mean, I tell other people's stories. It's just a job."

She frowned, thinking about Travis's *Once an artist, dear, always an artist* but chose to keep the thought to herself.

"Are you an artist?"

"Used to be," she said with a nod toward a watercolor she'd hung on the wall. "That's one of mine." It was the image of a mom waving her kids off on the school bus. It wasn't painted from memory—her mother never walked her to the bus—but it captured something she'd always wanted. Something she strived to give CJ now.

His eyes widened. "Wow. It's good." His gaze lingered on her artwork. It made her feel . . . she wasn't sure what. Exposed?

"I haven't painted in a long time."

"Why not?"

CJ dropped his fork onto his plate with a clang. The sound was so jarring, Emma gasped. "CJ!"

"Sorry, Mommy." He looked at her with his big eyes. "Can I be done now?"

She surveyed his plate. He'd eaten less than half of what she'd served him. "Two more bites."

He obliged, then turned to her, eyebrows raised in expectancy. She wiped his mouth and hands. "Okay, go play."

He ran off, leaving her sitting at the table, alone with a man whose presence was doing a number on her nerves more than a set of toy cars ever would.

"Sorry about that," she said. "I should probably be firmer with him, but some days it's so much work."

"I bet," Jamie said. "He reminds me of my nephew Henry."

She set her drink down. "You have a nephew?"

"I have two nephews and a niece," he said. "My older sister Hillary's kids."

For no good reason, she added that to the list of reasons she wasn't crazy for hiring him straightaway.

"I've never interviewed anyone before," she said. "I'm not sure what else I should ask."

"Well," he said, "I'm not looking for somewhere permanent, and I do have experience with small renovation projects. Mostly I've built set pieces for photo or video shoots. What exactly are you looking to do in the apartment?"

"I'm looking to clean it out," she said. "But I'm not looking to be the one to do it."

"Understood."

"Also, I need to go through the boxes up there, but I don't want to throw anything away."

He frowned. "What do you want to do with the contents?"

"Maybe organize it and stash it in the garage?" She knew it was a faulty plan, but she couldn't bear to part with any of Cam's things. Not even the old sweatshirt she still wore to bed every night—and it had three holes in it.

He looked like he wanted to ask her a question—probably *"Have you had your mental health checked recently?"* But he refrained.

"My husband was killed overseas," she said, as if blurting it out would make it less painful. Like ripping off a Band-Aid or jumping straight into a cold pool without testing the water.

"Wow," she said. "That's the second time I've had to say that today. I suppose that's the downside of moving somewhere new."

He didn't respond.

"This move is me making a go of it on my own." She balled up her napkin in her fist. "I tell you that at the risk of sounding genuinely pathetic."

"It's not pathetic." His voice had gone soft. Tender. He pitied her, like everyone else. She hated that. She'd earned their pity, of course, given that she'd become a pitiful creature, but that's not who she wanted to be anymore. Not in *The Year of Emma*.

"I don't think I'm quite ready to face his things," she said. "I know it's crazy. He's been gone five years."

"There's no statute of limitations on grief," Jamie said matter-of-factly.

She found him watching her, and this time, instead of kicking up her nerves, his attentiveness calmed something inside her. Something that had been stirring for a very long time.

"Do you think you can make the apartment inhabitable?" she asked. "It needs some updates. Maybe a lot of updates—I don't actually know."

"I can try," he said.

She stood and stacked the empty (and in CJ's case, not empty) plates, then walked them into the kitchen.

She hadn't expected him to follow her, but after she set the plates in the sink, she turned to find him behind her, holding the bowl of leftover pasta and the bread basket. "How'd you land here? In Nantucket?" he asked.

"Cam's grandparents left this place to him." She fished a Tupperware from the cupboard, planning to scoop the pasta inside, but he took it from her before she could. "So by default, when he died, it went to me."

That she'd been given Cam's beloved cottage still made her feel guilty, but she didn't say so. Some topics weren't proper after-dinner conversation, especially not with strangers.

"But you just moved in."

She could see Jamie trying to piece together the puzzle that was her life. She rinsed the plates and filed them in the dishwasher. "I was pregnant when he died. I stayed with his family. They saved me, really. But it was time to take my life back. Part of that is making the apartment ready for renters. Earning my own way."

"'The Year of Emma.'" He nodded toward the list hanging on

the refrigerator, laying her innermost desires naked in front of God and everybody.

"Right," she said miserably, snatching the list from the fridge. Had he read the whole thing? With her luck, he'd be some kind of speed-reader who now knew more about her than anyone else in her life.

"I think it's awesome what you're doing," he said. "I'm impressed."

She folded the paper and flicked it across her fingers. "Well, don't be. It's taken me way longer than it should've. My poor kid—"

"Seems perfectly happy to me," he said, cutting her off.

She took the container of pasta from him and stuck it in the refrigerator, and his words turned themselves over in her chest. Why did a simple comment from a man she didn't even know bring tears to her eyes?

When she closed the door of the fridge, she found him standing at the sink, rinsing out the cups. "You don't have to do that."

"I don't mind," he said. "Unless you want me to leave." He turned the water off. "I can head out."

"Jamie, do you have a place to stay tonight?"

Surprise washed across his face. "Yeah, I'm fine."

She squinted at him. "I saw you go into a hotel this afternoon. I assume if you'd gotten a room, you wouldn't still be carrying your bag around?"

He half laughed, half sighed. "I knew you were as smart as you look."

"I am an employed, independent woman."

That warranted a smile, though it was fleeting. "Look, Emma, I'll be fine. Don't worry about me."

"Don't be silly," she said. "I'm sure we can clear a spot in the apartment for you to stay tonight. It won't be cozy, but it's something."

He dried his hands on a kitchen towel and chewed on a response. "Well?"

"You're sure it's no trouble?"

"I'm sure," she said.

"Okay." A beat. "Thanks."

Once upon a time, Emma had loved helping people. She'd been the recipient of so much help these last few years, she'd forgotten how good it felt to be the helper and not the helpee. Still, as she ran upstairs to find blankets and pillows that would suffice for the evening, a part of her felt slightly guilty, like she was betraying her husband.

Because Jamie Shaw had awakened something in Emma that she'd long commanded to stay asleep.

# CHAPTER FOUR

JAMIE AWOKE WITH A START AND A GASP, the sound of the explosion still fresh in his mind. The nightmares were unrelenting. Every other night or so, they were back. The same thing over and over. Dr. McDonald swore EMDR therapy would help him. Said he had PTSD, but how was that possible? PTSD was something soldiers experienced.

And he wasn't a soldier.

He shook the thought away and rolled over, punching the pillow underneath his head. It smelled like Emma—something he shouldn't know but did thanks to their conversation in the kitchen the night before.

Emma smelled sweet like cinnamon. He forced that memory out of his head. He didn't have the right to commit her fragrance to memory.

Pale light tinged with blue filtered in through the window near the front door. The apartment over Emma's garage had a lot of potential, he'd discovered when he arrived last night. She hadn't walked him out. She'd given him a stack of blankets, pillows, and towels and said a hurried good night, locking the door as soon as he stepped outside.

It had to be weird for her, allowing someone in the space so clearly occupied by her husband—or at least by the memory of him.

A few framed photos of a young and happy-looking Cam had been hung on the wall across from the bed, which had been buried and surrounded by boxes. When a person died, all that was left of them were things that could be stuffed in boxes and packed away to be dealt with on another day.

Given his conversation with Emma at dinner last night, though, it seemed that day had yet to arrive.

He pushed himself up onto his elbows and slid out from under the covers. No sense staying in bed and wishing for sleep when he was certain it wouldn't come. He knew better. The nightmares were unkind that way. It's why he'd gone to see Dr. McDonald in the first place.

It had been years—shouldn't he have gotten over it by now? It was Hillary who'd made his appointment several months ago now. No way he was going to actively seek out therapy. She said she was worried about him, that she could tell he wasn't sleeping, that he wasn't himself, and she made a compelling case that he needed professional help.

It pained him to think she might be right.

Mostly he went to shut her up. She'd been relentlessly on his case for months.

He'd had three sessions before Dr. McDonald told him to get a dream journal. He didn't want a dream journal. He didn't want to chronicle his pain.

He wanted to forget it.

Two sessions later, when the journaling was deemed "an excellent tool to sort through your emotions," Dr. McDonald gave him homework.

"A lot of your guilt seems directed toward the survivors," she'd said.

"Right," he said. Why was she saying that like it was a revelation? Of course his guilt was directed toward them.

"Let's try something different this week."

Inwardly he groaned. Could they try *not* doing therapy? That'd be great.

"I want you to try writing a letter to one of the families," the doctor said. "Say whatever's on your mind, whatever's in your heart."

He hated when she talked like that. He didn't want to put down on paper what was in his mind, and he certainly didn't need her dissecting what was "in his heart." How he'd managed to get through that session without an eye roll remained a mystery.

Still, he'd gone home that night, and he'd done as he was told on the off chance Dr. McDonald wasn't a quack. He wrote a letter to Mary Beth Winters, the mother of a young soldier named Freddy. Sometimes Freddy showed up in his dreams. One minute he'd be smiling, laughing, cracking jokes—seconds later, he was on the ground, eyes open, blood pooling near his temples.

Freddy didn't have any other family, which meant Mary Beth didn't have any other family either.

That thought had run him ragged.

So ragged that when he started writing, he couldn't stop. His hand raced across the page, pouring out his apologies and regrets, begging for her forgiveness.

He'd sealed the letter and sent it, and when he told Dr. McDonald about it at the next session, she looked shocked.

"You weren't supposed to *mail* the letter," she'd said. "This was just an exercise—for you."

But it was too late. It was gone. And with it, a measure of the heaviness he carried around with him.

Two weeks later, he received a response in the mail. Mary Beth Winters thanked him for his kind note and invited him to her house. And he went. And when he met her, she said the letter had given her closure—something she'd desperately needed.

Then, against all logic, she said she didn't blame him for what happened, even after he told her the whole story. When she hugged him, he wept, and the tears felt like a much-needed release.

Maybe that's why it had seemed so important to him to come here in person. Sitting with Mary Beth had helped him more than anything else he'd tried, more than the email he'd received in reply to the letter he sent to the other widow, Alicia Birch, only a few days after sending Mary Beth's.

Perhaps he was looking to re-create that same feeling now. Her words had been like a balm to his soul, though the relief was somewhat short-lived. He was haunted. Tormented. Never mind that Mary Beth's words had reminded him of how he'd felt learning that God was a forgiving God and that while he was a sinner, he could be absolved of his mistakes simply by praying from the heart. If he wanted forgiveness, it was a gift to him.

Why was he finding it so impossible to reach out and take it?

*Because you don't deserve it.*

He wove his way through the boxes to the sink and peered out the window toward the main cottage. A single light was on in a room on the second floor. Maybe Emma had a hard time sleeping too.

He fished through his bag for track pants and a T-shirt. If he was going to stay here for a while, he was going to need a few things.

But not today. Today he'd make do with what he had and get going on this apartment.

He flipped a light on and looked around. It had a lot of promise. He wasn't a carpenter, but he was handy, and he knew how to google whatever he didn't know. Jamie had been raised by a DIY enthusiast, which meant he'd picked up a lot over the years. He'd always appreciated that his father took the time to teach him how to snake a clogged drain or lay a hardwood floor. It had saved him money over the years and given him a much-needed distraction. When he moved into his apartment in the suburbs, he'd had plans of renovating, but he'd never gotten around to it. Most of his time and effort went into the business and the office space.

He'd see this project for Emma through, though. He owed it to her.

He turned and took in the space. The studio apartment was one large carpeted room. The kitchenette was at the front of the space, the window over the sink looking out toward the main house and, beyond Emma's yard, the ocean, a few blocks away. The rest of the room was open, meaning they could arrange it however they wanted. There was a bed and an old couch, but if Emma was really going to rent this place out, everything would need an upgrade.

Did she know this wasn't a simple, low-cost project?

His phone dinged from the nightstand, where it was still plugged in.

He walked the length of the room in just a few long strides and picked it up. *Dylan.* His business partner wouldn't be happy when he learned Jamie wasn't on the ferry back to the mainland.

"Hey, man," Jamie said.

"Hey, you're never going to believe who I just got off the phone with."

"Who?" Jamie rarely got excited. Work was work. Business was business. He did everything he could to make sure his clients were happy with the job he did, but he felt no emotional attachment to any of it.

His days of being emotionally attached to his work were over.

"Jerrica Danielson."

Jamie sat on the edge of the bed. "The fitness lady?"

"Jamie." Dylan didn't hide his disapproval. "She owns FitLife. And she wants to hire us."

"Like, it's a done deal?"

"Pretty much," Dylan said. "She's got a whole plan for rebranding. She wants us to tell the company story and launch a whole new ad campaign. We're talking photo shoots, video, the works."

Jamie rubbed his free hand over the back of his neck.

"Why aren't you saying anything?"

"No, man, it's great," Jamie said, though even he knew his response was less than enthusiastic. "When does she want to start?"

"Soon," Dylan said. "A couple of weeks, I think, but that means we need to storyboard the project and get her our ideas. When are you back in the office?"

Jamie hadn't thought this through. It wasn't too late to slip the letter to Emma under her door and take the next ferry out of town. She'd find someone else to help with this apartment—he'd go back to his life, having said his piece, and that would be that.

There was a knock at the door.

"Look, Dylan, I gotta call you back," Jamie said.

"Okay, I'll email you the details." Excitement rose in his partner's voice. And it should—this was a huge get for their business. They'd been praying for a partnership like this one for a long time. Because Jamie knew if Jerrica Danielson liked their work, it could mean job security for a lot of years.

"Great," Jamie said. "I'll be in touch."

He clicked the phone off and walked toward the door, pulling it open to reveal Emma, wearing pajama pants and a white T-shirt. Her chestnut hair was piled in a messy bun on the top of her head, and her face was makeup free.

Man, she was pretty.

He pushed the thought away.

"Hey." He was surprised he managed even one word—the sight of her had him tongue-tied again, just like yesterday.

He told himself this attraction he felt toward her was nothing more than his guilt working overtime.

But as she lifted her chin and looked him straight in the eyes, he knew what he told himself was a lie.

And that was going to be a problem.

# CHAPTER FIVE

EMMA ROUTINELY AWOKE BEFORE DAWN. If she were more inclined to take better care of herself, she would've used that time to work out or meditate or pray.

Actually, she'd attempted the prayer-in-the-morning thing many times, but she found it impossible to concentrate. Impossible to converse with a God who took her husband away. But that wasn't quite right, was it? In truth, she feared Cam's death was her punishment, because she'd let God down long before he'd returned the favor.

She needed a distraction, and making breakfast for the man staying in the apartment along with all of Cam's earthly possessions seemed as good a distraction as any.

If Elise were here, she'd have something to say about Emma's act of kindness. But Elise wasn't here, and when Jamie opened the door, Emma said a silent prayer of thanks for that.

He stood in front of her, his thick hair tousled and messy, sleep still evident in his eyes.

Or maybe it was a lack of sleep that she saw? Maybe Jamie had demons that kept him awake at night too.

From her spot outside the door, she had a line of sight into the apartment, and a ray of sunshine lit a direct path to the unmade bed.

The intimacy of that caused a brief hiccup in her otherwise-steady pulse.

"Sorry to barge in on you," she said.

"You own the place." He wore a worn gray T-shirt with a Chicago Cubs logo on the front and a pair of black track pants. Thank goodness he was fully clothed. The unmade bed and a bare-chested Jamie might've been more than her heart could handle.

She didn't deserve to have these thoughts. It wasn't fair to Cam. *Enough, Emma.*

She held up the tray she was carrying. "I know there's no food up here, so I thought I should bring you something so you don't starve." There. That sounded neighborly, right? She had a perfectly legitimate reason for being here. If this were a bed-and-breakfast, the hostess would make the morning meal. It wasn't so out of the ordinary.

Never mind that he could easily run down to Island Coffee and pick up coffee and a bagel. If he'd thought the same thing, he didn't say so.

He pushed the door open wider so she could pass through, but she hesitated for *one-two-three* before finally walking through the door. She knew she couldn't avoid the apartment forever, but being in here was almost too much. She was well acquainted with anxiety, and she feared the space might be a trigger.

She allowed herself a scan of the room. "Wow. I haven't really been in here since—" She turned to him. "The movers brought everything here right after—"

Sometimes the grief struck at the most inopportune times. Just yesterday she'd told two different people her husband was killed in combat. Today she couldn't even say the words out loud. The tray shook slightly, her trembling hands unable to hold it still. At the sound of the silverware vibrating against the glass of orange juice, Jamie reached out and took it from her. He set it on the counter.

"This was really kind of you," he said.

She nodded, thinking that perhaps he should've used the word *stupid* instead of *kind* because right now, *stupid* was how this idea felt.

"I was going to stop by later, actually," he said. "I figured we should work out a timeline and budget and get an idea of what you're wanting to do in here."

Right. A timeline. An idea. A budget. She really hadn't thought this through. Her arms hung loose at her sides as she finally took in the apartment. "I didn't realize it was so outdated."

"It could use a little TLC," he said.

"You must think I'm so naive," she said, avoiding his gaze.

"Why would I think that?"

"Because I put out an ad saying I needed someone to clean out my apartment and maybe paint some walls—I didn't say anything about installing new floors or drywall." She turned to him. "I may have gotten ahead of myself."

Emma didn't often get embarrassed. Or at least, she didn't used to. She used to be so confident, so self-assured. She knew what she wanted and she went for it. Cam's death had stolen that from her. It had turned her into a person that questioned her every move.

"I think it's actually kind of brilliant," he said.

And apparently it had turned her into a person in dire need of affirmation because that one little sentence lit something inside her that she hadn't felt in years.

She hoped he didn't notice. "You do?"

"Even if you don't get many rentals this season, you can't go wrong with a rental property on Nantucket. It's a good investment."

That was true. If she did this right, she could book this place for the entire season and maybe even at Christmas. That was pure profit right in her pocket.

*I can take care of myself.*

Jamie moved toward the kitchen and started rummaging through the drawers. With his back to her, she took a moment to study him. He was tall but not towering. He was muscular but not bulky. He was good-looking but not fussy, and his skin was a warm bronze color. His nearness caused her nerves to buzz—she seemed to have a heightened awareness of his presence.

He turned and found her staring. He held a sheet of scratch paper and a dull pencil. "Like you, I'm a list maker."

Was she blushing? She didn't mean for him to see her *Year of Emma* list. Especially not number nine, which had been added by Elise without her permission.

"Number nine," Elise had said, writing in a pink glitter pen she'd found in her purse. "Go on a proper date."

"No." Emma tried to snatch the notebook away from Elise to no avail.

"Em," Elise said. "You deserve to be happy. Cam wouldn't want you to be alone."

Emma had rejected the idea outright and should've scratched it from her list. There were some things even Elise didn't know about Emma, namely the reason that she absolutely did not deserve to be happy.

"Let's make a list of what it would take to make this happen."

He picked up a box off the rickety kitchen table and set it on top of another box, clearing a space for them to both sit.

"Your food is going to get cold." She didn't love cooking, so she hoped he appreciated the eggs, bacon, English muffin, bowl of fruit, cup of coffee, and glass of juice she'd assembled in the name of *kindness*.

"And if you don't eat the bacon, I will, so save my waistline and eat while we make this list." She picked up the tray and set it in front of him. "I didn't know how you liked your coffee. Or if you like coffee."

"I do," he said. "Black."

"Perfect," she said.

"Thanks for making this," he said. "I'll get to the store today so I have my own food."

She responded with a smile. "Where do we begin?"

He took a drink of the orange juice and surveyed the mess in front of them.

"Do you know anything about renovation?" she asked. "I know exactly zero things."

He laughed into the glass, but it was enough to light his hazel eyes.

"I know some," he said. "My dad's a college professor, but he loves all that DIY stuff, so he's taught me a lot. His thought was never pay someone to do something you could do yourself."

"That's a good thought," she said. "So where would you start?"

"Depends on the budget, I guess." He took a sip of coffee. "This is good."

"Island Coffee. It's my favorite."

"I think we need to start by getting everything out of here."

Right. That.

"I'm guessing there's a lot here for you to go through."

"Can we just move the boxes into the garage?" *Can I just avoid dealing with this a little while longer?*

"Sure," he said.

They were quiet for a long moment. Then she finally said, "What do we do after that? If the budget weren't a factor?"

Surprise registered on his face.

"Hypothetically," she said.

"Hypothetically, I'd rip out the carpet and put down hardwood. Dark, wide-planked. Hand-scraped if we can get it. I'd paint the walls gray so the white woodwork in here pops. I might do an accent wall over there." He pointed to the wall behind the bed. "Backsplash in the kitchen. New appliances. Curtains. Artwork."

She raised a brow. "Are you an interior designer too?"

He laughed again. It was a nice laugh. "Not even close."

She chewed the inside of her lip. "So a lot."

"To make it Nantucket worthy, yeah."

She hadn't factored any of this in. When had she become so

foolish? What did she think, they could move the boxes out and instantly have renters lined up for the season? It was silly at best and idiotic at worst.

"That'll take a while."

He nodded.

"Do you have other work? Your business, I mean."

His jaw twitched. "I have some time off."

She regarded him for a moment. He'd cleaned his plate and finished the juice and now turned the mug around in a circle on the table.

"What are you doing here anyway?" she asked. "I mean, you obviously weren't planning on staying in Nantucket."

He shifted in his seat and pushed the plate away. "No, I really wasn't."

"You're not on vacation, are you?" she asked. "Because working on this project does not seem like a very relaxing way to spend your time off."

"No," he said. "Not exactly." Jamie took a quick sip of the coffee, then set the mug down. "Emma—"

"Mo-om!"

The sound of CJ's impatient holler drew Emma from her seat. "Oh, shoot. He's awake. He's probably scared."

"Mom! Mom!"

She rushed to the door and yanked it open. "I'm right here, buddy!"

He wore his red race car pajamas and a look that perfectly blended terror and sadness. In his hand, he carried the well-loved teddy bear he'd gotten the day he was born.

"I'm here." She turned back to Jamie, who was standing beside the table, a strange look on his face. "Sorry. We'll finish talking later?"

He nodded and she rushed down the stairs, anxious to assure her son that the parent he had left was still alive and well.

Well, alive anyway.

The "well" part remained to be seen.

# CHAPTER SIX

"WHAT ARE YOU THINKING?"

Jamie knew telling Hillary why he was still in Nantucket was a mistake. It had been four days since he'd arrived, and that was four more days than he'd planned to stay. His sister wasn't the only one anxious for him to return. Dylan had called three times that day.

At some point, Jamie was going to have to talk to him. At some point, he was going to have to admit he wasn't finished here.

And at some point, he was going to have to tell Emma the truth.

That revelation twisted like a knot in his belly.

"I'm thinking I can help out here," he said.

"This is a bad idea, Jameson." In the background, one of her kids started crying.

"Anthony, can you get your son?" Hillary hollered. If she'd put her hand over the phone to muffle the sound, it hadn't worked.

"Look, you don't need to worry about me," he said. "I've got this under control."

"Is that right?"

"Yes." He didn't tell her that he'd eaten dinner with Emma and CJ again last night or that he waited until her bedroom light turned off before going to bed. Who did he think he was, her guardian angel?

Yet he couldn't shake the overwhelming need to protect her.

"What's your endgame here, Jamie?"

Hillary's question annoyed him. He didn't want to think about his endgame. He didn't have one. All he knew was that clearing out this apartment and helping her become independent felt good.

"You need to stop punishing yourself." Hillary must've felt the need to fill the silence left by his inability to respond.

"I'm not punishing myself."

"You are." She paused. "And it's not healthy. You shouldn't even be there. You need to come home."

"I will," he said. "When I'm done here, I will."

She sighed. "Jamie, how do you think she's going to react when you tell her the truth?"

Another zinger. Leave it to Hillary to lay it all out there, without a single coat of sugar.

"I don't know," he said dumbly.

"You have to tell her before she starts thinking of you as a friend—or worse. Oh no, Jamie, do you have the hots for this girl?"

"It's not like that," he said.

*It's not like that,* he repeated to himself because he needed to be reminded. Truth be told, he *was* drawn to her—he told himself it was his guilt, the need to do right by her, but he wasn't so sure. Was it guilt that made him imagine what it might be like to slip his arms around her? Was it guilt that had him wondering about the girl behind those wide eyes? Or replaying the sound of her laughter as he drifted off to sleep at night?

"What is it like?" Hillary's pointed question served as an angry wake-up call.

"I'm just helping her out," he said. "And finally—finally—I don't feel helpless, for the first time in five years."

Another sigh. "I'm worried about you."

"Yeah, well, don't be."

"Keep me posted," she said. "I have to go drop kids in Anthony's lap because apparently that's the only way to get him to pay attention to them."

Jamie laughed. "All right. Love you."

"Love you, too. A whole lot."

He hung up and tried to shove the conversation aside, but it proved impossible. Hillary was right. She was always right. He needed to tell Emma the truth.

He sank onto the bed in the small, outdated apartment and sighed. This wouldn't go his way. He already knew it. And the thought of her hating him was almost worse than the guilt he'd come to find absolution for.

~

It turned out Travis Butler was a perfectionist, which meant Emma had to be a perfectionist too. She'd been working at the gallery for a week now, and every day she was there, she learned a little more about what he needed.

She learned this primarily by making mistakes.

In just under two months, Gallery 316 would participate in the Nantucket Art Festival, a celebration of new local talent and Travis's favorite event of the year.

"I'm known for bringing the best and brightest to the festival every year," he told her that morning as they were going over the class schedule for the following week. A sculptor named Bess Winthrop was going to be in studio teaching, and Emma was trying to find a way to attend.

She didn't like leaving CJ at night, but Bess Winthrop was a renowned artist—and Emma had always wanted to learn more about sculpture.

"Which is why this morning's news is so upsetting." Travis had paused for dramatic effect, and Emma realized she'd allowed her mind to wander.

"Wait. What news?"

"The news that Marco St. John isn't coming to the festival."

Emma scanned her mental database. She didn't know who Marco St. John was. Had Travis mentioned him? "And who is that again?"

"Marco St. John was our headliner," Travis said as if she should've known. And to be honest, she probably should've known.

"Why did he cancel?" she asked.

Travis flicked the air with his wrist. "Something about a car accident and his girlfriend being in the hospital. I don't know; I didn't read the email closely."

"That's terrible. Maybe I can help?" The words were out before she had a chance to think about them.

"You?"

"You said I might need to help find new talent," she said. All the while, a tiny voice at the back of her mind was screaming for her to stop talking.

He regarded her for a moment. "You really think you can do this?"

She nodded. "I know I can."

"Fine," he said. "But you cannot mess this up."

"Understood."

"We need fresh and fabulous," he said.

"I'm on it."

A bell dinged to signal someone had entered the gallery from off the street.

"Customer." Travis gave her a pointed look.

She stood and moved from the classroom to the main gallery, her mind spinning. What was she doing—sabotaging herself? How was she going to find a new artist to impress Travis?

He had the highest standards and was very hard to win over.

But she had high standards too. The old Emma certainly had it in her to do this—surely that fearless girl was still in there somewhere. She didn't know how, but she wanted to save the day, to make herself indispensable, to be good at her job.

If only she knew where to begin.

# CHAPTER SEVEN

~~~

AFTER WORK, EMMA PULLED INTO the driveway just as Jamie was parking a truck in front of the garage.

She knew he'd cleared out Cam's boxes because she'd noticed they were stacked in the garage, but she wasn't sure what the next step in the process was. She'd sort of been avoiding discussing it because, frankly, she now realized she didn't have the money to do what needed to be done. And telling Jamie was going to be humiliating.

*Sorry you came here for a job I posted, but surprise! There's no job anymore, so I assume you'll find a new place to live. Good luck!*

Yep. This was a great way to get herself in over her head.

She parked and got out of the car. She wasn't going to be able to avoid him now.

CJ barreled out of the back seat and ran straight for him. "Hey, wanna play trucks with me?"

When her son had warmed up to the stranger living above the garage, Emma didn't know. Possibly at their second dinner together? Chicken stir-fry. Once again, CJ had been fascinated by

Jamie—watching with complete interest as their guest prepped his bowl of chicken, rice, and vegetables for eating, then copying everything he did right down to the salt and pepper he shook onto his food a bit too enthusiastically.

It was slightly disconcerting.

"CJ, Mr. Jamie is busy," Emma said so quickly it was as if she was going for a record.

"Maybe we can play later, bud."

"Go wash your hands," Emma said. "We're going to eat soon."

She watched as her son raced toward the door. She should plan something fun for him. Wasn't that part of *The Year of Emma*?

*3. Have more fun. Make more fun.*

She stifled a groan.

"Did you get a new truck?" She looked at the brand-new Chevy sitting in her driveway.

"Rented it," Jamie said. "Is it okay to park it there?"

She nodded.

"Figured if I'm going to get anything done in the apartment, I was going to need a way to buy supplies and bring them home from the hardware store."

She chewed the inside of her lip.

"Can I show you something?" he asked. "Do you have time, I mean?"

She tossed a glance at the house. CJ was probably in front of the TV. "If I hurry."

He nodded, then started up the stairs.

Would it ever get easier going inside this apartment?

She followed him through the door and looked around. Already the place looked bigger, brighter—better. But still not rentable. It might be clean, but it was still outdated and very much looked like a college kid's hideout, not like a beach escape.

"I picked up some paint samples." He pointed to the empty wall in the kitchen area. He'd painted four rectangles in varying shades of gray. "And a few different options for the backsplash."

Her eye was instantly drawn to the white subway tile. She knew it was overused, but she didn't care. It was classic, and she liked it. She went over and picked it up, holding it next to the gray rectangles on the wall.

"This one looks perfect." Emma pointed to a box that wasn't too blue or too brown or too lavender. It was a true gray.

"I like that one too," Jamie said. "It looks good with that subway tile." He turned. "And here are a few options for the floor." He pointed to the kitchen table, where small squares of hardwood flooring samples were situated. "You could do tile, but I think the wood will give it a homier feel."

"Wow," she said. "You've been busy."

"It's been good to have a project," he said.

His phone buzzed on the counter. He picked it up, looked at the screen, then silenced it. She knew nothing about his personal life. Had he come here to sort out a tricky romance? Was he nursing a broken heart? Running away from old mistakes?

It was not her business. She really shouldn't even be thinking about Jamie and romance in the same sentence.

She pushed the thoughts aside. What she needed to consider was how to navigate this project on a shoestring budget. The things he'd picked out were perfect but way too expensive. She didn't have to crunch numbers to know that.

"At the risk of sounding like an idiot, I need to tell you something," she said.

He straightened, watching her attentively. Too attentively, in fact. And she liked it a little too much.

"I didn't realize how much needed to be done in here initially, you know, when I first met you."

"It was hard to see under all the boxes."

Emma hated how dumb she felt that she'd so thoughtlessly gotten him involved in this project in the first place, especially with zero funding.

"Is something wrong?"

She scrunched her face. "I'm sorry, Jamie. I don't have the money for this after all. I thought I did, and I thought it was going to be a really good source of income, but I don't. I underestimated everything that needed to be done."

Hadn't she watched enough HGTV to know these projects were never simple? It was never as easy as anyone thought. Running a Clorox-soaked sponge over every surface wasn't going to cut it. Especially not here in Nantucket.

"I think I'm going to have to put the project on hold." She frowned. "You can stay the rest of the month, of course."

That was the other thing. Without this project, Jamie would leave. That shouldn't bother her, but it did. Whether she'd admit it or not, she liked having him there.

"Maybe we can figure something out," he said.

She shook her head. "It's pretty impossible."

"Have you been to the bank? Maybe a small loan?"

"I'm not sure it's smart to go into debt."

He looked genuinely disappointed as his eyes fell to the table, where the hardwood floor samples sat, cheerily waiting to be picked out.

"I'm really sorry."

He shook his head. "It's okay." He lifted his eyes to hers. "I can leave the samples for you, for when you're ready."

She nodded. "Thanks, Jamie."

~

A few nights later, after dinner, Emma loaded her dishwasher and glanced through the window toward the apartment above the garage. The lights were on. There was a man up there.

In Cam's apartment.

It wasn't something she'd gotten used to. And her curiosity about her guest was another thing she hadn't gotten used to. It had been years since she'd felt even the faintest attraction to a man. That was intentional—and, she reminded herself, that was how it needed to stay.

She didn't deserve to get lost in all the fluffy feelings of first love. She'd forfeited that right a long time ago.

It was for the best that the rental project wasn't going to happen, and Jamie had to leave.

So why did it feel so dreary in her heart?

Elise had called that morning to arrange for a time to come visit, and against her better judgment, Emma told her about Jamie.

"He was just going to help me with the apartment," she'd said, though she did sound like she was trying a little too hard to be convincing.

"Is he hot?"

Emma could practically hear her friend's eyebrows wagging. "He's not . . . unattractive."

Elise squealed. Why did this whole conversation make her uneasy?

Because Jamie was there to help her fulfill a dream Cam had left behind? Because Emma wasn't in the market for romance? Because Elise's teasing was a smidge too close to the truth?

Now, standing at the sink, water running over dishes that were long rinsed, her mind wandered to the man in the apartment. Jamie was still a stranger to her, and yet, over the last week and a half, he'd occupied far too many of her runaway thoughts. She'd invited him for dinner the night before, and he'd stayed behind to load the dishwasher while she gave CJ a bath.

He'd outlined each step of what it would take to make the apartment renter-ready, even though he knew she couldn't move forward with the project right now. He reasoned one day she'd be ready to take the plunge, so this way, she'd have everything she needed to make it happen. And this afternoon, when she ran home from work at lunch, he was out mowing the lawn.

She'd opted not to invite him for dinner tonight simply because her feelings were turning to a jumble, and she needed to get them under control.

She finished in the kitchen, picked up her laptop, and sat on the couch in the living room. The cottage had been well-maintained, thanks to Cam's parents and the property manager that had been handling everything for the last several years. She knew that even with a job and a potential rental income, she wasn't really independent. Without Cam, without this cottage, her world would be entirely different. It was a blessing, and she wouldn't lose sight of that.

She pulled a white-and-blue vintage quilt from the back of the couch and onto her lap. It was soft and worn, the way fabric turned when it had been well-loved. Thanks to some nonchalant probing at dinner the night before, she'd learned that Jamie and his business partner, Dylan, owned a business in Naperville, Illinois, called Graystar. It was about the only piece of personal information she'd managed to get out of him, other than the fact that he had a sister with three kids and a husband who liked to drink beer and watch sports.

Jamie wasn't forthcoming with information about himself. In fact, he'd been downright cagey when she asked him again what had brought him to Nantucket in the first place.

"Would you believe me if I said I was answering your ad?" He'd smiled then, and she had to look away, but the aftereffects rippled the nerve endings throughout her entire body.

She flipped the laptop open and typed in *Graystar, Naperville, IL*.

A sleek, modern website appeared on the screen—and a muted photo of two men, dressed in hiking gear, standing on a cliff overlooking a body of water, mountains in the background. She navigated straight to the "Who We Are" section. The screen filled with a hazy image of Jamie and another man, sitting on the hood of a Jeep on a dirt road in front of another mountain range.

Jamie wore a black ball cap and a zipped-up North Face jacket, cargo pants, and hiking boots. His eyes stared straight into the lens of the camera, as if they had a story to tell.

"What is your story, Jamie Shaw?" she said under her breath.

She looked around on the website, marveling at the stunning photos and videos in various portfolios. She didn't know much about business or telling a client's "brand story" (whatever that meant), but she did know a good artistic eye when she saw it. This man had it in spades. Maybe that's why he'd been able to pull together samples for the apartment so easily.

She moved to the search bar and typed *Jamie Shaw*. Google loaded a number of pages, but none of them were her Jamie Shaw. She quickly dismissed that thought. Jamie Shaw was no more "hers" than the crown jewels. She'd be smart to remember that.

She typed *Jamie Shaw, photographer*.

A different offering appeared.

She scrolled down to a page with the words *Jameson Edward Shaw, Photographer* highlighted and clicked. The page seemed to be several years old, but at the top were the words *The Art of Jameson Edward Shaw*. Maybe it was a different Jamie.

The images on the screen were every bit as stunning as the ones on the Graystar site, but they had a different quality to them. The colors were vibrant, the composition unique. Jameson Edward Shaw had an artistic eye that was truly rare. And he seemed to have traveled the world.

The image of a woman in tribal dress, nestled alongside a full-grown elephant caught her eye. A series of tribal portraits followed, along with a number of documentary-style photos of various foreign countries.

A group of schoolchildren playing in a dirt yard outside an African school. A mother holding a baby while standing in a river, a lush, green mountain range in the background. A close-up of a bicycle, which she gathered wasn't ridden for enjoyment but for work.

They were the kind of photos that made a person want to know more, the kind that dared you to look away.

She navigated to the "About the Photographer" page and clicked. The image of a man, shown in profile, camera slung over his shoulder, appeared on the screen. She looked closer. That could be Jamie, but it was hard to tell at this angle, as if the photo were intentionally mysterious. She scanned the bio.

Jameson Edward Shaw is an award-winning photo adventurer. He sees the world through a unique lens and strives to capture the story behind each image. His work has appeared in *National Geographic*, *Travel Magazine*, *Vogue*, the *Wall Street Journal*, and more. For inquiries or collaboration, contact Selma Day.

The work was stunning, the kind of photographs you'd see in a gallery. And those were some impressive credentials.

All at once, an idea formed.

If this was Jamie's work, could she convince him to show his art at Gallery 316? What if he was the first new artist she discovered? Maybe she couldn't follow through with the renovation plans, but was it possible Jamie was there for something else entirely? Something so much better? Travis had given her the job, and truth be told, it was the part she was most excited about. Not that answering phones wasn't exciting.

Who knew that the man helping her renovate Cam's old apartment was an authentic artist? And possibly her ticket to job security.

# CHAPTER EIGHT

TWO DAYS LATER, Jamie stood on the porch of the cottage, trying to work up the courage to knock.

He knew what Emma had said about the apartment, and he respected it, but he also had the overwhelming need to fix things, especially for her.

He had a feeling she wasn't going to like what he was there to say.

He pulled the letter out of his pocket and turned it over in his hand. When he'd written it, he had no idea who Emma was. She was a name and not much more. He never expected to have any reason for not wanting to give it to her.

But now he did.

This apartment project was his chance to help her, to ease his guilt, to put what he could right. It was a dumb thought. As if renovating an apartment could right such a wrong.

The letter was looking shabby from all his handling of it, proof of his indecision.

The light flipped on, and he turned to face the door just as

Emma pulled it open. He stuffed the letter back in his pocket and forced a smile.

She frowned. "What are you doing out here?"

"Uh, sorry." He searched for an excuse for why he'd been standing out there without knocking for a solid three minutes, but he came up empty. He wasn't good on the spot.

She watched him for a beat—was his squirming visible?

"I, uh, have an idea," he said, finally getting his bearings. "About the apartment."

"Come in." She stepped back and let him pass.

He did his best not to inhale the fragrance of her. He failed. Cinnamon and something else—vanilla maybe?

CJ ran into the entryway. "We're going to the beach tomorrow! Wanna come? We can build sandcastles!" He jumped up and down like a kid who'd had too much sugar.

"Oh, buddy, let's not bug Mr. Jamie with the beach," Emma said. "I'm sure he's got a lot going on."

"I have exactly nothing going on," he said. "And I'd love to come." He found her watching him. "If it's okay, I mean."

She paused, then mumbled something that sounded like "Uh, sure."

"Great. Text me the details?"

She nodded, then looked away. CJ ran up the stairs with a cheer, leaving Jamie standing there with Emma. Alone.

Sometimes being alone with her felt perfectly normal. Now was not one of those times.

"So what did you want to tell me?"

The question filled the space. *So many things.* What was he doing here? He was an honest person—why hadn't he told her the truth from the start?

"Jamie?"

"Right." He gathered himself. "I was thinking about the apartment."

"What about it?" She moved toward the kitchen, motioning for him to follow. She wore a pair of jeans, a loose T-shirt, partly tucked in at the front, and a pair of pig slippers.

"It's hard to have a serious conversation with you when you're wearing those." His gaze drifted to her feet.

She kicked one foot up. "Meet Peppa." Then the other foot. "And Pig." She grinned. "CJ named them."

"Nice," he said.

She pulled the plug from the drain, the sink full of dishwater. "Your idea?"

Right. His idea. "I don't think you should give up on the apartment," he said. "You don't owe anything on it, right?"

"Right."

"So after you cover your expenses, whatever rental money you bring in is pure profit."

"Yes." She took the lid off the teakettle and filled it with water. "Do you want some tea?"

He almost grinned. Did he look like the kind of person who drank tea? "I'm okay, thanks."

"Are you sure? Chamomile is supposed to help you sleep."

He frowned. "You think I need help sleeping?"

She cocked her head and sized him up. "Definitely."

What gave him away? "What makes you say that?" He leaned against the doorjamb of the kitchen and watched her.

She shrugged. "A hunch, I guess. You have this tired-behind-the-eyes thing going on."

He didn't know it was that obvious. Or maybe she was just that observant.

"Do you sleep?" She leaned against the counter, her stance matching his.

"Sometimes."

"Me too."

He hated knowing that stress and grief kept her awake at night.

"So?" Expectancy raised her eyebrows.

"So?"

"What are you suggesting?"

He'd given it thought. Plenty of thought. The trouble was, he was fairly certain she wouldn't go for it. "You should let me help out."

She took a mug down from a shelf on the wall and fished a tea bag out from a nearly empty cupboard. "I thought we talked about this."

"We did," he said. "And I understand you don't want to go into debt. But what if I spotted you the up-front money?"

She turned and faced him. "Absolutely not."

"It would be like an investment," he said. Something inside him pleaded with her to let him do this for her.

"How would that even work?"

"I'd buy the materials and do the work, and then when it was done, you'd rent it out."

She frowned. "So you pay for everything, do all the work, and make none of the money?"

He shrugged. "You could pay me back over time, once the rental started doing well."

The teakettle whistled. She took it off the burner and poured steaming water into her mug. "I don't think that's a good idea."

"Why not?"

"Because I don't even know you," she said. "And you don't know me, so why would you even offer such a thing?"

He looked away. The letter practically turned to a flame in his pocket. He should tell her. He had to tell her.

Why couldn't he tell her?

Their eyes met.

*Oh. That was why.*

"Look," he said, "I've got some extra money, and I've been looking for a project. This is a great financial move. I think we'd make back our initial investment within the year."

"*Our* investment?"

He didn't respond.

She dipped the tea bag low into the mug, studying it thoughtfully.

"It's not really an investment if you don't make money on it down the road."

"Maybe *investment* is the wrong word."

"What would be better? *Charity case*?"

"It wouldn't be charity."

"You're right. It wouldn't be, because I'm not going to let you pay for it."

"I already bought the flooring."

Her eyes darted to his. "You what?"

"I don't have anything else to do right now," he said. "So I bought the flooring. And the paint."

"Jamie."

"You can pay me back or not," he said. "But I'm not returning it."

She removed the tea bag from the mug and stirred milk and sugar into the drink. "Why would you do this?"

Another shrug. "It's a good distraction."

Which was the opposite of what Emma was—not a good distraction.

"You need a distraction?" She picked up the tea and took a sip, then added a little more sugar.

"I guess you could say that, yeah."

"Working some stuff out?"

If only she knew the half of it.

She eyed him for a beat too long. "Fine, since you are stubborn and pigheaded, I'll let you do this, but only if it's a true investment, which means I'll pay you back for the renovation supplies, and then you'll make money on the rental same as me for an agreed-upon length of time."

"Like six months?"

"Like a few years," she said. "At least. I'll let you do this, but only if it's a legitimate investment and not a charity case."

He studied her for a long moment, certain this had something to do with that list she'd pinned to the fridge. This was about her independence, her pride, which was every bit as important to her as his absolution was to him.

She stuck her hand in his direction. "Deal?"

He hesitated.

"This is my final offer," she said.

"Half the renovation supplies," he said.

She raised her eyebrows.

"My final offer."

She rolled her eyes. "Fine."

He took her hand and shook it. "Fine. Deal."

The second their skin touched, a wave of energy zapped down his spine. She gave one firm nod, then pulled her hand away so quickly he wondered if she felt it too.

"I'll have my lawyer draw up a contract," she said.

"You have a lawyer?"

She took another sip of tea. "Actually no, but didn't that sound professional when I said it?"

He laughed. "It was very impressive."

"I was just going to find a contract online and change the words so they worked for this agreement."

"I'm sure whatever you come up with will be fine," he said.

"I guess this means you'll be staying around for a little while longer."

He didn't dare look away. He was reading so much into that simple statement. Was she happy about that? Annoyed? Indifferent?

*Seriously, Shaw. Knock it off. She was someone's wife.*

"If that's okay," he finally said.

She shrugged as if it didn't matter one way or the other. "Fine with me."

He nodded. It was a perfectly acceptable response from a woman who had no interest in him romantically, which was what she was, a fact he'd be smart to remember.

"Are you sure about the beach tomorrow?" she asked.

"I don't have to go," he said. "If it's a mother-son bonding thing. Or whatever."

"Oh, you're not getting out of it now. You said you'd build sand-castles, and that kid is not going to let you off the hook." She smiled.

He smiled back. He couldn't help it. Her smile lit up the whole room. Like someone finally turned the light on after he'd been searching around in the dark for years. "I'll be there."

"I have to work in the morning, so is lunchtime okay?"

"Works for me."

"See you then."

He didn't move for *one-one-thousand, two-one-thousand, three—* then finally forced himself to go.

Whatever these feelings were, he needed to squash them quick.

Or he'd find himself head over heels in love with Cam Woodson's widow.

And that was absolutely not the reason he'd come to Nantucket.

# CHAPTER NINE

THE NEXT DAY, Emma arrived for work twenty minutes early. Travis was already there, and judging by the look on his face, something was wrong.

She hung her purse on the designated hook and joined him behind the counter.

"You look stressed." She slid the white chocolate mocha she'd picked up for him on the way into work across the counter.

"Godsend," he said, picking up the drink. "Is it that obvious that I'm stressed?"

"Kind of. You've got a really deep wrinkle in your forehead."

He glared at her. "And now I have wrinkles on top of everything else. Great."

Travis, she'd learned, was slightly dramatic. And this gallery was usually the source of all his emotions. Last week, when he'd found out Milton Maxwell had agreed to show a piece for the Nantucket Art Festival, Travis had been beside himself in excitement. Today it seemed the pendulum had swung back in the other direction.

"What's wrong?" she asked. "Can I help?"

He frowned. "Have you found me a sensational undiscovered artist?"

The image of the tribal woman with the elephant popped in her mind.

Before she could respond, he was talking again. "I want to make sure you understand the importance of this job you volunteered for." He paused, as if waiting to see if he had her undivided attention. "The Nantucket Art Festival is riding on this," he said. "This is the premier cultural event of the summer."

She wasn't sure that was true, but she didn't say so.

"And Gallery 316 has a reputation for finding *the* artist who is the talk of the entire event."

She knew this. It was becoming clear that though he'd agreed to let her find a replacement for Marco St. John, he didn't actually trust her to do so.

"Won't that be Milton Maxwell?" she asked dumbly.

She knew it was "dumbly" because of the instant look of exasperation that came her way.

"Miss Woodson," Travis said. "You cannot be that dense."

"I'm not from here, Travis," she said. "Enlighten me." She took a sip of her own coffee. So she'd assumed Milton Maxwell was going to be their headliner. Did that make her a complete idiot?

"Milton Maxwell is not a *discovery*," Travis said. "He's already a successful artist. The festival is also one of the best ways for new artists to emerge onto the art scene, and every year, without fail, Gallery 316 has launched one of these artists from oblivion to stardom. It's what we're known for."

She didn't bother to remind him that he'd given her this job. It was evident he was intent on worrying about it, so maybe it was better to pretend their previous conversation had never happened. "So what's the problem?"

"The well has run dry," he said. "There are no undiscovered artists deserving of this honor. Not a single one."

She frowned. "I know that's not true."

He held a hand up. "Before you tell me to take another look at your portfolio, you should know I never choose employees for this honor."

She shook her head. "I didn't mean me." Though she was slightly offended at his reaction to the idea that she did. "I just mean in general. There are lots of incredible artists out there."

"I had the perfect person to replace Marco," he said. "A photographer named Rajah, like the tiger in the movie *Aladdin*."

"Rajah who?"

"Just Rajah," Travis said. "Apparently he only needs the one name."

"So what happened?"

"As of this morning, he's no longer undiscovered." He turned his laptop around to reveal an article from the *New York Times*. Rajah was showing at a high-end art gallery in the city and receiving all kinds of critical praise.

"Is it the end of the world if Gallery 316 doesn't discover a new talent this year?"

Again he looked at her as if she'd just said the stupidest thing possible. "Are we in the same conversation?"

She didn't respond.

"Yes, it would be the end of the world," he said. "I thought I had this taken care of, and now I'll have to step away from my work in order to start the search all over again. These things don't just happen overnight, Emma." He said her name as if it had an unpleasant taste.

Emma knew that this reaction was part melodrama and part legitimate concern. She also knew she had a real opportunity to make herself indispensable. After only a couple of weeks at the gallery, she already knew this was a job she loved and wanted to keep, despite her boss's penchant for acting like the star of his own telenovela.

"I thought this was my job." She proceeded with caution. "You hired me to alleviate stress. That only works if you actually hand some of this stuff over to me."

He frowned at her. "Did I really agree to let you take this on? What was I thinking?"

She tried not to be offended. "I do have a good eye. You said so yourself."

"I never said that." Travis took another drink as he walked toward the front of the gallery to push the door open and welcome any passersby inside.

"You did," she reminded him. "Two days ago, when I rearranged the back wall."

He didn't let on, but she could tell by the twitch in his eye that he remembered. "Well, have you come up with anybody?"

"Maybe." It was a foolish thing to say, especially since she didn't know (a) if "Jameson Edward Shaw" was the Jamie who'd become her accidental business partner practically overnight, and (b) if Jameson Edward Shaw was still taking photos like the ones she'd marveled at online.

"Maybe?"

"I think so."

Travis looked annoyed.

"Can you give me a few days to figure it out?"

"I don't have a few days," Travis said, returning to his melodrama.

"Fine, a day," she said. "Give me a day."

"Fine," he said.

"You won't book anyone else?"

He flicked a hand in the air dismissively.

"I won't let you down," she said, knowing full well it was a promise she had no business making.

An old couple walked in, and Travis nodded at Emma as if to remind her she had a job to do. She welcomed the couple to Gallery 316 and invited them to look around. As she took a step away to give them their space, she glanced outside.

Sunshine shone through the trees and onto the sidewalk, highlighting patches of cobblestone in the street. Nantucket had many great qualities, and she was beginning to learn them for herself. A pang of gratitude welled up inside her. Life had certainly not gone as planned, but she was here, and she was okay. And in a few hours, she'd be at the beach, relaxing.

Or maybe not relaxing. With Jamie joining them, there was a good chance every nerve ending in her body would be on high alert.

~

Emma returned home at lunchtime with CJ to find Jamie sitting on her porch, a picnic basket beside him. He'd made lunch?

CJ was out of the car seat practically before she turned off the engine, and she watched as he ran toward Jamie like a dog who'd been let out in a field to play.

Jamie lit up at the sight of them, his navy-blue-and-white board shorts showing legs that were tanner than she expected. Tanner and more muscular. The guy either worked out regularly or had really good genes.

"I'm gonna go find my suit!" CJ hollered as he disappeared inside the house.

Jamie's grin turned lazy as he faced Emma, who now stood at the bottom of the porch stairs.

"Can I show you what I did this morning?"

She shifted her purse from one shoulder to the other. "Does it involve a picnic basket?"

He followed her gaze to the basket at his feet. "No. That was just a bonus. I figured you might be hungry."

"I was going to make peanut butter and jelly sandwiches."

He shrugged. "Now you don't have to."

"All right," she said, trying not to linger on his thoughtfulness. "Show me what you did this morning."

He strolled down the stairs, and she fell into step beside him as he led her toward the garage. "I hope you like it, but if you don't, I can do it over."

"I'm sure I'll love it. Whatever it is."

She followed him up the stairs, and he opened the door to the apartment. For the first time, she wasn't hit with feelings of sadness over all that she'd lost. Instead, there was a twinge of excitement for what was to come.

Should she feel guilty for that? If she dwelled on it, she certainly would.

The light poured in through the uncovered windows and door, revealing the gray paint she'd chosen on every wall.

"I didn't paint in the kitchen area because we'll do the backsplash, but what do you think?"

"I think it's a ton of work," she said. "You did the whole thing today?"

"Two coats." He moved back, giving her more space to take it all in. "I started really early."

She glanced at him. "How early?"

He grimaced. "Four?"

She shook her head. "You should've had the chamomile."

"But if I had, you would be looking at a partially painted apartment."

"Touché." There was something sweet in the way he'd presented the space, like he was a kid seeking approval on a graded paper he'd brought home from school. "It looks pretty awesome."

"I was hoping you'd think so," he said.

She smiled. It mattered to him what she thought. But why? She wouldn't delude herself into thinking anything about his being there was normal.

"Why are you doing this?" She'd blurted the question before she could decide if she actually wanted to ask.

"What do you mean?"

"I mean, it's a little weird, right?" This was a flash of the old Emma. The pregrief Emma. The one who spoke her mind and didn't back down from hard conversations. That Emma had been on hiatus, and since she moved here, since declaring this year *hers*, she'd been reminded more than once of the person she used to be.

"What's weird?" He shifted, a look of discomfort washing across his face.

She remembered this. She remembered that most people didn't quite know how to take her. She was forward and blunt. She liked to tackle problems head-on.

Somewhere along the way, she'd lost all of that.

Moving here had reminded her of it.

"You're a perfect stranger. You answered an ad. When it wasn't what I told you it was, instead of getting annoyed, you offered to pay for the renovations."

"I offered to invest," he said.

"You pretty much offered to pay for it," she reminded him. "I was the one who insisted you invest."

"Have you been thinking about this a lot since last night?"

She shrugged. "Some."

"So that chamomile didn't really do the trick then, huh?" He smirked at her.

She responded with a friendly eye roll.

"Nothing's changed," he said. "Except now you have gray walls."

"I just wondered why," she said.

"Because gray walls are very in style."

She smiled. "I'm serious."

He looked away. "I'm looking for people to help, I guess."

"Why?" Now she was more than curious. "Did you used to be a bully or something?"

Their eyes met, and he paused. Finally he said, "Isn't it a sad commentary when altruism is met with suspicion?"

"I guess it is, yeah."

She heard the screen door open and slam shut, followed by CJ bellowing, "Mom!"

"Let's go to the beach." Jamie opened the door and walked outside. Emma took another look around the apartment. Nothing in her life had returned to normal.

But she no longer felt like everything in her life was broken.

She supposed she had Jamie to thank for that, though she wasn't sure why. And maybe he'd never tell her. And maybe that was okay. Maybe his arrival in Nantucket had helped her remember who she was before she'd forgotten who she was.

And maybe that was all that really mattered.

# CHAPTER TEN

~~~

JAMIE HAD BEEN IN NANTUCKET FOR TWO WEEKS, but he'd barely caught a view of the water. If he was smart, he'd make a point to stare at it daily—he had a feeling it would calm his nerves. Besides, how many more days would he be able to claim the ocean as his backyard? It was an entirely different world here than where he was from.

Island life had an altogether different feel than being in land-locked Illinois. It was the air that made it so. Or the smells. Or the sounds. Or all of it mixed together.

As they walked off in the direction of the beach, he and Emma lugging along anything they could possibly need while they were there, Jamie realized he might have accepted CJ's invitation too hastily. Being here, like this, with Emma and her son . . . well, it was different from working on her apartment or even allowing her to feed him the occasional meal.

This felt less like business and more like . . . a date.

Especially with this stupid picnic basket in tow. Jamie had packed lunch mostly because after he'd finished painting, he needed something else to do. It turned out downtime was his enemy. Too many unwanted thoughts, and if a thought popped in his head, like, say *She's going to hate you when she finds out who you really are*, he couldn't help himself but to run it down to the end.

He'd consider each possible scenario from the most mundane to the most disastrous, and he'd play it out as long as his imagination would allow. It was something Dr. McDonald had warned against. Apparently, at least according to her, he was in control of his thoughts. A thought might enter his mind without his permission, but he didn't have to dwell on it. For whatever reason, he found that impossible.

They reached the beach and CJ let out a squeal of delight. Oh, to be a kid again, without a care in the world. The boy kicked up the sand as he ran ahead, and Jamie almost lost his breath at the sight of the ocean.

It had been so long since he'd allowed himself to coexist with nature without feeling the guilt of his past mistakes. But like a beauty queen on a stage, the beaches in Nantucket demanded attention.

Jamie was good at ignoring beauty. He'd become the kind of person who focused instead on facts and details.

He plodded through the sand, quiet, thoughtful, aware that Emma was watching him.

He glanced over at her, and though he couldn't see her eyes behind her big sunglasses, he knew she was sizing him up. Making assumptions. Wondering about him.

It was as scary as it was thrilling. He wanted her to like him, but her watchful eye was proving difficult to avoid. She asked whatever questions popped into her head. She had no hesitation in being forthright.

And he'd been anything but.

Worse, she was making ignoring beauty a whole lot more difficult.

CJ dropped his towel in a heap in a clearing.

"I guess we're stopping here," Emma said.

Jamie set up the two chairs he'd carried, and Emma set down the picnic basket.

"I haven't brought him down here because it kind of stresses me out," she said.

Jamie watched as CJ filled a bucket with sand. "What does?"

"The beach." She held up a hand to block the sun and drew her attention to him. "I sometimes worry about CJ getting pulled under or running off somewhere."

"I'll keep an eye on him," Jamie said.

"Oh, I wasn't saying that so you'd offer. Just thinking out loud."

"I know." Jamie would never tire of looking for ways to make Emma's life easier. "But I don't mind."

"You're a good swimmer?" She studied him. Her glances had turned to gazes. He couldn't avoid her questions forever. Thankfully, this was an easy one.

He smiled. "I'm a great swimmer."

"In the ocean? Because it's different in the ocean than it is in a pool."

"I've done a lot of swimming in the ocean."

"When you used to take pictures for all those magazines?" She sat down in the chair and kicked off her flip-flops.

The question caught him off guard. How did she know about that?

"I didn't check your references, but I did google you," she said, leaning back. "You *are* Jameson Edward Shaw, photographer for *National Geographic* and *Vogue* and all those other fancy magazines, aren't you?"

Jamie stared out at the ocean. In the distance, he could see a lighthouse with a red stripe around the middle of it. She was one step closer to finding him out. If he was smart, he'd tell her the whole sordid story right now.

Why wasn't he smart?

"Sorry. Did I say something wrong?" she asked.

He glanced at her. "No, sorry. I got distracted by the lighthouse."

"Sankaty lighthouse," she said. "We can hike over there and go up to the top if you want. I bet the view is amazing."

"I bet you're right," he said, aware that a hike to the top of the lighthouse would feel even more like a date than a day at the beach.

"Before we moved here, my friend Elise made a list of all the things we *had* to do once we got settled in. Touring the lighthouse was one of them."

"How many of the things on the list have you done?" he asked, thankful that the conversation seemed to have steered away from his former life as a photojournalist.

She watched CJ closely. "Zero."

He wanted to change that. He had absolutely no business wanting it, but he did. The thought scared him, as did most of his thoughts where Emma was concerned. He felt like a nerdy middle schooler with a crush on the popular girl. He wanted her to like him, and it was wholly consuming him.

It was his guilt. Or it had started out that way. Now he feared it was something else.

CJ stood and turned the bucket of sand over. It spilled out in a disappointing pile. "This is a lame sandcastle."

Jamie pulled his gray T-shirt up over his head and tossed it on the chair. "Let's get some water and build this thing right."

He picked up another bucket and trudged down to the shore, CJ close at his side. Cold ocean water licked his feet. Guilt nipped at his heels.

What was he doing here? Why was he embedding himself in Emma's life like this? CJ splashed in the water, then filled his bucket and threw it at Jamie. He gasped at the shock of cold against his warm, bare skin, picked the boy up, and threw him over his shoulder. CJ let out a shriek of laughter as Jamie propelled him down toward the water, headfirst. CJ's hands scraped the ocean, and he belly laughed.

Jamie turned him right side up and set him back down in the ankle-deep water. "You ready to build this castle or what?"

CJ looked back on the shore where Emma sat, watching them. Jamie stared at her for a beat, then noticed she swiped underneath her glasses. Was she crying?

He turned away. He was making this worse. He was dragging out the inevitable.

Yet nothing inside him told him to run away. In fact, every single nerve ending in his body told him to run *to* her. It was unfair, and he knew it.

"Mommy!" CJ called out. "Come out here!"

Emma stood and took off her cover-up. At the sight of her body in her red polka-dot bathing suit, Jamie forced himself to look away— but not before a brief moment of admiration for what she'd been hiding underneath that flowy white garment.

The same imagination that played out every possible scenario of a situation would also gladly play out the occasional fantasy about Emma if he allowed it to.

He wouldn't.

He couldn't.

*She's going to hate you when she finds out who you really are.*

The thought entered, unwanted, and for once, he took Dr. McDonald's advice and chose not to dwell on it. Because the last thing in the world he wanted to think about was the fact that Emma could ever hate him.

And that made him wonder if there was any way to keep her from ever finding out the truth about why he'd come to Nantucket in the first place.

Jamie decided to be present, for the first time in a long time. And something inside him seemed to awaken as the minutes passed. After they built an epic sandcastle, CJ announced he was hungry, so they reapplied their sunscreen and opened the picnic basket.

"Wow," Emma said. "This all looks amazing. Were you planning to feed everyone on the beach?" She grinned at him.

That grin could cause a power outage.

"I didn't know what you guys liked," he said.

She pulled out the sandwiches he'd bought at Bartlett's Farm earlier that day. Every single one of them looked good, and he'd had trouble deciding. In retrospect, he might've gone a little overboard.

"Can we split them?" Emma asked. "I kind of want to try more than one."

"I didn't peg you for the indecisive type." He unwrapped the chicken pesto sandwich.

"It's not indecision," she said. "I want to try it all. I have a hearty appetite."

Well, that was refreshing. He hadn't dated anyone seriously for a few years now, but his sister had set him up with two different women in recent months. Taking a woman out and paying for a dinner she didn't eat ranked up there as one of his biggest pet peeves.

"Cam used to laugh at how much I could put away." She seemed to say it without thinking. She quickly looked away, unwrapping the ham and Swiss. "Sorry."

"It's fine," he said.

"Here you go, buddy." Emma gave CJ half the ham and Swiss along with a small bag of chips, then glanced back at Jamie. "I'll be lucky if I can get him to eat three bites of this."

They ate in silence for a few minutes.

"Are you a pretty adventurous eater?" she asked.

He swallowed the bite in his mouth and stared out at the water. This topic could easily segue into his photography. His past life. His mistakes.

"Sorry. I just don't really know anything about you."

"Google wasn't helpful?" He tossed her a smile.

Her cheeks turned pink and the sight of it made him dizzy. Man, he liked her. Hillary would say he was drawn to her out of some odd sense of duty, but he didn't think that was it. She stirred something inside him, like a waking of the dead. He could practically feel himself reengaging in a life he'd all but walked away from.

Nobody had done that in years. He'd been going through the motions. Nothing more.

"Google left me with a lot of blanks to fill in." Her reply came out shy, which surprised him because Emma seemed anything but.

"When I was traveling, I really liked to try the food in the different countries," he said. See? A perfectly benign answer. No harm there. He wasn't lying. He wasn't giving himself away. An annoying thought at the back of his mind worked hard for his attention.

He ignored it.

"You don't travel anymore?" she asked.

"Not like I used to."

"When you were working as a world-class photographer?"

He stifled a smile. "When I was working as a photojournalist."

"Oooh, fancy." She shook her shoulders as she said it. He wanted to squeeze that tan shoulder, to feel the heat of her skin under his fingers.

*Enough, Shaw. Knock it off.*

"It's really not fancy," he said. How many nights had he spent sleeping on a dirt floor? How many days had he gone without a shower and a proper meal? His work was adventurous but grueling. And lonely—it was often, always, lonely.

A twinge of desire twisted in his belly. He found that much harder to ignore.

He'd gone all this time without missing it—nothing had changed. He didn't get to mourn that loss when others mourned so much more.

And yet . . . it felt like something inside him had shifted.

"What was it like?" she asked.

"Which part? The traveling or the photojournalism?"

"All of it." Her eyes were wide, and she'd practically abandoned her meal. He had her full, undivided attention. And he wasn't sure he wanted it.

He shrugged and tossed the crust of a turkey sandwich on its wrapper. "It was a job."

She looked disappointed.

"That's not true, actually," he said, not wanting to lie to her. "It was incredible. I don't think I ever felt more alive than when I was finding new stories to tell." That creative rush, that deep desire to locate beauty and share it with the world, was something that fueled him. He could've lived on that feeling for decades if things were different.

"Why'd you stop?"

He propped an arm over his knee and looked at her. "Not all of the stories I found were good ones."

She went still.

"I guess I was looking for a quieter, simpler life," he said.

That was God's honest truth. Yet there was a huge part of the story he was choosing to keep to himself. And he was choosing that because he was selfish. Emma deserved to know everything, but the fear of losing her had grown even bigger in just the last few hours.

How could he sacrifice that already?

*How could you not?* It was wrong, keeping it to himself.

"Emma, look—"

"Mom, I'm done!"

Her eyes darted to CJ, who had eaten approximately four bites total. She shook her head. "You eat like a bird."

He grinned up at her.

"He really favors his dad," Jamie said.

Emma let out a tiny gasp as she met Jamie's eyes.

His pulse quickened. Why had he said that? He quickly backtracked. "In the photo on the wall in your entryway, I mean. The one of you two on the beach."

She stilled. "Oh."

"CJ looks like him."

She nodded. "Yeah, I think so too."

He regretted his careless comment, especially because it seemed to upset her. "Sorry, I didn't mean to—"

"No, don't be silly." She stood. "It's totally fine." She was wrapped up in a huge towel, which she shed as she held her hand out to her son. "Let's go back in the water for just a little bit, CJ." She looked at Jamie. "You coming?"

"I'll clean up here first; then I'll head down."

He watched as the two of them started off toward the ocean. CJ bent over to pick something up, then waved it in the air. "Mr. Jamie! I found a seashell!"

"That's great, buddy!" Jamie called back.

He repackaged the leftovers and put them back in the picnic basket, then settled into the chair, the sun overhead, high in the sky. Emma and CJ chased the waves as they lapped the shore, and Jamie watched, the sound of the boy's laughter filling him from the inside out.

He leaned forward, elbows on his knees, watching as life played out right in front of him, and for the first time in five years, he did something that used to be so common. He composed a photograph from the scene in front of him—Emma, wearing her red bathing suit and a floppy straw beach hat, framed by the bright light of the shining sun, leaning in toward a little boy, love so evident on her face it could fill a thousand oceans.

He picked up his phone and tried to capture it, but it wasn't right. The zoom wasn't powerful enough to maintain the clarity of the image, and the story slipped away.

And the disappointment that showed up in its place was surprising and palpable.

The memory of an artist long since forgotten returned with such swiftness it nearly took his breath away.

Finally, a subject that had captured his artistic desire so much so that he wasn't sure he could ignore it.

# CHAPTER ELEVEN

~~~

BY LATE AFTERNOON, Emma could feel the sting of the sun on her shoulders. They packed up their things and practically dragged CJ away from the ocean. Apparently he was going to be a kid who loved the water.

Just like Cam.

The similarities were clear—even Jamie said so. And CJ often reminded her of her late husband, though these days, it was harder to conjure him. When she forgot the way his smile made her feel, she found a book of photos to fill herself back up with him. When she forgot the sound of his laugh, she found their wedding video and played it as she fell asleep. When she forgot the sound of his voice, she listened to the recorded outgoing message on his old phone, which she still paid for, solely for that purpose.

But she didn't turn to her son for reminders of Cam.

She wasn't sure she could trust what she saw.

They walked back to the cottage, CJ on Jamie's shoulders along with their beach chairs. He'd insisted on carrying them, leaving her with a bag of sandy towels and the picnic basket containing their leftovers from lunch.

"Thanks for coming with us," Emma said, determined to keep things from becoming awkward with him, even though he'd artfully dodged her questions about his life as a photojournalist. She wanted to know more to assess his willingness to participate in the art festival, of course, but the job itself fascinated her. She'd never known an artist who'd been so successful.

Why would he give that up?

And why didn't he want to talk about it?

Her mind played through a series of the photos she'd seen on his old website. They told so many stories, but none of them were about the storyteller.

They reached the cottage, and Jamie hauled CJ off his shoulders and down onto the porch steps.

"Wanna play trucks?" CJ asked.

"I think you're going to take a little nap, mister," Emma said.

"Mo-om!"

"Inside. You can lie on the couch."

CJ stomped off, his lower lip formed in a considerable pout.

"That kid," Emma said, shaking her head.

"He's a good one." Jamie faced her. "You've done a good job with him."

Heat rushed to her cheeks. "I wish I could take all the credit. His grandparents are largely responsible."

Jamie watched her. Studied her. Was he formulating her story behind that artistic lens?

"Listen, I had a sort of ulterior motive for probing you about your photography," she said. Might as well come clean. At least about this.

"Oh?" He leaned the chairs against the porch steps. She tried to ignore the way he moved, but it was impossible. It was graceful and strong at the same time. It was hard not to notice the reaction in her body.

*Good grief, Emma, he's just setting down the chairs. Get a grip.*

When she realized she had his attention (how unnerving!), she told him about the art festival. About Travis. About what the job meant to her. About her promise to find someone amazing.

"When I told Travis I could find someone, I was thinking of you."

Jamie shifted, a look of discomfort clear on his face. "Oh, that's flattering, but I don't really do that anymore."

"Your website says you showed in a gallery once. In Chicago. This would be like that."

"I didn't even realize that website was still up," he said. "It's old. It's from a different life."

She frowned. *What happened to you, Jamie Shaw?*

"It would really help me out if I could deliver the best new artist of the festival," she said. "It's a big deal to my boss." As if she had the right to ask him for a favor. As if they weren't still mostly strangers. As if he wasn't already helping her by getting her apartment ready to be rented and paying for it too.

Who did she think she was, anyway?

"Why don't you submit your work?" he asked.

She scoffed. "What work? I haven't painted in ages." She was kicking herself for mentioning that fact about herself during one of their dinners early on. Leave it to Jamie to commit the tidbit to memory.

He shrugged. "I haven't taken artistic photos in ages."

"That's fair," she said. "But you *are* still working in photography."

"Yeah," he said. "But it's always someone else's vision. It's just business."

"But why?" She watched him. "I mean, you're obviously gifted, and you have an impressive résumé. Not many people have found that kind of success. It seems like such a waste."

He looked away. "I'm sorry I can't help. I wish I could. It's just not something I do anymore. I wouldn't even have anything to submit."

"You're living in one of the most beautiful places in the country," she said, aware she was being pushy. "You could come up with something."

He didn't respond.

"My boss said, 'Once an artist, always an artist.'" She tried to keep her tone light, afraid she'd offended him. He'd gone serious and a little broody. "And you're an artist. It's a shame we don't get to see the world through your lens." After a beat, she added, "Just think about it, okay?"

"Sure," he said, "but don't get your hopes up."

She nodded, but it was too late. Her hopes were already up. And she was slightly afraid those hopes were about more than photographs in an art show.

Jamie intrigued her. There was something mysterious about him—something that made her want to know more.

Still, she could see he was done talking about it for today. If she was going to learn anything else about him, it would have to wait.

"Thanks for coming with us today," she said. "And for helping with CJ."

"Anytime," he said.

She didn't move for a moment, and he didn't either. It was as if there was more to be said, but she wasn't sure what. She just knew she liked it better when he was around.

"I should go check on CJ," she finally said.

Jamie nodded, and Emma told her legs to move. They obeyed, barely. She went inside and found her son already asleep on the couch. The heat plus a full day of play had done him in. She envied the peace he seemed to have such easy access to. How long had it been since she'd been so carefree? To simply fall asleep on the sofa in the middle of the day?

She moved toward him, noting his rhythmic breathing.

Jamie said he looked like Cam when he smiled. Did he? She hoped so. She wanted to see her husband in her little boy, but as the years went on, her memory turned foggy. And the older CJ got, the less of Cam she saw.

Maybe it was her fear that blotted out the similarities?

Or maybe there were none.

She went into the kitchen, where she put away the day's leftovers and tried not to think about Cam. About their last conversation. The look on his face. The way she'd broken his heart.

She could shove the thoughts aside, of course, but she knew they'd be replaced by a whole different set of unwanted musings—the ones where she dreamed up stories about Jameson Edward Shaw.

Twice she'd found him watching her after lunch. He sat in his chair—shirtless, she noticed—and watched her play with CJ. But not in an unsettling way. In a way that made her wonder if he was dreaming up stories too.

She couldn't explain why, but she felt it was her duty to convince him to do this gallery show. Not only because she was certain to impress Travis, but because she couldn't shake the feeling that a big part of Jamie was missing without art and creativity in his life.

She tried to explain that to Elise on the phone later that evening when her friend prodded her for details about her "mystery man."

"It's not your job to save everyone, Emma," Elise said. "You need to be focusing on you."

But that was the thing. Somehow thinking about Jamie, about his art, about what she theorized was missing in his life *was* helping her focus on herself. She had a hunch that she had a lot in common with the man.

"Can we go back to talking about how he looked without his shirt on?" Elise teased.

"It's not like that," Emma said in protest.

"I think it's exactly like that, and that's a good thing. You sound happy."

Emma went silent. She didn't deserve to be happy. Not like this. She'd vowed to grow old alone, to make being CJ's mom enough for her.

That had never been a problem before.

"It's been a lot of years, Em. It's okay for you to move on."

The words came at her like an unwanted and annoying poke to the ribs. She'd planned to never move on. It wasn't something she wanted to try—not even in *The Year of Emma.*

"I can practically hear you overthinking this," Elise said. "What if you just went with it?"

"Went with what?"

"Whatever it is. Whatever happens. If you feel like kissing him, then kiss him. If you feel like ignoring him, then ignore him."

"That'll never work," Emma said.

"It doesn't have to be complicated."

"But it is," she said. "I have so much baggage." So much more than even Elise knew.

"Whatever. I think you're scared."

*I am.*

"He sounds like a great guy. I think you should go for it."

She'd hung up the phone feeling unsettled and out of sorts. She'd take a melatonin, but it had stopped working—anything stronger and she wouldn't be able to function the next day.

Sleep eluded her. She stared at the ceiling, wondering if she should turn on the TV. She tossed. Turned. Tried to make her mind go blank.

Nothing was working.

Around 3 a.m., she got up and went down to the kitchen to make herself a cup of tea. It didn't always help despite what "they" said, but there was something about the ritual that calmed her nerves. In the dark, she filled the kettle with water and put it on the stove to heat.

She told herself not to look up at the apartment above the garage, but her curiosity proved too strong. As she suspected, a light was on.

Jamie was either still awake or he'd forgotten to turn it off before falling asleep.

The clock on the wall clicked off the seconds as she watched for some sign of life in the apartment. After a longer time than she'd ever admit, she saw a shadow pass by the window. She rushed into a corner, breathless.

Ridiculous.

What was she now, a girl walking down the halls of her high school, hoping to steal a glimpse of her crush?

The list on the refrigerator caught her eye. She should probably tuck that dumb thing away somewhere so it didn't taunt her every time she looked at it. Because it was definitely taunting. Especially *9. Go on a proper date.*

She moved back to the window and looked up. The light in the apartment had gone off. She said a quick, silent prayer that Jamie slept what was left of the night. And then she felt something inside her turn.

She hadn't prayed much lately. Not about CJ or about moving or about her job. Not about her guilt and all she'd yet to forgive herself for. And yet here she was, praying for Jamie.

Because she could see that something inside him was broken.

And for some inexplicable reason, she wanted to be the one to put him back together.

# CHAPTER TWELVE

~~~

AFTER RETURNING FROM THE BEACH, Jamie went back to the apartment and tried to forget his conversation with Emma.

The truth was, he would've done anything for her. Anything to make her life easier or win her points with the boss of this new job that she actually loved. Anything to make her smile.

Anything except what she was asking.

Showing his work in a gallery had always been a dream. And while he had shown two pieces in a gallery in Chicago, it hadn't been a solo show. It was barely a blip. Sure, he'd claimed it on his website, but once upon a time, he'd wanted so much more.

And now this beautiful woman he couldn't stop thinking about was offering him the opportunity to see that dream fulfilled—and he couldn't bring himself to take it.

He wasn't the same photographer as the man who'd shot those images on his old website.

He opened his laptop and navigated to the web page that had told Emma more than he wanted her to know. As he scrolled through the photos, the memories returned—he was on an African safari, then eating with a couple in Thailand, then surfing off the coast of Mozambique. He was finding people with interesting faces and even more interesting stories. He was sharing a meal with a tribe in the mountains of India.

He was alive.

Each image was a moment in time. A moment he'd captured. A story he'd discovered. Each photo, proof that he'd been a witness to something special. Or maybe he'd created something special.

On the beach, he'd been overwhelmed by the desire to compose that shot in the viewfinder, to preserve the moment between Emma and her son. What did that mean?

From where he sat, the camera, securely fastened in his bag, seemed to be calling out to him. He'd stopped marveling at the way it felt in his hands. He'd stopped allowing his knowledge of the settings, the aperture, the white balance, the composition, the lenses and equipment to be anything other than facts that could inform his work.

It was work.

Not art.

And that was part of his penance.

His index finger jumped; the muscles in his legs twitched. He wanted that camera. He wanted to take it out of the bag and explore Nantucket with it. He'd never been on the island before, so there was a whole world that was unknown to him. And while he didn't want to admit it, Emma was right—it was one of the most beautiful places he'd ever been.

He hadn't done a lot of exploring, but he'd done enough to know there were two different sides of the island—the side that attracted tourists and the side that only locals knew about. He wanted to discover Nantucket for himself—not what he read in some travel book.

Find the stories. Dig out the hidden gems. That had always been his way.

There was so much beauty here, waiting to be captured.

Before he could change his mind, he retrieved the camera bag from the other side of the apartment. He unzipped it and took out the familiar piece of equipment. It felt like an old friend in his hands. He knew that camera inside out. It had been with him through everything, and here it still was.

He unscrewed the cap keeping it free of dust, then found his favorite zoom lens, clicking it into place with a turn.

He walked over to the window and looked outside. Emma and CJ were on the porch. The boy's hair was slightly mussed, probably from a nap he'd been unable to avoid taking. The sun shone through the trees as it made its slow descent in the western sky.

The light captured them perfectly, lassoing itself around the exact spot where they sat. He held the camera up to his right eye, closed the other one, and watched them with the assistance of the zoom lens.

He couldn't re-create the moment on the beach, but this almost felt more personal. More intimate. More special.

He snapped a few pictures, looked at them on the screen at the back of the camera, and then quickly turned it off and put it back in his bag.

No. As much as he wanted to help Emma, this wasn't the way. This wasn't what he was here for. He'd come here for one reason—to give Emma his letter. How he'd gotten so far away from that, he had no idea.

As was typical, he struggled to fall asleep that night. Between replaying his day with Emma at the beach, marking each line of her face in his mind, preparing for the moment he had to say goodbye to her and thinking about that overwhelming need to feel his camera in his hands again, he was unsettled. Then there was the usual fear of falling asleep because he didn't want to relive the horrors of trips that weren't about sharing meals and finding the best places to surf.

He'd seen so much good. And so much bad.

At some point in the middle of the night, he'd drifted off. He was certain his sleep was fitful, but at least he hadn't been woken by a nightmare.

He got up the next morning and plodded toward the kitchen, where the letter caught his eye. He was stupid to leave it out on the counter like that—was he just asking for Emma to find it?

Maybe subconsciously he thought that would be better. Then he could put this whole thing behind him. She'd take back the offer of helping him show his work and remove any trace of her affection from him, making it much easier for him to move on.

He could take it to her now, put an end to this entire stupid charade. He picked it up and glanced outside. The morning sun hadn't quite broken through the clouds, bathing the yard in a light-gray hue. Her kitchen light was on, and if he closed his eyes, he could imagine the sounds of her morning.

He glanced down at the letter. He'd nearly confessed everything so many times since he'd been there, but something always stopped him. This had gone on long enough.

He opened the door, determined to explain himself this time, but as he stepped out, he nearly tripped on a small basket sitting on the landing. He looked up, but the yard was empty. He picked up the basket, took it inside, and set it on the counter.

Inside was a mug, a box of chamomile tea, sugar packets, and a card that said: *Saw your light on at 3 a.m. Might be time to try the tea.*

He smiled.

How long had it been since someone had given him a gift like this? Thoughtful and kind and personal?

Years.

It shouldn't make him feel the way it made him feel, but it did.

*You're not here for this.*

He shoved the thought aside. He didn't care why he was here. For the briefest moment, the rest of it didn't matter. Why he'd come. How he knew her. What the letter said.

All that mattered—just for a beat—was Emma.

He couldn't have predicted this. When he'd met Freddy's mom, he'd felt almost no personal connection to her at all. He'd remained appropriately detached throughout their conversation. It was a step toward absolution, nothing more. Same with his brief but cordial exchange with Jimmy's widow, Alicia.

He'd stupidly thought this would be the same.

But Emma wasn't Mary Beth Winters. Emma had stunned him from the moment he saw her.

If he'd wanted to take care of her before, that feeling had only multiplied.

He was in trouble, and he knew it.

～

The next morning, Emma followed CJ out the door to day care. The boy raced onto the porch and stopped.

"CJ, we're going to be late." Emma pulled the front door closed behind her and locked it.

"Someone left a present."

She peered over the armload of bags and lunch boxes. On the ground was a large brown paper bag, and her name had been written in black marker right at the top.

Emma frowned.

"What is it, Mommy?"

"I'm not sure."

"Is it your birthday?" CJ asked. "I didn't get you anything."

She smiled down at CJ. "No, buddy, it's not my birthday. Why don't you run to the car and buckle in?"

"I want to know what's inside."

Regrettably, Emma did too. She set her armload down and picked up the bag. A small white envelope was taped to the inside. She opened it and read:

*In case you find yourself up again at 3 a.m.*
*Once an artist, always an artist.*

She stifled a smile and removed the two pieces of tissue paper on the top, letting out a small gasp when she saw what was inside.

A large pad of watercolor paper, brushes, paints—and not the cheap ones, the artist-level, premium ones. Underneath was a palette for mixing colors, and there was even a small container of brush cleaner. At the bottom of the bag was a small box, and inside, everything she could possibly need to start painting again. Pencils. Tape. A kneaded eraser. A board with clips for her paper. It was like Jamie had asked a watercolor artist what all she could possibly need and then bought everything on the list.

And then he'd given it to her.

Artist to artist.

Her eyes welled with inexplicable tears.

"What's wrong, Mommy?"

She glanced down at CJ, then tousled his hair. "Nothing, kiddo. Absolutely nothing."

But it wasn't true, was it? Something *was* wrong. She'd begun to have feelings for a man who was turning out to be far better than she deserved. And she'd sworn to herself she wouldn't do that.

How did a person reverse these feelings once they were there? She needed to find out. And fast.

Elise's words rushed back at her.

*"What if you just went with it?"*

For a moment, it didn't seem like the craziest thing in the world. It was. And she couldn't. But it was nice to pretend what it would be like not to have all of her hang-ups.

What it might feel like to lay down all her regrets and move forward.

After Cam died, she'd gone to talk to someone—a therapist named Kyle Morganstern, someone her in-laws knew from church. She'd had no hope of talk therapy making a lick of difference in her life, but there were still days when she thought back on what the man had said.

"You're going to have to learn to forgive yourself, Emma." Kyle handed over a box of tissues.

She wiped the tears from her eyes and cheeks, knowing it was okay to cry but hating how powerless it made her feel. "What if I can't?"

"You can't go back and change the past. You can only learn from it and move on." Kyle sat there in his khaki pants and his tucked-in button-down shirt and watched her. His one leg was crossed over the other, and he hardly moved. She thought it must be a condition of employment as a therapist that a person wasn't easily ruffled. That meant very limited expression, at least in Kyle's case. "You know if you ask, God forgives."

"If I do penance or something, right?"

He shook his head, a slightly amused expression on his face. "No. You don't have to work for forgiveness. He just gives it to those who are truly sorry."

She'd rejected the thought immediately.

She hadn't grown up with God—not in her heart or in her house. Her father had left when she was young, and her mom created messes that seemed too big even for God to clean up.

What she had grown up learning was that when you messed up, you were punished. There were consequences. And she deserved whatever punishment she got.

That was the day she decided that if Kyle wasn't going to give her a list of consequences, she'd assign them to herself. Not pursuing romance was a given, but she'd also subconsciously decided that she shouldn't be allowed happiness of any kind.

She realized it only now, standing on the porch holding a gift from a man who was too kind, too thoughtful. She rushed her son into the car and started toward day care.

She might not deserve forgiveness. She might not deserve happiness. But CJ did. And wasn't she doing him a disservice by allowing herself to stay trapped in this muddy puddle of regret?

She pulled up in front of the day care center and sighed. She had no answers, only more questions, perhaps the most perplexing one *What on earth am I going to do about Jamie Shaw?*

# CHAPTER THIRTEEN

~~~~~

THE GALLERY WAS SLOW, giving Emma a chance to peruse submissions that had come in for the Nantucket Art Festival, on the off chance Travis had overlooked someone. Of course, even if she found a promising artist in the previously discarded list, there was still the question of whether or not the artist would be available. They were coming down to the wire in finding a replacement headliner, yet she was still holding out hope.

She scrolled through email submissions, bored by what she saw. Perfectly serviceable art. But nothing with the "wow factor" Travis was looking for. Which explained why none of these artists had been selected when they first came in. Travis had picked the one he wanted, and now that Marco St. John was no longer available, it was up to Emma to find someone just as good, if not better.

She pulled up Jamie's old website and compared the work of each potential artist with his. His photos consistently stood out. None of these others held a candle to him.

Not the performance artist who used tinfoil as her primary "artistic medium" (which mostly just meant wrapping random objects in tinfoil and calling it art). Not the oil painter who was quite talented, but not very inventive—more a copy of Georgia O'Keefe. Not the sculptor whose work bordered on pornographic.

No, none of these came close to the moving photographs that filled the computer screen. Jamie's work drew her in. It begged to be studied and admired.

So she studied and admired it. It was like she couldn't look away.

Around noon, her boss strolled in, looking slightly disheveled. Typically Travis dressed like a very fashionable Nantucket businessman. Today he wore jeans, a T-shirt, and a pair of sneakers.

She would not have guessed he even owned a pair of tennis shoes.

He must've noticed her once-over of him because he shot her a look. "Don't say a word."

She held up her hands as if in surrender. "I'm not. You look . . . comfortable, is all."

"I've been working. Sculpting. It's glorious."

"Why are you here?" she asked.

"Uh, because I own this place."

"No, I mean, why did you stop in when you're supposed to be creating?" She leaned against the counter. "You know I have everything here under control."

"We have a class this weekend," he said. "I came to check supplies."

"I already did," she said. "We were low on clay, so I ordered more, but everything else looked good."

"Did you contact Bess to be sure you didn't forget anything?"

"Yes," Emma said. "She said she's excited to be teaching again and she can't think of anything extra she needs. I also sent out a newsletter advertising the class, and we got three more people signed up."

His eyebrow quirked. "Impressive." His gaze moved from her to the computer behind her. "What's that?"

She turned around and saw Jamie's gallery on the screen. "Oh, I was just looking through the submissions for the art festival."

"Why? I already vetoed all of those people." Travis took a step toward the computer, toggled the mouse, and began scrolling. "Oh. This one is new." He squinted, eyeing Jamie's work. "You don't need to look at anyone else. This is the winner." He beamed. "Good work, Emma. I have to admit I wasn't sure about your ability to recognize exceptional talent, but clearly you understand how to spot a standout. Once again, Gallery 316 will reign supreme. I'm impressed." He chuckled, eyes still focused on the scrolling images. "How did I miss this submission? These photos are exceptional."

Emma's heart sank. "They are, but this is not one of the artists who submitted."

Travis frowned. "What do you mean?"

She stuttered a lame reply. "It's—he's a photographer I'm pursuing."

Her boss faced her. "Has he been discovered?"

"No."

"Won a Pulitzer?"

"No."

"Become a household name in the art community?"

"No."

"Then he qualifies. What's the problem?"

"He doesn't shoot these kinds of photos anymore," she said. "He mostly does branding for businesses—advertising, that sort of thing."

Travis grimaced. "So he's a sellout."

Emma sighed. "I don't think so. I think something must've happened to make him quit. People who are this gifted don't simply stop creating, right?"

Travis watched her with a little too much interest. "You tell me."

She pressed her lips together thoughtfully. "I reached out to see if he would consider it."

"And?"

"He said no."

Travis flicked a hand in the air. "And here you got me all excited. Who else do we have?"

Emma navigated to the submissions, showing Travis their dismal options.

"This can't be all," Travis said.

"I'm afraid so."

"Then you have to stay on this—" he squinted down at the screen—"Jameson Edward Shaw. Can you get him to change his mind?"

Emma shifted. "I'm not sure."

He studied her, peering through his round glasses. "Get him."

"But—"

"Prove to me you can do this job," he said. "Part of it is working with artists who are insecure. You have to continuously tell them how wonderful they are in order for them to work up the courage to share the work of their soul."

"But—"

"And in a couple of months, I'll probably need you to tell me how wonderful I am and build up my courage to share my work too." He nodded at her. "If you're still here in a couple of months, that is."

She knew it wasn't a threat—Travis wouldn't fire her if she didn't get Jamie to show his work at the gallery. But convincing him *would* go a long way with her boss.

And more importantly, for Jamie. It wasn't right to have this kind of talent and hide it from the world.

"So you'll do it?" Travis had moved toward the back door.

Emma nodded weakly.

"That's the spirit," he said. "I have faith in you. The success of Gallery 316 at the Nantucket Art Festival is now on your shoulders." And with that, he was gone.

While Emma was grateful Travis had at least some faith in her after only a couple short weeks of working in the gallery, she was also quite certain that faith was blind and misguided.

Because no matter how much she wanted to believe that she could convince Jamie, she wasn't sure. How would she show him that this was a good idea? How could she prove that his gift needed to be shared, that his work would move people on a deep, emotional level?

She scrolled through the images for the thousandth time and landed on one of two dark-skinned children, their black hair wet against their heads as they peered up at the sky, mouths open in search of the raindrops frozen in midair by Jamie's camera.

His work was textured. The colors in his photos were muted yet vibrant. How did he do that? She scrolled until she found another image, this one of an old woman in Bangladesh. The deep lines on her face were wonderfully clear as she grinned, showing off her toothless smile. An image of a young boy jumping from one roof to another, shot from below, made the child appear to be flying.

The photos, when all pulled together, were connected by more than Jamie's signature style. They were connected by a singular emotion—joy.

And that's when she got the idea.

It would be her last-ditch effort to prove to him that she was right. And if it was his insecurity that caused this artistic standstill, she'd show him the truth.

No more lip service.

It was time for Jameson Edward Shaw to see just how incredible his talent really was.

# CHAPTER FOURTEEN

~~~

WITH THE WALLS PAINTED and a new butcher block countertop installed, Jamie was moving on to the backsplash in the kitchen. Not only would this be a great decorative addition, it would help delineate this room from the rest of the space a little more clearly.

The only reason he knew how to install the white subway tile Emma had picked out was because his business partner, Dylan, had insisted on tiling the bathroom walls in their photography studio and office.

Jamie agreed, but only if he and Dylan did the installation themselves.

Dylan lasted one session before giving up, but Jamie had been determined to figure it out and do it well. In the end, the job had turned out really nice, and now that he was standing back and surveying the changes he'd already made in Emma's apartment, he was thankful he'd taken the time to learn. It would save them both a chunk of money.

"I can already tell that's going to look amazing." Emma's voice broke into his thoughts.

He'd left the door open, along with all the windows, to try to coax a breeze into the stuffy apartment. It was fully summer now, and there was no air conditioner. He made a mental note to find a window unit. No way she could rent this place without AC.

It was Nantucket, not a campground.

"Hey." He faced the doorway, where she stood. "You're home early."

She shrugged. "Travis had a meeting at the gallery, so I got off a couple of hours early."

"You like it so far?" He'd installed a new light fixture over the sink, and the new appliances still had a plastic coating on them, but it was enough to visualize its potential.

Emma surveyed the space with a nod, then gave him a once-over, and he suddenly felt naked. He probably shouldn't have taken his shirt off. He noticed, though, that she wasn't quick to look away. He fetched his T-shirt off of the chair where he'd tossed it and pulled it over his head.

"Sorry."

"I probably shouldn't just barge in on you," she said.

"Yeah, how rude to walk through an open door."

She smiled at him. He felt it at the backs of his knees.

"Can I help?" she asked. "CJ had an outing with the day care group. They're going to see a movie and then for ice cream, so I've got the night off. I figure if we're doing this together, I can't let you do all the work."

He surveyed the space. "I was going to start on the wall behind the sink."

"Are you patient?" she asked.

He shrugged. "Patient as the next guy."

"Patient enough to teach someone who has never done this before?"

She'd fastened her dark, wavy hair in a pile on top of her head. Her face was almost free of makeup, and she wore a pair of cutoff jean shorts and a red tank top. Her bronze shoulders were a reminder of their day at the beach.

And he wanted to kiss her.

He'd been fighting off that particular thought for days. Best to keep fighting.

"I'm patient," he said, wondering if she caught the subtext. In that moment, he thought he might wait for Emma forever.

"Then I'm here to help." She smoothed her hair and tugged at the bun. Her blue eyes had catchlights in them, as drawn to the light as he was to her.

He was doomed. He was starting down a path, feeling helpless to change direction.

"Okay, but feel free to quit at any time," he said. "I promise I won't think less of you."

She squinted at him, a smile playing at the corners of her mouth. "I'm in this for the long haul, Shaw."

He turned away to conceal a smile. He liked her. Too much. He should reject her help and spend the afternoon alone.

But he didn't want to.

He didn't want to admit what he wanted to do.

"The first thing we have to do is clean the wall." He picked up a sponge and a spray bottle of cleaner.

"I can handle that." She took both from him.

"Have at it."

While she worked, he opened a box of tile and then covered the countertops with cardboard scraps. He caught her watching him twice, but he couldn't think of a single thing to say. His mind had gone blank.

Probably because today she didn't smell like cinnamon. Today she smelled like something sweet and fruity. He liked it. But it was messing with his resolve.

He heaved the bucket of adhesive up onto the counter and took out the trowel just as Emma tossed the sponge back into the bucket.

"I'm basically already a pro," she said.

Jamie gave her a side-eye. "You wanna handle this alone? There's a pizza place downtown I've been wanting to try."

She grinned. "If you want a big mess on this wall when you get back, sure."

"Can't have that." He took measurements while she watched, marking up the wall so they didn't make a mistake.

"There's a lot of math involved in this, huh?"

He shrugged, calculating in his head. "Some."

"And you're good at math?"

"I'm okay." He smirked as he finished off the measurements. He was great at math, but he wouldn't brag.

"Usually creative people aren't," she said. "At least that's what I used to tell myself."

"We all have our gifts." He put the tape measure away.

"Speaking of that," she said. "Thanks for the paint stuff."

He'd kind of hoped she wouldn't bring it up. He didn't want to discuss why he'd bought her those art supplies. He didn't want to talk about feelings or anything resembling feelings. He would've been perfectly happy to pretend he hadn't located an art supply store on the island. That he hadn't looked up "supplies a watercolor artist needs" online and taken that list to that store, where he then bombarded the salesgirl with questions about which brushes were good for what and was this type of paper better than that other kind.

"It wasn't a big deal," he said. "Just a thank-you for the tea."

"Of course," she said.

"I was thinking if you started to paint again, you'd realize that you should be the one doing that gallery show."

"You don't even know if I'm any good," she said. "I could be terrible."

He found her eyes. "Not a chance."

Attraction zipped between them. Did she feel it too?

"How can you be so sure?" She crossed her arms over her chest.

"Are you bad?" he asked, opening the bucket of adhesive.

The corner of her mouth turned up, so slightly he almost missed it.

"That's how I know," he said.

"I didn't say anything." Her face brightened. She smiled. He'd made her smile.

"Besides, I've seen your work, remember?" He checked to make sure the wall was dry, then spread the adhesive on a patch of it, right in the middle. "Hand me a tile?"

Before she did, she opened a junk drawer next to the sink and Jamie's heart somersaulted. The letter lay, facedown thankfully, right on top. She found a Sharpie, slammed the drawer shut with her hip, and laid two tiles on the counter in front of him.

His heart raced. That was a little too close of a call.

"We have to leave our mark," she said. She signed the back of one tile, then held the marker out to him. "Your turn."

He took it and scribbled his signature on the other tile, then stuck it to the wall. He nodded at her tile, still lying facedown on the counter. "Your turn."

Her eyes widened. "You want me to put it on the wall?"

"It's not hard, I promise."

"If it can be messed up at all, I will mess it up."

He laughed. "That's the spirit."

His hands were still holding his tile in place as she picked hers up and stuck it on the wall next to his. They stood like that—silent, side by side, fingers nearly touching—for a count of three.

Finally he glanced over at her. She was staring out the window, past the yard toward the house. He wanted to ask her what she was thinking about. What kinds of things went through her mind these days? Was she still consumed with Cam, with his death, with how her plans had gone horribly, terribly awry? Not so much in this moment, but often, when he looked at her, he swore he saw sadness.

"You know how else you could leave your mark in here?"

She blinked a few times, then looked at him, a question behind those big blue eyes.

"Paint something for that spot right next to the door." He nodded toward the open space. "Personalized artwork is a really nice touch."

"We seem to have something in common," she said.

"I'm no painter."

"No, but you are an artist." She pulled her hands away from the tile and picked up two more. They continued to adhere the tiles to the wall in a pattern, making sure they were level.

"So what do we have in common?"

He looked at the tile she'd just stuck on the wall. It was completely crooked. He waited for her to realize it. She didn't.

"Do you mind grabbing me a bottle of water from the fridge?" he asked.

"Not at all." She turned around and he straightened the tile before she returned with a water he didn't want but took anyway.

"Thanks."

"To answer your question—we seem to each want the other one to do something creative. That's what we have in common."

"Something other than tile the wall?"

"Yes, because I clearly can't do it in a straight line." Her face turned smug. "I saw you fix it."

He smiled and looked away. "Sorry."

"It was actually really sweet of you to try and preserve my pride." She picked up the charm on her necklace and tugged it side to side. "I'll make you a deal."

He leaned against the counter and crossed his arms over his chest. "Okay?"

"I'll paint something if you take one new, non–work-related photograph. The kind you'd be proud to show off."

He should've expected something like this.

"Is this about the art festival? Because I—"

"No," she said. "It's not. I mean, I haven't given up on that, but this is just about art."

"Why does it matter so much to you?" he asked. "Whether or not I'm taking photos?"

She searched his eyes, and neither of them moved for several seconds. It was as if time stopped for a moment, and somehow she could see straight through him. Everything he was trying to conceal from her—did she see it all?

"I guess because I know how it is, when you're a creative and you're not creating." She looked away—finally. "It's like this whole part of you is dead."

It was exactly like that. "And that's how it is for you?" he asked.

She kicked at something invisible on the floor. "Number ten on the *Year of Emma* list: 'Start painting again.'" She shrugged. "There was a reason I put that on there, I guess."

After a beat, she finally met his eyes again. An understanding passed between them. It wasn't about attraction this time, though. It was a deeper knowing that came with being a creative. They understood each other in a way that many people wouldn't.

"Okay," he said. "Deal."

Her eyes lit. "Yeah?"

"Yeah."

"Great," she said.

"Great." He paused. "When does this have to happen by?"

She chewed the inside of her lip thoughtfully for a second. "End of the week?"

"Okay." He turned back to the task in front of them. "Should we finish this wall then?"

"I'll just hand you the tiles," she said. "You can put them up."

He nodded as she handed him a tile. More adhesive. Another tile. And the overwhelming feeling that he'd just made a terrible mistake.

~

Emma and Jamie worked nonstop for a couple more hours, and when they finished the wall behind the sink, they both stood back and stared at it.

She'd expected working this closely with him would do a number on her nerves, especially after seeing him shirtless upon her arrival. But they'd settled into a comfortable rhythm, and now that they were done, the primary emotion tugging on her was disappointment. It wasn't like she had a million reasons to be here in the apartment, especially not now that it was evening.

"Do you want to get a pizza?" She blurted the question out without thinking. "I mean, you mentioned there was a place you wanted to try. And we could eat it in my kitchen since it's a sauna in here."

"Should probably get some AC."

"Agreed," she said. "Put it on my tab."

He smiled. It was a nice smile, and she had the feeling he reserved it for special occasions. It wasn't like he trotted it out to get whatever he wanted or anything, even though it would be a very effective bargaining chip.

"Uh, sure," he said. "Maybe let me shower quick and clean up, and then I'll head down?"

She tried to pretend that the idea of him showering had zero effect on her, but her mouth had gone dry at the thought.

"I'll order the pizza," she said. "What do you like on yours? I like sausage and green olives."

She was being pushy. She'd apologize for it if she wasn't so thankful that this side of her still existed. She'd spent the last five years in such a fog, she'd stopped having opinions about everything. While pizza wasn't a presidential election, it was something.

And she had a preference.

"I hate olives," he said.

Her eyes darted to his. Apparently she wasn't the only one with opinions. "Oh no. We can't be friends after all."

"I mean, I can pick them off, but—"

She held up a hand, a purposefully melodramatic look on her face. "No, I'll order my half with olives and yours . . . without."

He shook his head, amusement on his face. "Then can you get my half without sausage too?"

"Cheese pizza?" She widened her eyes. "That's your preference?"

"Disappointing, right?"

She waved him off. "We all have our flaws."

He laughed and she turned to go. "See you in what, half an hour?"

"Should be good."

She raced outside and down the stairs, trying to ignore the flip-flopping of her heart in her chest. She had a sort-of, kind-of, okay-maybe-not-really date with a man she was finding it more and more difficult to resist.

And that had her insides buzzing.

*If you feel like kissing him, then kiss him.*

Elise's words taunted her again. She did feel like kissing him. A lot. And for the first time in years, she wondered if Elise was right. If she should just let things happen as they would instead of fighting it every step of the way.

She might not deserve it, but she couldn't deny it.

She was falling for Jameson Edward Shaw. And the inclination to pretend she wasn't was lessening by the minute.

She ordered the pizza, then raced upstairs for her own quick shower. Afterward, she reapplied her lotion and mascara and studied herself in the mirror.

She'd forgotten how it felt to be kissed, but she wanted to remember. What if she was so rusty she was bad at it? What if she made a complete fool of herself?

"Knock it off, Emma," she said to her reflection. "You're getting way ahead of yourself."

She didn't even know if Jamie wanted to kiss her. And she certainly wasn't going to make the first move.

But as she went downstairs to wait for him, she realized that she desperately hoped he did.

She wanted to be kissed. She wanted to be loved. She wanted to be worthy.

And she wanted to forget she'd ever done anything to make those things impossible.

# CHAPTER FIFTEEN

~~~~~

THE PIZZA ARRIVED THREE MINUTES BEFORE JAMIE.

Emma opened the door and the scent of him wafted straight at her like a wall of yumminess.

He'd showered, and that dark-blond wavy hair still held on to enough moisture to make her wonder if it would stick up when it dried. Jamie was unfussy. Rugged. Handsome. His features were chiseled, and while she found his sense of humor wonderfully appealing, she realized in that moment there was a shyness about him. Something unassuming, as if he was always asking permission.

Jamie's presence was the opposite of imposing or overbearing. He was gentle. Kind.

And he had the most perfect hands she'd ever seen.

Long fingers. Nicely manicured nails. Veins in the top of the hand that for some reason made her think of strength. She wondered if he'd ever played the piano with those hands.

"Hey," she said after realizing she'd been staring.

"I'm starving."

"The pizza just got here."

It wasn't their first meal together. She could tell herself it was just like the other times he'd come over for dinner. But it wasn't because this time CJ wasn't there being the constant ball of chatter he normally was. This time they were alone.

She hadn't been alone with a man since—

She cut the thought off before finishing it.

"Do you mind if we eat in the living room?" she asked. "I make a point to eat at the table when CJ is home. I don't want to set a bad example. But it feels a little formal."

*A little too much like a date.*

And it wasn't a date.

"I don't mind," he said.

The polite conversation lulled, and Emma motioned for him to follow her into the kitchen. Maybe she hadn't thought this through. What were they going to talk about all evening? Without their usual conversation buffer, they had only each other to occupy the moments.

The thought sent a shiver down her spine.

She *definitely* hadn't thought this through. Emma handed him a plate, then turned toward the refrigerator to grab two cans of Coke from inside the door. Her nerves danced a jig in her stomach. It was that blasted conversation she'd had with herself before he arrived.

Because of that, all she could think about was kissing him.

They dished up their pizza, grabbed their drinks, and walked back to the living room, where for one awkward beat neither of them seemed to know where to sit. He ended up on the couch, and she sat in the armchair.

Part of her regretted it instantly. The reckless part. The sensible part of her knew the distance between them was good. Though that was a pretty presumptuous thought. For all she knew, Jamie was involved with someone. Or simply not interested in her.

"What do you like to watch?" she asked, picking up the remote control and pointing it at the television.

"Period dramas," he said.

She glanced at him. He'd just taken a bite of pizza, and his long legs stretched out in front of him. He looked good on her couch. She had a feeling he'd look good anywhere, though. "Really?"

"No." He smirked. "Mostly I watch sports."

"How original," she teased. She flipped a Red Sox game on and leaned back in the chair.

"We don't have to watch this," he said. "I do watch other things."

"Like?"

"Marvel movies."

She eyed him. "Anything more interesting than what I would absolutely expect you to watch?"

He thought for a moment. "*The Great British Bake Off*?"

"You watch that?"

He took another bite and nodded. "I love it."

"Okay, that is a surprise."

"It's relaxing," he said. "And it makes me want to bake."

She navigated to Netflix and found the show. "Have you watched the latest season?"

He shook his head. "I've mostly been painting and tiling lately. And my apartment doesn't have Netflix."

He wasn't looking at her when he said it, but the gleam in his eye was clear. She didn't know how to respond, so she found the show and turned it on. They watched. They ate. They barely spoke. And she tried—hard—to pay attention to the television, but it was nearly impossible with him in her living room.

"Do you have baking stuff?" he asked after the first episode ended.

"I think so," she said. "Why?"

"Let's make our own *biscuits*," he said.

"You mean cookies? Because when you say *biscuits*, I think bread."

"I mean cookies."

"You bake cookies?"

"It's been a while, but yes." He set his empty plate on the coffee table.

"I thought you were being ironic when you said the show made you want to bake."

He shrugged. "I'm full of surprises."

He was, but she wouldn't say so. This conversation was feeling a little too much like flirting. "Okay, let's." Anything other than sitting in the same room not talking.

"When do you have to pick up CJ?"

She glanced at the clock on the wall opposite the television. "He's getting a ride home. I think they said it would be about an hour."

He stood, picked up both of their plates, stacked their empty soda cans on top of them, and walked out of the room toward the kitchen.

Emma told herself to breathe. *Breathing is good. Breathing is key.*

By the time she reached the kitchen, he'd already gotten the butter and eggs out of the refrigerator. She hoped she'd be more help with the cookies than she was with the backsplash. Jamie had fixed more than one of her crookedly placed tiles. He never said a word, just quietly straightened her shoddy work.

"What kind of cookies are we making?" she asked.

"What kind are your favorite?"

"Oatmeal," she said without thinking.

"Okay, the real question—" his face turned serious—"raisins or butterscotch chips?"

She narrowed her gaze as if to challenge him to disagree with her. "Never raisins. Always butterscotch."

"Good answer." He smiled. "After the great olive debacle, I'm not sure our friendship could've withstood another great divide."

"I don't have any though, so these will have to just be plain oatmeal." She pulled the rest of the ingredients from the cupboards and lined everything up on the counter. Suddenly the room felt small. Too small. And he was everywhere. His presence filled the entire space.

*"If you feel like kissing him, then kiss him."*

She begged Elise to get out of her head as she grabbed a bowl from a cupboard below the kitchen island. Without a word, Jamie started measuring ingredients. This attractive, talented world traveler baked cookies. Who would've thought?

"Don't you need to look up a recipe?" she asked.

He stuck the bowl of butter in the microwave and turned it on. "I have this one memorized."

She never would've guessed.

He looked at her with a raised brow. "I take my baking very seriously."

Emma surveyed the orderly scene he'd laid out on the counter. "I see that."

For the second time that day, they found a rhythm. They could tile a backsplash and bake cookies. What more did a couple need for a successful relationship?

Whoa. A "couple"? A "relationship"? She needed to knock that right off immediately. It was possible to have a very attractive, platonic male friend.

Depressing but possible.

Not at all what she wanted but possible. And preferable. She reminded herself of the litany of reasons why she'd committed to a single life.

Once the first batch of cookies went in the oven, Jamie leaned against the counter and looked at her. "This has been a good night."

She faced him. "It has, hasn't it?"

"Unexpected."

"How so?"

He shrugged. "I don't know. I guess when I first met you, I didn't know we'd become friends."

The word hung there between them. It was a nice word. In any other circumstance, she would've been thrilled to have a new friend. Goodness knows she didn't have many these days.

She didn't exactly want to be Jamie's friend. But that's what they were. It's what was best. The only thing she'd told herself she'd allow.

"Friends," she repeated. "Right."

He watched her. She knew this moment. She'd seen it in movies. She'd lived it a time or two herself. But it had been so long. It was that moment where the air between two people changed. Where it snapped with an electrical current that demanded not to be ignored.

"Or maybe . . . ?" His unfinished question seemed to knock the word *friends* right out of the air. She could practically hear it shattering on the ground. And the new question pulsed with promise. With hope. With desire.

She lifted her eyes to his.

They were only a few feet apart. Him, casually leaning against her kitchen counter, an air of confidence surrounding him. Undeniably sexy. Her, standing in the center of the room, unsure what to do with her hands.

She forced herself not to break eye contact. Did he feel that? The spark between them? It threatened to ignite and set her on fire.

"Maybe . . . ?" The dot-dot-dot punctuating her sentence turned the word into a question she wanted him to answer.

He uncrossed his arms and reached toward her, catching the hem of her shirt between his fingers. He gave it a soft tug, drawing her closer. "We should probably keep this professional."

His eyes held her captive. They were almost gray. Stormy. There were stories in those eyes. She wanted to know them.

"Probably," she said.

His hand wound up the back of her neck, into the tangle of hair. His other hand grazed the side of her arm, and her body responded to his touch. He studied her as if memorizing every detail of her face—every line, every freckle. Had anyone ever looked at her so closely before?

She traced the edge of his chin with a trembling finger, and her knees weakened. She could feel his desire, and yet he was unhurried, as if he wanted to take his time with her.

He framed her face with his hands gently, then pulled her closer, and she knew that while she might be the more forward of the two of them, he was the one in control at that moment. For all her independence, she found that she liked that he was.

She watched as he moved closer, thinking she should close her eyes but not wanting to miss a moment of him. His gaze was so intent on her, she felt it at her core.

She couldn't pretend she hadn't imagined a moment like this, but when their lips finally met, she realized her mind hadn't done it justice. He watched her for a brief moment before his eyes closed and his lips explored hers with a firm and delicious curiosity.

After a moment of disbelief that this was actually happening, Emma wrapped her arms around him, drawing him closer, inhaling every bit of him as she gave in to his kiss so wholly, she was sure it would fill her dreams every night from this day forward.

Jamie stood straighter as his tender kiss turned intentional, and Emma's mind raced ahead of her. She liked kissing him—a lot. Jamie wasn't someone she was looking for, but she couldn't deny she had feelings for him, feelings that were hard to sort out.

His kiss made her want to be alive again.

But just one room over, hanging on the wall, was the image of a man she'd promised to never betray. Most people wouldn't understand why she'd vowed to keep that promise long after Cam was gone, but she had her reasons.

And this kiss broke that promise.

As Jamie deepened the kiss, she reminded herself this *wasn't* wrong. It wasn't a betrayal. Cam was gone. He'd been gone for five years. He wasn't coming back. And while she knew it was natural to feel a sense of strangeness in starting over, she couldn't convince herself that what was natural for other widows applied to her.

Because she had secrets that warranted punishment. She didn't deserve to fall in love again.

She wouldn't allow herself.

Jamie's mouth searched hers, then trailed sweet, wonderful kisses from her cheek down the side of her neck and back up again. Under the weight of his full attention, Emma's gaze fell to the floor.

She pressed her hands against his chest and took a step back. This was the part where they should laugh at how they'd jumped straight over the line of "professionalism" but neither of them cared because that kiss had been so electrifying, so enticing, it was worth breaking a few rules.

But the lightness, the flirtation—they were gone.

He must've sensed the shift. "I'm sorry," he said, watching her.

"No," she said. "It's fine. I mean, it was good. I mean, I liked it." She looked away. Why did she feel embarrassed now on top of everything else?

His hand slid to hers and he squeezed it. He pulled her into a strong embrace and Emma remembered how it felt to be held. She hadn't realized how much she'd missed it. How long had it been since she'd even allowed another person besides CJ to hug her?

She laid her head against his firm chest and drew in a deep breath. He kissed the top of her head, which fit nicely underneath his chin. She wanted to be with him—and not in a platonic way. She wanted to kiss him whenever she felt like it. She wanted to walk downtown holding his hand and spend her evenings watching British television with him.

Behind him, on the refrigerator, she spotted the *Year of Emma* list. How annoying that it haunted her so frequently. As if she'd given herself a code to live by, tasks to achieve, and if she didn't deliver, it meant she'd failed.

Or maybe it wasn't that at all. Maybe it was simply a reminder of what she wanted. She wanted to live. She wanted to be an active participant in her life. She wanted her son to know that she was happy. She wanted to feel loved again.

She wanted to be worthy of love again.

Would she ever be?

"Was that a mistake?" he asked.

She lifted her gaze to his, searching her mind for an answer to his question. Maybe. Maybe it was a mistake. But in that moment, it didn't feel like one.

In that moment, she thought the only mistake would be severing this connection, which was stronger and deeper already than her connection to anyone else she knew except CJ. She'd purposely closed herself off. She'd told herself it was for her safety, but she knew it was more than that.

She'd believed that she wasn't allowed to be happy because of her mistakes. She'd told herself it was wrong, a betrayal of her husband, for her to have a second chance when she'd so obviously messed up the first one.

But what if that had been rash and misguided? What if she could find a way to get past it?

Could she ever get past it?

"Emma?"

She shook her head. "It didn't feel like a mistake."

The smile radiated from behind his eyes. "No, it sure didn't."

The oven timer beeped and Jamie pulled himself from her arms. He slid the oven mitt on and checked the cookies, the smell of cinnamon and vanilla filling the room.

She turned from him, trying to get her bearings. Trying to understand how, without her having to say a word, he'd sensed that she wasn't okay. That hug wasn't for him, and she knew it. He'd stopped to check on her. He'd looked at her with such concern it nearly brought her to tears.

She didn't deserve this man—that much she already knew.

He put the next batch of cookies in the oven and turned to her with a sigh.

"What's wrong?" she asked. Did he already regret their kiss? She should, but she didn't—not yet anyway. Tonight, when she was replaying it in her head, she might. But now? Not a bit.

He shook his head. "Just thinking how much I want to kiss you again."

"Is that bad?"

He watched her. "I don't know. You tell me."

Before she could respond, there was a noise on the front porch.

"CJ," she said. "Guess you're going to have to wait for that kiss."

"Like I said before, I'm a patient man."

Why did she find that incredibly appealing?

"I should probably go anyway," he added. "I don't really trust myself to stay. I'm patient, but I'm still human." His smile held a bit of mischief.

She shook her head, hiding her own smile as the front door flung open and CJ ran inside. "Mom! I got *three scoops* of ice cream!"

Emma met him in the entryway just as Sadie, one of the other day care moms, showed up on the porch. They'd met a few times dropping the kids off or picking them up. Sadie always struck her as the kind of mom who had everything together.

"They had so much fun tonight," Sadie said. "We need to get them together again because Stella *loves* your son." She smiled, and Emma felt a wave of gratitude roll through her. CJ had a friend. "She's an only child, so this day care program is a godsend, and she sure has taken a shine to CJ. Such a sweet boy."

CJ spotted Jamie in the kitchen. He let out a shout and raced toward him. "Three scoops, Mr. Jamie! One was blue."

Jamie laughed. "I see that all over your chin." He met Emma's eyes. "Let's see if we can clean that up."

Emma turned back to find Sadie practically salivating on her porch. "Your boyfriend sure is something to look at."

"Oh, Jamie is just a friend. He's helping me get our apartment ready for renters."

Sadie's eyebrows shot up. "Oh? CJ said he was your boyfriend."

"He did?"

"If he's not, do you know if he's single?" Sadie grinned. "My sister just went through a terrible breakup. I have to say, I think that man would cheer her right up."

Emma frowned. "Sorry about your sister, but, uh, I don't think Jamie's the guy for her."

Sadie opened her mouth like she had more to say, but Emma cut her off.

"Thanks again so much for giving CJ a ride and for chaperoning the trip. Hopefully I can come to the next outing. Good night!"

Sadie lifted her hand in a wave as Emma closed the door, dreading the conversation she had to have with her son. Because not only did he think Jamie was her boyfriend, but she wasn't sure she wanted him to be wrong.

# CHAPTER SIXTEEN

~~~

HE TOLD HILLARY ABOUT THE KISS.

He shouldn't have, but he did. Who else was he going to tell? Dylan? His business partner wasn't exactly happy with him right now. He'd insisted that Jamie fly home for a meeting with Jerrica Danielson and the FitLife people, but Jamie kept putting him off.

Shirking his responsibilities.

Living in a dreamworld.

So now, midmorning on a Friday, he was getting an earful from his sister.

"What were you thinking?" Hillary asked—and not kindly. "Jamie, this is a disaster. You're usually so levelheaded."

"You're the one who told me to get back out there," he reminded her. And she had. Multiple times. "I thought you'd be happy for me."

"If it were anyone else, I would be," she said. "There are literally thousands of eligible women out there—why her?"

Jamie thought about the kiss. He'd fallen asleep thinking about it. He'd woken up thinking about it. He wanted to keep thinking about it—at least until he could relive it again. "She's not like any-one else, Hill," he said. "She's confident and insecure at the same time. Like, she's trying to remember what it felt like to speak her mind, but it still feels foreign to her. She's smart and witty and she's such a good mom. I didn't think that would matter, but it does. When I see her with CJ, it makes me think about things I never thought of before."

"Like what?"

"Like the future." He'd never minded traveling. He loved it, in fact. Opening his business had been less about settling down and more about survival. But even still, something in his soul had remained unsettled.

Emma calmed that in him.

"So what happens when she finds out the truth?"

Hillary's words were like a bucket of cold water.

"And when are you going to tell her?"

He sighed. "I've tried. A few times. I keep trying."

"And what? You keep chickening out?" Hillary had never been one to mince words.

"It's complicated."

"Well, it is now," she said. "It shouldn't be. You can't do this, Jamie. You're going to break her heart."

Those were the words that did him in. He'd known it—he'd always known it. The second he stepped onto the ferry to Nantucket, he knew he wasn't coming here to give Emma the warm fuzzies. His presence could shatter her. When had he forgotten that?

When had he convinced himself that she would be immune to what he had to say?

"I'll tell her," he said, making up his mind to do so.

Now Hillary sighed. "Look, Jamie. Nobody wants to see you happy more than me. You know that. But I don't want to see you or anyone else get hurt. And I'm afraid that's where you're headed. I'm just trying to save you the pain down the road."

"I know," he said.

And he did know. Of course he knew. He just didn't want to think about it.

"It's not that simple," he said.

"It *is* that simple, Jay."

"No, it's not." He looked at the apartment. It was still torn up, and he had a ways to go before it would be ready for paying renters, but it occurred to him he might've been purposely dragging his feet. It wasn't like he wanted to leave any sooner than he had to.

Man, he was really messing this up.

"She can find someone else to help her with that apartment," his sister said, as if reading his mind.

"I took a picture the other day," he admitted.

Hillary went silent. She knew—more than anyone, she knew what that meant.

He thought about the photo he'd snapped of Emma and CJ in the yard. About the way being around her not only made him happy, it made him want to be creative. That part of himself that he'd allowed to die, or maybe, more to the point, the part of himself that he'd murdered—it had been resurrected. And not because of their deal.

But he didn't tell any of that to his sister.

"A picture-picture?" she asked.

"A photograph," he said, certain she understood the difference between what he'd been spending his time doing and what he used to spend his time doing.

"Of what?"

"Of her." *Of Emma.* "Her and her son."

Hillary didn't respond right away. Finally, after a long pause, she said, "Just be careful, okay?"

He nodded but didn't respond into the phone. He couldn't. Because he'd already been the opposite of careful, and he wasn't sure how to go back now.

After he hung up, he planned his day. He would work on the apartment through the morning and early afternoon, then head out in search of that one perfect photo.

Truth be told, he'd rather wait until Emma got home and go exploring the island with her, but if he was going to get reacquainted with his camera, he should probably do it in privacy. Their relationship was a tumultuous one, and they needed time alone together to heal.

And yet he wondered if he could repair what was broken without Emma's influence. She'd truly awakened something inside him— something he might need in order to be creative.

Emma was good for him. Even Hillary couldn't deny that, now that she knew he was taking photos again.

The real question, though, was whether or not *he* was good for *her*.

And he had a horrible feeling he already knew the answer, that heartbreak could come at any moment.

It was reckless to carry on this way. Selfish.

But he didn't want to lose her. Maybe if he waited just a little bit longer to give her the letter, to reopen old wounds, she would be invested enough in their relationship that she'd forgive him.

Was that too much to hope for?

~

Travis wasn't coming in today. He'd called and left her a message with a list of tasks. It was 10 a.m. and she'd finished them all. Well, all except *Solidify that photographer for the art festival—we're running out of time!*

Right. That. She did have a plan, but it was difficult to think about Jamie today. More to the point, it was difficult to think about Jamie and *not* think about that kiss.

Had she ever been kissed like that before?

She wasn't sure she had. Or maybe she was just lonely. Pitiful.

But now wasn't the time for daydreaming. Now was the time for doing. On her way into work, she'd picked up her special delivery from the post office, and now she had to implement the next phase of her plan.

Emma laid the cardboard cylinder out on a worktable in the classroom, keeping one ear on the door in case anyone wandered in from off the street. Mostly people treated the gallery like a museum, but not during the art festival. That event brought in buyers, and according to Travis, it was a surefire way for an artist to make a splash. It would be great for the gallery and for her boss, of course, but it could be even better for Jamie.

She opened the package, then unrolled its contents, the three images she'd selected from Jamie's website. She'd purchased the hi-res digital versions, something she assumed Jamie had automated once upon a time. Then she had them enlarged and printed, and now she would have them framed.

Of course, these wouldn't be part of his actual gallery show—Travis would want new art for that—but it would show Jamie the potential. If she did it right, it would make him understand the impact his work could have if displayed correctly.

She laid the photographs out on the table, even more stunning in print. The joy he'd captured—she envied it. These people, who likely had very little by the world's standards, were happier than she'd felt in years. Happier than most people seemed, too, if she was honest.

She picked up the image on top, the one of the toothless old woman, and studied it.

"New artist?"

Emma turned. She hadn't heard anyone come in, but now, through the doorway, she spotted a neatly dressed couple standing in the gallery.

She laid the print back down on the table.

"Sorry, just a project I'm working on."

The pair walked toward her. "We're always on the lookout for new talent," the man said. "Travis always calls us first when he's found someone worth investing in."

Emma made a noise that sounded like a nervous laugh as her mind spun with all the ways this could go wrong.

"But Travis has been radio silent lately," the woman said. "He's not hiding his discovery from us, is he?"

"No, actually," Emma said. "He's working on his own art."

The man grimaced. "Oh, I thought we'd talked him out of that."

Emma knew this couple. Not literally, but she knew people like them. Elite art collectors who sneered at anyone they deemed "less than." She said a silent prayer of thanks that (a) her own portfolio was carefully tucked in her bag, and (b) Jamie wasn't here to see them eyeballing his photographs.

"So spill." The man had moved toward the table and now shifted the top image to reveal the one underneath. "These look promising."

Emma resisted the urge to smack his hand away. Didn't he know it wasn't polite to touch things that didn't belong to you?

"These aren't really for the public." Emma rolled the photos back up.

"The public?" The woman's expression told Emma she'd said something wrong. She looked at her partner, then back at Emma.

"I can have Travis give you a call when he's back in," Emma said, certain she would do no such thing.

"We can call Travis," the man said. "But first we'd like the name of this artist."

"I'm happy to share it as soon as I get permission," Emma said.

"Permission?" The woman stared at her.

"From the artist."

"Miss, any undiscovered artist in his or her right mind is going to want their work on our radar. We launch careers."

Funny, Travis had said the same thing. Was it possible they all worked together to make their artist of choice the "next big thing"?

"I'll be sure to pass that along," Emma said, wishing these people would leave. She felt like she was holding bricks while treading water. And these two kept adding more weight.

The woman lifted one neatly waxed eyebrow and peered down at Emma, who felt three feet tall in her presence. "You really won't tell us the name of this photographer?"

"I don't have permission for that yet, ma'am, but as soon as I do, I can make sure you're the first to know."

"Fine," the man finally said.

"If you'll just leave your name and number—"

"You really don't know who we are?" The woman's forehead crinkled in disbelief.

Emma felt her jaw go slack. "I'm new here," she stuttered.

The woman closed her eyes and shook her head, sighing the most exasperated sigh Emma had ever heard. "Travis has not trained you well."

"We'll take it up with him," the man said.

"No, I—"

"Good day."

The sound of the woman's heels clicking on the sleek hardwood floor haunted Emma until finally they opened the door and stepped out onto the street, muttering something about "the nerve of that girl."

How had Emma missed that clicking when they'd come in?

She sighed. Three minutes later, her phone rang.

*Travis.*

She could ignore the call, but he'd show up in the gallery, so what was the point? She clicked the phone on, but before she could say hello, Travis spoke. "Do you have any idea what you've done?"

Her heart sank. "No?" Her voice was small. It occurred to her that it shouldn't be. She'd done nothing wrong.

"You've just offended two of the biggest collectors in Boston, thereby putting our entire festival entry in jeopardy."

Emma didn't know anyone else in the world who used the word *thereby*. Somehow Travis pulled it off.

"I'm sorry. I just—"

"You just nothing," he said. "Caroline and Mark David Heyward want direct access to the artwork you're preparing. What artwork are you preparing in *my* gallery, Miss Woodson? I didn't authorize any purchases."

"It's a project I'm working on," she said, knowing that being dodgy right now was only going to make matters worse.

"Miss Woodson, any project you're working on should be approved by me," he said.

"It is," she said. "In a way. It's about the photographer for the art festival. And I haven't spent any of the gallery's money."

"So you got him to agree?" For a brief moment, Travis sounded hopeful.

She chewed the inside of her lip. "Not exactly. Not yet. I'm still working on it. If you give me a little more leeway, I know I can make this happen."

"You do realize our relationship is still quite new, yes?"

"Yes?" It came out as a question because she was full of uncertainty.

"And thereby, you have yet to earn my trust."

"Yes." *Thereby I have not done so.*

"Why on earth did I allow you to be a part of this at all?"

"Because you want this photographer," she said. She glanced out onto the street, eyes scanning the tourists moving down the block. She'd yet to allow herself a day or two to be a tourist in Nantucket. She should do that; it might inspire her—give her an idea of something to paint.

Travis had gone quiet.

"He's really good, Travis," she said. "You saw his work. But he's going to need some coaxing if he's going to go public."

"Mark David demanded the artist's name," Travis said.

"But you didn't give it to him," Emma said, hopefully.

"I didn't," Travis said. "But we're going to have to."

"What if Jamie doesn't agree to show at the festival?"

Silence.

"Travis?"

"It's not an option," he said. "Thanks to you, Caroline and Mark David are taking it personally. They are critical to our success, unfortunately. And they feel they've been kept out of the loop and treated rudely."

"Rudely?"

"You really do have so much to learn about the way things work around here, Miss Woodson."

"Yeah, I guess I do."

"You can start by striking the word *yeah* from your vocabulary. You sound like an uneducated—" There was commotion on the other end of the line. "I have to go."

*Darn. I was really hoping you'd finish insulting me.* "Okay."

"You have until the end of the week to secure your photographer, understood?"

"I understand," she said.

"Your job is on the line here, darling."

"I understand," she repeated.

"Mark David and Caroline are—" More commotion. Was he raising chickens? What was that? "I have to go."

He hung up.

Emma set the phone down with a sigh that fogged the window. She looked out onto the street again, this time with a longing to break free from what now felt like a glass cage and run loose in the street.

But no, she loved this job. And she could do this—she just needed to figure out the best way to convince Jamie to share his art. For a brief moment, she imagined him in the same room as the Heywards. Somehow she didn't think he'd find a single reason to cater to people like that, which meant that making him their prized "discovery" could actually have adverse effects for everyone.

But this wasn't about a snobby, entitled couple. It wasn't even really about Travis or the gallery or Emma's job. It was about Jamie and his work. His stunning, incredible, moving work.

Across the street, in front of a ritzy boutique Emma had window-shopped many times, she spotted a familiar silhouette.

She froze, her muscles tense, her heart betraying her by racing along like it had just been asked to sprint. She moved toward the door and out onto the street.

A man—tall, wiry, with dark hair—stood on the street corner concentrating on the phone in his hand. He could be anybody. She walked a few steps down the street, still watching, but she lost him in the crowd. She strained for a better view, but he was gone.

Her nerves pummeled her from the inside out. She glanced down and saw a patch of hives around her wrist. She scratched at them, willing them away.

She told herself to calm down. It was nothing. There were hundreds of people on the street. It was just like her to think she saw the one person in the world she absolutely never wanted to see again. Her imagination had conjured it—of course it had. That's what she did. She thought too much.

She told that to herself over and over for the rest of the day, but as she went home that night, she still struggled to believe it.

Because as much as she wished she could, in six years' time, she still hadn't been able to erase the memory of that man from her mind.

# CHAPTER SEVENTEEN

~~~

DAYS HAD PASSED SINCE THEIR KISS, and while it hadn't happened again, Jamie had high hopes for tonight.

Tonight they would share their artistic creations in what felt a lot like a date.

Emma had insisted on making the arrangements, and he hadn't argued, though in his exploration for photo-worthy scenes, he'd spotted more than a few places he wanted to take her.

It wasn't surprising, really. He wanted to take her everywhere.

He'd even considered taking her back home with him for the meeting with the FitLife people, something he absolutely couldn't blow off, but that felt like a pretty big step. Besides, he couldn't predict how his sister would react to learning that he still hadn't taken her advice.

He arrived at Emma's house five minutes early, his printed photo carefully placed inside a portfolio case he'd bought from the art supply store, and found CJ on the porch, visibly upset. The boy looked up at Jamie with his big brown eyes and then looked away.

"Whoa," Jamie said, sitting on the top step next to him. "That's a pretty sad-looking face."

CJ shrugged.

"What's wrong?"

When the boy didn't respond, Jamie nudged him with his shoulder.

"Are you my mom's boyfriend?" CJ didn't look at him, just stared out at the yard.

"Oh." Jamie hadn't expected that. "Not exactly."

"Do you wanna be?"

*Yes.* "Grown-up relationships are complicated," Jamie said.

"But you like her," CJ said.

"Yeah, I do."

"And she likes you."

"Does she?"

CJ tossed an *are you kidding?* look at him that made the boy seem ten years older than he was.

"Stella said boyfriends don't stay very long."

"Who's Stella?"

"My friend," he said. "If dads don't stay and boyfriends don't stay . . ."

Jamie filled in the blanks in the silence. *Then who does?*

He wasn't prepared to have this conversation. His interactions with kids usually started with piggyback rides and ended with tickle fights. This was out of his depth. CJ was asking hard questions for a five-year-old.

"You know your dad didn't want to leave, right?" Jamie said. "That wasn't a choice."

"He died," CJ said.

"Right," Jamie said. "But I know he would've given anything to have met you."

"How do you know?" CJ's eyes waited for an answer—anything he could cling to.

Jamie wished he had the right words. He *did* have the right words;

he just couldn't say them—not yet. Instead, he shrugged. "Because look at how great you are."

The boy's grin was lopsided. "I am great, huh?"

"The best." Jamie mussed CJ's brown hair and gave him a playful squeeze. Then he glanced back and spotted Emma, standing in the doorway behind them, listening to every word he'd just said.

He played back the conversation in his mind—had he given himself away?

"CJ, Stella's mom is almost here," Emma said, her voice tight. "Go get your stuff." She stepped out onto the porch as her son ran back inside.

Jamie stood and allowed himself a moment to drink in the sight of her. Tonight she wore a strapless, multicolored sundress with diagonal stripes. The top of it was flowy, almost like a separate piece had been sewn on to create a swish whenever she moved.

Her tan shoulders drew him straight to the spot where her collarbones met. He tried not to think about kissing her there.

He failed.

He reached over and took her hand. With him on the step lower and her on the porch, they were eye level, and in a flash, he was lost. He was pretty sure she could ask him for anything in that moment, and he would've happily given it.

*My money? It's yours. My car back home? Yours. The office space I renovated with my own two hands? All yours. My heart? That's yours too.*

The thought sent a heat to his cheeks, and he forced it all aside. This was all happening too fast, and he reminded himself to slow down.

"Hey," he said, catching—holding—her gaze.

"Sorry about that," she said.

He shrugged. "It's fine. He's a kid."

She made a face. "But also, Jamie, and please don't take this the wrong way—"

"Uh-oh," he said.

She closed her eyes and drew in a deep breath. "No, it's not bad. I just—"

"Don't want me talking to your kid about us," he supplied.

"Don't want you talking about Cam."

The words hung there. She wasn't angry or accusatory. She was speaking her mind, and he liked it. But knowing he might've overstepped upset him just the same.

"It's not a big deal," she said.

"No, I get it." Jamie pulled his hand away with a firm nod. "I didn't mean to—"

"No, Jamie, seriously," she said. "It's just all really hard and confusing for him."

"Did I say something wrong?" He hated this. Hated knowing that there was so much more left for him to say.

She shook her head. "Forget I said anything."

He laughed softly. "Emma, it's cool. You're allowed to have your preferences when it comes to your kid and the guys you date."

Her eyes widened. "The guys I date?"

"Yeah," he said. "I'm sure you've had to explain boyfriends to CJ before, right? He's just older now, so he's got more questions."

Sadie's car pulled into the driveway, stopping in front of the garage. Emma's gaze lingered on Jamie; then she took a step back and waved at Sadie.

"He's so excited," she called. "Let me get him!"

While Emma popped her head back inside the house, Jamie avoided Sadie's prying eyes. The woman had no shame in studying every inch of him. Was this how women felt being ogled by men on the street? Some men might be flattered, but Jamie wasn't one of them.

He walked up onto the porch, trying to extinguish the unwanted thoughts that had accompanied his conversation with Emma. She'd looked so caught off guard at the end of their conversation—was he really blowing this whole night before it'd even begun?

Emma returned, CJ in tow, and he threw his arms around Jamie's legs and squeezed. "See ya later, Mr. Jamie." Then he looked up at Jamie. "Don't leave without saying goodbye, okay?"

Emma's face fell, and she pulled him away, walked him out to Sadie's car, and buckled him in the back seat.

Once they'd gone, she turned to Jamie and frowned. "Maybe this is a bad idea."

For a million reasons, it wasn't. And for a few very valid reasons, it was.

But Jamie didn't want to admit that—not to himself and certainly not to her. He'd given himself a deadline to finish the apartment, to do what he said he would do, to help Emma and CJ in a real, tangible way. After that, he'd come clean—and then whatever happened, happened.

If that meant he'd have to say goodbye to them, then so be it.

Even as he thought the words, though, he knew he was lying to himself. Saying goodbye might kill him. How could his feelings for Emma be so strong already?

Because they were tied up with so many other feelings?

Should he call Dr. McDonald to sort this out? Or was he avoiding her the way he'd been avoiding Hillary this week?

"I don't think it's a bad idea," Jamie said.

She crossed her arms over her chest and watched him. "There haven't been any boyfriends," Emma said.

He felt the pull in his forehead. "What do you mean?"

She looked away, pressing her fingers to the bridge of her nose, as if whatever she had to say was giving her grief. "I haven't dated anyone since . . ."

"Since Cam," he said, realizing.

She nodded, still studying the ground beneath her strappy sandal.

The charm on her necklace dangled right below that spot between her collarbones. He stepped toward her, aware that her vulnerability had heightened everything between them.

She hadn't dated anyone since her husband died. He was the first man she'd dared take a chance on. It wasn't all that different for him, though, was it? Trauma turned you off from intimacy like water from a spigot.

"Emma." He waited until she looked at him; then he smiled at her—his warmest, most tender smile. Would it properly convey the way he felt? Would it say *I'd wait a lifetime for you*?

"This is so stupid," she said. "Way too early for all these messy feelings."

He took one of her hands and softly tugged her closer. "You're not the only one with messy feelings," he said. "And it's been quite a while for me too."

"But five years?" She rolled her eyes in self-deprecation. "It's a little excessive."

"I saw the list on the fridge, remember?" He grinned. "This isn't exactly a surprise."

But that wasn't true, was it? He might've seen the list, even read number nine. But it hadn't registered that *he* might be the one she dated. It hadn't registered that number nine might've been on the list because she hadn't dated *anyone* in all these years.

"I guess if you're okay with knowing this is all new for me," she said. "Like, I feel like I've never done this before."

"It's not like riding a bike?"

She laughed. "So far, no."

"What's it like?"

A blush rose to her cheeks. "New. Exciting. Scary. Interesting."

"Scary?"

She shrugged. "Is that so hard to believe?"

He shook his head. No. He felt exactly the same way. "We can keep everything light and laid-back," he said. "We don't have to rush anything. For CJ's sake and for yours."

She inched up and kissed his cheek. "Thank you." The whisper sent a shiver down his spine, and he wondered if he'd just made a promise that would be impossible to keep.

# CHAPTER EIGHTEEN

~~~

EMMA HADN'T EXPECTED THE PREDINNER CONVERSATION to be quite so serious.

She wished she could rewind, go back to the moment when she'd overheard CJ talking to Jamie on the porch. She could've interrupted, shut it down.

But something had kept her frozen in place. And then Jamie said what he said—the absolute perfect thing for him to say at that moment, and she turned to mush.

Even now, nearly an hour later, sitting at the restaurant she'd chosen for their evening out, she wasn't sure she'd fully recovered.

"So how'd your painting turn out?" His question filled the unwelcome silence.

She picked up her water and took a drink. "Okay, I think." But just okay. Felt a little strange, if she was honest, like she needed more time to reacquaint herself with the brushes and paints. "Yours?"

"I'm happy with it," he said.

"Did it make you want to keep taking pictures?"

He studied the ceiling for a moment. "No."

She watched him as he brought his gaze back down to hers. "I don't believe you."

He smirked and took another bite of his chicken and risotto.

"How old are you?" she asked. "I just realized I don't even know."

"Thirty-three."

She made a face. "You're creeping up there."

"How old are you?"

"Thirty."

He grinned. "Ah, you're right behind me."

"Serious relationships?"

"Two notable ones," he said. "My last serious girlfriend, Amy, and my first Canon."

She smiled. "There must've been more than that."

He took a drink. "Why?"

"Because—" She allowed a gesture toward his face to be her reply.

He half laughed, seemingly modest, as if he had no idea how truly good-looking he was. That was unlikely, though. After all, he did own a mirror.

"You know, I could say the same thing about you," he said. "You are, well—" He copied her gesture, and she suddenly felt shy. Oh, the effect this man was having on her. It was every emotion all at once.

Emma liked looking at him. It was hard to pull her gaze away. His lips were so full and enticing, she could think of nothing but kissing him. In this light, his eyes were a steely gray, and the way he looked at her set her on edge and put her at ease all at the same time. But if she was honest, her pull to him had less to do with the way he looked and more to do with the way he made her feel.

Jamie was attentive and kind. And for all her independent ideals, he seemed intent on taking care of her. The longer that went on, the more she liked it. She didn't want to lose herself in him, but somehow it was like he made her a better version of herself.

"What happened with Amy?" she asked.

He chewed the bite in his mouth and swallowed. "Didn't work out."

She squinted at him, as if that might give her a better look—a peek inside the window into his soul. "Did you get tired of her?"

He scoffed. "Quite the opposite."

She reached over and covered his hand with her own. "Tell me."

*Stop pushing.* The voice was a firm reminder that she was often a bulldozer trapped in a small person's body.

He looked at their two hands for a beat, then turned his palm upward, lacing his fingers through hers. The simple connection—so sweet and innocent, practically lit her skin on fire. She'd be smart to be cautious. She was falling too hard, too fast.

She cleared her throat. "I'm sorry for being pushy. I just want to know everything."

His eyes danced, tracing a pattern on her face. "I want to tell you everything."

She forced herself not to look away, even though the conversation had grown weightier than she'd intended.

"When I gave up photography," he said, "Amy left. She said I wasn't the same person anymore."

"Without the art," Emma said.

He nodded.

"Was she right?"

He held her gaze. "Yes."

A sadness lingered after he spoke that one word.

"Favorite food?" she asked, trying to lighten the mood.

"Pizza," he said without hesitation.

"Right, but with just cheese." She made a face.

"Why spoil a good thing with vegetables?" He shrugged. "Favorite beverage?"

"Tea," she said. "Best vacation spot?"

"Nantucket," he said, squeezing her hand. "Should we get on with the evening?"

She made eye contact with their waitress and nodded for her to return to their table. "Yes, but the rest of the evening doesn't take place here."

# CHAPTER NINETEEN

~~~

STROLLING DOWN THE STREET with Jamie made Emma feel more than ever like they were a couple. He'd paid for dinner and ushered her outside with his hand gently on the small of her back.

Nothing had made her more certain that she was in a little too over her head than the way that simple gesture had made her feel— safe, protected, wanted.

It did not, however, make her feel worthy. And that nagging reminder was wholly annoying.

When she recounted this whole evening to Elise later on that night, she'd be certain to leave a lot out, because while Elise might be privy to Emma's thoughts about how handsome Jamie was or the way she felt when he took her hand for an evening walk on a romantic island, she was certainly not privy to the rest of it.

The kindness in his voice when he'd spoken to CJ. The way he'd jumped in to help her with the apartment. The fact that he'd gone to buy her art supplies when she suspected he knew very little about watercolors. And on and on.

Everything about Jamie told her this was a very good man.

But if she told Elise, she'd accuse Emma of falling in love with him. And, she reminded herself, that was not what this was. Emma was not allowed to fall in love with anyone. They were simply two people with a mutual attraction getting to know each other.

He traced the top of her hand with his thumb.

*Oh. Maybe this is more than that.*

They reached the back door of Gallery 316 just in time. She let go of Jamie's hand and went searching for her keys in her purse, her skin cool at the absence of him.

"This is where you work," he said.

She nodded, the keys jingling as she inserted one into the lock and turned, pushing the door open. They both walked inside, and she closed and locked the door behind them.

"Okay, one minute." She flipped the lights on and revealed the open space at the back of the gallery. "This is a staging area. And apparently where I reveal to you proof that I'm not above humiliating myself."

He shook his head, hands stuffed in his pockets, portfolio tucked under his arm. Truthfully, she'd been wondering what was inside that black case since he picked her up.

"How should we do this?" she asked. "Big reveal on the count of three?"

"You might be disappointed," he said. "I'm pretty rusty."

"Me too!" she said, a little more loudly than intended. "I felt like I was painting with my left hand."

He laughed. "You're really beautiful, you know that?"

Her skin tingled with a rush of heat to her cheeks.

"I guess that's why, even after an entire day exploring Nantucket—" He unzipped the portfolio and set it out on the table. "I came back to this." He lifted the cover to reveal a large print of an image so beautiful it took her breath away.

"Your photo is of me?"

Her and CJ, playing on the porch. She'd been completely unaware that he'd been watching, which should possibly creep her out but really only made her feel like she'd been a part of something very, very special.

"Truthfully, I'd wished I had my camera that day we went to the beach," he said. "There was a shot that would've been perfect, but—" He'd turned shy. Even really amazing artists sometimes struggled to share their work. "This one was even better."

He'd captured everything—joy, love, happiness—all things she sometimes felt had gone for good. But here it was in front of her. A visual reminder that joy and pain can coexist in a singular life.

"Do you like it?"

She could hardly see it anymore for the cloud of tears in her eyes. "No, I love it."

He looked pleased. A little embarrassed but pleased.

"Jamie, you really do have a gift," she said. "What you captured here—it's unbelievable." She studied the image. "The composition. The way the light is hitting. The focus on the emotions—you're a storyteller." *You're an artist.*

"I'm glad you like it," he said. "It's yours."

She would frame and hang it before the weekend was over.

"What about you?" he asked, pulling her attention, an unwanted reminder that she had to keep up her end of this deal.

"I don't even want to show you," she said. Her painting had been clunky and hard to complete. She didn't feel that artistic flow. It was forced—technically sound with none of her in it. She'd had to disconnect from that side of herself a long time ago—the less she felt, the better.

Which was a solid reminder why this excursion with Jamie should really remain about work, about the gallery, about the art festival— and not about the way he seemed to drink her in every time they were in the same room together.

"A deal's a deal," he said. "Is this it?" He turned to the easel behind her. She'd covered it with a sheet. Just a single sheet stood between her and artistic humiliation.

He took the bottom of the sheet in his hand and looked at her. "Are you ready?"

She groaned. "No. This was a terrible idea."

"No turning back now," he said. He swiped the sheet off, revealing her clumsy attempt at a painting. She'd completed it the night before, while CJ slept, haunted by the dim light that was still on in the apartment above the garage.

Now, watching him look at it, she felt so foolish.

Her version of Millie's restaurant seemed so elementary under the watchful eyes of a legitimate artist. She'd completed the rough sketch of the iconic Nantucket café earlier in the week, noting the wood doors that flung open to reveal the most perfect hue of light teal. Overhead, an orange sign boasted the restaurant's name and the traditional gray shingles were accented with white trim. She'd also added a few colorful paddleboards, a red life preserver, and a bike, leaning against the outer wall of the building.

She chewed the inside of her cheek, tilted her head, and gave it a good once-over. She tried to look at it objectively. The colors were good—deep, bold, vibrant. She'd done an excellent job of matching them to the inspiration photo, which meant the end result screamed "Summer in Nantucket." Watercolors were so unpredictable, and while years ago, she would've had a better handle on them, they'd gotten away from her a bit in her rustiness.

Nothing she could do to change it now; it was what it was. She dared a peek at Jamie, who was still looking thoughtfully at the painting.

"Is it that bad?" she asked.

He turned toward her. "Are you kidding?"

She proceeded to point out every single thing that was wrong with the painting.

"Emma," he interrupted her. "It's really good."

She went still. Why did that simple compliment warm her from the inside?

"And I know you're going to try to keep telling me it's horrible and you're out of practice, but I'm looking at it, and I think it's really good. I think you should show it to your boss."

"No," she said. "That's not why I'm here. I'm here for a job that I think I could really enjoy. I'm here to find new artists, like you." She glanced at the photograph he'd given her. "I don't know if you realize what a gift you have."

He went back to the watercolor. "I could say the same thing about you."

After a pause, she said, "I guess we're both just two reluctant artists."

He didn't look at her, but she saw the hint of a smile on his lips. He slid his hand into hers.

Emma loved the way her hand felt wrapped inside his. She loved standing close enough to him that if she moved just an inch or two, she'd find herself in his embrace.

After Cam died, she couldn't have imagined ever allowing herself to fall in love again. She'd declared she wouldn't. She'd promised herself, promised Cam—she'd gone to his grave a week after the funeral and sat at the end of it and wept. For what she'd done, for what she'd lost, for the baby her husband would never know. And she'd promised him.

How many promises to that man was she going to break?

Slowly she removed her hand from Jamie's, then tried to disguise the movement by turning back toward the table where his photograph still lay.

"You okay?"

Of course he'd caught on. That was the danger of his inquisitive eye. He seemed wonderfully, horribly aware of her every emotion, whether she wanted to share it or not.

"Jamie . . ." As much as she didn't want to ruin this new, tenuous relationship, she did owe it to him to be honest. She'd learned the hard way how important that was.

Still, when she looked up into his stormy-gray eyes, the words wouldn't come. She wanted to go on pretending, and if, months down the road, they discovered this was all make-believe, then so be it.

The plan was faulty, and she knew it, but she chose to ignore that. Instead, she had something else to share with Jamie. Her nerves started buzzing at the thought.

"I have something to show you," she said.

"Okay." He eyed her suspiciously, and she forced herself to smile.

New love shouldn't be so heavy. Why couldn't she simply "go with it" like Elise had instructed her to do? She did her best to shove every single weighted, regretful thought from her mind.

"I need you to keep an open mind," she said. She held up one finger as if to instruct him to stay put, then walked into the gallery and turned on the dim lights illuminating the back wall. Then she inhaled and let her breath out slowly. *Here goes nothing.* She said a silent prayer that Jamie wouldn't bolt the second he saw what she'd done.

"Okay, you can come in here," she said.

He strode from the back room into the main gallery, stepped into the light, and turned toward the back wall, where she'd hung three of his photographs that evening after the gallery had closed.

She studied his face as he focused on the grouping, and she handed him a mock-up of the brochure she would've put together if this were a real gallery show. She'd created a logo of his name—*Jameson Edward Shaw*—and added the details of the show, which she'd titled *An Expression of Joy* in a sleek, modern font.

He read the paper carefully, then glanced back up at the images. She couldn't tell if he was irritated or amazed or something else entirely. His expression had turned unreadable.

"What is this?" he muttered.

"I wanted to show you what it might feel like to see your photographs on the wall of an actual gallery," she said cautiously. Had she made a terrible mistake? "When I was looking through your work, I saw a theme that connected so many of the images—joy. Not fake joy, either. You've captured people who have almost nothing in their happiest, most joyful moments." She pointed to the eyes of the old woman Jamie had frozen in time. "Look at that. She's smiling with her whole face." She stilled. "I don't know many people that smile with their whole face. CJ does, I think. But I've never captured the image of it."

At her side, Jamie shifted.

"I know I said this wasn't about the art festival, and it's not." She turned to him. "It's about your art. It's about how good you are."

His jaw twitched. His eyes scanned the photos on the wall. "You shouldn't have done this, Emma."

Every nerve ending in her body went on high alert. She recognized the way her body processed dread—the fear that she'd messed up. Again.

"I'm so sorry, Jamie. I just thought—"

Commotion behind them silenced her. A key going in the lock. A door opening. A threesome walking in.

Travis. And behind him—Caroline and Mark David Heyward.

The dread intensified.

"Travis." Emma's mumble was barely audible. "What are you doing here?"

He shot her a look as if to say, *I own this gallery. What are* you *doing here?* She understood and snapped her jaw shut.

"We came to see the new installation." Caroline pointed her long, straight nose in Emma's direction. "The photographs you wouldn't let us see earlier. You could've mentioned you were waiting to share them until they were in their proper setting. We would've respected that." She sashayed toward them and waved a hand toward Jamie's work—a grand, sweeping gesture.

Emma instantly understood that this was not a woman who was used to being told no. Caroline Heyward was the queen of her own existence, and as such, they should all bow to her every whim. Why did that make Emma want to do the exact opposite? To snatch Jamie's photos from the wall and run?

She'd made a terrible mistake. Why had she thought she could get away with this?

Travis and Mark David joined them, and now they were a five-some, staring at the wall of photos that could only be described as "stunning." She glanced at Jamie. Make that a foursome. Four of them were enamored with the photos. Jamie's gaze had set and stayed on her.

And while his face was still slightly unreadable, she didn't think whatever he was thinking was good.

Yes, she'd botched this up royally, as if she couldn't help but make a mess of things.

*Badly done, Emma,* she thought in Mr. Knightley's chastising voice.

She deserved the reprimand too. This was not the way this was supposed to go, but she should've predicted this was the way it would go. Sabotage at its finest.

She wasn't sure how to convince Jameson Edward Shaw that she really did have his best interests at heart. Not with Caroline and Mark David eyeballing his images right in front of him.

She internalized a groan and wished the evening could end in that exact moment, while at the same time steeling herself for whatever was about to unfold in front of her.

# CHAPTER TWENTY

"AH, YES." THE STUFFY MAN wearing the pink button-down was surveying the photographs with a kind of scrutiny that made Jamie want
to excuse himself from the room.

Had this been Emma's plan all along? Had she set him up? The
thought of it turned something inside him. He hadn't expected her
to go to such great lengths to get her own way, and frankly, he was a
little irritated to learn that she had.

Though she had seemed genuinely surprised when her boss
strolled in.

Still, she'd gone to the trouble of enlarging and framing his prints.
She'd even matted them underneath the perfect shade of white. The
photos did look stunning, just like she said they would. And for a
brief moment, seeing them lined up on the wall, pulled together by
a theme she'd recognized—but he hadn't—had almost made him
remember a dream he'd long abandoned.

But this—standing here while these people critiqued his work—
reminded him that the abandoned dream didn't need to be unearthed.

"You must be the artist." The one who was Emma's boss turned toward her. He wore a neatly tailored navy-blue suit, a blue-, pink-, and white-checkered shirt, and a pink bowtie.

Did everyone here wear pink?

Jamie tried not to feel like a slouch in the clothes he'd thought were "nice," a pair of black dress pants and a simple blue button-down, sleeves now rolled to his elbows.

"This is Jamie." Emma put a hand on his arm. Yep, that touch still had an effect on him, despite his feelings being a little uncertain at the moment.

"Brilliant," the other man said. "I'm Mark David Heyward, and this is my wife, Caroline." He stuck a bony hand out toward Jamie, and after a quick beat, Jamie shook it.

"Good to meet you," he said.

"Jamie, we saw your work earlier and are so thrilled you'll be participating in the Nantucket Art Festival." Caroline flashed a smile, her teeth white against the red of her lips.

He started to respond, but Emma's boss beat him to it.

"Mr. Shaw is something of a holdout, Caroline." Travis quirked a brow in Jamie's direction. "I hoped maybe hearing your thoughts on his work might possibly sway him." He gave Emma a pointed look. "I told you there was a good reason my assistant held you off earlier today."

Jamie had a feeling he was missing something. He knew Emma was tasked with finding a new artist, but how crucial was it that it was him?

The three art lovers were looking at him now. Was he supposed to say something?

"What could possibly be holding you back?" said Mark David. (Two first names felt like overkill, but who was Jamie to say so?)

His mind flashed with images of a firefight. An ambush. A mistake. All pictures he'd seen in his nightmares too many times to count.

"I don't really shoot like this anymore," he said. "I guess I've become more of a commercial photographer."

"But you have such a gift." Caroline touched his arm, her hand lingering there. "It would be a shame to keep it from the world."

As if that would convince him. He didn't feel like he owed the world anything at the moment—not after what had been stolen from him.

"We were thinking maybe a new series," Mark David said. "Featuring some of our favorite Nantucket landmarks and hidden spots. Nantucket art always goes over wonderfully at the festival. Folks do love to celebrate our little island."

"Landmarks like Millie's restaurant?" Jamie asked with a quick glance at Emma, whose face was so red he thought she might explode.

"Sure," Mark David said. "If it inspires you."

"I should go." Jamie felt like he'd been set up, and he didn't like it.

"Mr. Shaw," Caroline said, "I don't think you understand what this could do for your career. We are in the business of turning young, undiscovered talent into stars. It's happened every year for the last decade."

He leveled his gaze at the woman. "Mrs. Heyward, I don't want to be a star."

"I'm so sorry, Caroline," Emma's boss said. "It was my mistake to leave this in the hands of an amateur. I'll be handling the talent scouting from now on."

Emma's eyes fell to the floor under the weight of her boss's glare.

Caroline was still focused on Jamie, like a lioness eyeing her prey. He didn't like it. He didn't like feeling he was there to be swindled. And he had Emma to thank for it.

"It was nice meeting you all," he said (a lie) and then turned to go.

"Emma," the boss said behind him—and not quietly, "I really thought you could handle this."

"I'm sorry, Travis."

Jamie pushed the door open and stepped out into the warm night. She wasn't the only one who was sorry.

The walk home at dusk played with his senses. The smell of the sea mingled with the smell of food from the restaurants whose doors were flung open, invitations to passersby to come in, sit, stay a while.

The sounds of chatter filled the air, and as he walked, he caught bits and pieces of conversation—not enough to make any assumptions about anyone but enough to get his imagination going.

And everywhere he turned, there was another image begging to be captured. The cobblestone streets mixing with the storefronts—*click*—the passersby on their way to dinner or to a party or down at the beach—*click-click*—pots of flowers spraying happy color out onto the street, glowing in the warmth of a waning sun. *Click-click-click.*

As much as he'd tried to avoid it, that scratch of creativity had returned.

Ever since he'd taken that photo of Emma and CJ, he'd been seeing images everywhere. He'd been miming the action of clicking the camera more than he cared to admit. He'd composed so many untaken shots, heard the shuttering of the camera, imagined the end result.

And yeah, maybe even thought once or twice about the idea of showing in that gallery.

Why, then, had he been so quick to leave?

Because something about the way Emma had convinced him to go there felt like a betrayal. Weren't they just two art lovers on a date? Weren't they using their deal to connect to each other—and to a part of themselves they'd each allowed to die a long time ago?

He sat down on a bench at the corner of a busy intersection and instantly saw four new images that would be perfect in an art show featuring scenes from Nantucket.

Someone else's show. That wasn't why he'd come here.

But falling in love had never been on his agenda either, and he had a bad feeling he was well on his way to doing that.

"Jamie."

He turned and found Emma, standing on the street, looking horribly upset and beautiful at the same time. Her dark hair was coming loose from the long braid that snaked over her left shoulder. Her blue eyes were wide and concerned.

All at once, her intention was clear. She hadn't meant to betray him, only to show him a life she thought he might love.

Because she could see the remnant of a dream that had once been.

That's how well she already knew him.

That's what scared him to death.

"I'm really sorry," she said. "Can I sit?"

He nodded toward the empty end of the bench.

"Look, I didn't mean to overstep. I had no idea they were going to show up tonight. I only wanted you to see what I had in mind, since we'd be working together on the art festival, if you agreed to do it. But I went about it the wrong way."

"Yeah, you did," he said gently.

She folded her hands in her lap and stared at them. "I'm so sorry. I know how personal art is. It was a misguided idea."

He paused. A boy and his dad crossed the street, the man's hand wrapped around his son's for safekeeping. *Click.* Emma glanced up, a halo of light behind her as the sun dipped down in the evening sky. *Click.*

"Can you forgive me?"

"It *was* a misguided idea." He inhaled a slow breath. "But it was an effective one."

Her eyes shot to his. "What do you mean?"

"Would it help you if I did the show?"

The line of worry etched in her forehead faded slightly. "This isn't about me, Jamie."

He turned back toward the street. "This place is alive." *It makes me feel alive.* "Ever since that day at the beach, I've been . . ."

She didn't press him. She didn't move. He wasn't sure he wanted to explain any of this to her. Inevitably the conversation would lead to his reasons for shelving his artistic side, and that, he couldn't disclose. Not until he'd finished the apartment. Not until he'd done something to make her life better, easier.

More bearable.

The colors of red brick meshed beautifully with the cobblestone. This was Nantucket. The Nantucket everyone saw. What if he could take images of this and mix them with images of the Nantucket most people didn't know existed? Surely there were places on this island that the locals kept to themselves.

*Nantucket: Seen and Unseen.*

A study of the island that seemed to bring people back to life. The ideas were endless.

"I've been wanting to take photos again," he said. "Creative photos."

Her soft lips crawled to a slow smile. "You have?"

He nodded. "So much, it kind of scares me." Had he really just said that out loud?

"I get it," she said. "I mean, I think I do. I'm assuming there's a reason you stopped in the first place." She paused, but he didn't fill in the blanks. "I can only imagine the things you saw while you were traveling. But this is part of who you are, Jamie. It makes sense that it wouldn't stay asleep forever."

He sat with that. "So would it help you?"

There were tears in her eyes. She looked away, possibly to conceal them, but it was too late.

He reached over and took her hand.

"Why are you so good to me?" she asked. "I don't deserve it."

He pulled her closer. What would the two of them look like to him if he were outside of his own body? Would he take time to compose this shot? Would his finger tap lightly on the button of his camera before finally finding the perfect exchange of emotion between the two of them, the one that told the story, that made the viewer curious?

He kissed the top of her head. "You deserve every good thing, Emma."

She swiped the tear that had escaped, wiping her cheeks dry. He held her, drinking her in, feeling like the most conflicted, luckiest man alive.

Because of her, this creative spark that used to fuel him had been reignited.

How could he repay that when he owed her so much already?

"I'll do this," he said. "But I don't want to have to talk to those people again."

Emma laughed, then drew her eyes to his. "I can't make any promises. They want to make you a big star."

He tucked her hair behind her ear and shook his head. "I don't want to be a star. I just want to be creative again. I owe that to you."

She touched his hand. "No. Give me none of the credit, especially after I messed up so badly tonight."

He leaned forward and kissed her, right there on the street, because he'd been resisting the urge for hours and he just didn't have the strength anymore. Her lips were full and fresh, and he was certain he would never tire of tasting them.

After a moment, she leaned back. "Are you sure about this?"

He nodded. "I've already got more ideas than I know what to do with."

She smiled. "And you'll let me help? I learned how to mat and frame. And I can find a better printer than the one I used for the rush job."

"Details," he said. "We'll work it out."

Her eyes shifted, catching something across the street behind his shoulder. He turned to see what she was looking at but only found a crowd of tourists not unlike the one he'd looked at when he first sat down.

"What is it?" he asked, turning back to her.

"No, it's nothing," she said. But the color had drained from her cheeks.

"You okay?"

"Yeah." She stood. "Do you mind if we try to catch Travis before he leaves? Tell him the good news?"

"If we must," he said. "But don't expect me to be polite to those people."

Her smile looked forced as she turned in the direction of the gallery. "You're the talent now," she said. "You don't have to be polite."

He slid his hand around hers, and she stiffened to his touch.

And Jamie couldn't help but wonder if this was the coldness he would feel when the ghosts of the past finally caught up to him.

# CHAPTER TWENTY-ONE

~~~

WAKING UP BEFORE DAWN THE NEXT MORNING, Emma thought perhaps she'd been hasty in agreeing to accompany Jamie on his quest for "the perfect morning light." There wasn't enough coffee in the world to combat her lack of sleep.

She'd lain awake longer than usual last night, playing and replaying the moments of the night before, right down to the kiss on the bench that had been sweet, yet toe-curling at the same time.

The moment Jamie agreed to do the art festival was quite possibly the happiest moment of Emma's post-Cam life.

It meant that (a) he'd forgiven her for her botched attempt at convincing him to do it in the first place, and (b) she could go back to Travis and redeem herself after the stern talking-to she'd gotten the moment after Jamie had walked out of the gallery. Right in front of Caroline and Mark David, who watched with matching looks of pretention on their faces.

She'd relished telling him and the Heywards that they would, in fact, be able to claim Jameson Edward Shaw as their "big find" this year almost as much as she relished the moment Jamie told them he would only deal with Emma.

Travis had been taken aback, but he recovered quickly.

Then Jamie took all three of his "Joy" photographs off the wall and said, "And these aren't for sale," and that had nearly turned her giddy.

Something about the look on Mark David's face—it was nice to remind a snob that they didn't always get their own way.

Yes, she'd relished it too much, and while she should probably feel badly about that, she didn't. She was too happy. She now had weeks of working with Jamie ahead of her, and she had every intention of making sure his show was exactly as perfect as she knew it could be.

She owed it to him.

Which was why she was pulling herself from her bed at this hour when she was pretty sure even God wasn't awake yet. That and the fact that his excitement over the prospect of shooting that morning stirred something inside her.

Truthfully, his newfound creativity was inspiring her too. She'd never be the kind of artist Jamie was, and that was okay. She could paint for fun and throw herself wholly into this accidental career of being a gallery assistant. At least for now. She enjoyed it. She was around art all the time, and she got to do what she was good at. Nothing about it felt like she was settling.

In fact, the idea of helping put together the show was exciting. Something told her she'd be good at it. She liked people. She wasn't shy. She was good in a crisis. And she loved art. She was born for this job.

She just needed to prove it to Travis.

As long as she could continue to ignore the way her eyes had played tricks on her twice now and the sinking feeling that had followed, she'd be good to move forward.

*Your past is going to catch up to you.*

Jamie walked out of the apartment just as the tinge of first light appeared on the horizon. She sat on the porch, a thermos of coffee and a bag of muffins in hand. CJ had spent the night with Stella, and while she knew that girl-boy sleepovers wouldn't last long, she was thankful to have this time for herself.

Did that make her a terrible mom?

She stood and lifted a hand. "You're cutting it close, sailor."

He smirked. "You have coffee."

"I'm a goddess."

Now a full-on smile. He leaned in for a kiss, which she gladly gave. After a brief moment, she took a step back and found his eyes, open and on her.

"You smell minty," she said.

"You look like you didn't sleep."

She frowned. "Ouch."

"Still beautiful, of course." He took the coffee and they walked toward his rented truck. "Okay if we take this?"

She nodded and they got in. He tucked the camera bag on the seat between them, and she noticed he treated it with the same care she treated CJ.

"Why'd you bring that with you when you came to Nantucket?" she asked as they made their way out onto the street. When he looked at her, she nodded toward the camera. "Were you expecting to work?"

"No, not really." He focused on the road. "I'm not sure. Habit?"

"Can you work while you're here?"

His jaw tightened. "I've done some things here. Zoom calls and that sort of thing. But I'm going to have to make a trip home soon to touch base."

What was keeping him here? He hadn't exactly been forthcoming with his reasons for being on the island in the first place. She considered asking him again but decided against it. She didn't want anything—not even her overactive curiosity—to ruin this morning.

Neither of them knew the hidden places of the island, which Jamie had explained was part of the concept for this series. So today they would visit the typical tourist areas, but before the rest of the island awoke.

She imagined he would take several different approaches to photographing Nantucket—busy streets, empty streets, hidden places, tourist favorites—and then put the show together once all the images had been captured and he selected his favorites. She hoped she got to be a part of that process.

They parked the truck. "You sure you don't mind me tagging along?"

He glanced at her. "You're the whole reason I'm doing this."

She smiled. "That's a good thing, right?"

He squeezed her hand, then pulled the camera from its bag. "A very good thing."

"So how does one go on a photographic walk?"

He riffled around in the bag for a moment, then produced a smaller model of the camera in his hand.

"What's that?"

"Your camera," he said.

"Uh, no." She could feel the frown crinkling her forehead. "My artistic expertise starts and ends with watercolor. And these days I'm not even sure about that." It wasn't exactly true. She'd dabbled with other mediums, but she always returned to the one she felt more comfortable with.

He shook it, indicating that she should take it. "I'm going to teach you."

The camera was light in her hands. "But why?"

He shrugged. "Maybe it'll shake loose the creativity you've been suppressing."

"I haven't been—"

But his knowing look stopped her. "Don't think I don't know that rendering of Millie's wasn't your best effort. I mean, it was good, but there was something missing."

Well, shoot. "How do you know?"

"I might've looked at your portfolio."

Her eyes widened. "You what? When?"

"The second day I met you." He ran a hand over his stubbled chin.

Her jaw went slack.

"Sorry." He looked anything but apologetic. "You showed me that one of the mom at the school bus, and I was curious. I had a hunch, and I was right. You're really good."

She hated that the compliment had an effect on her.

"So we'll stretch a different creative muscle and just see what happens. No pressure."

She rolled her eyes. "Creative people think they know everything." She turned before he saw her smile and let herself out of the truck.

They walked down Main Street, angling their cameras *just so* to get the exact shot they each saw in their minds. Twice Emma had caught him pointing his lens at her, and twice she'd been unsure how to react. How many images had he captured of her without her even realizing it?

After about twenty minutes, they made their way past Children's Beach and out toward Brant Point lighthouse. Emma marveled at the poofs of giant purple hydrangeas in the lawn outside several of the gray-shingled cottages with white trim. One cottage on the corner had a huge wraparound porch and a cheery teal door that practically begged to be photographed.

She lifted her camera and clicked.

Jamie had crossed the street, aiming his lens at the ocean, where a sailboat bobbed in the water and, closer to the shore, a man and woman balanced gingerly on paddleboards.

He pointed and clicked, not stopping to check the settings or the light. She supposed he knew instinctively if he was capturing what he wanted.

She lifted her camera and zoomed in on him, crouched down and eyeing the horizon, camera poised for another shot. Even dressed in shorts and a faded T-shirt, he looked like a pro. She clicked. Zoomed in closer and clicked again.

She'd never tire of watching him work.

They continued on toward the lighthouse, then strolled down to the beach. His camera hung around his neck, his hand bearing the weight of it. He slid his free hand in hers.

"This was a good idea," he said.

If she wasn't careful, she would get used to this. She couldn't deny how much she liked being near him. She wouldn't try to pretend she didn't love that he was creative, that he understood that part of her.

Cam hadn't, sadly. Her husband had been a genuine good guy, the best kind of guy, but there were ways in which she knew they would never connect. Her art was only hers. He didn't understand or appreciate it. On many levels, they almost felt mismatched, but he'd loved her so well.

And she'd loved him—with the whole of herself.

A person only got one true love in a lifetime. If she'd already had hers, did she and Jamie have any hope? Maybe if she could keep her feelings from getting tangled, they could keep things casual. Friendly. Fun. Didn't they both deserve some fun?

Her chest tightened at the thought. *But that's not what you want.*

She ignored the thought and followed Jamie across the street to Island Coffee, where he ordered a cup of coffee, black, and she ordered an iced coffee with loads of cream and more sugar than she'd ever admit out loud.

Afterward, they headed back to his truck. Even in the quiet, Emma felt something she hadn't in years—contentment. There was no pressure to fill the silence, no need to be someone she wasn't. There was only a soft understanding and an agreement not to over-analyze a relationship that had only just begun.

Not the easiest feat. If overthinking was an Olympic sport, she'd have more gold medals than Michael Phelps.

Jamie flipped on the radio—a sports station with two men talking—then quickly turned it off. "You probably don't want to listen to two guys talk about baseball."

She clicked the button to turn it back on. "I don't mind at all."

She rolled the window down and inhaled the salty air, pretending for just a moment she had no job to get to and no responsibilities.

The daydream came to a screeching halt when he pulled into her driveway. A blue Camry sat parked next to her car.

"Were you expecting company?" he asked.

Her mind raced back to the man she swore she'd seen on the street, not once but twice. She'd convinced herself it was only the ghost of her regret, but what if it wasn't? What if he was here?

"Emma?"

She shook her head. "I don't know who it is." Her throat went dry, like someone had wiped away her saliva with a thick ball of cotton. She opened the door, camera still hanging from her neck, and walked around the front of Jamie's truck, aware that he'd exited the vehicle and now watched her with more interest than she wanted.

As she approached the Camry, the passenger door opened and a familiar wisp of a woman got out.

*Nadine.*

Cam's mom was small in stature but big in personality—and apparently she saw nothing wrong with the surprise visit.

Emma's pulse quickened as Nadine tossed a once-over at Jamie. Emma wasn't ready to define her new relationship to herself, let alone to her late husband's parents.

Why did she feel like a high schooler who'd just been caught sneaking back in the house after a night of sin?

"Good morning," Nadine called out cheerily as Emma walked toward her. "We arrived on the first ferry." She reached for Emma and wrapped her in a tight hug. She lowered her voice. "Are you just getting in?"

Emma stepped back from her mother-in-law's embrace. How this must look. "No, we left early for a photography walk." She glanced at Jamie, who stood near the truck, wearing an undeniable expression of uncertainty. "This is my friend Jamie. He's a photographer."

Jerry hugged her now, clapping her on the back with his beefy, Cam-like hands. "Good to see you, sweetheart."

Some people didn't connect with their in-laws. Emma was not one of those people. Her own family was broken and dysfunctional, and Jerry was the closest thing to a father she had. He'd treated her like a daughter from the moment Cam announced their engagement. And she'd needed to be treated like a daughter given that her own father had left when she was a girl, and her mother had never quite gotten her life back on track.

Would it hurt them to see her with someone new? Her heart twisted at the thought.

"Good to see you too, Dad," she said.

"You didn't mention a new friend, Emma." Nadine walked toward Jamie, whose eyes widened. "I'm Nadine Woodson."

Jamie straightened and took a step toward her. "Jamie Shaw." He stuck a hand out in her direction, but she instantly pooh-poohed it.

"Oh, Jamie," she said. "I'm a hugger."

It was something to watch tiny Nadine manhandle Jamie like he was nothing more than a child in need of a hug. Over the older woman's head, Jamie looked at Emma, who only grinned.

Nadine pulled back and studied him. "You sure are a handsome one." She tossed a look over her shoulder. "Emma, where'd you find him?"

Jamie's face flushed a color she hadn't seen before.

"Picked him up on the street," Emma said as her mother-in-law squeezed Jamie's bicep.

"Good decision." The older woman waggled her eyebrows.

Jerry, Emma noted, was much quieter.

"We're sorry to drop in on you unannounced," Nadine said. She practically dragged Jamie across the driveway to where Emma and Jerry stood. "We missed you and CJ, of course. Is he still asleep?"

"He spent the night with a friend," Emma said.

Nadine leaned in closer. "Did *you* also spend the night with a friend?" Despite leaning in, she'd failed to lower her voice.

"No!" Emma said, a little too quickly. How did she show the appropriate amount of horror for the question without coming across as guilty?

Nadine held her hands up. "Sorry to pry."

"You're not sorry," Jerry said. "It's what you do."

He reminded Emma of Cam, who got his football player genes from his father. A wide, stocky man, Jerry Woodson had played college ball back in the day, and Emma had never met a man prouder of his son than Jerry.

She'd envied their relationship at first. Then she'd fallen into her own relationship with Cam's dad, and she realized that love was something he gave freely. The thought of disappointing him made her feel anxious in a way she hadn't in a very long time.

Sure, she wanted to impress Travis, and she wanted Jamie to like her. But with Jerry—it was something else she sought. She wanted him to be proud of her. To approve of her. Of her relationships.

It was crucial that he gave his blessing.

And if he found out about her last conversation with Cam, it would absolutely break his heart.

"When will our boy be home?" Nadine asked.

Emma filled them in on CJ's typical routine while she was at work, and her mother-in-law pooh-poohed that idea too.

"Can we take him for the day? Maybe we can meet you for lunch?" She looked at Jamie. "Both of you?"

Jamie straightened. "Actually, I've got a full day."

"Jamie's going to be showing his work at the art festival this year," Emma said. "Plus, he's helping me renovate the apartment."

"The apartment?" A shock of concern rose to Nadine's eyes.

"Yes," Emma said. "But don't worry. All of Cam's stuff is in the garage, still in boxes."

The older woman's jaw twitched. "Right. We should probably go through that."

Emma didn't want to agree to that. She was sort of hoping those boxes would simply go away. Searching through Cam's things wasn't something she had strength for.

"How about dinner then?" Nadine turned to Jamie. "I'll cook. Give you the night off. We'll all sit down, and we can get to know your friend."

Emma looked at Jamie, who stared back at her as if waiting to follow her lead.

"Um, I'm good with that," she said. "If you are?"

He nodded. "Sure."

"Perfect," Nadine said. "We'll take CJ to the market, and he can help me in the kitchen."

Emma smiled. She hadn't realized until that exact moment how much she'd missed them.

Jerry popped the trunk of the Camry. "We don't want to keep you, Emma. We'll get ourselves settled in the guest room, and you can get ready for your day."

Emma glanced back at Jamie, who'd gone pale as a sheet. Was "meeting the family of the woman you're sort-of-maybe-kind-of dating" too much for him?

Nadine settled on a time for dinner, instructing them both to come hungry. Then she and Jerry picked up their suitcases and walked off toward the house, leaving Emma and Jamie standing there, both a little bewildered.

"Sorry," she said. "They're really great people. They just want to know everything about everyone all the time." She smiled.

Jamie looked like he'd swallowed a bird.

"You okay with this? I can tell them you can't make it if it's too awkward."

He shook his head. "No, it's fine. It'll be good to get to know them."

Her eyes narrowed. "You sure?"

He nodded. "But I do have a lot to do, so I'll see you tonight?" He gave her a quick kiss on the cheek, hoisted his camera on his shoulder, and strolled off toward the garage.

# CHAPTER TWENTY-TWO

~~~

AFTER A FULL DAY OF WORKING on the apartment and trying not to think about the fact that Emma's in-laws were on the island, Jamie showered and dressed for dinner.

The day had taken a swift turn, and he was unsure how to process it.

He and Emma were new, and getting to know her inside this little bubble they'd put themselves in had been ideal. How would the outside world react to the two of them? More to the point, how would her former husband's parents react to the two of them?

Should he make his feelings for Emma known? Hold her hand? Steal kisses when helping her do the dishes?

Jamie stopped in the kitchen before walking out the door. He opened the drawer, the place where that stupid letter had been banished, and took it out.

*You're betraying them all.*

The thought turned around inside him like a persistent gymnast trying to land a backflip on a balance beam. He stared at the envelope, her name on the front.

"Emma," he whispered, as if he hadn't practiced the speech before. Only, it had been easier before. He hadn't known her. He hadn't developed feelings for her. "I didn't come here because I saw an ad. I came here to tell you it's my fault your husband was killed."

The words, whispered in the silence of this empty apartment, haunted him.

He wanted to leap to his own defense, but what else could he say? He *was* at fault. If he'd listened, Emma never would've lost her husband.

"It's my fault," he whispered again.

And now he was going to sit at the table with that man's family— his parents, his son, his wife—and eat dinner like he belonged with them. Who did he think he was?

He absolutely needed to tell her the truth he'd been avoiding for so long. He'd been selfish and thoughtless entering into a relationship with her the way he had.

His phone buzzed on the counter in front of him. A text from Emma: Hey, can you bring that French bread I know you've got stashed up there? We forgot to grab some.

It felt so normal. So casual. They were friends on their way to becoming more. This precarious, precious relationship was the best thing in his life, and he was going to lose it because he was a coward.

Which was the same reason those men had lost their lives.

*Coward.*

He hated the word. He hated that it defined him.

He replied, Of course, then grabbed the bread, stuffed the envelope back in the drawer, turned off the light, and decided the charade ended tonight.

Tonight he would tell Emma the truth. And if it meant that he lost her . . . Well, he didn't want to think about that, though he knew it was a very real possibility.

He walked downstairs and onto her porch, knocked quietly, then pushed the door open.

He could hear voices in the kitchen. Emma was telling them about the gallery, about her job, about the show.

"Honestly, Jamie is saving my life here." He could hear the smile in her voice. "You will not believe how talented he is." Papers shuffling. "Look at this photo he took of me and CJ."

A quiet gasp from Nadine. "That's stunning."

"And that's nothing," Emma said. "I'll show you his website later." Jamie made a mental note to take that website down.

"What brought him to the island?" Nadine asked.

After a brief pause, Jamie called out, not wanting to add "eavesdropping" to his list of sins. "Hello?"

"Oh, he's here." Emma rushed out of the kitchen and into the entryway. She smiled at him. "I didn't hear you come in."

"Sorry," he said. "I knocked but figured you guys didn't hear."

She took the bread, and he told himself it was a bad time for kissing her hello. CJ raced into the room, appearing, as usual, out of nowhere, and shoved a photo in Jamie's direction. "This is Margot. She's going to be my dog."

Emma put a hand on CJ's and pushed it down carefully. "They visited the animal shelter today." Then to her son, "CJ, I told you we can't have a dog right now."

The boy's face fell, his lip shoved out in a pout. "That's not fair."

"Go wash your hands," she said. "We're going to eat."

He stomped off, and she sighed, then looked at Jamie. "You okay? You look . . ."

"Are you about to insult me?"

"And tell you that you look like you didn't get much sleep?" She smiled wryly, calling back his comment from that morning. "I wouldn't dream of it." She turned back toward the kitchen. "Do you want a drink?"

"I'm good, thanks." He wasn't good, actually. His throat was dry. His palms were clammy. He wanted to teleport to a different time and place.

But no, that wasn't right either. Another time and place might not have Emma in it. Now that he knew her, how would he survive a life without her? He shoved away the thought because he had a horrible feeling it wouldn't be long before he found out.

# CHAPTER TWENTY-THREE

DINNER WITH HER IN-LAWS, her chatty son, and her new love interest. What could possibly go wrong?

She'd texted Elise earlier in the day to fill her in on this latest turn of events, and in reply her friend had sent back: Good luck, my friend. And Godspeed.

Emma had no idea how to interpret that, but the fact that her friend felt compelled to send well-wishes made the situation feel even weightier than it already did.

Now, sitting at the table, which looked like it had been set for a holiday meal, thanks to Nadine, Emma told herself to relax.

*It's just dinner.*

CJ and his grandmother filled the space with stories about their day of adventures—they'd collected seashells in the morning, eaten pastries midday, visited the animal shelter (darn them!), gone shopping for their meal (lobster rolls, one of Nadine's specialties), and bought Nantucket sweatshirts that they found at one of the shops.

"I know it's a very touristy thing to do," Nadine said. "But I don't care. The sweatshirt was soft, and I like the idea of telling the world I was on the island."

Never mind that Emma could count on one hand the number of times she'd seen her mother-in-law wearing a sweatshirt.

Jamie was quiet. Too quiet. How was he feeling about this? Awkward and out of place, she imagined. It didn't matter that Cam had been gone five years or that her in-laws were handling everything beautifully—it must've been strange to be in this mixed company.

"Were you able to look through your photos from your excursion this morning?" Jerry looked at Jamie.

"I was, actually," Jamie said.

"Ooh, did you get anything good?" Nadine asked.

His eyes darted to Emma. "A few nice images."

For some inexplicable reason, she wondered if he was referring to the photos he'd taken of her. What a cocky thought.

"I can't wait to see them," she said.

"Emma says you have a business near Chicago?" Nadine asked.

As Jamie told them about his business back in Naperville, Emma told herself this was simply friendly conversation, not the third degree, not an assessment of him in any way. Just people getting to know each other.

"And what brought you here?" Cam's mom asked. "To the island?"

Jamie shifted. The pause turned pregnant and Emma frowned. She'd asked him this same question before, and he'd deflected. She'd brushed it off at the time, but now—did he really not have an answer?

"Can I be 'scused?" CJ asked. "Mr. Jamie and I are going to build a train track."

The unanswered question hung in the air.

"Mo-om-my?" CJ turned the word into three syllables.

"Sure, buddy, go ahead."

CJ hopped down and grabbed on to Jamie's arm. "Come on, I got a new train today! I'll show you!"

Jamie pushed back from the table and stacked CJ's plate on top of his. "Thank you for dinner. It was really good."

The lightness in the air had been replaced by something heavy, and Emma's gaze fell to her plate as he exited the room.

Nadine picked up her glass and sipped.

"Emma, how much do you really know about this man?" Jerry's quiet words were thick with concern.

"Enough, I think," she said. "I mean, as much as a person can know in just a few weeks' time."

Jamie had joined CJ upstairs, and Emma could hear the sound of trains racing along the wooden track. It was unlikely he could hear their conversation, but she kept her voice low just the same.

"You said he answered your ad?" Nadine asked.

She nodded, a sick feeling needling its way into her stomach. "He's helped me a lot. The apartment. The art show. Even with CJ."

"He does seem like a good guy," Jerry agreed. "And it's obvious he really cares about both of you."

Nadine frowned. "But there's something a little . . ."

Emma held her breath.

"Off."

"How do you mean?"

The older woman shook her head. "I don't know. I can't place it. I just feel like he's hiding something."

Emma's muscles tensed.

*Aren't we all?*

~

Jamie had tried to find a good time to speak to Emma. He'd folded the letter and tucked it in his back pocket, placing a hand on it every time he stood, sat, or moved to make sure it didn't fall out. He could easily leave it on her nightstand and disappear on the first ferry the next morning.

But no, that would only make things worse.

He wasn't aiming to break her heart.

He'd considered pulling her into the bathroom and unloading the whole sordid story while CJ put his pajamas on and Cam's parents retrieved their collection of DVDs of their favorite Nantucket-set television show, *Wings*. Not surprisingly, that didn't feel right either. He would've been smart to tell them all at dinner when the question came up, but he thought he owed it to Emma to share the truth with her when they were alone.

Which, he was quickly realizing, wouldn't be until after Cam's parents left.

This could go on forever, and all it was doing was intensifying his guilt.

After the third episode of *Wings*, the one where pilot Brian ignores a thick fog to go after his ex-wife, Carol, who was moving to London, Jamie extracted himself from the sofa.

"Are you leaving?" Emma stood.

"I should," he said. "I have some work projects tomorrow, and I want to get a shoot in later in the day."

Her face softened. Had he imagined a coolness from her ever since dinner? "I'll walk you out," she said.

He thanked her in-laws again, told them he'd see them tomorrow, then followed Emma through the kitchen and out the back door.

The light next to the door of the apartment shone dimly across the yard, only a few feet from where they stood. That and the moonlight were the only two things cutting through the darkness.

"Thanks for coming tonight," she said. "I know it was probably weird."

"A little." It had been, in fact. Being there, in the midst of her family, a place he very clearly did not belong, only highlighted the things that were wrong between them. Things she didn't even know.

But here, when it was just the two of them in the quiet, the very faint sound of waves lapping the shore in the distance, all of that fell away.

"You handled the inquisition pretty well," she said. "I hope you didn't feel too on the spot."

He reached for her hand. "It's obvious how much they care about you."

"They treat me like I'm theirs," she said. "Which is good because my own parents sure didn't."

He frowned at this, realizing and relishing that he still had so much to learn about her.

"A story for another day," she said, sensing his curiosity.

"I want to tell you all about why I came here." His gaze fell to their feet.

*Coward.*

He'd practiced this in the mirror. He had a plan to come clean. But it wasn't only about Emma, he realized in that moment. It was also about him, about what he'd witnessed, about what he'd caused. Saying that aloud had never grown easier, not in the entire five years since he'd returned from that trip to Africa. In all that time, he'd only recounted the story three times—once for Hillary and his parents, once for Freddy's mother, and once for Dr. McDonald. He didn't count the email to Jimmy's widow, Alicia, because writing it out hadn't required nearly as much strength as saying the words aloud.

She waited until he looked back up before smiling. "Is that also a story for another day?"

"Maybe," he said.

"I don't mind waiting," she said. "I'm a patient woman."

At the reminder of his own words, he smiled, and when she inched up on her tiptoes and pressed a soft kiss to his lips, he closed his eyes and drank her in, aware that in all of heaven and earth, he did not deserve this woman's love.

"Good night, Jamie," she said.

He kissed her again, then watched as she slipped inside through the back door, so close and yet just out of his reach.

A hush falls over the lush, green vegetation. A hush that signals danger.

He can't explain how he knows, but he knows. The unit knows. They all know. They are driving into a trap.

*Maybe we should turn around.* He thinks the words but doesn't say them. It's too peaceful. Too eerily quiet for nothing to be wrong.

The truck ambles on, kicking up the dust of the dirt road that leads to the village up ahead.

He lifts his camera, looking through the viewfinder at the horizon, searching—for what?

Everything goes still.

And then—a single gunshot. Followed by a series of gunshots. A noise he will never forget rings out into the quiet.

The truck goes limp, a tire flat with a bullet wound. They hop into action. They're trained for this. But he isn't. His heartbeat thuds in his chest, a quick staccato. The chaos in the truck grows. They're yelling. Barking. One of them—Cam—takes control of the situation and gives out the orders.

To Jamie, he says, "Stay close to me."

More gunfire. An explosion up ahead. Flames. Heat. They've been hit. They exit the truck and search for cover. The trees provide a canopy, a hiding place.

They run. His legs tense. It's hot. The truck is engulfed in flames. His muscles ache, but he forces them to go on.

"Stay here."

The soldier has hold of Jamie's vest.

"You hear me?"

He nods. His temples ache. He squats down in the brush and hides.

"You're safe here."

But it isn't safe. Nowhere is safe.

"Stay here." The words rush back, feeling like a death sentence. "You hear me?"

Another explosion. A long, loud clatter of shots pierce through the air. The soldiers are shouting, swearing. One of them is injured. One of them is dead.

Jamie's heart pounds, battering against his ribs like a log being driven into a locked medieval gate.

"You hear me, Jamie?"

The words play on a continuous loop.

"You're safe here."

He should've listened.

*"You're safe here."*

~

Jamie awoke with a start, forehead wet with sweat. He gasped for air while he got his bearings.

He wasn't in the Congo. He was here, in Nantucket, in Emma's apartment. He was safe.

*"You're safe here."*

Truth was, he hadn't felt safe since that day.

Not talking about it had become his safety net. Pushing it all aside, pretending it didn't happen—it was the only way to deal with the unconscionable, knowing that it wasn't a nightmare—it was a memory.

He padded to the sink, found a glass, and filled it with water. His eyes roamed toward the window he knew to be Emma's bedroom.

A slight, if misguided, sense of peace wove its way through him at the thought of her. In that moment, he realized he'd avoided speaking the truth—that his actions had led to Cam's death—because from the moment he saw her, she calmed the haunting shame inside him in a way nobody else had. She saw him—not for who he was, but for who he was trying to become.

And her belief in him, in his talent, in his goodness, had fueled something in him that had gone missing. How could he give that up?

How could he break the silence that had been his saving grace since the moment he'd witnessed a tragedy, the pain of which he would never outrun?

He emptied the glass and set it on the counter, then returned to the bed, where he stared at the ceiling, praying to a God who'd seemed to abandon him that day.

# CHAPTER TWENTY-FOUR

~~~

AFTER A WEEK WITH HER IN-LAWS ON THE ISLAND, Emma found herself falling back into familiar patterns of letting them handle tasks she really needed to be handling.

Parenting CJ, mostly, but other things too. Cooking meals. Planning outings. Other women might resent their presence, but Emma's heart was full every morning when she woke up and found Jerry out on the back deck, thick Bible splayed open in his lap, cup of coffee on the table at his side.

This had always been Cam's dad's morning routine. Wake before the sun, make a pot of "the good stuff," which, she found out later, was actually poorly brewed Folgers, and spend a bit of time with Jesus.

Cam hadn't been as steadfast in his faith as Jerry, but after his death, when Emma moved in with them, she hadn't been able to avoid the question of her own faith.

Her pregnancy bladder had her up early in the mornings, and before long, Jerry was pouring two cups of coffee and making it clear she was welcome to join him. Sometimes they sat and talked. Sometimes he prayed silently while she tried not to fall back asleep. Sometimes he shared a passage from a book that was so much more than words to him. And Emma marveled at how his faith was so real, so genuine, so much so that she started to want it for herself.

Seeing him on the porch now, for the fifth day in a row, she was convicted with the reminder that she'd given her heart to Jerry's God. She'd made him *her* God. And since she'd struck out on her own, she'd all but abandoned him.

Why was that? Didn't she need him now more than ever?

Same way she'd needed him back then, in the wake of Cam's death and everything that had gone before.

Jerry had helped her understand forgiveness. He said God would wipe her slate clean. She'd tried to believe him—she wanted that more than anything. But she'd struggled. And she'd yet to really put her past behind her.

She poured herself a cup of coffee and pushed the back door open, walking out in her pajamas like a daughter anxious to sit attentively with her father as he shared whatever was on his heart that day.

"Morning," he said.

She dropped into the empty Adirondack chair beside him and stared out across the backyard. "Morning."

"You're not sleeping," he said.

"Nope."

"Why's that?"

She sipped the warm drink and tried not to spit it out. She'd forgotten how bad "the good stuff" was. "I'm not sure."

"Could be that man living above your garage."

Jamie *had* been occupying a lot of her thoughts lately. "Could be."

"Feeling guilty?"

The words twisted around, turning a somersault inside her. *Guilty* was something she always felt. She reminded herself that Jerry didn't know about any of that. He was referring to the present, not the past. "Maybe."

"It's awful hard to lose someone you love," he said. "But moving on is a natural part of life. Doesn't mean you forget the person you loved. Doesn't even mean you stop loving them. Just means you stay among the living. You haven't really been doing that up until now."

No. She hadn't. Jamie seemed to have pushed the oxygen back into her lungs, awakening something inside her that had long since fallen asleep.

"It's strange having feelings for someone other than Cam," she admitted.

His face turned gentle, every bit the wise father she'd grown to love. "I understand."

"I guess I'd sort of sworn off romance."

"Because you don't want to get hurt again?" he asked.

*That and other reasons.* She only nodded.

He took a drink, then rested the mug on his thick leg. "Risk is part of living, kiddo. After spending a few days with you, I have to say, it's nice to see you doing that again."

The unwanted tears were back. If someone could've just warned her that every step forward would be accompanied by a fresh supply of tears, she would've felt more prepared.

"And whatever else you're holding on to," he said, "it might be time to let that go too."

She looked at him, straight into the eyes that seemed to read her as if she were as clear as the text on the pages of his old Bible. What was he saying?

He rested his head back against the chair and closed his eyes.

"What do you mean?" she asked quietly.

He drew in a breath. "You're carrying something that isn't yours to carry." His eyes fluttered open. "Time to put it down."

She frowned. "What makes you say that?"

He shrugged. "Take it up with the Holy Spirit. That's what he told me to tell you today."

She couldn't imagine the Holy Spirit was overly concerned with the deep regret she'd saddled onto her shoulders, but she didn't say so. Surely he had other things to worry about.

He? Was the Holy Spirit a "he"?

The light in the apartment flicked on, and Emma's heart followed suit. Jerry didn't seem to notice, but somehow their conversation validated her feelings for the man above the garage. Despite her reservations, she'd grown attached to Jamie.

If Cam's dad was giving his blessing, then maybe this whole relationship could become more than just a casual "date for fun" kind of thing. As if it had ever been that to her in the first place. She'd erected all kinds of walls around herself, but Jamie had penetrated every single one. Knocked her resolve straight to the ground.

"I should go." She stood. "Busy day."

"Us too," he said. "I think we're taking CJ to the beach." He winked at her. "You're doing good, Emma. That one's not the Holy Spirit. That one's me."

The simplicity of his acceptance warmed something inside her. "Thanks, Dad."

He took another sip. "Coffee's good, right?"

She grimaced. "Good? That might be a stretch."

He waved her off. "You're just too used to your fancy, overpriced drinks."

"That, and I prefer to keep the sludge out of my coffee mugs."

He feigned an arrow to the heart. "That cuts deep."

She smiled as she left the porch, thanking God for that man. If anyone had told her that her husband's death would bring her closer to his family, she never would've believed them, but what a gift they'd become. One of her favorite gifts.

She showered and dressed for work, anxious to get going because today was the day she would receive the first few images of Jamie's show. He'd texted her yesterday to let her know he'd made progress (most likely in the wee hours of the morning) and could he take her to lunch to show her?

Of course she'd fired back an Absolutely!!! And she could hardly wait to see what he'd come up with.

The morning was busy. She'd coordinated their next art workshop, a study in oils with award-winning painter Madeleine Farrar, conversed with three different collectors who were anxious about the new artist that would be featured at the festival, and she'd even rearranged the back wall of the gallery. Travis would likely change it back to the way he had it, but it was fun to mix it up just the same.

When lunchtime rolled around, her stomach gnawed in emptiness, and as she put the finishing touches on a mock-up brochure for Jamie's show, the door to the street opened. She looked up, expecting Jamie, but was faced instead with a ghost.

"You look good, Emma," he said, as cocky as ever.

And as usual when it came to Blake Simpson, she had absolutely no reply.

# CHAPTER TWENTY-FIVE

~~~

JAMIE MADE HIS WAY DOWN THE STREET toward Gallery 316, portfolio under his arm, thinking about the images he'd printed for Emma to see.

While he was clear on his artistic vision, he knew that her keen eye and attention to detail were invaluable. Despite his initial reluctance, after spending the last two weeks photographing the island, he couldn't deny that a part of him was excited about his first real gallery show.

He sidestepped a group of slow-moving tourists and rounded the corner toward the gallery. Through the glass window, he saw Emma, standing at the center of the room, a pained look on her face. In front of her was a man—tall, bulky. And he had a grip on her arm.

What the . . . ?

Jamie made quick work of the distance between himself and the front door. He pulled it open and the man turned toward him, dropping Emma's arm. She turned away.

"Emma?" Jamie ignored the guy and focused on her. She refused his eyes.

The guy looked back at her. "I'll be in touch." He turned and walked out, glaring at Jamie as he passed by.

Once he'd gone, Jamie moved toward Emma, who was doing a terrible job of pretending she wasn't rattled. "Who was that guy?"

She shook her head. "Oh, just an old friend."

He frowned. "That conversation didn't look friendly. Are you in trouble?"

She dragged her eyes to his and put on a smile. "No, nothing like that."

"What's going on?"

"It's nothing, Jamie," she said firmly. "Can we just drop it?"

His heart twitched. No, they couldn't drop it. The image of her in possible danger wasn't something he could simply erase.

"Emma—"

"Look, there are things you aren't telling me, right? About why you came here—a story for another day, remember?"

He stilled at the mention of it. "Yeah."

"So this is my *other* story for another day," she said. "I don't want to talk about it."

He couldn't argue with that. What could he possibly say? He knew how it felt not to be ready to share the dark parts of yourself with someone else, no matter how badly you wanted to.

He moved around the counter and pulled her into his arms. "I'm sorry. I'm just worried about you."

She bristled at his touch, then finally relaxed into him. "I'll be okay."

He inched back and forced her gaze. "You sure?"

She nodded. He supposed it would have to do for now.

~

Blake's threats tangled with her shame, leaving Emma panicked and broken.

She tried to focus as she and Jamie looked through his photographs—beautiful, stunning images of an island that was becoming her home. He'd known something was wrong, but he was respecting her request not to press.

Did she really think her secret would stay hidden? She'd been such a fool to assume she could simply start a new life, as if the old one wouldn't catch up to her. A fool to believe that God wiping the slate clean meant there would be no consequences for her actions.

*I'm such an idiot.*

"Do you want to do this another time?" Jamie asked. "I don't mind waiting. I have a few things to do in the apartment anyway. You're awfully close to being able to rent it out."

Why did that make her sad? Of course she wanted the apartment ready—but once it was, he'd be gone.

She needed to tell him the truth. She didn't want a relationship that was built on lies. But it would change everything between them. It would change the way he saw her. He might even break things off with her once he heard what she had to say.

*Where's that forgiveness now, God?*

"Maybe," she said. "Is that okay? You can leave these here with me, and I'll look them over, but I think I just need a break."

He nodded. "I'll head back to the apartment. I'm almost done installing the flooring, so I can work on that. Stop by later?"

She nodded. He kissed her goodbye. She watched him go.

And as soon as the door closed behind him, the dam broke on the well of tears she'd been holding in. Her mistake was too big to hide, and she realized now she couldn't outrun it.

It would ruin her entire life to come clean, and she knew it. She would lose everything and everyone she loved.

But what choice did she have?

# CHAPTER TWENTY-SIX

TWO DAYS LATER, EMMA FOUND HERSELF in the middle of a perfect storm.

She'd successfully avoided Jamie ever since he left the gallery after walking in on the tail end of Blake's visit, but as she hung up the phone now, she knew her days of avoidance were over.

With her in-laws off for a short trip to Martha's Vineyard, Sadie and Stella on the Cape for the week, and CJ's day care closed since both staff members had come down with "that dreaded summer cold," Emma had no choice but to beg yet another favor from Jamie.

She made a mental note to get out and meet more people. People who might be willing to watch her son in a pinch.

She walked up the stairs to the apartment and knocked on the door. Moments later, he opened it and stood in front of her in a pair of pajama pants, hair messy like he'd just woken up.

Her body responded to him, that traitor, but how could it ignore the tanned and toned torso, the piercing hazel eyes, the lazy, teasing smile?

She'd been married—she knew how things worked between men and women. And while Jamie had been more than patient with her, she couldn't deny there was an attraction to him that made her want to push her own boundaries.

That scared her. A lot. Because she'd jumped straight over those boundaries in the past, and it had only brought her heartache and shame.

*I don't want anyone else to get hurt.*

"You're just about the best thing I could imagine seeing first thing in the morning," he said.

"I'm not here to flirt with you," she said flirtatiously.

He took her hand and pulled her inside. He smelled of mint and yesterday's aftershave. He closed the door and backed her against it, leaning in, his arm pressed firmly into the wall behind her.

"I have a favor," she said, her voice barely audible.

He grinned, then kissed her cheek. His free hand slid across her collarbone as his lips trailed down to her neck. She closed her eyes and let herself get lost in him. Just for a moment.

His lips found hers, and she straightened at his attentiveness to her.

"What's the favor?" he whispered before deepening the kiss.

She opened her eyes and studied him for the briefest moment.

*I love him.*

*Oh no.* The thought had entered her mind without warning, but there it was, followed by the clear knowing that she didn't want to hide anything from Jamie. She wanted him to see her, completely and honestly, for who she was.

She'd been avoiding it, but it was time to tell him the truth. Not now, of course, when their conversation would be rushed, and she had somewhere else to be. But tonight. She'd tell him everything, because like it or not, Blake Simpson was a part of her past, and he wasn't going away. Jamie deserved to have all the facts before he decided if he loved her back.

Besides, she wanted him to know her—not just a squeaky-clean version of her—but the real her.

And that scared her to death.

"I need a sitter for CJ," she said, pulling back ever so slightly. "Today?"

She grimaced. "Yes. I know it's short notice."

He kissed her again, lingering for a moment as he inhaled. "I can do that."

"Are you sure?"

He walked over to the bed and picked up a rumpled T-shirt she assumed he'd taken off during sleep. He pulled it over his head and down around his torso.

*Shame.*

He smiled, realizing he had her full attention.

The air between them snapped, and her hand searched for the doorknob. "I have to go get ready, but can you be down in half an hour?"

He hadn't broken eye contact with her, and his grin had only grown flirtier by the second. "Yep."

"See you then." Emma closed the door behind her and let out a deep breath. It was getting more difficult for her to resist this man.

~

Jamie had relished the small victory of being the person Emma turned to for help when she found herself in a jam. He'd happily rearranged his day to bail her out.

That morning, he took CJ exploring and even taught him to use the old camera Emma had used on their photo walk. CJ's perspective, lower to the ground and a little off-center, was kind of perfect, and he imagined her looking through the images her son had taken with a smile.

He lived to see that smile, to be the reason for it.

Just after lunchtime, they strolled down to Children's Beach so

CJ could run off some energy. As they stepped onto the sand, Jamie's phone rang.

*Dylan.*

He'd been putting his business partner off, and he knew Dylan was getting frustrated. Sure, they'd exchanged plenty of emails, and Jamie had managed to stay mostly on top of things, but his attention had splintered and he knew it. Dylan was not getting the best of him at the moment.

Their last exchange had been a week ago, before Jamie got an idea for the FitLife campaign while out shooting for the gallery show. He'd been surprised to find that the two different kinds of photography weren't completely separate in his head, as he'd originally thought.

Had he been fooling himself this entire time thinking that commercial shoots were without any artistic merit? Perhaps he'd been an artist all along.

He swiped to take the call. "Hey, man."

CJ let go of Jamie's hand and raced off toward the water.

"Don't get too close," he called out after him.

The boy turned and pointed to his feet as if to ask, *"Is this good?"* Jamie gave him a thumbs-up. "What's up?" he said into the phone.

"Hard at work, I hear." Dylan's words carried a tense tone.

"I'm just doing Emma a favor," he said. "Her sitter bailed."

"Well, can you do me a favor? Our client is going to bail if you don't come up with a plan."

He thought back to the images he'd shot with Jerrica Danielson in mind. A whole campaign about using what you had to get fit. No weights? Use your own body. No gym? Use the beach. It was right up her alley, and if he could get a little more time with it, he was sure he could make it good enough to present.

"I'm working on it," he said. "I can send over some images next week."

Dylan sighed. "I'm not sure images on a computer screen are going to sell her. She's losing faith in us."

Jamie understood the subtext. She was losing faith in *him* because he was here and not back home. Instead of building brands for their clients, he was building sandcastles.

He glanced up at CJ, who was burrowing his feet into the sand gleefully.

"I'm going to need you to come back and present this in person—whatever it is," Dylan said, stealing Jamie's attention. "We never set things up for you to be gone this long, and the emails and online meetings are fine for some clients, but not for her. You're going to have to charm this one, Jameson."

He knew it was coming, planned on it even, and still, he found himself frustrated by it. Annoying when real life and adult responsibilities got in the way.

"Did you hear me?" Dylan asked, impatience in his tone.

He sighed. "I'm not finished here yet."

"Well, get finished. The business depends on it."

He hung up, and Jamie turned back toward CJ. The boy was sitting in the sand, and the man Jamie had seen in the gallery with Emma knelt beside him.

"Hey!" Jamie raced across the beach as the man stood. "Get away from him."

The man stiffened. "Whoa, slow down there, mate."

"No, I don't think I will." Jamie positioned himself between CJ and the stranger. "Look, I don't know who you are, but I know Emma wouldn't want you around her son."

A smile crawled across the man's lips. "I wondered if she'd told you about me. Should've known she hadn't. Emma's always been good at keeping secrets." He winked. "See ya soon, kid."

"No. You won't." Jamie spoke through gritted teeth.

The man's eyes narrowed. "Oh, I think I will." He strolled off, leaving Jamie standing dumbly in the sand, the boy at his side and a bunch of questions he wasn't sure he wanted answered floating around in his head.

"Do you know that man?" Jamie asked CJ, who'd freed his feet from the sand and now stood upright beside him.

CJ shook his head. "He said he was a friend of Mommy's."

Jamie tossed another glance in the guy's direction, his figure shrinking as he strode off down the beach.

And a chill of concern turned his insides cold.

# CHAPTER TWENTY-SEVEN

~~~

AFTER WORK, EMMA RACED HOME to relieve Jamie, who'd stopped answering her texts a few hours ago. She assumed he was busy keeping CJ occupied, or maybe even working, but his silence had set her on edge.

She opened the back door, and instantly the smell of garlic hit her nostrils. She inhaled.

"What in the world . . . ?"

Jamie was at the stove and next to him, her son, standing on a chair and stirring a pan of red sauce.

"What is this?"

"We made dinner!" CJ grinned, then flicked the spoon, sending a splatter of sauce across the wall behind the stove.

"Whoa, buddy, careful." Jamie wiped up the mess, then gently took the spoon. It didn't escape her how patient he was with her son. "Go play, and we'll call you when it's ready."

CJ hopped down.

"Mister?" Emma hollered after him. When he turned back, she

knelt down and pointed to her cheek. CJ raced back, pecked her on the face (and not gently), then ran off. Emma stood, wiping her cheek dry with the back of her hand. "You think he'll still do that when he's sixteen?"

"Not a chance." Jamie smiled. "I hope you're hungry."

"I'm starving. I worked through lunch." She couldn't hide her wide smile. "But I think I came up with the perfect configuration for the pieces in your show."

"Oh?"

She pulled her laptop from its case and set it on the counter. She navigated to the document where she'd mocked up the walls of the gallery—she'd inserted each of Jamie's images exactly as she saw them in her mind.

She scrolled across the page, explaining her vision for the best way to display Jamie's photos so each had the maximum impact and told the story she hoped he wanted to tell. "We start with what's seen, the Nantucket everyone knows and loves, though I have to say, a lot of your pictures are still showing a different side to what's right there in front of our faces." She glanced at him and found he wasn't looking at the screen. He was looking at her.

"Are you paying attention?"

"Not really," he said.

She swatted his arm and closed the laptop. "We'll go over it later."

"Good." He kissed her just as the oven timer beeped. "It's ready."

Jamie took a lasagna from the oven and walked it over to the dining room table. Then he poured the red sauce into a bowl and explained garlic bread was better when dipped. She didn't argue.

Emma called for CJ, and the three of them sat down—almost, she realized, like a family.

He asked about her day and let her blather on and on about a renowned watercolor artist named Danielle Donaldson, whose work she'd admired since her time at the university. "I spoke with her assistant, and this afternoon I got an email saying she would consider coming in to teach a workshop."

"Your way of getting back in the classroom?"

She scrunched her nose. "Too self-serving?" She'd been unable to attend any of the other workshops they'd hosted, but this one would be different.

Jamie laughed and pulled a piece of garlic bread from the basket at the center of the table. "I think it's brilliant."

"She's brilliant," Emma said. "I hope she says yes."

"We met your friend at the beach today," CJ blurted.

Emma frowned. "What friend?"

"I was going to talk to you about that after dinner." Jamie had lowered his voice.

"Talk to me about what?" Emma's pulse quickened and a wave of nausea rolled through her, because even without a single detail, she knew exactly who they'd met on the beach.

She glanced down at CJ's plate. He'd eaten four bites of lasagna and half a piece of garlic bread. His face was caked in red sauce, and he was blowing bubbles in his milk.

Jamie stood. "There's a wet rag in the kitchen with your name on it, kiddo."

CJ jumped off his chair and followed Jamie into the kitchen while Emma sat in silence in the dining room, the remnants of their cozy little dinner practically mocking her.

*You're just pretending.*

She'd been pretending this whole time. And the past had finally caught up with her.

He returned a few minutes later and informed her that CJ was happily playing in the other room, a Pixar movie on the TV. "I thought it would be good if we talked for a minute, alone."

Emma folded her hands in her lap as Jamie sat back down beside her.

"What's going on?" His voice was so concerned. He was so worried about her. It shamed her.

She closed her eyes and forced herself to take a deep, slow, calming breath. Her nerves twittered in her belly, and her palms were clammy and cold.

*Here goes nothing.*

Her mind raced back to the day it started. The day she went from loving wife to adulterer. It wasn't the day she slept with Blake. It was the day she returned his flirtation after a meeting at work. That's where it all began, really.

An "innocent" flirtation acted as an open door.

She'd taken a job at a bank—not at all a job she wanted, but the only one available to her at the time. Blake Simpson was an investment banker, much higher on the totem pole than Emma, and all the women she worked with seemed to melt when he walked in a room.

After two weeks there, Emma had a fairly clear picture of the kind of guy he was. Arrogant. Entitled. Flirtatious. And for whatever reason, he'd taken a shine to her.

She looked at Jamie now, too embarrassed to continue. Nothing in his eyes said "judgment," so she found the courage to go on.

"Cam and I had a good marriage," she said. "We really, really loved each other. But there were things—" this was the part that hurt—"that came between us."

Jamie reached for her hand. "You don't have to tell me this, Em."

"No," she said. "I want to tell you. I don't want any secrets between us."

At that, Jamie looked away, something unreadable passing over his face.

"I had a really hard time getting pregnant," she said. "Cam was gone so much, and when he was home, there was so much pressure to make everything line up at just the right time. It took such a toll on us." She drew in a deep breath, remembering those days she'd tried so hard to forget. "By the time I had my third miscarriage, he just sort of tuned out. It was like he couldn't figure out how to comfort me anymore, so he just stopped trying."

How was it possible for someone she loved so much to become so unreachable, like a stranger to her? After the third lost baby, she'd shut herself off, sure, but Cam had made no effort to go looking for her. He'd taken no steps to try to pull her back into his world.

Instead, they began to feel more like roommates. On the days it was too much for Emma to process, she stole away into the bathroom and had a good cry, not wanting to be even more of a burden. Cam never asked if she was okay. Not even when she emerged with red eyes and tearstained cheeks.

Maybe she was just that good at hiding her sadness, but she didn't think so. More likely, he was just that good at ignoring it. Emma had never felt so alone in her life.

"I was so mad. At him. At God. At myself. I thought there must be something wrong with me if my body is rejecting life like this. A fundamental part of being a woman, and I couldn't do it. It was humiliating." She didn't dare look at Jamie. He hadn't moved or shifted or even hinted that he was still breathing, but she knew if she looked at him, she'd lose her courage. "Not long after that, I ran into Blake on the way out of the bank after work one night. He said I looked like I needed cheering up." A tear streamed down her face. "He was handsome and attentive, and honestly, it was nice not to think about everything I'd lost. It was nice to just be Emma for a change. Not 'Cam's wife, who couldn't stay pregnant.'"

Jamie's thumb moved slowly over the back of her hand, a slight encouragement that he hadn't completely rejected her.

Could she tell him the rest? Did she have it in her to explain?

The affair started so innocently and not at all innocently. Looking back, she knew she could've seen the red flags and warning signs all around her, but she'd been so intent on ignoring them, so focused on herself.

The gap between her and Cam deepened, and she mourned for what they were losing, the relationship that was slipping right through her fingers. At the same time, Blake was there, attending to her whims, keeping things light and fun and without complication.

And then something shifted.

"Cam didn't like to lose. Not on a football field or a golf course and definitely not in his marriage. I don't know what changed, but he came to me and told me he didn't like our relationship anymore. He didn't like the tension between us, and he felt like he was losing me." Her eyes clouded with unshed tears. "He said he would fight for me, no matter what. That I was the most important person in the world to him."

A quiet sob escaped at the memory. Emma had been so ashamed of what she'd done, of the way she'd hurt their marriage, a precious treasure she had vowed to cherish. To hear him recommit to her so wholeheartedly was a painful reminder that if it all fell apart, she would have only herself to blame. She broke it off with Blake immediately, but the guilt clung to her like a tick, burrowing in.

She drew in a breath. "I hate crying." She pressed her palms into her eyes, willing them dry. Jamie said nothing, but his silence encouraged her to go on.

"A little over a month later, I found out I was pregnant again, and Cam was a completely different husband. He was kind and attentive. We prayed together—do you know we never did that before? We prayed for the safety and health of our baby. He laid his hand on my stomach and begged God to keep his son or daughter safe."

Finally she met Jamie's eyes.

"And I didn't have the heart to tell him I didn't even know if the baby was his."

An unmistakable look of surprise sprang to his face, but he quickly replaced it with one of concern.

"Not at first," she said.

Seeing that plus sign on the test had sent her insides swirling. *Not again.* A dread festered at the base of her stomach. How could she go through this again? Her dread wasn't replaced with a quiet hope. This time, it only multiplied because she didn't know if this baby belonged to her husband.

She and Cam were finally back on track, and this could derail everything. In an instant, she could be completely alone. What man would forgive this transgression?

She had begun to hope they had a real future, but she knew that would only happen if she was honest with him. She had to tell him the truth.

"He found out he was going to be deployed," she said. "His unit was sent in to help with some protective detail in Africa. It wasn't supposed to be a long trip—just a few weeks."

At her side, Jamie straightened. His thumb stopped. *The reality of this must be hitting him finally.*

She pushed her chair back from the table and cleared the plates, walking them into the kitchen and dumping them in the sink. He would never forgive her for this gross indiscretion. She was a horrible, terrible person, and she knew it. How could she have done such a thing to such a good, good man?

Jamie was probably wondering the same thing.

She spun around and found him standing there, arms loaded with the rest of the dishes. "I wasn't sure what you wanted me to do with these."

At that, she broke.

"You're helping clean up?" Her voice cracked at the realization.

His face fell. "Should I not?"

"Jamie, you don't have to pretend anymore," she said. "I know what you must think of me."

He set the dishes on the counter and stared into the sink for a beat. "I think you made a mistake," he said softly.

"I did!" she shouted. "And I pay for it every day."

He made a face that told her to be quiet—CJ was just a room away.

She obeyed. "Every time I look at my son, I don't know if I can trust what I see. I don't know if that's Cam's smile. The way his ears stick out—did he get that from Cam? And that chin—I *think* it's the same, but what if I'm just seeing what I want to see?"

Jamie leaned against the counter and faced her.

His coolness angered her. She deserved to be yelled at. She deserved his disgust. Heat flared to her cheeks. "Well?"

He frowned. "Well, what?"

"Tell me what you think of me." Her pain turned to hysteria. "Tell me I'm a horrible, awful person. That I should be ashamed of myself for what I've done."

"No," he said simply. "Why would I do that?"

"Tell me!" she shouted the words, willing him to tear her down the way Cam had refused to do. "Tell me what you really think of me, Cam!" She felt her legs give out underneath her.

Jamie sprang forward and caught her, holding her up—his strength, at least for the moment, enough for both of them.

She sobbed, a deep, horrible, years-overdue sob, and he stood, unmoving, bracing himself against the counter, holding her in his arms, and let her cry.

After a long moment, she calmed herself.

"I told him the truth the night before he left," she said quietly into Jamie's chest. "I was ready for him to yell at me. To tell me he'd never forgive me. To tell me to pack my things and go—we were done. I wanted him to say those things because I deserved it." She wiped her cheek with the back of her hand, working hard for the memory she'd buried a long time ago.

The look on Cam's face after she finally got the words out would haunt her until the day she died. It wasn't anger, like she'd expected; it was hurt. Raw, genuine, horrible hurt. And *she'd* been the one to inflict it on him.

"Say something, Cam," she'd begged.

He looked at her, then looked away. "I should finish packing."

She followed him into their bedroom, his silence so much worse than the fight she'd prepared herself for.

"Cam?"

The muscles in his back tensed. "Do you love him?"

Tears sprang to her eyes. "No! I told you it's been over for weeks."

He waited a beat, then quietly went back to packing.

"Shouldn't we talk about this?" she asked, wanting him to put her out of her misery. She'd imagined this moment so many times. She'd played every possible scenario to its bitter end. She couldn't let him leave without knowing where they stood.

"When I get back," he said. "We'll talk when I get back."

"No, Cam!" She shouted the words. "We need to talk about this now. I know you're mad. Just tell me—tell me what you think of me!"

But he didn't. Instead, he shook his head and kept packing. He refused to engage, and it irritated her to no end. She needed to be cut down, put in her place, broken. It was what she deserved.

She looked up at Jamie. "He left the next morning. He kissed me on the front porch before the sun came up, and then he walked away. It was the last time I ever saw him."

He loosened his embrace and she inched back, wiping her cheeks and smoothing her hair.

"And you never found out for sure about CJ?"

She shook her head.

"You could get a test done."

"Absolutely not."

"Emma—"

"The day they told me about Cam, I decided that was it. This baby was his, no matter what. I would raise him knowing that his daddy loved him—that he was a hero."

"That's fair." Jamie folded his arms casually over his chest and watched her.

"But Blake . . ." She couldn't finish the sentence. The man had all but threatened her.

"What about Blake?" A tight line appeared across Jamie's forehead.

"He wants to know if CJ is his," she said. "He said he found me when I reactivated my social media profiles. Someone at work commented on how cute my son was. The profile picture is me and CJ. He said CJ has his eyes." She choked on the words. The decisions she'd made had haunted her this entire time, but now . . . The threat of having it all revealed, of Cam's parents finding out. Of CJ finding out. The thought of disappointing everyone gnawed at her more than anything else.

"Did he threaten you?" Jamie's jaw twitched.

Emma's shoulders slumped as if the wind had been let out of her by way of a hidden valve. "Sort of."

Jamie tensed at her side.

"He said if I didn't get the test myself, he'd have the court order me to do it." She'd been so shocked to see him there in the gallery and even more shocked to hear that he'd approached CJ on the beach. "Jamie, I don't think he's going away."

Jamie ran a hand over his chin. "Then maybe you should send CJ away."

She frowned. "What? I can't do that."

"He could go stay with his grandparents," Jamie suggested. "They'd probably love it."

"He should be here, with me," she said.

"Just until you figure out what to do," he said. "It'll buy you some time at least."

That was true. It was a good point. It wouldn't solve anything, but it might give her some breathing room. "It's not a bad idea," she said. "I'll ask them when they get back from the Vineyard."

They were still in the lull of conversation.

"You're really beating yourself up over this, aren't you?" he asked.

She scoffed. "I deserve to be beaten up over this." The list on the fridge caught her eye. "Why do you think that stupid list is so aggravating to me?"

"I'm not sure." He looked at her, nothing but genuine concern for her in his eyes.

"Because I don't deserve to have a year devoted to myself," she said. "I don't deserve to get back to living. Cam doesn't get to, and he didn't do anything wrong."

"Emma—"

"You know what the worst part of this is?" she cut in. "Cam couldn't even be excited at the idea of being a dad." A lone tear streamed down her cheek. "I stole that from him, along with everything else."

"I'm sure he was excited," Jamie said.

Her gaze hit the floor. "But we'll never know, will we?"

# CHAPTER TWENTY-EIGHT

THE FOLLOWING MORNING, Jamie awoke with fresh resolve.

He knew exactly what he needed to do.

It wasn't a great time to fly back to Chicago, but after hearing Emma's confession, he knew he didn't have a choice.

He'd been humbled by her willingness to share this with him, the secret that obviously tormented her. He was shocked, of course, to learn that Emma—*his Emma*—wasn't exactly who he'd thought she was. And yet he knew a little something about holding on to a secret, didn't he?

Truthfully, after hearing her confession, he hoped maybe she would be more understanding with his. It wouldn't be long before he found out.

He called Dylan and gave him the details of his trip. It wasn't only about his business—there was something else he needed to do there. Something for Emma. It would require him to be wholly open with her, in a way that might cause his internal wounds to bleed.

But she was worth it.

His only concern was leaving her on the island alone. Especially if this Blake guy was still around.

He peeked outside the window and saw Emma and her in-laws in the yard. There was a tiny red suitcase at her feet. He didn't think he should interrupt the moment, but he also didn't want to miss the chance to say goodbye to CJ—if everything went south, he might not get another chance, and he'd promised him he wouldn't leave without saying goodbye.

As strange as it was to admit, the kid had really grown on him.

He pulled the door open and walked outside carrying a mug of coffee.

At the sound of his door, the trio in the yard turned toward him. Smiles all around, though Emma's seemed guarded.

"Morning," Jamie said. "You guys heading out?"

Jerry nodded. "We're taking CJ back to the Cape so Emma can focus on the art festival."

Emma glanced up at him. "I didn't like the idea of working long hours and leaving CJ in day care."

He nodded. It wasn't a lie—Emma would be busy. CJ would've been with a sitter. But they both knew there was more to it than that.

"Can I say goodbye before he goes?" Jamie asked.

Emma's face softened. "Of course."

"Let's go hurry him along," Nadine said. "We don't want to miss the ferry." She smiled at Jamie, then put an arm around Emma's shoulder and walked her back toward the house, leaving him standing there alone with Jerry.

Jamie shifted his weight and searched his mind for something to say, surprised when the older man spoke first.

"You really care about them, don't you?"

The question took Jamie off guard. After a beat, he glanced at the man and found they had a connection. They both loved Emma and CJ and would do anything to protect them.

"I really do, sir," Jamie said. "And I would never hope to take your son's place, but I do want what's best for them."

"Me too." Jerry drew in a breath. "You think she's doing okay here?"

"I think so," Jamie said, shoving aside the thoughts of smarmy Blake and his threats. "I think she's finding her way."

"Thanks to you," Jerry said.

Jamie smiled. "No, I think she's just that strong. But she needed to figure that out for herself."

"I think you're right," Jerry said. "Though these past few days, she seems a little off."

Jamie prayed her father-in-law didn't ask him any questions about Emma's emotional state as of late. He didn't want to lie to the man, but he wouldn't betray her trust.

"You make her happy," Jerry said. "It's obvious. And I haven't seen her happy in a really long time."

Jamie hoped that didn't change after he returned from Chicago.

"Guard her heart, son." Jerry stuck a hand out in Jamie's direction.

Jamie shook it with a nod, but a wave of guilt rolled through him. "I will."

"She's one of the good ones."

The back door flung open and CJ ran out. He wore a small yellow backpack, a baseball cap, and a wide smile. "Mr. Jamie! I'm goin' on a 'venture!"

He ran straight over to Jamie and wrapped his arms around Jamie's legs and squeezed.

Jamie felt the hug around his heart.

He told himself to stop obsessing. He had a plan to tell Emma everything—he just needed a few things to help him explain.

They gave hugs, handshakes, and *see you soon*s and after they'd gone, he and Emma stood in the driveway, alone.

"I hate this," she said.

"I know." He slid his hand in hers. "Can I do anything?"

She hugged him. "Just this."

"Have you decided what you're going to do?"

She pulled back. "Not yet. I'm going to put Blake off a little while longer to try and figure it out."

"Hey, do you think he's dangerous?"

She frowned. "Why?"

"Because I have to go back to Chicago for a few days, but there's no way I'm leaving you if that guy is a real threat."

She waved him off. "No, he's not that kind of threat. He's just arrogant and bossy. He'd have no problem ruining my life, but he wouldn't actually hurt me."

"Are you sure?"

She nodded. "You have to go back for work?"

He hated that he did. "Yeah, Dylan's trying to nab a pretty big client."

"Maybe it'll be good. I've got everything you sent over for the festival, and I really am going to be busy. Plus, the timing might work out really well. I got a call from a couple of old friends last night. They've been wanting to come out for a visit, so maybe they can get away last minute. I wasn't sure how I was going to explain you to them anyway."

"You just tell them you've met a dead sexy, top-rate male specimen and you can't imagine a single day without him." Jamie grinned at her.

She responded with a kiss. "They'd never believe that."

"They would when they saw me."

She gave him a playful shove. "How long will you be gone?"

"A few days for sure," he said. "Maybe a week?"

"And you leave when?"

"Tomorrow."

"Maybe I can put some finishing touches in the apartment while you're gone? And you can photograph it when you get back?"

"Sure," he said. "I bet you we'll be able to rent it out before the season is over."

She practically beamed. "I never thought it would be ready in time for that."

He shook his head. "You had so little faith in me."

Emma's face turned serious. "You really don't hold it all against me? What I told you last night? I guess I kind of thought you'd be mad."

He took her face in his hands. "Give me some credit, Em. We all mess up. We all have regrets—I know I do. If I held that against you, it would be totally hypocritical. Besides, it's not for me to judge. I know you had a life long before you met me."

"Long before?" She eyed him. "Are you saying I'm old?"

He smiled, thankful some of the playfulness between them had returned. He kissed her fully and deeply and with all the tenderness he could find.

"I have a secret too," he said.

She wrapped her hands around his wrists and brought her gaze to his. "Oh?"

"I think I'm falling in love with you."

Her eyes filled with tears, and as she blinked, one trailed down her cheek. He swiped it away with his thumb.

"After what I did, I never in a million years thought I would ever hear those words again," she said. "I know I don't deserve this."

He pulled her into him and held her there. She'd said the same thing before, more than once, words he could relate to because he felt the same way about himself.

No, they weren't worthy. None of them were. But love didn't come with strings attached. He could see that for Emma—could he ever believe it for himself?

# CHAPTER TWENTY-NINE

~~~

EMMA STOOD AT THE DOCK, watching the ferry pull away from the shore. Jamie was on the deck of the ship, looking at her, and she tried to remind herself that this wasn't the same as when Cam left for Africa.

*He's not going anywhere dangerous. There's no militia in Chicago.*

As the ship grew smaller, she waved, still holding on to the sight of him. He waved back, and her heart turned to a deep ache. She missed him already.

Sure, she had plenty to keep herself busy, but she wouldn't have him. His laugh. His kindness. His kisses.

She rolled her eyes and turned away from the ocean. Had she really become this person? So caught up with a man that she couldn't bear the thought of being apart for seven measly days?

She was an independent woman now, embracing the second chance and standing on her own two feet. She would be absolutely fine.

Still, she'd called Elise and arranged for a spur-of-the-moment visit with her and their friend May. They'd been talking about a trip since they found out Emma was moving to the island, and this seemed as good a time as any. Ever since Jamie had asked if Blake was dangerous, she'd felt uneasy about being on the island alone knowing he was there. She wasn't afraid of him—not by a long shot—but she didn't like knowing he was around.

She got in her car and drove over to the Jared Coffin House, where she knew he was staying. She parked and went in to the front desk, gave them her name, and asked them to call up to his room. She waited until they got the okay to give her the room number.

"He's in the Ada Suite." The woman behind the counter gave her directions. Emma thanked her, then walked away.

Blake opened the door before she could knock on it. "Fancy meeting you here like this," he said, a smug, mocking look on his face.

"I came to tell you to leave," she said. "And to leave me and CJ alone."

He sighed. "Don't be unreasonable, Emma."

"I'm not."

"Come in." He opened the door wider to allow room for her to pass by.

She hesitated.

"Nothing's going to happen," he said. "We're past that, right?"

"Long past." She couldn't for the life of her figure out what she'd ever seen in the guy in the first place. Now divorced and with a receding hairline, Blake was still as cocky as ever.

He closed the door behind her.

"Look, Emma," he said. "I don't want any trouble. I told you I just want the chance to know my son. Liz and I didn't have any kids—CJ may be my only shot at having a kid of my own."

Her stomach turned. The very idea that this was even a remote possibility infuriated her.

"I just want to know," he said. "You owe me that much."

"I don't owe you anything," she said. "Because of you, my marriage almost ended."

"Don't blame me, darling." His voice had turned cold. "Nobody was an unwilling participant in our relationship. Besides, I really cared about you."

She ignored that. She knew it wasn't true.

"It was wrong," she said.

"But it's not wrong now." Blake wore jeans and an untucked striped button-down, and he was wholly unappealing to her. He was still good-looking, she supposed, but his insides were ugly. Why couldn't he just go away? "We're both single." He took a step toward her.

She inched back. "I'm not, actually."

He scoffed. "You mean that Boy Scout I saw at the beach? That's not gonna last."

"Shut up, Blake."

"You think he's going to stick around if he finds out the truth?"

Emma's anger flared. "He already knows."

Surprise splattered across Blake's face. "The whole truth?"

"All of it."

"Impressive, Emma." His tone mocked. "I didn't think you had it in you."

"Just go, okay? That's why I came here—to tell you to leave."

"Well, I came here to tell you to get the kid tested or I'll call my lawyer."

She didn't even know if he had a legal leg to stand on, but he seemed pretty sure of his case. She felt like an animal, locking horns with its prey. What if she got CJ tested and he wasn't Blake's? Then she could move on—free and clear. Unloading everything to Jamie had already made her feel a hundred pounds lighter.

But what if the test proved that CJ was Blake's?

Then her entire world would come crumbling around her. The ramifications of that were unbearable to consider.

The fear of the unknown stuck to her bones. She didn't know if she had the courage to unravel this.

"Look, I'll give you a couple of weeks," he said. "If I don't hear from you soon, you'll force me to take this to the next level. And once that happens, there's no keeping it quiet."

"This is a lot, Blake," she said. "I need some time to work this out."

He inhaled slowly. "How much time?"

"I'm not sure," she said. "Can you just back off for a little bit?"

He watched her for a long moment. "Okay, Emma, but don't take forever. I really need to figure this out."

"Fine." She turned on her heel, but Blake grabbed her arm. She stopped cold.

"We could still make this work," he said. "We could be a real family."

Her heart wrenched at the thought. She forced herself to look at him. "We'll never be a family, Blake. We never should've been anything at all. That stupid affair is the biggest regret of my life, and no matter what happens with this test, you need to understand that there is not now, nor will there ever be, anything between us again."

He lifted his hands as if in surrender, letting her know she'd made her point.

She stormed out and made her way back downstairs, the realization that none of this was going away hitting her squarely in the chest.

Tomorrow she'd welcome her first Nantucket guests, women she hadn't seen in over a year. She'd focus on Jamie's artwork today and her guests tonight, and every breath in between, she'd pray for wisdom because her life had become unbearable all over again.

~

Good morning from Chicago.

Jamie's text came in as she was waiting at the ferry for Elise and May. She smiled.

You miss me already?

I missed you before I even left.

She sent back three heart emojis and tucked her phone in her pocket, turning her attention to the harbor, where the Hy-Line Cruise was docking.

Before the ferry stopped moving, she spotted her friends on the deck of the ship. She waved. They squealed. And she swallowed the lump at the back of her throat.

She'd missed them. What they'd lived through together had been horrendous, but it had brought them all closer. They were bonded together forever.

They raced down to the street, and Elise flung her arms around Emma. "I've missed you!"

Emma couldn't help it. She cried. When she pulled back and turned toward a much calmer and more dignified May, the oldest of the three of them wiped her tears away.

"You look wonderful, Emma," she said. "You look happy."

"Thanks." Emma smiled. "I'm so glad you're here."

"Are you kidding? Free lodging on Nantucket Island? Who could say no to that?" Elise linked her arm through Emma's as they walked off toward the parking lot where she'd left her car.

"So what do you want to do while you're here?" Emma asked.

Elise grinned. "Drink wine. Eat food that I don't have to prepare. Catch up with you two. It's been too long."

Emma pointed toward her car. "This is us." She popped the trunk. "So you don't care about seeing the island at all?"

Elise stopped. "Oh. That too, I guess."

They laughed, piled into the car, and Emma drove them back to the cottage, a million thoughts racing around in her mind.

"So are you going to tell us about your new boyfriend?"

May's question stopped all the other thoughts from spinning.

Emma chewed the inside of her cheek. She'd talked to Elise about Jamie. It wasn't like she'd kept him a secret. But these women, more than everyone she knew, knew how difficult the topic of new love was.

"You can't keep silent about him, Em," Elise said. "Do we get to meet him?"

"He's out of town," she said. "Had to go back to Chicago for work."

"Even better," Elise said. "We can talk about him all we want and not worry that he'll show up unannounced."

Emma pulled into her driveway. "I'll show you what he's done in the apartment. I know you didn't see it before, but it's amazing. Maybe you guys can help me decorate?"

"Oh, that sounds fun," May said.

"Soon I can start renting it out," Emma said. "It'll be a good little side income."

"And then what happens to him? Is he going back to Chicago?" May's question was valid, but that didn't mean Emma wanted to consider it.

She opened the car door and got out. "We haven't gotten that far."

Her friends both frowned.

"It's still kind of new," Emma said.

Elise waved her hand fitfully in the air. "No, yeah. Of course. These things have a way of working themselves out. Now, take us inside and show us to our rooms. I call the one closest to the bathroom. Two kids later and my bladder is the size of a pea."

Emma led them toward the house, but she couldn't shake the feeling that everything was about to change. She'd just been hit with a healthy dose of reality, the real world colliding straight into her with all the force of a Mack truck.

And the little bubble she and Jamie were curled up inside of had been popped.

# CHAPTER THIRTY

~~~

JAMIE'S MEETING WITH JERRICA DANIELSON couldn't have gone better.

The queen of her own fitness empire and a motivated entrepreneur, Jerrica didn't need to be charmed. She needed to be treated like a woman with a good head for business.

Jamie wasn't going to try to flirt his way into a deal with her. Instead, he pitched an artistic vision inspired by his time in Nantucket.

"I like it," she said. "A lot. Thank you for not pitching me the same old fitness branding that everyone else is using. I want to stand out."

"I think the idea of 'use what you've got' is a bold move," Jamie said. "It will make people trust you. You're telling them, 'We've got plenty of equipment and clothing and supplements, but we can also work with what you've got and still help you get in shape.'"

Jerrica was a tiny, solid woman with a long red braid and 0 percent body fat. "My clients are smart women, Mr. Shaw," she said. "Thanks for not treating them like they aren't."

"I know a lot of strong, smart women," he said with a smile. "I wouldn't dare insult their intelligence." He thought of Emma.

Stronger than she realized. She wouldn't have been swayed by faux charm. She would want facts and figures, just like Jerrica.

"And we'll shoot there, right?" She nodded toward the image on Jamie's laptop—two women doing yoga on the beach with the Sankaty lighthouse in the background.

"Oh, these are just sample shots," he said. "We can do them by the lake."

"Let's do both."

He frowned. "That'll be expensive."

"We'll do shoots in cities and on beaches with some of our favorite landmarks in the background."

"And we could roll them out one by one as the campaign goes on," Jamie said. "It's a good idea."

She beamed as she turned back toward the laptop. "There's something special about this place, though."

"Nantucket?" he mused. "Yeah, there is."

*Her name is Emma.*

"I'll have to come on that shoot. You can show me and Joey around."

Entertaining Jerrica and her husband on Nantucket? He could handle that. "I'd love to."

They closed the deal with a handshake and Jerrica's signature on the paperwork Dylan had prepared, and after the woman and her assistant left, Dylan finally showed an expression other than professional attentiveness.

"Dude, that was amazing," he said. "Brilliant."

Jamie couldn't help but smile. There was a satisfaction knowing he was helping business owners, even if it wasn't the traditional artistic endeavor. "I'm glad she liked it. It was a little risky. And I didn't have a plan B."

"So good to have you back, man," Dylan said. "We've got some inquiries to get through, and there's that dog food company that needs some new shots—"

"Dylan, I've been thinking." Jamie took a basketball off his shelf and palmed it, then sat back down behind his desk.

"Don't even say it." Dylan sank into the chair opposite him, a deep frown setting in.

"You don't even know what I'm going to say," Jamie said, knowing full well he probably did.

"I wondered how long it would last," Dylan said, his tone even.

"What do you mean?"

"This was never going to be enough for you," Dylan said. "I knew it when we started this place. Brand building isn't exactly your passion."

"No," Jamie said. "But it's good work. And we're good at it."

"We're great at it," Dylan said. "But even I know you're wasting your talents here."

"I'm not leaving," Jamie said. "I don't want out."

Dylan frowned. "You don't?"

"No. I just want to change my role, maybe. Expand a little. Work from Nantucket."

"How would that work?"

Jamie had given it a lot of thought. He and Dylan didn't work exclusively with clients in the Chicago area. Thanks to the Internet, they'd been connected with businesses all over the country. Was it possible that he could make a new home base? He laid out the plan for Dylan, what he knew of it anyway. And to his surprise, his partner didn't immediately reject the idea.

He could keep things running here, in the Midwest, and Jamie could relocate and foster a new client base on the East Coast. They'd stay connected over the Internet, of course, and they'd arrange for regular meetings throughout the year.

"She must be some woman," Dylan said now, leaning back in the chair.

"This is all a bit premature," Jamie said. "No telling how long it'll be before she realizes she's too good for me. I guess I just wanted to know if it was an option—working remotely. It might even be a good way to expand."

"I'm all for it," Dylan said. "But you're going to have to hire me an assistant."

Jamie laughed. "Can't handle things on your own, buddy?"

Dylan rolled his eyes. "No, I'm bored. It's horrible here without you."

"Well then, you'll have to make the trip to the island next time. It's incredible. The views, the restaurants, the beaches." He pulled out his phone and scrolled to a photo he'd taken of a pair of sailboats at sunset.

"That's awesome," Dylan said. "Maybe I could learn to surf."

"Then . . ." Jamie scrolled through the images, and a selfie of him and Emma appeared on his phone.

Dylan grabbed the device from his hand. "That's her?"

Jamie didn't bother trying to wrestle the phone away. "That's her."

Dylan did a slow whistle. "Gorgeous."

Jamie shrugged. "You're talking about me, right?"

"What is a goddess like this doing with a troll like you?"

"I have no idea," Jamie said—and he meant it.

Dylan waited a minute, then handed the phone back. "It's good to see you happy, man."

Jamie didn't linger on the sentiment. Happiness, he knew, was a precarious thing. Fleeting and not something he wanted to cling to. How quickly the tide could turn and it would only be a distant memory. "Let's get some work done."

After a full day at the office, Jamie drove to his sister's house. She'd promised him a proper home-cooked meal, and he wasn't about to turn that down, even though he knew it would be served with a side of guilt.

The evening turned out to be mostly bearable. Good food, wrestling with the kids, conversation that he managed to steer away from Emma and onto other topics. After dinner, with the kids occupied and Hillary's husband, Anthony, stretched out in front of the television, Jamie settled on to the back porch with an iced tea and a plate of Hillary's homemade milk chocolate chip cookies.

"You made these for me, right?"

Hillary picked one up and took a bite. "Think what you want."

He grinned. "All right, I've braced myself for whatever lecture you're about to unleash. Lay it on me."

She rolled her eyes. "No lecture. I'm not Mom."

No, their parents had retired to Arizona, lived a life that consisted of shopping and golf, and still saw fit to dutifully address topics ranging from religion to politics to the frequency of his haircuts. Hillary, at least, stuck to the important issues. Like breaking the heart of the woman he loved.

"I am a little worried about you, though," she said.

"I've got it under control," he said, knowing it was a hope more than a fact.

"You still haven't told her."

"You make it sound like it's easy, Hill," he said. "It's not easy."

"I know it's not, but it's been six weeks. That's long enough to develop some real feelings."

He looked away.

"Jamie." He knew that tone. He hated that tone. "Tell me you haven't developed real feelings."

He reached into his back pocket for the flyer Emma had designed for the art festival. His name and a photo she'd snapped of him out on their photo walk were prominently featured. He handed it to his sister.

"What's this?" She looked it over. "Jamie?"

"I'm doing a show." The words came out shy, like he wasn't sure he had the right.

Her eyes widened. "You're doing a gallery show? Like, in a real gallery?"

He tried to play this part cool, but he failed. He was excited about the show—why hide it?

"Jamie!" She tossed half of a cookie back on the plate and raced inside to tell Anthony, who—Jamie was sure—could not have cared less. "Anthony, look at this! Jamie's doing a show! In a gallery!"

Anthony's groan sounded confused, like she'd woken him. Jamie picked up a cookie and took a bite. They were perfect, as usual. Hillary always slightly underbaked her cookies, just the way he liked them. Not at all perfect by the standards of the judges on *The Great British Bake Off*, who preferred their biscuits crispy, but perfect for him.

She rushed back out. "Why didn't you say something?"

He shrugged and polished off the cookie. "I just did."

"But before now? You've been here for two hours—you should've led with that." She looked at the invitation, undeniable pride in her eyes. But it was more than that, and he knew it. It was a sign that her little brother was emerging from this hole of hibernation he'd been living in. Doing something he loved, something he'd denied himself of for too long.

"I'd never be doing that if it wasn't for her," he said.

Hillary went still.

"She's good for me, Hill." He brushed the crumbs from his fingers. "She makes everything better."

"Oh, my gosh." Hillary's shoulders dropped. "This is worse than I thought."

He frowned. "What do you mean?"

"You're in love with her."

"Don't say that," he said, though protesting was probably futile. She always could read him like a book. "I just really like her."

His sister set the invitation down on the table. "Then what's your plan?"

"What do you mean?"

"I mean, you're gonna tell her the truth when you go back, right?"

He looked away.

"You're going to tell her."

"Yes, I'm going to tell her," Jamie said firmly. "You act like it's easy, like it's no big deal to tell someone, 'Hey, I'm the reason your husband died.'"

She went still. "Jamie, it wasn't your fault."

"It *was* my fault," he said. "Cam told me to stay put, and I didn't listen. I was scared, and I didn't trust him, and I thought I knew better, so I moved. And he had to come after me, and that's what got him killed." Jamie's voice broke. "That man died because of me. And so did Freddy, and Mike lost a leg." Hillary knew the men by name. She knew because she was one of the few people he'd talked to about what had happened when he was embedded with the unit. Even Dylan didn't know the whole story.

She didn't respond. She knew he didn't like talking about it. Telling her in the first place had nearly killed him and, to his dismay, had landed him in Dr. McDonald's office.

"Look, when I went there, when I saw her, all I could think was— maybe I can help her. Maybe I can do something to make her life better. To take some of the difficulty away—hardships she wouldn't have if it weren't for me. So I agreed to renovate the apartment. It would help her out. That was all I wanted to do."

"But you fell in love with her."

"But I fell in love with her," Jamie confirmed. "And if I lose her . . ." He looked away. "If I lose her because I was too big of a coward to be honest from the start . . ." A scoff then. "Well, I suppose maybe that would serve me right, wouldn't it?"

"Don't say that."

"But it's true."

Hillary picked up her discarded cookie and took another bite. "So let's hear the plan."

"What plan?"

"Your plan to make sure she doesn't hate you after you tell her."

He sighed. "You really think she'll hate me?"

Hillary's shrug was the reply he didn't need.

His plan, if you could even call it that, was simple. Tell the truth. Which was what he should've done on day one.

And yet, if he had, there was a really good chance they never would've gotten to know each other at all—and it was impossible to wish that away.

~

His apartment in the suburbs didn't even feel like home anymore.

Anywhere without Emma didn't feel like home.

He went inside and dropped his workbag in the living room. Then, without thinking, he went straight to the desk, opened the drawer, and found the abandoned memory card.

He turned it over in his hand.

Years of work had come and gone on that card. A catalyst for moving images from camera to computer.

He'd never looked at the photos he now held in his hand. It was a little surprising he hadn't destroyed the card, now that he thought about it, but he was grateful he hadn't. Maybe a part of him knew he'd need it one day.

He pulled out his laptop, hooked up the card reader, then stuck it inside, giving it time to connect to his computer. Giving his nerves time to simmer inside him, as if they'd just been plugged into an electrical socket.

His heart lurched as the first image jumped onto the screen.

The memory of that day came at him hard and fast. He tried to emotionally detach as he scrolled through the images until he found the one he was looking for.

He studied it. Stared at the photo for so long he started to see double.

*"Stay here."* The sound of Cam's voice echoed in his mind.

*"You hear me, Jamie? You're safe here."*

A sob formed at the back of Jamie's throat, and he didn't even bother to try to make it go away.

"I'm so sorry." His voice broke as he spoke the words. "I'm so, so sorry."

Tears fell.

This was the release he hadn't allowed himself to have. He'd been haunted and plagued and tortured, but he'd never been free. He wouldn't allow it.

Now, more than ever, he needed to make amends. He needed forgiveness. He needed redemption.

Were those things for sale? Why were they so hard to find?

Jamie bent over the desk, head in his hands, overcome by grief—his grief, Emma's grief, CJ's grief. And the deep fear that in trying to right this wrong, he'd only made everything worse.

# CHAPTER THIRTY-ONE

~~~

BEING ON THE ISLAND WITH FRIENDS was an entirely new experience. Because Elise and May had never been to the island, and because Emma had never really taken the time, they purposed to become tourists, and they weren't even ashamed of it.

They tried top-rated restaurants and spent too much money in upscale boutiques. Both of her friends stocked up on Nantucket-themed gifts—sweatshirts, blankets, a shot glass for Elise's husband, Teddy. They went to the Nantucket Whaling Museum and climbed the steps of the First Congregational Church. And in the evenings, they walked the beach, watching the sunset and marveling at how much their lives had changed.

By the middle of the week, they'd collected enough throw pillows and rugs and artwork to get started on decorating the apartment, and all Emma could think about was how much Jamie would love it when it was all done and pulled together.

May really was a whiz at making a space feel like a home, so mostly Emma and Elise did whatever she told them to do.

"This is an incredible space." Elise plopped down on the couch, tucking a pillow under her head.

"You should've seen it before Jamie got in here," Emma said. "It's unrecognizable now."

"Right, but you helped." Elise dipped into the bowl of Hershey's Kisses that Emma had set on the new coffee table.

"I picked things out," she said. "But he did almost all of the work."

Elise waggled her eyebrows. "Sounds like a keeper to me."

Emma felt a blush rise to her cheeks. She turned away, hoping it went unnoticed, and pointed to the corner opposite the bed. "I was thinking we could do a little reading nook over there with some of the artwork we bought."

"That's a great idea," May said.

Emma pulled out the watercolor she'd done based on one of Jamie's prints and laid it on the bed. He'd asked her to paint something for the spot near the front door, but that would come later. This one seemed to go better in the nook she'd created in her head.

May picked it up. "Oh, wow, where did you find this?"

"Oh, that's one of mine." Emma walked to the kitchen area, where their takeout was still sitting in bags on the counter. She started to unpackage everything so they could have lunch—sandwiches from Bartlett's Farm. She'd try not to think about Jamie and their trip to the beach while she ate, but she had a feeling she would fail.

She looked up and found she had both of her friends' attention. "What?"

"You're painting again?" Elise swung her legs onto the ground and reached for the frame.

Emma unwrapped the chicken salad. "It's not a big deal."

"The heck it isn't," Elise said.

"It's a very big deal, Emma," May said. There was a proud, maternal flicker in her eye. "You're painting again."

"How did that happen?"

Her friends knew all about her artistic aspirations. They also knew that she'd hung up her brushes the day Cam died. It felt so frivolous after that.

"It was Jamie, actually." She unwrapped another sandwich. "One morning I woke up and there was a box on my porch full of art supplies."

Elise gasped. "He bought you paints?"

"And brushes and watercolor paper and, really, just everything I needed." She smiled at the memory. "I don't think I would've ever picked up a brush again if he hadn't pushed me."

Elise sank back down on the sofa. "Emma, that is so sweet. This guy is the real deal."

She glanced at May as if seeking her approval.

"You like him," May said.

Emma stopped messing with the food. "I really do."

"But you're holding back?"

She shrugged. "A little, I guess."

"Why would you hold back? Sounds like your new boyfriend is perfect." Elise popped another chocolate into her mouth.

"It's scary, though," Emma said. "When I lost Cam, I swore that was it. I never wanted to love anyone like that again. It hurt way too much."

May moved toward the counter, and Elise sat up straight on the couch.

"Emma, there's always a risk when it comes to relationships," May said. "But if you don't let yourself leap every once in a while, you'll miss out on so much."

"It was time for you to get back out there, Em." Elise joined them in the kitchen.

"Sometimes it feels wrong," she said. "Like I'm betraying Cam."

"But it's not wrong," May said. "It's okay to be happy. It's okay to enjoy your life."

"It's more than okay," Elise said. "Not just for you, but for CJ."

Emma nodded. "I know."

"This is a good thing, Emma," May said. "A very good thing. And we couldn't be happier for you."

She smiled. "I have the best friends."

"You really do," Elise said.

They laughed.

"I've missed you guys," Emma said.

Emma had brought plates over from her house. She pointed to the food. "Dig in."

They each took a sandwich and ate their lunch standing right there at the counter in the apartment Jamie had renovated. And for one delicious moment, Emma realized that for the first time in a very long time, she was undeniably happy, right down to the bone.

~

Jamie had been gone for a week.

And while Emma had very much enjoyed her time with Elise and May, she missed him. She missed his arms around her. His laugh. His quiet demeanor and their witty banter, their connection. She missed watching him with CJ, treating him like a kid he loved to be around and not like an annoyance, which, let's be real, was exactly what he sometimes was.

She'd spent a good amount of time working on the art show, and she was proud of what she'd done. Travis had even complimented her—twice! And when he mentioned bringing the Heywards by the gallery for an early viewing, Emma absolutely refused and made him promise not to.

He'd reluctantly agreed but said it was very unorthodox for them to keep the artwork from his best collectors.

"Jamie hasn't even seen it yet," she said. "I'm not going to show it off without his approval."

Travis had flicked his hand in the air with a clear eye roll, but in the end, she was glad she'd put her foot down. She couldn't be sure, but she thought that might've even impressed her boss. He'd given her more responsibility at the gallery and even praised her for booking Danielle Donaldson, who was in very high demand.

When she was working, Elise and May explored the island, and when she wasn't, she savored every moment with them.

Tomorrow Jamie would return. The day after that, CJ would be back. And she realized that what had once felt like an empty, sad little life had grown rich and full of love and possibility.

Blake had returned to Colorado—thankfully—though she knew she couldn't avoid his request forever. She'd yet to decide how to proceed, though he texted frequently with reminders that he expected her to comply. Mostly she wanted to pretend he didn't exist, though she knew that wasn't going to happen. She could only hold him off for so long.

Maybe she'd find the courage to face it all when Jamie was back.

How ridiculous. She didn't need a man to prove she was strong. But he was the only other person in the world who knew the truth. It would devastate Elise and May if they knew. It was sacred, being married to a soldier. How could she be unfaithful when Cam was risking his life for the good of their country?

There was no forgiveness for that.

Yet Jamie had forgiven her.

While it wasn't the same as Cam forgiving her, it was something. And it made her feel like maybe there were second chances, even for her.

As she was closing up the gallery, she heard a noise at the back door. Travis had been spending more and more time in his home studio, and while he'd yet to bring in any completed projects, Emma could tell he was glad to have time to work on his own art.

That's how it was for artistic people. If they didn't create, it was like they walked around as a shell of themselves. She'd been doing that for years, and now that she was sketching again, stealing time to paint, filling her creative tank, a part of her had been reborn.

She had Jamie to thank for that.

She moved through the gallery, expecting to find Travis coming in, but instead, she found Jamie standing in the doorway.

It took her a second to register that he was here—in the flesh—but when she did, she let out an embarrassing squeal and threw herself into his arms.

"I thought you weren't back till tomorrow?"

He hugged her body close and lifted her off the ground. He said nothing, only held her, inhaled her, made her feel whole again.

When he set her down, she pulled back and found a tight line of worry creasing his forehead.

"What's wrong?" she asked.

He studied her with such intensity, it was as if he were trying to memorize the placement of every freckle on her face. He shook his head. "Just missed you, is all."

Her heart leapt as the words registered. He missed her. Her hands found his and she smiled at him. "I missed you too."

He took her face in his hands and kissed her, so sweetly it nearly undid her.

"You've got good timing," she said. "Elise and May are dying to meet you, and they're picking me up for dinner. It's their last night here."

He grinned. Wow, it was even more striking than she remembered. "They're dying to meet me, huh? You've been talking about me?"

Her cheeks flushed. "I might've mentioned you once."

"Just once?" Another kiss.

"I'm glad you're here," she said, pulling away. "I want to show you how things are turning out for the show."

She'd mocked it all up in the workroom, using it as a staging area. She flipped the light on and motioned toward his photos, hung in the order she'd chosen.

"What do you think?"

She really, really wanted him to love it.

Jamie turned toward the wall and studied each one. A close-up of the cobblestone, taken from down low, the blurry images of Nantucket shops in the background. A drone shot of downtown with the ocean in the background, countless boats dotting across the water. A lone rowboat in the middle of a pond. A close-up of CJ's chubby hands building a sandcastle.

He'd captured the peaceful side of the island so wholly it made her never want to leave. He walked a slow line from the start to the finish without making a sound.

At his silence, she started to panic a little. She'd so wanted to please him, to do his work justice, but as she followed him across the room, she worried she'd missed the mark.

"Is it okay?" If only she could read his thoughts.

He went still.

She held her breath, waiting for his reply.

"It's perfect." The words were quiet. "Well, almost perfect." He faced her. "Can you leave space here for one more image?"

She eyed him thoughtfully. "You're holding out on me?"

He shrugged. "I found one I really love."

She wrapped her arms around his neck and kissed him again. She was so captivated by his return, she didn't hear the gallery door open. She didn't have any idea they weren't alone until she heard Elise's voice behind her.

"Should we come back?" her friend asked.

Emma pulled herself from Jamie's arms and spun around to face them. Her hand wound down into Jamie's, who seemed to tense at her side. It was probably a bit nerve-racking for him, meeting her friends, though it occurred to her she hadn't shared much about them. When they were together, it seemed they only talked or thought about each other.

"Guys, this is—"

"Jameson." The look of shock on May's face turned to confusion.

"Jamie." Emma squeezed his hand, but he stood, unmoving, a look of—what was that? fear?—on his face.

Emma's gaze pinballed from Jamie to May to Elise and back again. "I don't understand," she said. "Do you guys know each other?"

"Jamie is Jameson?" Elise asked.

His hand went limp inside hers; then he pulled it away.

Emma frowned. "Yes, Jamie is Jameson." She hadn't shown them his website or even told them his last name. When she talked about him, he was always just "Jamie." Dread pulsed inside her, down deep in a place so unreachable it couldn't be soothed. "How do you know him?" Another look at Jamie. "Jamie?"

They all seemed to be sorting something out, something she wasn't a part of. Worse, Emma couldn't decipher a single one of their expressions, but she knew something was desperately wrong.

"Someone explain." Emma felt anger well within her.

"Emma—" Jamie's voice told her something was wrong. Something was very, very wrong.

All at once, she wanted to run somewhere safe to hide.

Whatever it was, she didn't want to know.

She had the horrible, aching sensation that her entire world was about to change. Again. And she wasn't sure she was strong enough to handle it.

# CHAPTER THIRTY-TWO

～～～

JAMIE'S HEART POUNDED SO LOUDLY in his head it might as well have been the bass drum in a rock band. The joy of seeing Emma—that look of surprise on her face—had been so swiftly wiped away, like words from a whiteboard, that he wasn't sure he'd ever recover.

He stood like he was in a trance, putting it all together.

"May" was Mary Beth. Mary Beth Winters, Freddy's mom, and the recipient of the first letter Jamie had sent. The only other one he'd met in person. The day he met her, Mary Beth had been kind and forgiving, but under the current set of circumstances, it was likely she would be neither. After all, it looked like he'd pulled one over on Emma. It looked like he'd lied.

Because he had. *Oh, Emma, I'm so sorry.*

And his lies were going to make everything so much worse.

*Why wasn't I honest from the start?* His stomach roiled at the thought.

He'd figured this all out on the plane back to Boston—exactly how he'd tell her. The letter. The photo. The whole haunting memory card if she wanted it. He was going to give it all to her and answer every single question she had.

But how would he do that now?

He'd anticipated that none of it would go well, but being blind-sided by this information was so much worse than even he could've imagined.

"How do you know May?" Emma's question hung there, begging an honest answer, her eyes, broken and wide, fixed on him.

He glanced at Mary Beth, who seemed to be urging him to go on and tell her, but the words were stuck somewhere between his head and his mouth.

"I didn't know your Jamie was the same man," the older woman said into Jamie's silence. "And I'm sure he didn't know that I was your May."

Of course they knew each other. Why hadn't Jamie considered this could be a possibility? Emma was bonded forever with the wives and mothers of the other soldiers in Cam's unit. It only made sense.

Which meant Elise was likely married to one of the other men who had been there that day. Was she Mike's wife? Or Teddy's? Or Dane's? After perusing the images on the memory card, their faces were all so fresh in his mind. Whatever had gone foggy over the last five years had become clear again, like a cloud that had disintegrated midair.

"Emma, I can explain." Even as he said the words, it sounded like every single horrible movie line where some idiot guy who screwed everything up finally gets caught.

She took a step away from him. "Somebody needs to."

"I met Mary Beth several months ago," he said. "It was an exercise I did—I wrote her a letter of apology, and she invited me to her home to meet her in person." He stopped. Mary Beth's face softened, but only slightly. "And I went."

Did she remember that day as clearly as he did? Did she remember opening the door to a stranger whose first words were "It's my fault your son is dead"?

He'd blurted it out without thinking, and while he'd expected her to smack him or push him or call the cops on him, she hadn't done any of those things.

She'd opened the door wider and invited him in for a cup of coffee and a conversation.

She had his letter out, and she reread it while he sat there and watched. Afterward, she covered his hands with hers and told him it wasn't his fault. He'd cried at those words. He'd cried in her arms.

They'd mourned together.

Why didn't he think that Emma's reaction could've been the same? Why hadn't he given her the chance?

Because he was selfish. Because he was scared. Because something about her had captivated him from the moment she mistook him for a man answering her ad.

Because he wanted to make things better for her.

*Well, congratulations, buddy. The only thing you did was make everything worse.*

"Jamie was embedded with the unit in the Congo," Mary Beth said quietly when Jamie failed to continue. "He was there the day they died."

His gaze fell to the floor. The slick hardwood had been finished with a high shine. The world stopped moving. The earth stopped spinning. Every single fear he had unraveled right there in front of him.

"What did you just say?" Emma's voice brought him back to the moment.

He turned to her. "I wanted to tell you. I tried to tell you."

"When did you try to tell me?"

"So many times, Emma." It was true. So many times he'd tried to find the courage and failed. What a coward.

*I'm such a coward.*

"You were there?" Her voice cracked.

"The first day I showed up at your house," Jamie said gently, "I wasn't there about the ad. I didn't even see the ad."

Emma's eyes widened. "What?"

"But you needed help, and you said nobody else had responded. So I thought, *Here's something I can do to help her.* I just wanted to make your life easier."

She shook her head. "I don't understand."

"I knew who you were," he said. "I came to the island for you." The words sounded wrong. Like he was a stalker or something. He quickly corrected himself. "I mean, I came to apologize to you." He pulled the letter from his pocket. "I wrote you a letter too, not very different from the one I wrote Mary Beth and the other widow, Alicia Birch."

The color had drained from Emma's face. This was bad. This was really, really bad.

"I can't hear this now." She backed away, then looked at Mary Beth. "You never told me about a letter."

"We don't talk about Cam and Freddy," Mary Beth said. "We don't talk about that day."

Emma's eyes drifted to Elise. "And you knew too?"

"I didn't lose what you lost," Elise said. "May told me about the letter, but we didn't think you'd want to know. Em, it's not like you're big on discussing what happened."

Emma's shoulders slumped. She shook her head as if trying to sort through what she'd just learned—and Jamie knew it was too much for her right now.

He wished he could rewind. He wished he could tell her on his own terms, the way he'd planned, only he wished he'd done it weeks ago.

"You lied to me," Emma said, turning her attention back to him.

"No." But even as he said the word, he knew it was true. He *had* lied.

"Go," she said.

"Emma—" Mary Beth said.

"No, it's fine." Jamie held up a hand. "I understand if you don't want to see me right now."

Slowly she lifted her chin and locked onto his eyes. "I don't want to see you ever again."

The words were like bullets to his heart. "Please don't say that."

Tears streamed down her face. "Get out of here, Jamie."

He looked at Elise, then at Mary Beth. Neither would make eye contact with him. "I'm so sorry, Emma."

She turned away, an action that spoke far louder than words.

And Jamie walked out into the warm Nantucket night, a new pile of regrets heaped onto the old ones that were already too much to bear.

# CHAPTER THIRTY-THREE

~~~

IT WAS A BAD DREAM, RIGHT? A horrible, awful, *I need to wake myself up right now* dream.

Tears streamed down her hot cheeks as she processed through the feelings of betrayal stabbing her from every direction.

Was everyone in her life hiding something from her?

Her mind whirled, trying to make sense of it. She collapsed in a heap on the floor. Her friends were at her side, but she recoiled. "No." She didn't want them touching her. They both inched back.

"Why didn't you tell me?" she asked, as if it were their fault, as if knowing May had received a letter would've changed anything.

May knelt down beside her. "Anytime I've tried to talk to you about Cam, about Freddy, about that day—you have made it very clear it wasn't a topic you wanted to discuss." May took her hand. "I thought I was doing the right thing keeping it to myself."

Emma's eyes darted from one friend to the other. "But you didn't keep it to yourself. You told Elise."

Elise's husband had been in the unit too, but unlike Cam and

Freddy, he'd returned in one piece. For a long time, Emma had struggled with that. Why did Elise get to keep her husband when Emma did not?

In the end, she decided it was because she didn't deserve to be happy. After all, look at what she'd done.

The memory of her indiscretion nagged her. Jamie knew about that, and he hadn't judged her. She'd kept that secret, and she never would've come clean if Blake hadn't forced her hand. Was this really so different?

No. She wouldn't justify this. Not this. He should've told her. Her friends should've told her.

"Tell me what he told you," Emma said with a firm look at May.

The older woman had been like another mother to Emma and Elise. The world had broken them all, and they'd vowed to forever be in each other's lives. It's what happened with traumatic events, they reasoned. Nothing would change that. Emma knew these women loved her. If they didn't tell her something, it was with good reason. Of course it was.

*Maybe the same can be said of Jamie?*

No. Why was she trying to make this seem okay? It was different. Jamie had pulled her in, made her believe in love again when she saw now that she'd been right all along. Love was nothing more than a fairy tale. A way to ensure a broken heart.

"Em," May said kindly, "I will tell you everything, but I think maybe you should let Jamie tell you."

"I never want to talk to him again."

"You don't mean that," Elise said.

"Ever since we got here, Jamie is all you've talked about," May said.

"It would be annoying if it wasn't such a huge answer to prayer," Elise said.

Emma frowned. "What do you mean?"

"You've been so sad since Cam died," May said. "And we've been so worried about you."

"And when we made that list on your birthday, I had no idea you'd take it to heart. But you did. And look at you. You've got a great job that you absolutely love. You've made plans for the future. You're happy. He made you happy." Elise sat down. "It was just what we've prayed for."

Emma shook her head. "It was all a lie."

"It wasn't *all* a lie," May said. "That man loves you. And you love him. Give him a chance to explain."

"He was there," Emma said sadly.

"And don't think he hasn't had a lot to deal with himself, Em," May said, knowing more about Jamie than Emma in that moment. "We spent an afternoon talking, and I know it sounds crazy, but somehow it was exactly the closure I needed. He filled in a lot of the blanks about Freddy's death. Give him a chance to do the same for you."

He could've explained weeks ago. Before he became a part of her. Before she allowed herself to fall for him.

How did she extract feelings she never should've had in the first place now that they'd grown so deep and real?

May squeezed her hand, and Elise wrapped an arm around her shoulder, and as good friends do, they let her cry for a good long while before helping her up and taking her home.

Jamie wasn't there, of course, and the hollowness that realization carved in her chest nearly dragged more tears from a dry well somewhere deep inside.

May and Elise got her to bed, and in the darkness of her bedroom, she overheard them talking. Should they extend their stay? Was this going to set her back to where she was? *Just when she was finally showing signs of life again.*

She closed her eyes and willed it all away.

On the table next to her bed was a photo of her with Cam. A close-up shot that highlighted how happy they'd been once. Her betrayal had nearly destroyed her, might've destroyed their marriage completely, she didn't know. Was he planning to leave her? Would he have returned from the Congo and served her with divorce papers?

But this felt like insult added to injury. She'd betrayed him again by allowing herself to fall for Jamie, a man who'd been there the day he died. A man who wasn't at all what he said he was.

"I'm so sorry, Cam," she whispered.

The light in the hall turned off, leaving Emma in the darkness, exactly where she'd been until she moved to Nantucket. Until she started *The Year of Emma*. Until she met Jamie.

Was May right? Should she let him explain?

She rolled over, her mind conjuring the way it felt to sink into Jamie's arms at the end of a long day. The emptiness inside her matched the emptiness in the room, and a different kind of grief settled in her belly.

Now that she knew him, how could she live a life without him?

But she didn't know him at all, did she? How could she live a life with a man who'd kept so much of himself a secret?

~

She slept terribly, and when she woke up the next morning, she felt worse than she had before she'd gone to bed.

Somehow she knew it wasn't lack of sleep that tugged at her nerves but the sorrow she felt in facing the end of her relationship with Jamie.

But were her friends right? Should she at least hear him out? She didn't even know where he was. Had he found a hotel to stay in? Or an Airbnb?

And what about the art festival? She'd banished him from her life, which meant he might be gone by now.

Which meant he wouldn't be back for the showing.

Which meant she could kiss her job goodbye.

She picked up her phone and found their last string of text messages. He'd likely been on the ferry returning to the island when he typed them, but he'd wanted that to be a surprise, so he hadn't let on.

One more day till I get to see you. I've got some exciting news.

It occurred to her then that she'd never given him a chance to tell her what it was. She'd texted back: Hurry up and get here. I can't wait to hear all about it and show you how amazing your photos look on the wall!

She tossed her phone aside with a groan just as there was a light knock on the door.

"Come in," she called out, pulling herself up to sitting.

May's face appeared in the doorway. "I brought you some coffee." She held a steaming mug in both hands.

"Thanks."

May came in and sat down on the bed next to her. "How are you feeling?"

Emma took a sip of coffee and shrugged. "Awful."

"Are you up for a visitor?"

Emma frowned. "Why?"

"Because you have one," May said. "Jamie is downstairs."

Emma's stomach turned over. "No. Make him go away."

May was still as if chewing on something she wasn't sure she should say aloud. Emma could always count on her to be forthcoming—why was she holding back now?

"Say it," Emma said.

May looked at her.

"I know you have thoughts."

She shifted, still seeming unsure. "When you lost Cam, a part of you died. We all saw it happen. Like a light went out from your eyes."

Emma remembered the first time she'd met May. Freddy's mom lived near the base in Colorado Springs, and she'd hosted more than one get-together for the entire unit. They'd been together for two years, and in that time, they'd all become family. They used to tease Freddy that he could never find a wife, because no matter what, she'd never be as good a cook as May.

Freddy had such a great smile. The kind that lit up the whole room. He would've made someone such a good husband. *It's so unfair.*

"You stayed like that for so long, Em," May said. "Just like I said last night—we were worried. But every time Elise or I have talked to you in the last two months, you've been different. Back to your old self. You're painting again. You're leaving the house again."

"I'm living again," Emma said. "I know." Why did the thought suddenly make her miserable? Because she knew she had to give it up?

"That's no small thing," May said.

Emma set the coffee down and pulled her legs up, hugging her knees. "When he came to your house and said whatever he said—" Her voice broke. "You just listened?"

May nodded. "And I thanked him. It took a lot of guts for him to come talk to me given what he had to say."

Emma frowned. "What did he have to say?"

May put a hand on Emma's shoulder. "Go hear for yourself."

Emma hated this. She didn't want to make any more decisions. She was better off alone and she knew it.

"Emma, don't you have questions about their last mission?" May asked now. "Don't you want to know anything about the day Cam died?"

Emma squeezed her eyes shut. No. She didn't want to know. She wanted to block it out and pretend it never happened, to make the pain of it go away.

And yet that wasn't true, was it? She did want to know. Because when Cam left for Africa, he left behind a big question mark. Would he come back to her? Would he accept this baby as his own? Did he still love her?

*Did he forgive me for what I did?*

"Jamie is a brave man for being here," May said.

"Then why didn't he tell me from the beginning?"

"Would you have let him help you?" May asked. "With the apartment? With the art show?"

Emma stared at the floor. "I don't know." What would she have done if they could rewind back to that day when she'd met him outside the mailbox? She didn't know because she had no idea what it was he'd come here to tell her in the first place. But she supposed a part of her had to entertain the idea that she would've listened to his story and then sent him away.

Jamie said he'd wanted to help her. This was his way of making amends. She couldn't fault him for that.

"He's downstairs," May said. "Elise is keeping him company, so if I were you, I'd hurry."

Emma watched her friend go. Jamie had come here with a secret—and Emma couldn't deny she wanted to know what it was. She'd also come to Nantucket with a secret, and Jamie hadn't judged her for it.

She brushed her teeth and splashed some water on her face, then picked up her mug and walked downstairs, not bothering to change out of her pajamas. She found Jamie on the couch in the living room, alone.

He stood when she walked in. She was surprised to find him alone. Where were May and Elise?

"They went to get breakfast at a place downtown," he said as if reading her mind.

They were good friends, leaving her alone with this man who'd stolen her heart. But she wasn't sure being alone with him was safe for her right now.

She sat on the chair beside the couch, refusing his eyes. On the coffee table, there was an envelope with her name on it, the same one he'd had in his hand last night. Had he really been carrying it around in his pocket all these weeks? From the worn-out look of it, yes.

He sat down and rested his forearms on his knees, watching her.

She shrank under the weight of his gaze. He knew everything about her. Every secret she swore she'd carry to her grave. And she didn't know him at all.

"I'm sorry," he said. "For not telling you at the start."

Her eyes clouded over, and she begged the tears not to fall.

"When I met you that day, it was a little chaotic, and when you told me about the apartment, I realized I could help you. I wanted to help you. More than anything, I just wanted to make your life easier, and here I've gone and screwed everything up." He raked a hand through his hair, leaving it disheveled and sexy, and Emma found it terribly unfair that even in her anger and grief, she still found herself horribly attracted to him.

"I had the letter in my pocket that day," he said. "In my hand, actually, and then I put it away because, Emma, something about you—" He stopped.

"Something about me what?"

His eyes hooked on to hers. "I don't know. Something about you struck me right away. I wanted to know you. It was the most awake I've felt in years."

She knew that exact feeling. How many times had she said the same thing? How many times had her friends commented that she was living again—finally? Had she and Jamie brought each other back to life?

"I saw you and you stopped me in my tracks," he said. "And this isn't a line—for some reason, I knew I needed to know you." He paused. "Now I know I just need you."

Her gaze fell to the floor. "All that time we spent together. We talked about Cam—you said CJ had his smile." Her face crumpled and she covered it with her hands for fear of what her pain would look like to him. The realization that Jamie hadn't said that because of some photo he'd seen—something about CJ reminded him of Cam—it tugged at a string around her heart. It's what she wanted more than anything. For CJ to remind everyone of Cam. Because if he did, then it meant CJ was the product of a deep love—not of a horrible mistake.

"I went back to Chicago for work, Em, but there was something else I knew I needed to get."

She tried to calm the quiver in her jaw and watched as he picked up the envelope on the coffee table and turned it over. Every movement felt painful—not only for him, but for her. She was being hit in the face with everything she wanted to forget.

He pushed the letter toward her. "I wrote this weeks ago," he said. "Before I knew you. And this—this was the real reason I went back home." He opened an unsealed envelope, took out a photograph, and handed it to her.

Emma looked at the picture. A grinning Cam, sitting in a Humvee, holding up the ultrasound picture she'd tucked inside his bag. She'd included a note written on a pink note card that said, *Hurry home to us soon. I love you.*

She'd wanted to write *I'm so sorry. Please forgive me. I promise not to mess up again.* But she'd kept it short and simple because all of those things had already been said.

She'd always wondered if he'd discarded her note, but in the photo, she could see the edge of the pink card behind the ultrasound film in his hand. Her eyes drifted back to Cam's smiling face, and a sob caught at the back of her throat.

"Emma, you said you would never know if he was excited about being a dad," Jamie inched closer. "And I realized there was something else I could give you, something more important than new flooring or a success at work."

She looked up and found his eyes. They were sad but hopeful.

"I can tell you with absolute certainty that your husband was thrilled about this baby," Jamie said, the sentence a clear struggle to say aloud. He seemed to be willing away the tears pooling in his eyes. Tears for her, for them, for the brokenness that had pulled their two worlds together in the first place.

Jamie quickly found his composure and continued. "It was one of the first things he told me the day I met him. That he was going to be a dad. That after this trip, he was going to ask to stay home for a little while—so he could be there for you and for the baby. Said you guys were the most important thing in his life."

Emma's hand over her mouth couldn't contain the sob. It was just like Cam—she confesses an affair and her husband decides he wants to be there for her more. Did he blame himself for what happened between them? She looked at his face in the picture she held. *It wasn't your fault.*

"I know you blame yourself for a lot," Jamie said. "And I know there are things between you and Cam that I'll never understand. But I thought you should know that the man I met over there was deeply, madly, and completely in love with his wife and future child." Did it hurt Jamie to say so? If it did, he didn't let on. He seemed intent on making sure *she* was okay.

Nothing about this was about him—that should tell her the kind of man he was.

"And I never meant to hurt you, Emma." His hand twitched like he wanted to reach out and touch her, but he must've thought better of it because he pulled it back, folding it with the other one at his knees. "I'm so sorry I let it go on this long. The more I got to know you, the more I wanted to be around you. And I was so scared of exactly what's happened. That you would never want to see me again."

He stood, and everything inside her cried out, *Don't go!* But she said nothing, only stared at the photo of Cam and his son. The only photo of Cam and CJ that existed in the world—Jamie's gift to her.

How much personal pain did he have to mine to uncover it and hand it over? She didn't know the details of that day, but she did know Jamie had witnessed the deaths of three men and the life-altering injuries of several others. That couldn't be easy to relive.

He leaned down and kissed the top of her head—she closed her eyes and savored the moment. "Goodbye, Emma."

When he'd almost reached the door, she stood. "Jamie?"

He turned, hopefulness in his eyes.

"Will you be at the art festival?"

Disappointment skittered across his face, but he steeled his jaw. "Do you want me there?"

She looked away. "It would be better for the gallery if you came."

*Come to the show so I don't lose my job* was implied. *I can't bear the thought that this could be goodbye* was not.

He nodded. "I'll be there."

With that, he was gone. And so was the piece of her heart that had learned to hope again. He stoked a happiness inside her that made her want to believe in the reality of love.

How could she simply let that go when it had felt so real?

# CHAPTER THIRTY-FOUR

THE LETTER SAT ON THE COFFEE TABLE where Jamie had left it.

Emma stared at it but made no move to pick it up. Instead, she sank into the couch, holding the photograph of Cam.

Jamie had given her a gift nobody else in the world could've given her. And if he'd never come to Nantucket, she wouldn't have it.

*Cam was happy about the baby. He was going to ask for an assignment that gave us more time together. He loved me.*

In spite of everything she'd done, he still loved her.

Time passed and the door opened and her friends filtered back into the house, but Emma barely registered any of it.

She'd fallen into a haze, not unlike the one she'd walked around in for days after she learned of Cam's death, the one she'd remained in until only very recently.

"Emma?"

It was May. She had that unmistakable tone of concern in her voice. Emma stared past her.

Elise's eyes darted to the photo in Emma's hand. "What's this?"

"Jamie gave it to me," Emma said.

Elise took the photo and showed it to May, who sank onto the sofa next to her. "What happened?"

"He's sorry," Emma said.

"Of course he is," Elise said. "He really messed up."

May shot her a look and Elise shrugged. Emma shook herself from her trance and set the photo on the table. "He left a letter." She nodded toward it.

"Have you read it?" May asked.

Emma shook her head. "I don't want to read it. It'll only make losing him harder."

"Or maybe it'll keep you from losing him at all." May leaned over and picked up the letter, then handed it to Emma. But Emma didn't want to read anything that might change her mind. This was hard enough as it was.

"I have to get ready for work," she said. "And CJ will be back later. I don't know if I have time now to take you guys to the ferry."

Elise waved a hand in the air. "We'll be fine."

"But we could stay a little longer if you need us?" The concern in May's eyes was almost too much for Emma to process. Was it only a week ago she'd been feeling that her life was rich and full and wonderful?

"Don't do that," Emma said. "I promise I'll be fine. Cam's parents are coming this afternoon." She stood. Both May and Elise followed suit, and somehow they ended up in a three-person hug.

"I'm going to miss you guys," Emma said. "Come back anytime."

The hug lasted longer than Emma expected, and she understood what they weren't saying. They would miss her too. They'd all lived so much life, through so much pain, and they'd gotten through it together. It was hard to be apart after that.

When she pulled back, she saw that they were all three crying.

They laughed at their display, then wiped tears and cheeks and put on brave faces. Elise and May started out, but at the doorway, May stopped.

"Hey, Emma," she said, turning back to face Emma.

Emma glanced up.

"Read the letter."

Her gaze fell to the envelope on the table, and while she respected May, she still thought facing whatever words were written on that paper would likely be too much to bear.

~

Jamie hadn't gotten the chance to give Emma the memory card or share the rest of the photos with her. It was obvious he was making it worse by being there, and it killed him to think he'd brought her so much pain.

He still had so much to say.

He didn't know if she'd read the letter, but even if she did, would she understand what had happened? Would she understand how deeply sorry he was for his part in it?

He sat on the patio of a small coffee shop near the ferry dock. He'd promised her he'd stay for the art festival, but what was he going to do in the days leading up to it? He eyed the ferry like it was an escape route from heartache, as he considered leaving all of his belongings back at the hotel and jumping aboard.

But he couldn't do that. He couldn't let her down, and the art festival was only days away.

He looked at his open laptop. He'd promised to take photos of the apartment for Emma to help her get it listed on the rental sites. He'd finished the renovations before he left, but now what? Should he let her snap a few pictures on her phone and call it good?

He didn't like leaving promises hanging in the wind.

"Mr. Jamie!" In the distance, he heard a little boy calling out to him. He looked up and saw CJ with his grandparents, racing through the crowd to where Jamie sat.

He tried to smile, but he was afraid he failed. "Hey, buddy!" He braced himself for a CJ hug just in time, as the boy thrust his entire weight into Jamie's arms. Jamie squeezed him, aware that he might never have this chance again. A wave of emotion rolled through him and he forced it away.

"Did you just get back?"

"Yeah!" CJ squeezed him back—hard. "I missed you!"

Jamie edged back and gave CJ's baseball cap a tug. "I missed you too, kiddo." He looked up at Cam's parents. Did they know the truth? Had Emma told them? And if so, what had she said? He hadn't even had a chance to tell her everything that happened.

There was so much more to say. Would his explanation sound as trite as it felt?

Both of the Woodsons were smiling at him. He forced himself to do the same.

"Where's Emma?" Nadine asked.

He had no idea. He hated that he didn't. At the same time, if they were expecting her, did that mean she would show up here—on the dock? "I'm not sure."

Nadine frowned. "Oh?"

"I'm just doing some work here," he said dumbly.

Nadine and her husband exchanged a confused look, and then their attention was drawn away to something behind Jamie.

"Speak of the devil," Jerry said.

"Mommy!" CJ raced toward her and she scooped him up, clinging to him as if she might lose him. And he wondered if she felt like she might. Had she decided what to do about Blake? Would Jamie ever know the truth? It wasn't like she owed it to him to tell her. He wasn't a part of her life anymore.

The thought tied his insides into a knot.

CJ slid to the ground and gave Emma a tug toward the rest of them. Emma met his eyes, and he tried to force himself to steady his gaze, but it was hard and he was shaky. He wanted everything to be different. To have the chance to prove to her that his love for her was as real as the sky above them. He wanted to spend the rest of his life making it up to her.

But judging by the coldness in her glare, that wasn't going to happen. If she'd read the letter he'd left that morning, it hadn't changed anything.

"We should hurry," she said. "I have to get back to the gallery."

"Oh, that's right," Nadine gave Jamie's arm a squeeze. "Your show is this weekend." She looked at her husband. "I wish we could come back for it."

Emma frowned. "You're not staying?"

"We just made the trip to drop CJ off," Jerry said. "We're heading to Boston for a few days—we're going to be tourists."

Emma's shoulders slumped. "I thought you would be staying."

Nadine frowned. "Is everything okay? Should we not have brought him back so soon? Maybe you have too much going on at work?"

Emma shook her head. "No, of course not. It's fine."

"Are you sure?" A line of worry crept across Jerry's forehead.

She nodded. "Absolutely."

"Okay," he said. "We can change our plans. We don't mind."

"Don't you dare," Emma said with a smile that looked slightly less forced than the one she'd given when she first arrived. "You've already done so much."

They both smiled. "Good because we didn't even bring a day bag," Nadine said. "We're heading straight back on the next ferry."

Emma's face dropped ever so slightly. "Oh, wow. Okay." Her in-laws seemed not to notice her disappointment as they gave a round of goodbye hugs and squeezed CJ extra hard.

"We'll be back soon."

Nadine even stopped in front of Jamie and gave him a hug. "Good luck this weekend. Hopefully, we'll see your brilliance for ourselves one day soon." He hugged her back, surprised at her forcefulness given how small she was.

"Thanks," he said.

After they'd said their goodbyes, he found himself standing there near the ferry dock with Emma and CJ. He felt awkward and out of place.

"You okay?" he asked. Had it really only been hours since he'd seen her? It felt like a lifetime ago.

She looked at him, then smoothed her hair, pulling the ponytail in two pieces to tighten it to her head. "I'm fine."

He could tell she wasn't.

"Emma, I'm sorry."

"CJ," she called over to her son, who was vrooming his suitcase around Jamie's table with reckless abandon. "Let's go."

"Did you read the letter?"

She leveled her gaze at him. "No."

His heart dropped to his stomach. "Can we talk?"

"No."

"Emma, please," he said. "We need to have a conversation."

"I don't think I can."

He watched her. Her jaw twitched, tense and tight. "What about the apartment?" he asked, his only connection to her.

"What about it?"

"My investment . . ." Oh, man, was he really going to be that guy? What was he doing? But it was the last card he had to play.

Her face fell as if she'd just now remembered.

"I need to get in there and take some good photos of it for the listing."

She shifted. "Fine. Come tomorrow when I'm at work. Do you still have a key?"

He nodded.

"Great."

And that all went about as well as he should've expected it to. Everything good that had happened between them felt like a distant memory, like something that was so real yet only a dream. He'd lost her, and he had no hope of ever winning her back.

# CHAPTER THIRTY-FIVE

"WELL, WE KNEW THIS MIGHT HAPPEN." Hillary's sigh came through the phone loud and clear. She'd expected this.

Jamie's silence hopefully communicated that he had not. Or at least he'd hoped against it.

"So what are you going to do?" she asked.

"Get out of her way, I guess."

"Brilliant plan, little brother."

"What am I supposed to do? She hates me."

"She doesn't hate you," Hillary said. "And you don't hate her, so if she's worth it, then you've got to fight for her."

Jamie chewed on that now as he parked in front of the apartment. Her car wasn't in the driveway, so he really shouldn't be worried. She had told him to come by today.

Did it matter that he'd planned it so he was there at the very end of the day? Did it matter that he hoped she'd come home while he was still there—so maybe she'd give him just a little of her time?

"Listen, Hill, I'll call you back," he said. "I've got some work."

"Fine," she said. "And I'll keep thinking. There has to be a way to help her see you're not a bad guy."

He wasn't so sure, but he thanked her anyway.

He walked up the stairs to the familiar space, a space he'd renovated to make Emma happy. The whole process had been healing—not only meeting her, falling for her, but working on this apartment. It had been therapeutic throwing himself into improving it. He'd felt like he was doing something good, something worthwhile. Now he wondered if even that was a mistake. How would they sort through the messiness of his investment?

Truthfully, he'd happily walk away, let her make all the money on the rental—it had been his plan all along. But as it was one of the only connections he had to her, letting go of it was proving more difficult than he imagined it would be. Besides, knowing Emma, she wouldn't allow that anyway.

He opened the door and walked inside. The space was tidy and smelled clean. He'd spent a lot of hours ripping out the old and replacing it with new, fresh and shiny, and Emma had used the week he was away to finish decorating.

It looked perfect. Exactly like the kind of space someone would rent for a vacation or even a long stay on the island.

Exactly like the kind of space *he* would rent for a long stay on the island.

Was it really only two days ago he'd planned to return with news that he was moving his business here?

He pulled out the camera and started shooting. Wide-angle shots of the entire space, the brand-new kitchen, the backsplash, the new appliances. The gleaming hardwood shone in the afternoon sun that streamed in through the window. The bed had been made up with white bedding, then topped with colorful throw pillows.

A gray couch and white armchair sat in the center of the space, perfectly situated for an evening in front of a large-screen television. He moved into the bathroom, which he'd retiled. The sink and toilet were new and the shower had been resurfaced. Emma had hung peacock-colored towels on the brushed nickel towel bar, along with three pieces of matching whimsical bathroom-inspired artwork, stacked on top of each other—a toilet paper roll with the words *That's how I roll* artistically positioned underneath, a clever sketch of a toilet and the words *Put a lid on it* hovering above it, and lastly, the outline of a toothbrush and toothpaste tube, along with the words *Squeeze my bottom.* He snapped a photo and smiled.

Leave it to Emma to add a touch of humor to the place. He ached a little as that thought raced through his mind.

He wandered back out into the main space and snapped a photo from this angle. He walked over to the corner of the living room where a stuffed chair had been positioned next to a tall shelf of books. Leaning on the top of the shelf was a familiar scene—a watercolor version of the photo he'd given Emma of her and CJ playing in the yard.

She must've used it as inspiration.

He took the frame from the shelf and studied it. It was miles better than the haphazard first attempt she'd shared with him that night in the art gallery—that had clearly not captivated her the way this one had.

This image meant something to her.

His image.

His heart squeezed at the thought of it. He returned the frame to the shelf, photographed the sitting area, then moved to the window and peered out into the yard.

His time here had been healing—he wasn't ready to give it up yet.

But he knew he was no longer welcome.

And that was perhaps the saddest realization of all.

~

Emma moved through the last few days leading up to the art festival like a zombie. Most of the work was done, thankfully; otherwise she was sure she would've messed everything up. It was hard to concentrate, and she was struggling with conflicting feelings about everything.

After running into Jamie near the ferry, her heart had become a complete and total traitor. She'd walked up and found him there, with Cam's parents and CJ, and she was sure he was leaving the island. The thought that he'd go without saying goodbye, despite her order that he do exactly that, was proving more unsettling than she expected.

It had led to the continuation of this trancelike state she was in, the one where she forgot to pack CJ a lunch to take with him on a field trip. The one where she made cookies to distract herself and completely forgot not one ingredient, but two. Cookies without sugar and baking soda went straight into the trash.

Two days after the fateful meeting at the ferry, Emma arrived for work, surprised to find Travis waiting for her. He was standing in the classroom, looking over Jamie's images a little too intently. She hadn't seen her boss in days—he'd gone down what he called "an artistic black hole" and couldn't be bothered.

It was a good thing too, because if he knew what a terrible job she was doing, he'd likely fire her on the spot.

But that wasn't true, was it? She was keeping up. She was ticking off all the boxes. The trouble was, her heart wasn't in any of it. This show she'd worked so hard on didn't seem to matter much anymore.

So much had changed so quickly, and really she just wanted everything to go back to the way it was. It wasn't the first time she'd thought that.

"I didn't expect to see you here," she said now to Travis's back. She hung her purse on the hooks by the back door and moved into the space next to him, trying to figure out what he was looking at.

Whatever it was that held his attention, it disappeared when Travis turned to her. He narrowed his eyes.

"You look terrible," he said.

She didn't respond. What could she say?

"What's going on with you?"

"Nothing, why?" Had someone said something? Probably that terrible Mrs. Matlock who'd shown up yesterday with a tiny little rat-dog in her purse. Emma had explained their "no animal" policy, but the woman refused to listen. Emma might've said something she shouldn't have, something like *Go ahead and let your dog pee all over the floor. What do I care?*

She'd regretted it the second the woman's blue-lined lids widened, but there was little she could do to change it now.

Travis waved a hand in the air and strolled toward the main gallery. "Jameson called me yesterday."

Emma's stomach dropped. "He did?" She followed him.

"Yes." Travis stopped behind the counter.

"Why?" Her mouth went dry.

"He had a couple of questions about the show." Travis gave her a side-eye. "I did find it strange he didn't reach out to you."

What was she going to say? *We aren't speaking? Turns out none of us really knows Jameson Edward Shaw after all? He's a big, fat liar, and I miss him so much I can't think straight?*

He turned to her. "And I was also surprised to learn he didn't know a single thing about the reception we've planned for tomorrow evening."

She frowned. Surely she'd mentioned it. Hadn't she? Her mind rolled through the memories of their last few conversations. The VIP, invite-only, black-tie affair had been an afterthought, but it was her idea—a way to placate collectors like the Heywards who would respond well to an early viewing.

"The idea was brilliant," Travis said. "But it only works if the featured artist actually attends the event."

"Right," Emma said. "I don't know what happened. I must've forgotten to mention it."

Travis flicked his hand in the air—his signature gesture—and moved toward the front of the gallery, where he unlocked the door. "According to Jameson, you did tell him, and he forgot to write it down."

Emma felt a blush rush to her cheeks at that. Jamie was still watching out for her, even though she'd been so cold to him. "Jamie is kind to cover for me, but the mistake was mine."

Travis turned toward her. "Oh, I know."

She looked away. "I'm sorry. It's been a hard week."

"Tell me about it. I've had to ditch three sculptures in the last two days alone." He sauntered past her and over to the wall where he straightened a frame that didn't need straightening. "You didn't tell me you were painting again."

She froze. "What?"

He pulled his phone from his pocket, scrolled to an image, and held it out toward her. She took it and there on the screen was a photo of the watercolor she'd hung in the apartment. Jamie must've seen it when he was there taking photos.

Last night, she'd received an email with twenty-five images for her approval for the listing.

Let me know if these are okay. If not, I'll take them again. And when I have your approval, I'll upload them and get the listing ready. Below you'll find the web copy my business partner, Dylan, whipped up. We can make any changes you like. We just need to add the prices. Let me know if we can move forward.

The email was kind but cold. Their relationship had become a professional one, and that realization had only made things worse. Her reply had been an equally cold *Everything looks good. We can move forward. Thanks.* She included her thoughts on pricing and hit Send.

And then she cried for a solid ten minutes. It had occurred to her that maybe she was overreacting about everything. That maybe she should take May's advice and read the letter or hear him out. She couldn't convince herself that Jamie would ever purposely hurt her when every single thing he'd done suggested the opposite.

But the reminder that he *could* hurt her whether he wanted to or not was enough to send her back into the bubble she'd carefully constructed around herself. She didn't want to feel that pain ever again. How had she let herself forget that?

"Oh," she said.

Travis snatched the phone back. "Oh?"

"It was nothing, really."

"It's wonderful," he said. "And I hate you a little for it. Here I am completely blocked, and you're over there casually pumping out masterpieces."

"Hardly."

"Your talented friend thinks so," he said. "He thinks you should be on display here."

"Jamie?"

Travis tossed her an exasperated look. "Yes, Jamie. Jameson. Mr. Shaw. He wants you to have a painting on display for the festival. This painting, in fact."

She shook her head. "I can't, Travis."

His eyes narrowed. "You can, Emma. And you will figure out a way to save this reception too. Apparently Jameson will only come if you are also being honored."

Her insides groaned. What was Jamie doing putting her on the spot like that?

"Oh, and before you get angry with him, he told me to tell you to go back and read number ten on some list?"

Emma didn't need to ask for clarification on which list Jamie was referring to. That dreaded *Year of Emma* list hadn't stopped torturing her since she wrote it.

"Apparently this is exactly what you want."

She also didn't need to find the list to remember what it said. *10. Start painting again. Submit to galleries.*

He was still trying to find ways to make her dreams come true, to help her accomplish the things on that blasted list. Anything she'd crossed off so far, she'd done so because of him.

But Jamie was wrong. This wasn't what she wanted—not anymore.

She wanted to quietly drift back into the shadows and live a life where nobody got hurt.

Was that too much to ask?

~

Emma texted Jamie that evening. I'm sorry I forgot to tell you about the reception. Can you make it?

His response came right away. It's fine. Your boss gave me the details. I already rented a tux. Not as cheap as the tux rentals back home.

I'll make it up to you, she promised.

How?

Emma wasn't sure how to respond. Luckily, another text came in from Jamie after just a moment: I'm kidding.

There was something else she wanted to bring up, though. You sent Travis a picture of my painting.

Yep.

You shouldn't have done that.

Why, didn't he like it?

He loved it.

Then I'm not sorry I sent it. I hope I see it alongside my photos on Friday.

Fine, but I don't want it to be a big deal. I don't want to be "honored" with the rest of you artists.

I guess it's a fair trade. But your work deserves to be honored.

# CHAPTER THIRTY-SIX

ALL DAY THURSDAY, Emma's nerves hopped around inside her like corn in an air popper. She'd made the necessary arrangements for the VIP reception, yet somehow she'd failed to invite the guest of honor.

The facepalm emoji seemed an appropriate description of her life lately.

The reception was a big deal—a party celebrating their artists. Jamie wasn't the only one; he was simply the headliner. The Heywards were thrilled with the chance to schmooze the artists and rub elbows with the collectors, and while she hadn't exactly figured out what their role in all of this was, she knew they were important.

Travis seemed intent on keeping them happy.

Angst welled within her at the realization that this night—this whole event—was supposed to be something they celebrated together. They'd put the show together. Heck, it was her stubbornness that led to him showing in the gallery at all.

He'd see she was right, of course.

It's just that she wouldn't get to celebrate with him.

She reminded herself this was better. Safer. *Protect your heart.*

Yesterday, after work, she'd gone shopping for a frock that wasn't found on the clearance rack at Old Navy. She knew that while the attention wouldn't be on her, she did need to make an impression. She wanted these people to see her as an equal, not as a gallery assistant. She wanted them to take her seriously. So she'd used her credit card and shopped for a bargain.

It would take her months to pay it off.

She took the black dress from the hanger and stepped into it, struggling to tug the zipper up to her neck. She finally got it and faced the mirror, admiring the woman looking back at her. She'd styled her long dark hair into loose waves and taken special care with her makeup. The dress fit her body effortlessly, as if it had been designed just for her, and she'd fallen in love with it the second she saw it in the boutique downtown.

High-necked with a lace overlay, the dress was banded at the waist, flattered by the tasteful cutout detail, a triangular shape ideal for every figure. The skirt flared out ever so slightly, the overlay weighing down the swish, extending just past the knee. She'd chosen the dress because it was slightly artistic but still classy. She'd chosen well. She loved this dress.

She looked . . . pretty.

Ever since her affair with Blake, she'd stopped looking at herself in the mirror. It was there to check her teeth for stray bits of lettuce and properly apply her makeup, nothing more. And while she'd never believed in admiring herself, she did want to like herself again.

What would it take for that to happen?

She slipped her feet into the red heels nearby, added a simple necklace and a pair of diamond earrings, the first gift Cam had ever given her.

Nothing flashy, but it suited her.

"I want to make peace with you, Emma Woodson," she whispered to her reflection. "But you're just so darn hard to forgive."

She shook the thoughts away, grabbed her red clutch, and walked out the door.

On her way to the gallery, Emma dropped CJ off at Sadie's house to play with Stella. Sadie assured her that she was thrilled to have him, claiming that the two kids entertained each other. "It's nice that she has someone else to build sandcastles in the backyard with," Sadie said with a smile. "A mother can only build so many castles."

At her wide *I know you know what I'm talking about* eyes, Emma smiled.

"Well, thank you," Emma said. "We'll have to have Stella come play one of these days."

Sadie put a hand on Emma's—a surprisingly personal gesture—and it took Emma off guard. "You have a job and you don't know many people here yet. I am happy to help out with CJ while you get settled."

The woman's kindness—and her innate sense of exactly what Emma needed—stunned her.

"You're doing great with him, Emma," Sadie said. "He's a wonderful kid."

Tears pooled in Emma's eyes and she quickly blinked, not wanting to ruin the makeup she'd taken far too much time to perfect.

"Now go knock that man off his feet." Sadie waggled her eyebrows.

Emma thought about explaining that there was no man to knock off his feet, but why bother? After this weekend, Jamie would leave Nantucket, and Sadie, along with everyone else, would realize that Emma was very much alone.

She parked behind the gallery, and before she got out, she reapplied her red lipstick—much bolder than anything she'd worn since her wedding day. Emma preferred to blend into the background—she supposed many artistic people felt that way.

They wanted their work to stand out while they watched from the shadows.

She closed her eyes and drew in a deep breath. This would be hard for her. Not only did she not fit in with Travis and his crowd, but she also couldn't spend the evening talking to Jamie.

Never mind that it's all she wanted to do.

She'd been carrying the unopened letter around for days, not wanting to read words that would make her question her decision to sever ties. It was the safe thing to do, and right now that was what she had to focus on. She owed it to herself and to CJ to stop being careless.

Another breath. Another long exhale. "You can do this." But as she opened the door and stepped outside, a flurry of doubt drifted through her.

She'd busy herself with work. There would be plenty of people to attend to. Plenty of people with questions. Plenty of other artists to schmooze. She'd do all of that. And nobody would notice if she avoided the handsome guest of honor.

Inside, there was already the buzz of activity. She closed the door behind her and spotted Travis in the main gallery with the well-dressed and perfectly coiffed Mark David and Caroline Heyward. They were standing next to a tall, unfamiliar statue she could only assume was the piece Travis had been working on. He hadn't come right out and said so, but his stress level had certainly skyrocketed as the date grew closer. Perhaps he'd finally finished a piece worth sharing.

Mark David caught her eye and raised a brow at her entrance. She couldn't interpret the look until she was close enough to see Travis's statue for herself. Mark David's expression accused, as if she had control over what her boss chose to display. As she studied the giant flesh-colored hand with a face carved into the back of it, she wished she did.

"Oh, wow," she said. "What's this?"

Travis looked at her, unmistakable pride on his face. "I finally finished it. Do you like?"

"It's really unique," she said.

Travis frowned. "Unique."

"Yes, uh, and very interesting." She tucked the clutch under her arm and wished she were small enough to hide inside it.

Travis's raised brow was interrupted by the jangle of the door and the entrance of another artist. He left them standing next to the statue, which was sadly positioned right at the center of the gallery.

And yet somehow it was appropriate.

"We told you to talk him out of this," Mark David said.

Emma laughed. "Why? I think it's perfect."

Caroline drew back in disgust. "It's so strange that someone with *such* good taste creates such terrible art."

"Darling," Mark David said, "Travis doesn't have good taste. He has people like us to tell him what to like." He eyed Emma. "Which is why your piece has already been sold."

Emma frowned. "What?"

She followed Mark David's nod to the wall of Jamie's photographs. Nearby, hanging in a very prominent place, was her painting, and next to it, the inspiration photo.

"I like the idea of showing both mediums together," Caroline said. "Was that your idea or Mr. Shaw's?"

She stared at the two pieces of art—so different yet with so many striking similarities. They looked like a perfect complement to each other.

"Uh, his," she mumbled.

He must've gone back to the apartment and taken the painting from the reading nook. "You said it was sold?"

"Well," Caroline said, "if it's for sale. We have a buyer, but apparently you're in the business of displaying art because you love it and not because you want to make money." She didn't hide her annoyance at this.

A bubble of laughter welled up within her. Someone wanted to buy one of her paintings?

The door opened again and Jamie walked in, a stunningly beautiful, tall, slender woman on his arm.

Time stopped. And Emma shrank back.

He brought a date?

At the sight of him, dressed in a tux that appeared to have been custom-tailored, hair tamed but still unfussy, she caught and held her breath.

Their eyes met, and she wanted to bolt straight out the back door, but soon she'd have to check on the appetizers and the waitstaff and the other artists and . . . Was he walking straight toward her? Where would she hide?

He joined their small circle, shook hands with Mark David and Caroline, then turned to Emma. Her spine melted and pooled in a puddle beneath her feet.

"Emma," he said.

Her name on his lips still evoked a physical response in her. *Darn it.* When was her body going to obey her mind?

"Jamie," she said.

"You look amazing." It set her nerves on edge to find herself under his watchful gaze.

Emma's eyes darted to the woman, who smiled widely, expectancy on her face. "I'm Hillary. Jamie's sister." She shook Emma's hand with fervor. "This is amazing." Hillary's eyes drifted past Emma to the photos on the wall. "Jamie, wow. Are those yours?"

Jamie looked away shyly.

"All except the watercolor," Emma said, eyes squarely on him.

He looked up. "I'm glad you agreed to show it."

"It kind of messes up the aesthetic," she said.

"No, it's perfect," Mark David said. "We have a buyer for both pieces. They want to display them as a set. He likes the whimsical take on the original piece. It's an interesting study in the unique interpretation of different artists."

Emma still hadn't broken eye contact with Jamie. Her heart sputtered, a cycle of questions spinning in her mind.

All at once, she wanted to read the letter. She wanted to know the truth. She wanted to ask him about Cam's final days.

But also she didn't.

Was she strong enough to hear whatever it was he had to say? Would it be the thing she needed to help her move on, or would it knock her straight back to where she was months ago?

What was best for keeping her heart safe? She didn't know anymore.

"Tell her to sell it," Caroline said to Jamie.

Jamie's eyes were still locked onto Emma's. "I don't think I'm the one to convince her."

Inside, her mind screamed. *This wasn't the way it was supposed to end! This cannot be goodbye!*

But she said nothing. Instead, she watched as he walked away, leading Hillary over to the stunning photos that lined the wall. In their absence, Emma stood there lamely with Mark David and Caroline.

Neither of them commented on the tension between Emma and Jamie, but it was clear on their faces it hadn't escaped them.

"Think about the offer, Emma." Caroline slipped a small piece of paper into Emma's hand. "That's what the buyer is willing to pay, though between us, I think he'd go higher."

Emma nodded but didn't look at the paper.

"That's without my fee, of course," Caroline added. "Twenty percent of any sale."

Emma frowned. "I don't understand."

"This is what we do," Caroline said. "We bring buyers and artists together."

"And we're the best at it," Mark David said. "You can certainly keep painting in your garage or wherever and hanging your work on the walls in your house, but we'd love to see you send it out into the world. Your style is very hot right now." He pulled a business card from his pocket. "We've already brokered a new show for Jameson at a gallery in Chicago. We could discuss your options, too."

She scanned the room until she found Jamie, standing near a corner with a single light shining on him from overhead, as if it had been placed there for just such a moment.

He looked back at her, and she wondered how that deal had come to be. And when Jamie became the kind of man to go into business with people he didn't even like.

Maybe she'd been wrong all along. Maybe Jameson Edward Shaw was nothing but a stranger.

As the expression on his face shifted, though, something told her that no, Jamie was exactly the man she knew him to be. Which would make walking away from him that much harder.

# CHAPTER THIRTY-SEVEN

~~~

JAMIE WALKED THROUGH THE RECEPTION on autopilot. He could usually handle himself in a social setting, but at the moment, having his work on display and being the center of attention was about the last thing he wanted.

The Heywards were chatting up the show they were planning for Chicago, and while there was nothing altruistic about that, he knew it was good for his career. If he wanted to make this a career, that was.

And without Emma, he wasn't sure he did. Without her, things were feeling a lot like they had felt before he came to Nantucket. Like he still had the heavy burden of regret tethered to him like a pack he was forced to carry on his back.

Twice she'd checked on him to make sure he didn't need a drink or an appetizer, and both times it was after Travis pulled her aside to tell her something, likely "You're doing a terrible job of attending to the talent."

It wasn't what Jamie wanted for the night. He wanted her there, on his arm, celebrating with him. He wanted her to be in a place of honor too. Instead, she seemed intent on dodging him and refilling champagne glasses.

Never mind that she looked stunning. Emma was beautiful, to be sure, but this was next level. He was used to seeing her casual, face free of makeup, cheeks naturally pink, and hair up and out of the way. She wasn't a woman who spent hours making herself look different than she did when she woke up—and he loved that about her.

But tonight, seeing her in a black dress that showed off her figure, her dark hair, long and wavy and falling to the middle of her back, those red lips and big blue eyes—he wasn't sure how to stop staring. She moved through the gallery effortlessly, like she was put on the earth to be admired, and he was happy to oblige.

"Go talk to her." Hillary was treating her quick trip to Nantucket like a vacation from her life. Since they'd arrived, she'd made three new friends, and Jamie had no doubt this wasn't the last time she'd see any of them. That's how she was. Extroverted. Social. Likable. Not like Jamie.

He would rather hide out in the deserted sculpture garden behind the building.

Jamie was holding a glass of champagne that a waiter in a white shirt and black tie had poured for him an hour ago. He'd barely sipped it. He didn't like champagne, but he needed something to do with his hands.

"Jamie."

For a moment, Jamie regretted inviting his sister for the weekend. She was so excited about the art show and wanted to be there to support him. He appreciated it, but right now, the plan felt faulty. Hillary was the one person he couldn't hide from.

He glanced at Emma. Well, maybe one of two people.

"She doesn't want to talk to me." He turned his attention back to his sister, who gave him a look that said *Don't be stupid*.

"She made it clear." Jamie hated that she had. If only she would let him explain—there was so much more to talk about than what he'd written. He'd never anticipated not being able to talk to her after she read his letter. Although he didn't even know if she'd read it. For all he knew, she'd thrown it away, unopened. "And I want to respect that."

Hillary didn't like that answer. "You can't leave next week without talking to her. Does she even know you were planning to move your business here?"

"It doesn't matter now," he said. "You were right. I waited too long to tell her. Now I'm a liar who can't be trusted. Not to mention the man responsible for her husband's—"

"Don't say that," Hillary snapped. "I'm sick of you saying that when it's absolutely not true."

"You weren't there, Hill." He set his champagne flute on the tray of a passing waiter. "You love me too much to think that my actions might've actually gotten someone killed, but I'm telling you how it was."

The thought that Emma might not even know all the details yet had him conflicted. On the one hand, he hated thinking that what had happened might still lie between them, like a bomb waiting to explode. On the other hand, did that mean he could still explain things to her? Better than he did in the letter?

"I've always believed if you put two people in a room, they can work anything out," Hillary said.

"Yeah, well, that's naive."

She bristled at his tone.

"Sorry."

She softened. "If there's love, then maybe there's common ground."

"We're not talking about a simple misunderstanding here," he argued. When he found he had the attention of a group of people nearby, he lowered his voice. "I was there when her husband died. It was my fault. And then I kept it from her for months."

"While you fell in love with her."

A man approached them. He had questions about "the upcoming show in Chicago." He lived in Milwaukee and wanted to know what kinds of photographs Jamie would be showing. As if Jamie had any idea. As if he even cared.

He forced himself to engage, to be friendly, to try to charm the man's wife, but his heart ached for Emma.

Nearly an hour later, after the crowd had thinned, he spotted her standing by herself, staring at an oil painting by an artist he'd met earlier. An older woman with wiry gray hair and a frumpy gray dress that looked more like something a toddler would wear.

Her fashion sense aside, the woman had a gift. The small piece reminded him of some of his favorites in the Art Institute of Chicago. Pastel blobs of paint had been transformed into figures on a beach in a scene painted as if the artist had a bird's-eye view. Reds and pinks became sailboats in the water and the white foam of the ocean stretched out to meet a tan-colored shore.

Slowly he walked over to the painting, to Emma, and stood next to her. He hadn't intended for their shoulders to be near touching or to be close enough to inhale the scent of her. It caught him off guard.

She didn't move away. Didn't move at all. She didn't even seem to be breathing. Was every nerve in her body aware of his presence the way his body was aware of her?

They stood as still as statues. He stared at the painting and yet saw nothing at all. His arm brushed against hers and the hair on the back of his neck rose like a weary child waking from sleep.

His eyes remained steady on the red blob of a sailboat drifting off to sea as his mind searched for something—anything—to say. Nothing came. He steadied his breath, tried to calm his racing heart. He clenched and unclenched his right hand, hanging loose at his side, a breath away from hers.

And then, as if acting on its own and without his permission, the skin of his knuckles brushed softly against the back of her hand. At his touch, he heard her breath catch, but a beat later, her trembling fingers moved, drawn to his like static electricity.

It was the slightest touch, like the hush of a breath, but his physical response to it was impossible to ignore. Her fingers searched his for a flicker of a moment, and he ached to know if she was thinking the same things he was. His mind flashed with memories of their short time together. Every stolen or freely given kiss, every knowing look traded in silence, every sweet conversation that he replayed as he closed out each well-spent day. The memories intertwined with his many hopes for their future, settling in a ball of disappointment in the base of his gut.

And then, like a wind that had snuffed out a candle, she was gone.

# CHAPTER THIRTY-EIGHT

~~~

THE DAY AFTER THE RECEPTION, Emma got a very slow start. Travis had told her to take the morning off. Since she'd worked so far ahead, they were ready for the kickoff of the art festival, and Emma was excited and a little sad the day had finally come.

She stood at the window in her kitchen, staring up at the apartment with a loneliness she'd like to drop-kick as far away from her as possible. She'd learned to be alone. Accepted it. Planned for it. And then . . . *Jamie.*

Jamie had set her back. Thanks to him, she'd have to relearn it all again.

Elise and May had tag-teamed her with a three-way call, and though she assured them she was fine, neither seemed to be buying it. As if they'd planned out what they were going to say, both of her friends insisted she go talk to Jamie or at least open the letter.

"We hate seeing you like this," May had said.

Emma silently cursed whoever invented FaceTime.

"You really do look awful," Elise added.

Emma thanked them and told them they had nothing to worry about before hanging up. Had she just told a lie? Even she was a little worried about what this had done to her.

Never mind that the photograph he'd given her, the one of Cam and the ultrasound film, had repaired something inside her that had been broken since the day her husband died.

Jamie had gone back to Chicago to retrieve that image for her. He knew how important it was because only he had the answer to the one question she wanted to know.

But that didn't make up for what he'd done, did it?

She'd just poured herself a cup of coffee when a familiar truck pulled into the driveway, and her stomach jumped to her throat.

Jamie.

What was he doing here?

Before she could find out, CJ spotted him and bolted out of the house like there was a fire in the kitchen. She watched from the window as Jamie picked him up and hugged him, trying to decipher the look of sadness on the man's handsome face.

Hillary got out of the passenger side and met them in the yard, and Emma found herself feeling like she was in middle school, desperately wanting the older "cool girl" to like her. It was silly, of course, since she and Jamie were no longer involved—so why was she straightening her hair and clothes in hopes of making a good second impression?

"Here goes nothing," she muttered under her breath as she opened the front door and walked outside, trying—failing—not to let her gaze linger on Jamie. Something inside her still sought out their connection. Would that ever change?

At the sight of her, he set CJ back onto the ground. "Morning."

"Hey," Emma said. "Hi, Hillary."

CJ ran a circle around the three of them.

"This is an amazing house," Hillary said.

Emma tossed a glance over her shoulder. "Thanks, we like it." It was small by Nantucket standards and nothing flashy, but in the past few months, it had become home. Would it feel so different after Jamie left?

"Jamie was going to show me the apartment, if that's okay?"

The apartment. Right. They still had to figure out how she was going to repay him for everything he'd done. On that front, she had no plan.

"Of course," she said weakly.

"I'll leave the key with you when we go," he said.

She shook her head. "No, it's fine."

He caught and held her gaze.

"I mean, you are responsible for the renovations, so maybe you should keep it for now?"

"Right."

"And I'm working on a plan to pay that all back," she said.

She stopped talking at his upheld hand, and she noted Hillary's curious look. His sister didn't know he'd footed the bill for the renovations, and judging by his expression, he didn't want her to know. She likely wouldn't approve.

Could Emma blame her? *She* didn't even approve. He'd sunk a lot of money into an apartment as a handshake deal with a woman he barely knew, and now that their relationship had become what it was, what would happen to that investment?

It wasn't a good business move on his part, but Emma was determined to keep their professional agreement, which meant she would pay back half of the renovation supplies and they would share the profits of her rental with him so she could cover his investment free and clear.

Or maybe she could pay back all of the renovation costs with interest and ask Jamie to let her off the hook for the rest of it.

"Are you happy with the way it turned out?" Jamie asked, the air tense between them.

She nodded. "It's really even better than I could've imagined."

After a pause, Hillary took a step toward Emma. "This is for you." She handed Emma a small brown bag with a cream-and-brown gingham bow tied around the handles.

Emma felt the pull of confusion on her forehead. "You brought me a gift?"

"It's just a little something for the apartment," Hillary said, and for a split second, Emma wondered if she wasn't the only one who wanted to be liked.

Emma glanced at Jamie, whose face was unreadable.

"Open it." Hillary smiled.

Emma pulled the tissue paper from the bag and found a large hand-poured soy candle. The clean, sleek label assigned it a fragrance called "Nantucket."

"I made it for you," Hillary said.

"You made it?"

"She makes candles," Jamie said.

"I wanted to do something island-inspired," she said. "Of course I was kind of guessing because I made it before I actually arrived. I'm happy with how it turned out though."

Jamie stuffed his hands in the pockets of his jeans. "You should look her up. Her business has really taken off the last two years."

Hillary pushed her shoulder into his. "Because of you."

He rolled his eyes. "Not because of me."

"He helped me with the branding," Hillary said. "Before it was just a hobby, but after Jamie and Dylan got their hands on it, business took off, I quit my job, and now I do this full-time. I'm a business owner."

Jamie's business was about so much more than branding. Emma could see that plain as day. He was in the business of helping people make their dreams come true. No wonder he insisted on Travis showing her painting. Despite her anger toward him, she was grateful for that much at least.

Emma took the candle lid off. The packaging was classy and upscale, the fragrance strong but not overpowering. It smelled like a day at the beach. "This is amazing."

Hillary beamed. "I'm glad you like it."

"I'll make sure we always have one in the apartment," Emma said. "And I'll buy some for the house."

"I'm working on a new Christmas scent now," Hillary said. "It's going to be delicious."

Emma smiled. She couldn't help it. She really liked Jamie's sister.

"Will you give me a tour?" Hillary asked, eyes on Emma.

"Oh, of course." She glanced at CJ.

"I can hang out with him," Jamie offered. "If that's okay?"

She hated the subtext of his question—*Is it okay if I spend time with your son?* It broke her heart a little more. "He'd love that." *He misses you almost as much as I do.*

She took Jamie's key and headed up the stairs, pushing open the door of the space that Jamie had once occupied. When she and Elise and May had decorated the space while he was gone, she had no idea he wouldn't be back there after he returned.

She showed Hillary every bit of the place, all her favorite details, and she realized there were pieces of her and pieces of Jamie everywhere she looked.

"It's pretty amazing Jamie did this," Emma said now as they stood in the brand-new kitchen. "I mean, he didn't even know me."

"Jamie's a really good guy." Hillary watched her a little too carefully.

Emma nodded. "I know."

"And he would kill me if he knew I said anything, but he was ready to pack up his business and move here." She paused. "For you."

"He was?" Emma frowned.

"He was." Hillary crossed her arms over her chest. "I told him this would all backfire on him, but I really do think his intentions were good. He was struggling to figure out how and when to explain it all."

Emma went still. She didn't have words.

"Did you read the letter?" Hillary asked.

Emma shook her head.

"You should read it. And I know this is hard for you, having the past brought back up like this, but—" She stopped as if considering her words. "It has been really hard on him too. A part of him died over there. He didn't come back the same guy he was when he left."

Emma didn't respond.

"But I feel like over the last few months, I got my brother back."

She tried to process what Hillary was saying, and it occurred to her, maybe for the first time, that whatever he'd witnessed that day had been bad enough to make him stop taking photos, something he was obviously created to do. Whatever had happened, it had profound adverse effects on Jamie.

Her heart twisted at the thought. What happened over there?

And what was Jamie's role in it all?

This whole time she'd been assuming he'd simply been there. But she'd never stopped to consider that maybe Jamie's life had been in danger too. That maybe the way the situation unfolded had left him broken and changed. That he was searching for a way to put the pieces back together.

The conflicted emotions tangled around her heart left her uneasy.

She didn't want to have sympathy for Jamie. She didn't want to think about Cam's death. She'd wanted to put it all behind her.

And yet she had questions. Questions that needed answers.

"Hillary, what happened over there?"

Hillary pressed her lips together thoughtfully. "It's not my story to tell. He wants to be the one to tell you everything. He had a whole plan to explain when he got back from Chicago. I know because I helped concoct it. He was going to let you read the letter, and then he was going to show you the photos."

"Photos? Plural?"

Hillary nodded. "He'd never even looked through them himself. Got back from Africa and stuffed the memory card in a box. If it weren't for you, I doubt he ever would've opened it again."

Emma had no idea.

"The plan just exploded," Hillary said.

Emma tried not to replay the night he'd returned from Chicago and everything went sideways.

"I'm not justifying what he did. It was wrong. But he did have his reasons," Hillary said. "He's leaving Sunday. And while I know Jamie has it in him to fight for what he wants, he's too much of a gentleman to fight if he thinks you don't want him to." She paused.

The sound of footsteps on the stairs pulled their attention. Jamie popped his head in. "Hillary, we should go. I've got that meeting."

Emma looked away.

"Thanks for showing me the apartment," Hillary said. "I'm going to go back to the Nantucket Hotel and get a massage." She winked at Emma. A clever way to insert the name of the place where she and her brother were staying. Just in case Emma had a use for that information.

She didn't.

"Of course," she said without emotion. "Happy to."

Hillary met Jamie at the door and walked out. Jamie stood there for a long moment like he wanted to say something, but instead he nodded at Emma and walked away, carving out a hollow spot in her chest where every good thing used to be.

# CHAPTER THIRTY-NINE

THE ART FESTIVAL KICKED OFF THAT NIGHT, and as expected, Jamie's work was very well received.

A little less expected was the fact that Emma's work was also well received. She'd brought in another piece, this one a painting of her favorite Nantucket cottage, inspired by another one of Jamie's photos.

It didn't escape her that his art fed her creativity.

Would she be able to paint after he'd gone?

Would she be able to breathe?

Jamie and Hillary attended the opening, of course, but Emma kept her distance. Her conflicted feelings and the dread of his departure were almost too much to bear.

At one point during the evening, Caroline and Mark David pulled both Emma and Jamie together near Travis's sculpted hand to ask if they'd made decisions about selling their work.

Emma had thought about it—the extra money would be nice, and she could always re-create the painting if she really wanted one for the apartment.

She looked at Caroline square in the face. "I'm open to selling," she said. "But at 15 percent commission."

Caroline looked offended. Jamie looked proud.

After righting herself, the older woman arched one penciled-in brow. "Eighteen."

"Sixteen."

"Fine."

"I'll do the same," Jamie said.

The Heywards shook their heads in unison. "Let's not get too big for our britches, shall we?" Mark David said with a pointed look.

Emma watched as they sauntered off. "I can't believe that worked."

"Guess that should tell you how talented you are," Jamie said.

She looked at him. She longed for him. "Thanks for everything, Jamie."

A shadow passed over his face like he was hoping for something more—something she didn't have the strength to give.

The next night, after the gallery closed, she went home and changed into yoga pants and a tank top and went up the stairs and into the apartment, the only place she might find she still had a closeness to Jamie. Her head pounded, drumming the beat of a song she didn't want to hear. A song her own mind made up to tell her over and over, in perfect rhythm, *Read the letter.*

She'd been ignoring it since she woke up, but now, in the dark quiet, with the letter sitting in front of her, she whispered a prayer for strength.

She didn't know what it was that the stranger had come to tell her that day. And she didn't know how she would feel after she read the words he'd written long before they'd met.

But she knew if she didn't find out, she would regret it.

She tore the back of the envelope open and pulled out the letter, handwritten on lined paper in a dark-black pen.

*Dear Mrs. Woodson,*

    *My name is Jameson Shaw, and I am a photojournalist who was embedded with your husband's unit as they worked an extension of the protective detail for American diplomats in the Congo five years ago. I spent two weeks with Sergeant Woodson and the rest of the men, and I was struck by what a close-knit group they were. I was also struck by their bravery and courage.*

    *On more than one occasion, I saw each of the men put themselves in danger in order to protect and serve another person. It was inspiring, and it made me want to be a better man.*

    *Which is, I suppose, one of the reasons for this letter. I returned from Africa unharmed. Your husband and several others did not. And I hold myself responsible.*

    *I know what I'm about to tell you may be painful to read, but please know it's not my intention to upset you, only to fill in some of the blanks of what happened and to explain the incredible heroism of your husband, a man who sacrificed his life to save mine.*

A tear fell onto the page, smearing the words. She folded the letter and stuffed it back into the envelope, her heart racing.

Without thinking, she scrambled down the stairs and sent a text to Sadie. Can you watch CJ for a little while?

Sadie texted back immediately, Bring him over! We're doing movie night!

The reply shamed her. She should be planning fun things for her son. She'd been so self-absorbed lately. And yet her newly built world was crumbling into a pile of rubble alongside her old world. It was time to face it, whether it snapped her in half or not.

And then she would get on with her life.

She dropped CJ at Sadie's and drove toward the Nantucket Hotel. She had no idea what room Jamie was in, but she'd knock on every door if she had to. She didn't want the letter to do the talking for him.

It would've been fine if they were still strangers, but she wanted the whole story, in Jamie's words, in Jamie's voice.

Besides, the letter was the easy way out. He didn't get to take that.

She parked and walked a block to the hotel, racing inside to the front counter.

"May I help you?" A young woman wearing a gray hotel uniform smiled at her.

"I'm wondering if you could call a guest for me?"

"Name?"

"Jamie Shaw," she said.

"Emma?"

She turned and found Hillary standing behind her.

"Hey." Emma tried to relax. She failed. She looked back at the clerk. "Never mind."

"I'm meeting a few new friends for drinks," Hillary said. "But I assume you're not here for me."

Emma smiled. "No, I'm not."

"Good." She nodded. "He's in room 218."

"Thanks." The beat of her heart pounded so strongly in her head as every emotion coursed through her veins.

She ran up the stairs, found his room, and stared at the numbers on the wall beside the door. What was she going to say? This conversation would surely break her heart.

Before she lost her nerve, she knocked on the door.

After a moment, he opened it, visibly surprised at the sight of her standing in the hallway.

She clung to her bag, wishing she'd taken time to change into real clothes before showing up at his door. She looked every bit the part of a woman falling apart.

"Emma." There was relief in his voice, as if he'd been hoping she would come.

She took the letter out and met his eyes.

He stepped out of the doorway and motioned for her to come inside.

"Sit." He pulled a chair out from under a small table in the corner.

She did as she was told. The air between them thickened in deafening silence. Finally she spoke. "I don't like talking about Cam. I don't like talking about what happened or about what I lost. I started reading this—" she held the letter up—"but I want to hear it from you." She lifted her chin and leveled her gaze at him. "I'm ready to know what happened."

He sat on the bed, their knees almost touching.

She was keenly aware of his nearness. In spite of everything, a part of her was still drawn to him.

"I will tell you everything you want to know," he said now, his eyes attentive and concerned and fixed on her. "Where should I begin?"

"I stopped when you said Cam saved your life." She handed over the letter.

His face went blank. "That's all you read?"

She nodded, then looked away.

He cleared his throat, then took the letter from the envelope, his eyes scanning words he'd written months, maybe years ago. Who knew how long he'd been wrestling with this? Likely since the day he returned from Africa.

He folded the letter and set it beside him on the bed. "The part you didn't get to is—" He stopped. "It's the hardest part, Emma."

She closed her eyes. She was afraid of that.

"I was working on a freelance assignment that would highlight some of the civil unrest in the Congo and the work of our troops in the area. A photo essay of the life of a soldier." He pressed his lips together, and Emma forced herself not to detach emotionally. Whatever he had to say, she would listen to it. She would feel the effects of it. She wouldn't run from it anymore.

"The unit—Cam's unit—they were a tight-knit group, and it only took a few days for me to understand the dynamic. Cam was the leader, for sure. The others all looked up to him, and I understood why. He was decisive and fearless and smart. They all loved him. They knew Cam would take a bullet if it meant saving any of their lives."

Emma blinked away fresh tears. She'd known this about Cam, but hearing Jamie say it was like realizing it again for the first time.

"He also watched out for me," Jamie said. "Made it his mission to give me space to work but only if I wasn't in danger. Never once did I worry about my life, and we were in a dangerous country. The unit was assigned to protect American diplomats, and I was there to capture it all. The soldiers at work or resting or interacting with locals—whatever they were doing.

"One afternoon—" Jamie's voice softened, as if feeling the memories all over again—"I remember it was hot. Really hot. I was wearing a T-shirt with a vest over it, then my camera, and Cam made me get a hat—said it would protect my face from the sun." He paused. "He was right." He dipped his chin, and Emma watched as he sorted through whatever was coming next, as if flipping through the files of his memory for the ones he'd stuffed at the back of his mental cabinet.

Visible pain appeared on his face, and Emma's heart was stunned at the sight of it.

All at once, she was filled with understanding—with empathy. They weren't on opposite sides of this thing. They were mourning the same tragedy. Perhaps that was why the undercurrent of their connection had pulsed so strongly from the very start.

"Uh . . ." His voice broke. "We were driving in the middle of nowhere, toward a small village . . ."

~

Jamie's mind latched on to the memory like a burr in a dog's coat. Just like that, he was there. He spoke the memory aloud as he replayed it in his mind, aware and not aware that Emma was in the room with him.

"The zoom lens gave me a close-up view of my surroundings. The lush green was deceptively beautiful, even peaceful."

He pointed his Canon, stabilized the camera, and clicked. Shot after shot detailing the part of the Congo that most people didn't see.

He'd been embedded with the soldiers for two weeks now, but this was the first time they'd left Kinshasa. So far things had remained mostly quiet, but as the truck rambled toward a small Congolese village, a feeling of dread fell over them.

He used the camera to scan the countryside. Nothing seemed out of the ordinary, but then did he know how to recognize "ordinary" in a foreign country? He'd traveled the world and had earned a reputation of one of the best photojournalists in the business, but every country was new to him. And "ordinary" changed with each plane that touched down.

The sound of gunshots cracked through the air, followed by the sound of men yelling. Inside the truck, the soldiers moved methodically—their training kicking in. A bullet left them with two flat tires, right there on the road. There was no time to pull off to the side—they slid to an abrupt halt, and the line of soldiers filtered out like ants. What were they going to do—draw gunfire? Go to battle right there on the outskirts of a village?

He'd been in danger before, but not like this. Adrenaline spiked, sending his mind into a staccato rhythm punctuated by fear.

The soldiers hopped into action. They were trained for this. But he wasn't.

There was yelling. Shouting. And then the quick directive from Cam—*"Stay close to me."*

Now Jamie stood and walked toward the window. Outside, a parade of people moved on with their lives. They walked in and out of stores or raced off toward the beach. They went to dinner with friends and then for ice cream on the dock. They were alive in a way Jamie hadn't been in years.

If they were bogged down with regret, it didn't show. And that only left him feeling more alone.

"There was so much noise," Jamie said, mostly to himself. "So much chaos. Sometimes when I close my eyes, I still hear the gunfire echoing through the canyon."

"That's why you don't sleep," Emma said softly.

He nodded but didn't look at her. Maybe it would be easier to speak to the window, to confess this part to the ether in hopes that the effects of it didn't unravel her in the way he feared it would.

He'd foolishly wished he could explain this to her, but now that he was here, he wished she'd read the letter—then she would already know the truth. He wouldn't have to speak it out loud. But he couldn't refuse her this. He owed it to her to be honest—finally.

"We ran toward the tree line, looking for cover, but nowhere was safe. The truck caught on fire, and I remember wondering how we were ever going to get out of there now. It was so hot. My chest burned and my muscles ached, but I forced myself to keep up with them, the other soldiers. In the distance, I heard a scream—someone had been hit. It was Jimmy Birch. Another guy—Mike—was injured, and it was bad." Jamie stopped, remembering.

*"Stay here."*

Cam had dragged Jamie into the wooded area several yards from the road and now pulled him closer by the vest.

*"You hear me?"*

Jamie nodded. His head pounded. He hid in the brush, careful to conceal himself as best he could.

*"You're safe here."*

Jamie choked the words out, grief and shame and regret mixing like chemicals in a vial at the back of his throat.

"I was such a coward." He broke as he said it, a sob like a brick in his windpipe. "If I'd listened, everything would be different."

He turned and faced Emma, whose cheeks were wet with a stream of tears. He knew she hated to cry. He knew after this last bit she would probably hate him too.

"I didn't stay where he put me. I panicked. I convinced myself I knew better, that Cam was wrong, that the situation had changed and the place where he'd left me was compromised. I got scared, I guess. So I ran—as fast as I could." He closed his eyes. "And when Cam saw me, he yelled at me to go back, but it was too late. He sprinted toward me, but we were flanked on either side. Pinned down." He went still in the memory of the exact moment he realized he'd been wrong to move.

*"You're safe here."*

*Why didn't I listen?*

"Everything went quiet, and I turned back and heard Cam shouting at me. The next thing I know, I'm on the ground, and Cam's body is on top of me, shielding me from the bullets raining down." He was shot six times in the back while Jamie wrestled to get out from under him, but he didn't say so. "He saved my life, Emma. I'm only here because he protected me."

He pushed the meat of his hands into his eyes, as if that could stop the flood of tears after the truth had poured out of him.

"It was my fault." Jamie sucked in a sob. "It was my fault he died."

She sat at the table, eerily quiet, a stunned look on her face.

And he braced himself for whatever was coming next, because he had a feeling it was going to hurt.

# CHAPTER FORTY

EMMA SAT, UNMOVING, AT THE TABLE, trying to digest the vivid portrait Jamie had just painted.

It was more than the military had told them. They'd received a report of the incident, but when soldiers die in combat, there's little blame to be assigned. A war zone wasn't as cut-and-dried as she wished it was. She'd accepted that. Cam had died in the line of duty. He'd been awarded medals and honored for his service. She'd made her peace with that, if not with herself over her actions.

But everything had changed in just a few moments' time. The peace she'd made had been disrupted, like a boulder thrown into a quiet stream.

She was overcome with the stark realization that the man standing in front of her, a man she loved, was only here because the man she used to love was not.

Jamie didn't move, strong arms hanging at his sides. How many times had those arms held her? Protected her? Made her feel safe?

And all this time, he'd been keeping *this* secret from her?

She'd wrestled with thoughts of understanding, of wanting to comfort him, because he, too, had lived a trauma and suffered at its hand.

But as she processed his confession, it wasn't empathy she felt. It was anger.

"How could you . . . ?"

His face faltered.

"How could you come here and keep this to yourself? How could you make me fall in love with you when you are only here because of Cam? Because the man I lost saved your life?"

As soon as she said the words, she saw the damage they'd done. She wanted to reel them back in, but her mind wouldn't allow it.

Something inside her had snapped, as if all the pain and emotion she'd forced herself not to feel had finally been let loose. The numb places were pulsing in anguish as she replayed the images she'd put to the story he'd told.

The gunfire. The explosion. Dragging Jamie to safety. The shouting. The terror. The swearing. The blood. And finally, jumping in front of a string of bullets to protect a man he didn't even really know.

Tears streamed down Jamie's face, and Emma's heart lurched with an unwanted empathy toward him. *They were mourning the same tragedy.*

But how? How could she mourn with the man who had stolen Cam's life? How could she forgive the way he'd become a part of her life, slipping in like a thief, taking even more from the man who'd saved him?

Everything about it felt wrong.

"I would trade places with him in a heartbeat if I could," Jamie said. "You have to know that, Emma."

She stood, clutching her bag and willing away the tears. "But you can't. Cam's dead. CJ will never know his dad." Even as she said the words, she grimaced. She looked away. "Why did you have to come here and bring this all back up again?" Her tone was tight, her words spoken through clenched teeth.

"Because I couldn't carry it anymore," he said. "There's not a day goes by that I don't think about Cam and the sacrifice he made for me. I am full of guilt and shame over what I did, over what you and Mary Beth and the others lost." His hand turned to a fist at his side. "But it's had way too big of a hold on me for too many years. I thought if I finally talked about it, if I asked for your forgiveness, then maybe it would lose some of its hold on me. Maybe then I could move on."

Another flash of anger whipped through her. "You don't get to move on!" She shouted the words, louder and angrier than she'd intended. "If I don't get to move on, then neither do you!" She rushed toward him, pushing him in the chest—hard. "How could you, Jamie?"

His hands flailed, but the impact of her anger hadn't even caused him to stumble.

She pounded again, the raw sound of her pain rising up from a deep place inside her. "How could you do this to me?"

He let her push and flail and smack; then finally he wrapped his arms around her—tightly—so she couldn't move an inch.

She collapsed into his chest, spent and weary and broken, and let herself cry.

"Emma," he whispered into her hair, his breath so close she could feel it on the side of her face. "There are so many things I would do differently if I could."

"Why couldn't you have just kept it to yourself?" She wished she didn't know. She wished they could go back to loving each other, back to believing that while life was cruel and unfair, it was also full of goodness and love.

He shifted. "The only way to heal is to face it—head-on."

After a moment, she pulled from his arms and wiped her cheeks dry, then looked at him with a newfound fury that burned white-hot inside her. "And that's what you're doing," she said. "You're facing it head-on."

"That's what I'm trying to do."

"Don't preach at me, Jamie."

This was the ugly side of her shame. It lashed out and hurt the people she loved. She'd seen it before, and despite trying to do better, at the moment she seemed to have no control over it.

"Don't you come here and preach truth and honesty to me after what you did." She practically spat the words. "This was so much worse than anything I could've imagined. You could've told me right at the start. You could've saved me the hurt of—" She waved her hands between them, as if to indicate it was their relationship she was talking about.

"I know, but, Emma, I'm not sorry for that," he said, his voice desperate. "I'm sorry I wasn't honest right away." A pause. "But I'm not sorry for loving you."

The words infuriated her. "How can you say that?"

"Because you reminded me there is good in this world," he said. "You reminded me of everything I love, and you made me want to stop calling what I was doing 'living.'" He took a step toward her, but she moved away. "I feel like I've been asleep ever since that day, and the moment I saw you, I woke up. You make me better, Emma, and I can't imagine a world without you in it."

She picked her bag up and slung it over her shoulder. "Well, you won't have to imagine it," she said coldly. "Because you'll be living it."

His face fell. She'd wounded him by refusing to forgive him. She didn't care.

She gave him one last lingering look, and then she walked away.

# CHAPTER FORTY-ONE

~~~

JAMIE LEFT NANTUCKET THE FOLLOWING DAY. Emma didn't get out of bed until CJ burst through the door and begged for her famous cinnamon rolls. The kind from a can.

She obliged, though her heart wasn't in it. And when he sneaked extra frosting, she didn't even object.

Hours drifted into days, and Emma tried to reconcile the Jamie she'd loved with the man who'd confessed his betrayal. It had been brave, in the end, to tell her the truth the way he had. While she hadn't appreciated it at the time, she appreciated it now, with days and distance between them.

Still, there was something about their conversation that had left her uneasy. Even as the weeks passed, she couldn't shake it.

The part where he told her the only way to heal was to face something head-on. She'd been angry at that because it felt like a slap in the face. Like he was using what he knew about her past to make a point, which he did not have the right to do.

And yet maybe it had been her shame that reached that conclusion.

Maybe what he'd said had nicked a wound, leaving it exposed, raw, and sensitive.

What if he was right? What if the only way to move on was to face it? Her stomach churned at the thought. She didn't want to face it.

~

Emma looked at CJ from across the table. Another breakfast, just the two of them. Why did it suddenly feel overwhelming? He dragged a piece of his waffle through the puddle of syrup on his plate, then lifted it toward his mouth. It fell off the fork with a splat. His big brown eyes—Cam's eyes, she thought—darted to hers.

"I think that's what happens when you have more syrup than waffle." She smiled at him.

He tried again, this time successfully, and swallowed the bite. Didn't she owe it to him to find out the truth? Sure, she could live the rest of her life not facing this fear that her mistake had stolen something so devastating, but she wouldn't have a moment of peace.

Look how it had already affected everything. The way it had wormed its way in, clamoring for her attention, taunting her, reminding her. *You should be ashamed,* it seemed to say, poking her in the ribs like an annoying twelve-year-old boy wanting to get a rise out of her.

She didn't want to be haunted by it anymore.

Maybe she thought she'd been walking around in the shadow of Cam's death, but really, she'd been walking around in the shadow of her own transgressions.

It wasn't because of Blake. He might've been the one to force her hand initially, but not anymore. This was about her.

This was about her putting down something that wasn't hers to carry.

This was about facing the truth so she could finally move on. So it finally lost its hold on her.

"I miss Mr. Jamie," CJ said abruptly.

It had been weeks, and CJ had only mentioned him a few times.

Did she really think he'd forgotten? In their time together, Jamie hadn't only loved her, he'd loved CJ—it was obvious at the start. Even more obvious at the end.

Emma glanced at the empty chair where Jamie sat when he ate dinner with them, then back at her son. "Me too, buddy."

It pained her to say so, but she did. And she feared she would for a very long time.

~

Another week went by. She'd booked the apartment for the rest of August and most of September. When the bookings came through, she desperately wanted to call Jamie and celebrate—it was working. The extra income potential was right in front of her. He'd made that happen.

Instead, she sent him a portion of what she owed him with a note that simply said, *I'll get the rest to you soon.*

He didn't reply.

~

Travis convinced her to hang two more paintings in the gallery. They went up without fanfare and sold the next day. She wanted to call Jamie and celebrate, but instead she deposited the money and sent a portion of it to him, asking him for a detailed invoice of what else she owed him for her half of the renovations.

He didn't reply.

~

The following week, Emma arranged for time off from work. Travis acted *very* put out, but she knew better. He didn't mind giving her what she asked for. She'd made herself invaluable. He didn't have to say so for it to be true.

It had been over a month since Jamie had gone. Her renter—
a single woman named Camille, who was writing a Nantucket-set
novel—had shown up as planned and fell in love with the apartment
and the artwork Emma had hung on the wall. She was particularly
fond of a photograph Jamie had chosen not to put in the festival show.
Emma had enlarged and framed it when she was decorating, and every
time she saw it, she remembered the day of their photo walk.

Back when things were simple.

Camille said the image instantly drew her in, and Emma could
see why. It showed an old couple on the rocks near Brant Point lighthouse, their hands intertwined like two young lovers.

"I bet they have a lifetime of stories to tell," Camille said.

How mortifying to think that when she first saw the photo, Emma
had hoped she and Jamie would last as long as those two. It's why
she'd chosen to put it on display in a place that reminded her of him.
She made a mental note to take it down after Camille checked out.

With summer nearly over, Emma called her in-laws to arrange for
a visit before CJ started school. They were, of course, thrilled, and for
the first time since she'd moved to Nantucket, she would leave the
island and return to her old life, if only for a week. But that wasn't
what had her insides swirling.

She'd also made an appointment to have CJ tested—a simple
cheek swab in a lab. Easy, the woman making the appointment had
said.

*Right. Easy.*

The night before their trip to the Cape, Emma scrolled through
her contacts and found Blake's number. She dialed, then inhaled a
deep breath until she heard his voice on the other line.

"Emma, wow. Long time."

"I'm going to text you the details on a lab in the Springs. You need
to show up there and get your cheek swabbed."

"Why?"

"Because, Blake, my husband is deceased, so I can't get a DNA
sample from him," she said, not concealing her irritation. "So we're

going to have to use yours. I've made arrangements with the lab to test your sample against one I'm going to send in from a lab in Chatham."

She'd jotted down the instructions on how to make this happen after talking with a nurse in Chatham. The nurse had assured her that the details would be kept private—the lab results would arrive in an unmarked envelope. She seemed to understand the prickliness of the situation.

After a pause, Blake said, "Okay, then."

She hung up and texted the details, saying a quick, silent prayer that whatever the results were, she was strong enough to handle it.

Emma made sure Camille had everything she needed, and then, the following day, she and CJ boarded a ferry for Hyannis. After an hour on the high-speed ferry, they arrived on the mainland and were met at the dock by her in-laws. Nadine threw her arms around Emma and hugged her so tightly, it brought tears to her eyes. She'd missed them. And nobody hugged like Cam's mom.

She pulled back and let Nadine look her over.

"We've missed you both so much," she said.

Emma smiled. "We've missed you too."

Jerry wrapped an arm around her shoulder and gave her a fatherly side hug. "Doing okay?" he asked quietly as Nadine picked up CJ's suitcase and led him toward the parking lot.

She put on her best smile. "Doing great."

But the expression on his face told her he didn't believe her. She should've known. He had a sort of sixth sense at reading her. Thankfully, he didn't press. She hadn't told them who Jamie really was yet—would they be disappointed to learn she'd allowed herself to get close to the man who'd cost their son his life?

She shoved the thoughts aside. She'd tell them, but not today. That would require an extra dose of courage.

The Woodson home was the oldest in a small town called Cotuit. Nadine's ancestors had founded the town, and though Cam's parents had upgraded and renovated, they'd kept most of the historical charm.

Emma relaxed at the sight of the big backyard overlooking the harbor and the quiet comfort of familiarity the moment Jerry pulled in.

Being here, she felt closer to Cam. She'd missed having such easy access to so many of their memories. Across the street, there was a small grocery store that doubled as a sandwich shop. She remembered the first time he brought her home to meet his parents—they'd eaten there twice, and it had become a favorite every time they were back in Cape Cod.

Down the block was the baseball field where the beloved Cotuit Kettleers played. The Woodsons were die-hard fans of the minor league baseball team. Once upon a time, Cam had dreamed of playing for the hometown team, but what little kid didn't? He'd later traded that dream for a life in the military. A life that suited him. Like Jamie said, he was a leader. Emma had no doubt he would've climbed his way through the ranks and made an excellent career for himself—and an excellent life for all of them.

Jerry unloaded their luggage and Nadine took CJ inside for some of her homemade sugar cookies, but Emma wandered to the edge of their property and stared out across the water.

Seagulls cawed overhead. A man fished in a small boat. A couple chased two small children down the beach, the sound of their laughter echoing through the air up to the bluff where she stood.

It was here that she'd healed after Cam died. In the home where he'd grown up, surrounded by photos and memories and the sound of his voice in the breeze.

It was fitting, she supposed, that she was here again, in need of healing. And selfish of her to seek it.

Nadine had prepared a feast for their arrival, and Emma ate until she was stuffed. The pot roast, potatoes, carrots, and fresh rolls reminded her of their many after-church Sunday dinners. She loved Nantucket, and she loved making her own way, but she'd missed this.

Emma slept in the guest room, which had been her room when she lived here. She'd chosen to give CJ Cam's room, as if that connection could bond her son to his father. Her sleep was sound, and she awoke early with the sun, the smell of freshly brewed Folgers filling the air.

She put a sweatshirt on over her tank top and walked downstairs, falling right back into her old tradition with a father-in-law who was a lot more like a father to her.

He'd left a mug and her creamer on the counter next to the carafe, as if to say, "I'm here if you need to talk." She smiled as she spotted him sitting on the porch, that thick Bible open in his lap.

Oh, to have faith like Jerry.

These days, she'd mostly given up when it came to her faith. She knew all about forgiveness. She knew God said he would forgive any sin if the sinner repented. But she'd done that—and she didn't feel forgiven at all. She could spend her whole life trying to make up for what she'd done, and it would never be enough.

She poured her coffee and joined Jerry on the porch.

He had his eyes closed, so she didn't say anything, assuming he was in deep communication with the Lord. Jerry had mastered the fine art of praying. Emma, for all her trying, typically got distracted within five minutes. Most of her prayers were short, sweet, desperate pleas for help.

After a few minutes and several sips of mediocre coffee, Jerry opened his eyes. Was he genuinely surprised to see her there? It was like he hadn't even heard her come outside.

"Morning, sunshine," he said with a smile.

She pulled her knees to her chest and smiled back. "Morning."

"I was just talking to the Lord about you."

On the inside, Emma groaned. She didn't know what she believed about Jesus or heaven or church, but every once in a while, her father-in-law claimed God had revealed something to him, and every single time he was right.

It would be creepy if it weren't so interesting.

At the moment, though, Emma preferred to keep her personal baggage zipped and stowed away. She didn't want God blabbing her secrets to Jerry, no matter how wise the man was.

"Oh?" She choked down another sip of coffee.

Jerry watched her. "What's going on?"

"Didn't God tell you?"

His face warmed in a smile. Jerry was amused, never put off, by her questions, her seeming doubts about God, her sarcasm where God was concerned. Her father-in-law seemed fascinated by the things she asked, always intent on letting her sort through it all for herself. He never forced his beliefs on her, which she appreciated, though some days it would be easier if someone simply told her what to think and believe.

"He told me to pray for you," Jerry said. "Seems like you're wrestling with something."

Was it that obvious?

"You haven't mentioned Jamie lately," Jerry said.

Sadness pricked the corners of her heart at the mention of his name. "No, I haven't."

"Do you want to talk about it?"

She closed her eyes. *No. I absolutely do not want to talk about it. But yes, I need to tell you something.*

"You don't have to," he said.

"I do actually." She looked at him.

He closed the Bible and waited as if knowing there was courage to be mustered.

"Jamie wasn't exactly who he said he was," Emma said. She drew in a deep breath.

Jerry's expression didn't change. He listened as she detailed the entire story, right down to the moment she'd stormed away from the hotel. She left nothing out. Not the letter or the betrayal or the fact that Cam—their Cam—had sacrificed his life for a man he barely knew. A man who later, in a sort of unfortunate twist, became a part of their lives. She knew it was as heartbreaking to hear it as it was for her to say it.

And when she finished, she prayed (really prayed!) that her father-in-law didn't break under the weight of it.

"I'm sorry it took me so long to tell you," she said. "I didn't know how to bring it up. I've been processing it, and I guess I didn't want you to be disappointed in me."

After a beat, Jerry looked at her. "So you've kicked him out of your life?"

She frowned. "I didn't really have a choice. He lied. And about something that really mattered. He's only here because Cam isn't. I don't know how to—"

She almost said, "Forgive." *I don't know how to forgive.* But she thought better of it. Forgiveness was such a tricky beast. Wrapped up in shame and guilt and pain, it was impossible to tease it apart.

"It must've been hard for him," Jerry said, a thoughtfulness in his tone that took Emma by surprise. "To live with that kind of guilt."

Emma hated that word—*guilt*. Always a reminder of her stupid mistakes.

*I'm guilty. Of so many things.*

But why this understanding of Jamie? Jerry should be irate. Livid. After all, he'd been kind to Jamie. They'd all eaten dinner together, and Emma's in-laws had made a real effort to get to know him. Didn't that tick him off?

"He probably wishes every day that he could take it back," Jerry said.

Emma stayed quiet. She didn't want to give Jamie the benefit of the doubt. And she felt a little annoyed that Jerry was.

"You know, Emma, Cam knew what he was signing up for when he enlisted." Jerry looked at her intently. "He had a job to do, and he did it. And if he were here today, I bet he'd tell you he'd do it all over again."

Emma hugged her knees to her chest. "But he's not here. Because of Jamie." *And she never got a chance to prove to him she could be the wife he deserved.*

"But Jamie *is* here," Jerry said. "Because of Cam."

Her eyes darted to his. "Doesn't that make you angry?"

He folded his hands and placed them on top of his Bible. "It doesn't."

She frowned. "Why not?"

"Because it was combat," he said. "Nothing makes sense in a war zone. Cam left on his first tour a naive kid from the Cape. He didn't like school, and this was his best option. The military promised him a future—and he excelled. Truth be told, it was an answer to prayer because for a while there I was sure he was going to go down the wrong path."

Emma knew Cam had fallen in with a tough crowd. He always said the Army saved his life.

"But when he came home, he wasn't the same. The things he saw out there changed him. Made him grow up—fast. And he rose to each challenge. Cam knew that when you're being shot at, when your life is in danger, you make split decisions. He was good at it. It's where he excelled." He set his Bible on the table between them. "Jamie made a split-second decision in a war zone, Emma. It wasn't his fault that Cam was killed in the cross fire. I'm proud of my son for saving that man's life—and if I ever see Jamie again, I'll gladly shake his hand and tell him so."

The words shamed Emma. She'd reacted so badly. She knew Jamie was in pain, and she knew what Jerry said was true. But having someone to blame for Cam's death—after years of only blaming herself—had eased some of her burden. She liked thinking that maybe someone else was at fault.

Another selfish choice.

"Can I tell you something else?" Jerry said, the kindness of a loving father evident in his eyes.

She nodded—genuinely ready to hear what he had to say.

"I don't know why Jamie didn't tell you the truth from the beginning. Only he knows that. But I imagine it wasn't an easy decision for him." Jerry paused. "All I know is that I saw you two together, and you were happy. I don't think you should be so quick to throw that away."

She didn't want to talk about Jamie anymore. She was up to her eyeballs in regret as it was. Besides, it was too late to change the past. She said what she said, and she was moving on. She and CJ.

"It was obvious," Jerry continued. "We left the island feeling so thankful—another answer to prayer. God had brought someone into your life who seemed to absolutely understand that being with you was a gift. I saw the way you looked at each other. I saw the light in your eyes. Do you know how many days I've spent in this exact chair praying for a way to turn that light back on?"

A tear streamed down Emma's cheek.

"It's your life, sweetheart," he said. "And I understand if you decide you can never see him again. But don't make that choice out of stubbornness or out of some misguided loyalty to Cam. He would want you to be happy."

"But it's all so messed up." She groaned as she wiped the tears away.

"It is. But that's life." He leaned forward and placed a hand on her shoulder. "Yes, you met under unfortunate circumstances, but does it matter? Does it matter what brought you together at the start?"

She looked at him. "Doesn't it?"

After a pause, he said, "Only you can decide that."

Emma didn't want to decide. She was tired of making decisions. "You'd really be okay accepting Jamie, knowing the truth?"

Jerry smiled. "We're all broken, Emma. Who am I to judge a man's past?"

It was so similar to what Jamie had said when he'd found out about her affair. Shame rose up within her. She'd behaved so badly.

"All I care about is who he is now," Jerry said. "And I think he's a good man."

He was a good man. Emma knew that was true. In spite of everything, that could not be denied.

The screen door opened and Nadine walked out holding a stack of mail. "Emma, why didn't you tell us Jamie was having another art show?"

Emma frowned. "What?"

Nadine handed over a card, printed on thick cardstock with the words *You're Invited* in shiny gold script.

A reception to celebrate
A Soldier's Peace
A photo essay by Jameson Edward Shaw
The Hubbard Street Gallery, Chicago

The date was September 24, one month from today.

"Are you going?" Nadine asked as Emma turned the card over and saw a note scrawled in Jamie's familiar handwriting.

*Mr. and Mrs. Woodson,*
*I hope you can make it to the showing. I realize Chicago is a bit of a hike for you, but I think you'll be glad you made the trip. I hope so anyway.*

*Jamie*

Emma stared at it, her conversation with Jerry still bouncing around like a pinball in her head. She didn't know how she felt or what she thought anymore. She only knew that even with weeks of distance between them, a part of her still ached for Jamie.

And she'd lost all confidence that would ever go away.

# CHAPTER FORTY-TWO

~~~

JAMIE HAD LEFT NANTUCKET WITH A PLAN.

He knew Emma didn't want to see him, and he respected that, but he also knew there was one more thing he needed to do. And while part of him wondered if it was selfish, another part of him knew this wasn't about him at all.

Now, weeks of planning and preparing—this time without Emma's help—had led him here. It might be his second gallery show, but it was far more nerve-racking than his first. This one would feature work so personal it almost pained him to put it on display. And the invite-only audience would be made up of members of Cam's unit and their families.

The idea had come to him as he perused the photos on the memory card. He'd never looked at the photos from that trip—never wanted to be reminded of the way it ended. But as he scrolled through the images, it occurred to him that there was a story to tell. A story of bravery and heroism and love and loss. It was a story of friendship and service, and it deserved to be told.

Still, he wished he could let the photos speak for themselves. Because this was a somewhat-unconventional art show, Jamie knew he had to make a speech to explain why they were all there. Maybe that's what made him the most uncomfortable.

Hillary had come alongside him, helping him with details like catering and decorations and invitations, while Jamie concentrated on the art. His final letter to the families of the men in that unit.

It was an hour before the doors would open, and Jamie thought he might come undone. Hillary told him she'd sent an invitation to Emma, but as of that morning, she'd yet to respond to it. He had no idea if she was coming or not, but the thought that she might had him on edge. Almost as on edge as the thought that she might not.

He missed her. He'd started missing her the moment she walked out of his hotel room that day, all those weeks ago now. He'd gotten a few messages about the apartment, all business, and checks he refused to cash. He didn't want her to pay him back. He just wanted her to be happy.

He'd spent a lot of time wrestling with that, because wanting to be happy and wanting to be the one making her happy were two different things. He'd finally come to terms with the fact that they might never be one and the same.

He'd been on two different freelance jobs, one in the deep woods of Minnesota and another covering forest fires in California. As he flew to each location, he reminded himself that his photos could mean something. His love of visual storytelling had been renewed, and he knew he had Emma to thank for that.

He arrived at the space he'd rented for this pop-up art show, the second floor of a renovated warehouse with high ceilings and rustic wood floors. It wasn't sleek or modern like Gallery 316, but it had its own kind of charm.

He hoped Emma liked it.

The thought that they might be in the same city at this precise moment sent a chill straight down his spine that he felt all the way to his toes.

He parked his SUV and walked up the stairs where he found Hillary bossing people around. She stopped midsentence when she saw him, gave his gray suit a once-over, and raised her eyebrows in approval.

"I admit I was worried what you might show up in," she said.

"It's not my first rodeo." He smirked.

She rolled her eyes. "Gosh, I'm surprised your big head fit through the door."

He followed her into a back room where the caterer was unpacking the appetizers. Hillary asked if the woman needed anything—she didn't—then returned to the main space.

"Well?" She motioned at the room. "What do you think?"

"I gotta hand it to you," he said. "You did a good job." Somehow Hillary had managed to take the photographs he'd printed and framed and display them exactly as he wanted. The story would unfold from one to the next, just like he remembered.

They'd created a sort of waiting area for guests, which would give him a chance to unveil his work to everyone at the same time.

"I still think you should open it to the public," Hillary said. "This is some of your best stuff."

He shook his head. "This one is personal. It's just for them."

White lights twinkled around the room. There were high-top tables draped with gray cloths and sprays of flowers throughout the space. It was perfect.

He looked at his watch. "It's almost time."

She frowned. "Why do you look like you're going to throw up?"

He swallowed. "Because I might."

Hillary squeezed his arm. "No matter what happens tonight, Jamie, you're doing a pretty amazing thing here."

He looked away. "It's not amazing. It's what I should've done a long time ago."

"Still."

A man dressed as a waiter appeared at her side. "Ma'am, we've set up the bar in the back, but we aren't sure about its visibility."

Hillary nodded. "I'll be right back."

He watched as she strode off and then turned his attention to the photos on the wall. Images that had been painful to print stared back at him. Men whose faces were etched in his mind, frozen in time and on display. Would it ease the pain of his regret?

Would it ease the pain of their loss?

The day he'd left Nantucket, something inside told him it was time to put Africa behind him. It was painful, and there were still days it haunted him, thinking that his actions had led to such tragedy and pain. But he was learning, slowly, to forgive himself. He only prayed that the people who would be attending that night would forgive him too.

But even if they didn't—even if Emma didn't—this would be his last act of repentance.

It was time to live again.

He buttoned his jacket and straightened a photo of Cam, Freddy, and the others, arms draped around each other, looking every bit the brothers they were.

"Lord," he whispered, "let this be a night of healing. Not just for me, but for these men and their families. For all of them."

He'd been praying a lot over the last several weeks. His conversations with God had started out angry, but eventually they'd found a little bit of common ground. He'd read something that stuck with him—*You either believe God is for you or you don't*—and he realized he wanted to believe that he was. He wanted to believe in a God who was good, and while he'd blamed himself for what had happened in Africa, he'd also blamed God for allowing it.

Why would a good God let good men die?

He knew any question that started with *why* would only frustrate him. He'd never know the answers, but if he believed God was for him, he had to believe that good could still come from pain.

Maybe tonight would be a sliver of good.

Hillary rushed through the space, past him, and into the back room just as the door at the main entrance opened and a couple walked in. He recognized the man as Mike Bouchard, one of the soldiers in the unit. His prosthetic leg was hidden underneath a pair of dress pants, and his limp was barely noticeable.

When he found Jamie's eyes, a broad grin stretched across his face.

And Jamie's nerves settled a little. This man had been there, also caught in the hell that rained down on them that day. Yet here he was, smiling. At Jamie.

Mike hurried over and stuck his hand out. Jamie shook it, surprised by the knot of emotion tied at the back of his throat.

"Didn't know if I'd ever see you again," Mike said. "How you been, man?"

"Good," Jamie said. "You?"

Mike filled him in on his latest, introduced him to his wife, and then asked what exactly they were doing there.

"You'll see," Jamie said.

The door opened and an older couple walked in. Then another. Soon the room had filled with people—some familiar, many strangers. Jamie worked his way around the space, knowing that in just a few minutes he'd have to call for everyone's attention so he could explain just what this art show was really about.

He kept one eye on the door as he chatted, but so far, no sign of Emma.

The waiters and waitresses moved through the room with appetizers and champagne for the toast he planned to give, and behind him, curtains concealed the images and faces and frozen moments in time that the people in this room could appreciate more than anyone else.

Hillary caught his eye from the opposite side of the space. She pointed to her wrist, likely aware that Jamie was stalling. *Just one more minute. What if she's on her way here?*

The door opened again. It wasn't Emma, but he did recognize the couple who entered. Jerry and Nadine Woodson.

His skin went hot at the sight of them. Where was Emma?

He wove through the crowd, and when he reached them, Jerry's face lit in recognition, Nadine's softening in what appeared to be pity.

That's when he realized Emma wasn't coming. That's when he
knew that while he'd said he was doing this for all of them, really he
was doing this for her.

"Jamie." Jerry shook his hand. "It's so good to see you again."

Had Emma told them the truth of who he was?

"It's good to see you both again, too," Jamie said.

Nadine gathered him into her trademark hug, so tight it almost
knocked him off-balance. She pulled back, tears in her eyes, and
smiled at him.

"How've you been?" he asked.

"We've been well," Jerry said. He looked around the space, rec-
ognizing some of the people in the room. "Anxious to find out what
we're all doing here."

Jamie forced a smile. "Hopefully you'll be pleased."

Nadine clapped her hands over his. "I'm sorry Emma couldn't
make it."

Jamie's stomach dropped. At least now he knew. "Oh, it's okay."

But it wasn't okay. It wasn't the least bit okay.

Jerry's eyes were kind. "I told her that if I ever saw you again, I'd
tell you one thing."

He braced himself for what was sure to be a bitter, angry word
that he very much deserved.

"She told me the whole story," he said. "What happened that day."

"So you know—"

"That our son saved your life?" The wrinkles around his eyes
deepened. "Yes."

Jamie stilled at the mention of Cam's sacrifice.

"And we know that you've been carrying around a lot of guilt over
that fact," Jerry said. "But we're here to tell you that we know our
son. And we are certain that if he had it to do over again, he wouldn't
have changed a thing. He did what he was trained to do. And we're
proud of him for it."

Nadine still had hold of Jamie's hand. She squeezed it.

"He was a good soldier," she said. "A brave man. And it was his honor to serve and protect."

Jamie tried—failed—to swallow the lump in his throat. Military families were some of the most amazing people he'd ever met. "I'm so sorry," he managed.

"He died doing something he believed in," Jerry said. "The best thing you can do is honor him by living your life to the fullest."

Jamie nodded. He hadn't been doing that. He would do better— for Cam and the other men who'd died or been injured that day.

"Jamie," Jerry said, "it wasn't your fault, what happened. But if you need to hear someone say it, then hear me now. We forgive you."

At that, Jamie broke.

Nadine pulled him into another hug, and he forced himself to breathe. He had to speak in a moment—he needed to pull it together.

"Thank you," he whispered. "Thank you both."

"Jamie." It was Hillary, undoubtedly aware that they were behind schedule.

Jamie stepped away and pressed his palms into his eyes, embarrassed at the show of emotion. "If you'll excuse me."

Cam's parents both nodded, and Jamie followed Hillary to the back room.

"You ready?" Hillary asked.

He shook his head. "She's not coming."

"But a whole lot of other people did come," she said. "And this matters as much to them as it would've to Emma."

He nodded. She was right. This was about more than one widow, no matter how precious that one widow was to him.

It was time to put the past to rest. Once and for all.

# CHAPTER FORTY-THREE

~~~

EMMA STOOD ON THE SIDEWALK OUTSIDE an old warehouse in the middle of Chicago, holding Jamie's invitation and trying to find the will to walk inside.

She'd returned from the Cape with a new resolve, and when she found the card in her mail, she'd tucked it away, determined to forget about it.

But as the date drew near, she couldn't shake the idea that she needed to be here.

Now, though, she wondered if she'd misunderstood her gut instinct. At her side, CJ, dressed in gray dress pants, a button-down shirt, and an adorable tie held in place by a circle of elastic, fidgeted. "Are we going inside?"

She took his hand. "Yes."

He gave her hand a tug. "Let's go!"

He didn't know what they were doing here. He didn't know that Jamie was only a single flight of stairs away. He didn't know that she didn't have the strength to face whatever it was he was planning to unveil.

He only knew they were on an adventure.

They walked inside the building, and Emma located the staircase. She felt like she was moving in slow motion as she opened the door and made her way to the second floor. Before they walked out, she stopped and knelt in front of CJ.

"CJ, I need you to be on your very best behavior," she said.

He nodded.

"Like, your *very* best." She looked into his big brown eyes and smiled. "This is a grown-up event we're going to, and it's important that you behave."

"I will, Mommy."

They walked into a hallway and followed the sound of voices into a room full of people, many of whom she knew. None of them were Jamie.

Elise and May rushed straight to her side as soon as they spotted her.

"We thought you weren't coming," Elise said.

Emma gave them a lame smile. "Surprise."

May squeezed her free hand. "It's good you're here."

Emma wasn't so sure. "Do we actually know what we're doing here?"

They shook their heads in unison. "But I think we're about to find out."

Cam's parents stood on the other side of the room. Jerry caught her eye and winked. He probably thought she'd made great strides by being here. She didn't have the heart to disappoint him with the truth—curiosity had led her through the door. Not some great sense of forgiveness or a willingness to move on, though she was working on both of those things.

Since returning to the island, she'd had a lot of time to think. And she'd finally (mostly) made peace with her past. She'd created a new life, and she intended to live it.

She'd laid down the pain of her mistakes, knowing it was time.

Now she was working on trading sorrow for joy. It's what Cam would want. She understood now that his sacrifice was freely given, and Jerry was right—he'd do the same thing all over again, even if he knew the outcome.

It hurt sometimes to think about it, but not as much as it used to.

The crowd began to quiet and everyone's attention was drawn toward the front of the makeshift lobby area. When she saw Jamie facing the crowd, Emma was thankful for a tall man to hide behind.

When he had everyone's attention, Jamie cleared his throat. She imagined he wasn't excited about talking in front of a crowd, but there he was, doing it anyway.

A wave of admiration rolled through her. In the space of the weeks away from him, the empathy she'd worked so hard against had found its way back to her, and somehow it had replaced the anger she'd been holding tightly with both hands.

"I want to thank you all for coming tonight," Jamie said. "Especially with so few details. It means a lot to me to see you all here." He paused. "Five years ago, I had the great honor to work alongside some of the bravest men I've ever known. While they served a protective detail of high-ranking American diplomats, I chronicled their lives. I expected my photos to reflect how seriously the men took their jobs. I didn't know that they would also reflect a deep sense of pride, bravery, and love.

"Over the course of those two weeks, I had a chance to get to know the men personally. I became friends with Freddy Winters, who the other men nicknamed 'Lover Boy' because he had a baby face that charmed women who didn't even speak the same language."

Soft laughter rolled through the group. Emma squeezed May's hand, and she smiled. It didn't hurt so much to remember Freddy now. Look how far they'd come.

"I played cards with the guys and learned that Mike Bouchard always has an ace up his sleeve—literally." More laughter.

"And I witnessed firsthand that Cam Woodson was the kind of leader every unit should have. Selfless. Fearless. And he loved his family more than anything else in the world."

Now May squeezed Emma's hand, and she realized it didn't hurt so much to talk about Cam anymore either.

"We all know how the tour ended—in tragedy," Jamie said. "And we've all mourned what we lost that day. Many of us have spent years blaming ourselves, replaying what we could've done differently, wishing for a Rewind button. I know I have." He paused. "But life doesn't work that way, and I suppose we all have to make peace with that. I'm still trying to do that."

Slowly Emma shifted, daring to look through the crowd, risking being seen.

"I had the idea to write letters to the families of the men we lost out there," he went on. "A way of making amends. But recently I realized that I wanted to share more than words. I wanted to share the moments I captured over there. To create a space, just for you, to remember, and maybe to put to rest, the pain of that tragedy."

Emma watched as Jamie's face twisted, sparking the empathy inside her again.

He'd beaten himself up for years over this. They both had. It was time to move on.

He lifted his chin as if guided by an unseen force and looked straight into her eyes. His face froze as if trying to determine if he was seeing something that wasn't there.

A rope of electricity held them in place as the seconds ticked by. He said nothing. Only stared. At her.

Finally she broke contact and looked around at the crowd as if to remind him he was supposed to be talking. After a beat, his gaze fell to the floor.

"Sorry," he said. "I lost my place." Another pause. "The images have been arranged in a specific order. When we pull the curtains back, you'll want to start on your left and work your way down the side, around the back, and over to the right." He motioned as he spoke the directions, then found Emma's eyes again. "My hope is that through these images, you'll have an even deeper understanding of the brave sacrifices that were made that day. That you'll share the stories of the men we lost and the friendships we found. That somehow, something good can come out of this unspeakable tragedy we all lived through—and maybe we'll all find the peace we've been looking for."

Emma didn't need to look around to know she wasn't the only one crying.

May tucked a tissue in her hand as Hillary pulled the curtain open and the crowd began to move. Emma stayed in place as her in-laws walked over.

"Can we take CJ?" Nadine asked knowingly.

Emma nodded.

"We'll catch up with you in a bit," Elise said as she and May walked off.

The crowd in the space outside the exhibit had thinned, and when she turned, she found Jamie standing only a few yards away. He seemed to be asking permission to approach her, and she remembered what Hillary had said about him being a gentleman.

His motives had been good from the start—she understood that now.

She walked toward him but couldn't speak.

"I thought you weren't coming," he said.

Her throat had gone dry. "I wasn't going to. I *really* wasn't going to, but I thought it would be good for CJ. I had a feeling what this was all about."

His hands were in his pockets, and he looked broken and out of sorts.

"I can't believe you put this whole thing together," she said, trying to lighten the mood. "Do the Heywards know?"

He smiled shyly. "They helped secure the space. I'm working on a new show, but it's a lot harder without you." He stuttered as if realizing he'd said something incorrect. "I mean, without your help."

She smiled.

"And without you." He inhaled. "Everything is harder without you."

She looked past him and spotted CJ, holding Jerry's hand and staring at one of the photos.

"Will this show be open to the public?" she asked.

He shook his head. "This one is just for the people in this room and the ones who couldn't make it tonight."

She knew that any one of his images could fetch a decent amount of money. He was forfeiting that in favor of their feelings.

*He's a very good man.*

"Jamie, I wanted to apologize," she said. "For the way I acted that day in the hotel."

He shook his head. "Don't."

"No, it was selfish of me," she said. "It took me a little while to understand that what happened over there didn't only happen to me. It felt like that for a long time. Me and May and Alicia Birch."

"Jimmy's widow."

She nodded. The other woman who'd lost a husband that day. Alicia had relocated overseas—her way of putting it all behind her, Emma assumed. Emma had heard she'd remarried and had a baby. She'd moved on.

Emma had not.

"I held on to that tragedy like it was mine alone," she said. "But it was yours to mourn too. I see that now."

He watched her so intently she felt it at the backs of her knees. "Thanks for that."

"I'm trying to move on," she said. "And I think part of it is accepting that bad things happen sometimes. And it's nobody's fault."

She saw that he wanted to protest. He firmly believed his actions had caused Cam's death—but he didn't argue. Clearly he was trying to put it behind him too.

"Emma," he said.

She gave him her full attention.

"Can we start over?"

Did that mean they had to erase everything that had gone before? Because some parts of their relationship were worth holding on to.

He held his hand out to her. She slid hers inside, and with that single touch, everything that was broken between them suddenly didn't feel so impossible to mend. Her skin tingled and her pulse quickened at the connection.

"Emma Woodson, my name is Jamie Shaw, and I was embedded with your husband's unit in Congo five years ago."

His hand tightened slightly around hers.

"I blame myself for your husband's death," Jamie said, sadness in his eyes. "I blame myself because it was my fault. He was a hero—and he saved my life."

He hooked the thumb of his free hand under her chin and lifted her gaze to his. "I'm sorry for what you lost that day. I'm sorry that it was him and not me. I'm sorry that I betrayed your trust. And I'm determined to make it up to you—if it takes me the rest of my life."

Emma went still, every nerve in her body on high alert. "It's good to meet you, Jamie. I've learned a lot over the past few months. Mainly that my husband's sacrifice was his to make, and I'm proud of him for making it. I miss him, and I'll always love him. And I've learned that living my very best life is the best way to honor his memory." She drew in a deep breath. "And I know my best life would be the one I would live with you."

It was like someone hit the Pause button on the rest of the room, and it was only the two of them and the beating of their hearts.

"You mean . . . ?"

The hopefulness in his eyes undid her. She laugh-sobbed and covered her face with her hands.

"You forgive me?" Jamie asked.

She looked at him again. "Don't get me wrong, Shaw—you *really* messed up. But yeah, I forgive you. I sort of even get why you did what you did. I tried to convince myself I could pretend we never met and move on, but I couldn't do it. I love you too much."

He smiled. "You still love me."

She laughed. "Against my better judgment, yes."

He pulled her closer and took her face in his hands. "Emma, if you let me, I will love you until the day I die."

She smiled. "I guess I'd be okay with that."

He shook his head as if marveling at the strange turn of events.

"Are you going to kiss me?" she asked.

"Do you want me to kiss you?"

Her gaze lingered, then dipped to his lips. "I want you to kiss me every day for the rest of my life."

"If that's a challenge, then I accept." He leaned down, his lips grazing hers softly, sweetly, as if she were something to be savored. As if he believed her to be more of a treasure than she ever felt she was.

His hands wound around her waist, and he pulled her body nearer, tighter, as if he couldn't get close enough. He studied her eyes, like he wanted to mark this moment in time, like he never wanted to forget how she felt the day she decided to believe in love again.

He watched her as he kissed her again and again, and the rest of the world fell away as she realized she never wanted to forget the day she decided to believe in love again either.

Her thoughts spun as she silently thanked God for second chances, vowing to spend every single day proving her love to this man, a gift she didn't deserve, an answer to a prayer she'd been too foolish to pray. She might not be worthy, but she was forgiven, and that, along with the gift of Jamie's love, were things she would never take for granted.

He leaned back and studied her, a smile playing at the corners of his mouth. "You've got my heart, Emma Woodson."

She kissed him again. "And I promise to take good care of it."

# EPILOGUE

EMMA STOOD AT THE GRAVESITE, looking down at the stone she'd helped pick out in the hazy days that followed Cam's death.

Jamie had taken CJ back to the car, giving her the moment alone that he must've sensed she needed.

He'd decided to relocate to Nantucket, and he'd already secured a small cottage with a usable office space. And while life could always throw another curveball, she thought they had a real shot at being happy. Genuinely, sweetly, wonderfully happy.

Cam had given them that gift.

And now she would give him the only gift she had to give.

She knelt down and wiped a leaf from the headstone, aware that the pain she felt was more of a dull ache than a sharp stab. Time healed wounds, to be sure, though she imagined she would always have the scar.

"Cam," she said quietly, "I don't know where to begin." She drew in a breath. "I've learned more in the last few months about the kind of man you were than in all the years I knew you when you were alive.

You were incredible. So brave and strong. And I hate what I did to you. You didn't deserve it. I was selfish, and I convinced myself that you didn't care about the babies we'd lost, about the way it made me feel. I know now that wasn't true at all. You cared so much you couldn't process it. I see that now."

A tear slid down her cheek, and she wiped it away.

"I've been beating myself up over what happened between us before you left," she said. "Wondering if I made a mistake telling you or if you'd ever forgive me. I think we would've worked it out. Not just for CJ, but for us, because when we were good, we were really good. And because we were worth fighting for."

She reached into her bag and pulled out a single sheet of paper. The lab results.

"I know it's a little late now, but I still wanted to make sure you knew that your son was definitely your son." She set the page down on the headstone, as if he could read it. "Every time I see him smile, I see you. And those eyes . . . and that mischievous streak is definitely from you." She laughed thinking about it. "He's a good boy, Cam, and I'm going to make sure he knows what a good man his daddy was. I promise you that."

She glanced back at the car, where Jamie stood, his attention split between her and her son, concern clear on his face.

"Then there's Jamie," she said. "I've been thinking lately that you saved his life and in so many ways, he saved mine. I hope it doesn't hurt you to hear that." She bowed her head as she spoke. "I will never stop loving you, Cam. A part of me lies here with you, and it always will, but I know I need to start living again, and I just wanted to let you know. Thank you for being so brave. Thank you for showing me what sacrifice looks like, for living and dying with honor. You inspire me, Cam. I pray you rest in peace."

She stayed still for a long moment and then finally pushed to her feet.

She walked slowly back to the car, back to CJ and Jamie, back to the promise of a new beginning.

As she stepped into his embrace, she cherished the strong arms that held her, and for the first time in a very long time, she felt the ease of a burden she'd been shouldering, a burden she needed to lay down.

And she believed—really believed—that she'd been forgiven.

For that, she was truly grateful.

# PROLOGUE

*Dear Mr. Boggs,*

*It's been five years since you died, and I've thought about you every single day since. If I close my eyes, I can imagine I'm ten years old and you're down at the beach building sandcastles with me and Cody.*

*None of the other parents ever wanted to play with us, but you were always more than willing. I mean, you couldn't have actually liked being buried to your neck in sand . . . but you let us do it. You even smiled for pictures like that.*

*I can't help but think that what happened was my fault. At least indirectly. I mean, don't get me wrong, I hate it in movies when people seem so broken up with guilt over something that's clearly not their fault—but what happened to you kind of was my fault, wasn't it?*

*Is it any wonder that I wish I could take it back? I wish I could say I'm sorry. I wish I could rewind and change everything about that night. I hurt you. I hurt Cody. I hurt Mrs. Boggs and Marley. I even hurt my own parents because the moment they told us you were gone, everything changed. It was like we'd been plummeted into a jar of molasses, like we were moving in slow motion, swimming through a thick cloud of sorrow.*

*Will the cloud ever go away? Will it always hang here, a sad reminder that the choice of a foolish girl could impact so many lives, destroy so many friendships?*

*I don't know. And I don't know why I'm writing. I know you'll never read these words. It helps, though, at least a little bit. It makes me feel better putting it out there into the world, the fact that I'm so horribly sorry for what I've done.*

*I pray one day you can forgive me. I pray one day you will all forgive me.*

*Love,*
*Louisa*

# CHAPTER ONE

This wasn't supposed to happen.

Not that there was time to think about it now. Not with the waves growing and the wind blowing and her paddle floating away, pulled out to sea by a storm she hadn't seen coming.

Louisa Chambers inhaled a sharp breath as the water swelled and a wave crashed over her head. Her legs kicked against the water of Nantucket Sound as she heaved her body up onto the paddleboard.

So much for a quiet morning out on the water.

She sighed. Her father would be so angry with her if she died paddleboarding.

"How many times have I told you to wear a life vest?" he'd say. "You don't challenge death, kitten."

He still called her kitten. She might actually miss that if she died.

She knew all too well the realities of death—she didn't need reminding. But maybe death needed to know she wasn't scared of it.

*I'm not scared. I'm strong. I'm stronger than I look.*

Again she willed herself to stay calm. Her paddle was officially gone.

She wasn't far from Madaket Beach—she'd hang on to her board and kick her way back. It was early, just after sunrise, but someone would be up soon. Mr. Dallas with his golden retriever, maybe. Or one of the McGuires.

But the wind intensified and pushed her in the wrong direction, sending her into deeper, choppier waters. The shoreline stretched on forever, and the water kept moving her farther and farther away from it.

Her hand slipped off the paddleboard, and she gasped as a wave smacked her in the face.

*How many times have I told you to wear a life vest?*

Her dad's voice echoed in her ear—louder this time—and rightfully so. She should've listened. She should've—*whack*. Another wave, this one bringing with it a mouthful of water. She spit it out and struggled back to her board, barely latching on to it as the current kicked up again.

She coughed, white-knuckling the paddleboard and scanning the shore, the horizon, the open sea.

*Nothing.*

That was when she began to realize she might actually be in danger. That was when she thought, *I could die out here.*

Who would handle the Timmons anniversary party if she died? How would she ever show Eric she was completely over him—even though, in reality, she wasn't sure she was? Who would water that stupid houseplant her mother had sent over from Valero and Sons "because you need practice keeping something alive if you're ever going to have children"?

She wanted to have children, so she needed to make sure that plant lived.

She draped her torso over the paddleboard and tried not to think about sharks. She tried to think about something happier.

*Beaches on Nantucket Close after at Least a Dozen Shark Sightings.*

It was the headline of an article she'd stumbled across online only two weeks prior. Were the sharks gone? Were they circling her at that exact moment?

And then, all of a sudden, the image of a smiling Daniel Boggs flittered through her mind.

*Is this how you felt, Mr. Boggs?*

That image had no business haunting her, not now when she'd been doing so well. But a wave tossed her forward, and she barely managed to hold on to the board, so she closed her eyes and prayed.

Because right about now, she needed a miracle.

Mr. Boggs had probably prayed for the same thing and look how that had turned out.

Maybe this was what she deserved. Maybe this was payback for what she'd done. Maybe this was God's way of reminding her that actions had consequences.

Actions like not wearing a life vest. Or breaking someone's heart.

She'd been working how many years to try to make amends for her mistakes? Would it ever be enough? Would forgiveness ever come?

It occurred to her that on normal days she was excellent at pushing these thoughts away. In fact, most days she didn't even have to work at it.

Apparently being faced with the end of one's life resulted in this. A deep dive into all the things she'd been successfully avoiding. As if there weren't more important things to be thinking about. Like staying alive.

If only she had a single clue how to do that.

"God, I'm pretty sure I don't deserve to be rescued, and I'm not in the habit of asking for help, which I'm sure you know. But it would be super awesome if you could maybe shift the wind and give me a push toward the shore."

The waves just kept pulling her deeper and farther away.

She supposed miracles were in high demand these days. And maybe it simply wasn't her turn. She clung to the board as fear welled up inside her. Panic buzzed somewhere down deep, and she tried to keep it from overtaking her.

She'd make a list like she always did to help sort out her anxiety.

A wave swelled, and she let out a scream (and she really was not the screaming type, so it surprised even her), but the water settled her back down, and somehow she still had hold of the board.

A list. Okay . . . what to list? *Things to do* seemed a bit pointless given her current situation.

Another swell, and she swallowed a mouthful of water. She coughed—hard—then drew in a clean breath.

> *Things I wish I'd done in my life. A bucket list made moments*
> *before my impending death.*
> - *I wish I'd worn a life vest.*
> - *I wish I'd checked the weather forecast.*
> - *I wish I had put on waterproof mascara (because when they find*
>   *my body, it would be nice not to look so dead).*
> - *I wish I hadn't wasted so much time on Eric Anderson.*
> - *I wish I'd said I was sorry.*
> - *I wish I'd mailed the letters.*
> - *I wish I'd made it to my golden birthday.*

After all, she'd spent twelve years wondering if he'd show. Or maybe that pact had been long forgotten, sucked down to the depths like dirt down a drain.

The next wave enveloped Louisa completely, heaving her under for so many seconds she was certain she'd lost the way back up and into the air. But no, another toss and there it was again—glorious oxygen.

She inhaled a sharp breath and coughed.

*I wish I'd fallen in love.*

She looked up at the sky, which had turned gray and dark. She hadn't realized she had so many regrets. Her teeth chattered and she started to tire. These waves were kicking her butt. She'd practically resigned herself to dying when she spotted a headlight—a boat out in the sound.

She tried to lift her arm, but it was so heavy. She tried hauling herself onto the board, but she didn't have the strength. Maybe she wasn't doing as well as she thought. Maybe she'd already half died. She looked for a white light in the sky but saw nothing.

Maybe white lights were only for people who weren't responsible for someone else's death.

She'd never get over that as long as she lived, though it seemed that might not be much longer. Unless someone in that boat was the answer to her prayer.

She had to stay awake. She had to hold on. They had to see her. *Please see me.*

The boat cut through the water, tossing in the wind, and again Louisa tried to wave.

*I wish I'd fallen in love.*

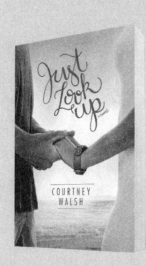

# A NOTE FROM THE AUTHOR

DEAR READER,

I've been carrying this novel around in my head and my heart for a very, very long time. In fact, it was one of the first ideas I ever had, but the timing never quite worked out for me to write it. I'm so very thankful that changed.

Emma and Jamie's story is a rare one, one that poured straight out of me so fast I don't think I could've stopped it. It was the kind of story that felt like a gift from God, like he cracked open my skull and dropped it inside. Not all books are like that. Most, in fact, are not. More often, there is a lot of angst, a lot of toiling, a lot of frustration, a lot of my husband asking, "How much longer until you turn this book in?"

But this one, for whatever reason, just made sense to me from the start. The characters jumped out of my head and onto the page, and I felt every bit of what they felt. Their pain, their elation, their joy, their hope, their shame. All of it. It all made sense to me.

Maybe because these are universal emotions. Maybe our need to be forgiven and our need to forgive other people burrows down so deep that we feel it on a soul level. Both of the main characters in this story were dealing with this in one way or another, and I really enjoyed the chance to explore this theme through their stories.

Writing is an escape for me. There's nothing like getting lost in another world, especially on the days when the real world feels a little too dark. I truly hope you find my books to be a source of light and hope in your life.

I would absolutely love to have you join my Facebook group, Courtney Walsh's Reader Room, or follow me on Instagram (@courtneywalsh), where I spend far too much time! And don't forget to sign up for my newsletter via my website, courtneywalshwrites.com, for all the latest news. I'd love to stay connected and I love to make new friends. I've been writing now for a handful of years, and I can honestly say that my readers are some of the very best people in the world.

I truly hope you enjoyed reading *What Matters Most* as much as I enjoyed writing it. Thank you so much for taking the time to read it. It means the world to me. I'm so, so thankful to you for being a part of my journey, for allowing me to share my stories with you, and for making my days brighter and so much more fun.

*Courtney*

# ACKNOWLEDGMENTS

AFTER A FEW YEARS OF WRITING, you begin to learn that your circle changes. People you thought were forever on the inside move to the fringes. Other people step in slowly and magically become a part of your life in a way that you never saw coming. Parts of my circle have changed. Other parts have stayed wonderfully consistent. And without the support and encouragement from these people, I would never finish a book.

Adam. For leaving me alone when I need you to. For not leaving me alone when I don't. For brainstorming, encouragement, and the occasional "tough love." You + me.

My kids, Sophia, Ethan, and Sam. I know you're basically self-sufficient these days, and I appreciate that this means extra writing time for me, but I also love the moments when you make me feel needed. And I'm so very proud of each one of you.

Katie Ganshert and Becky Wade. Truer friends have never been. I'm so thankful for our long chats, the brainstorming, the many laughs, and the constant gift of your friendship. So thankful God brought us all together.

Carrie Erikson. Just because you're my favorite sister, and I've still never found a single person who can make me laugh as hard as you can.

My parents, Bob and Cindy Fassler. For the support. The encouragement. The friendship. I am so thankful to you both.

Melissa Tagg and Deborah Raney. For your friendship, kindness, and support. I'm so thankful you are both a part of my journey.

Natasha Kern. For being a valued partner in an ever-changing world of publishing. I'm so grateful for your wisdom and guidance.

Rel Mollett. Thank you for being such a huge help and encouragement to me.

For our Studio families. For being such a huge, wonderful, important part of our life. You guys are some of the best people in the world, and I'm so glad to know you.

Stephanie Broene, Kathy Olson, and the entire team at Tyndale. For creating a space for my stories and always working so hard to make them better. I am forever grateful.

# DISCUSSION QUESTIONS

1. To help Emma move beyond her grief, her friend Elise helps her create a list of things she wants to do. How can a list of goals or dreams be helpful? Are there any drawbacks to creating a list like this? How did it help Emma?

2. Emma and Jamie's first meeting involves a misunderstanding. How would their relationship have been different if Emma had known why Jamie was really there? Should Jamie have tried harder to set the record straight? Have you ever had to clarify something with a friend or loved one when it would have been easier to let it slide?

3. Emma and Jamie both have supportive family and friends, including mature Christians who speak truth to them. Do you have a helpful support network? What are some things you can do to help develop and strengthen these kinds of relationships?

4. Emma moves to Nantucket for a second chance. She hopes to make a better life for her son, even though she doesn't believe she deserves anything for herself. Have you ever been motivated to make a change for someone you care about, even more than for your own benefit? Why is it often easier to take others' well-being into account than to make our own needs and wishes a priority?

5. Emma and Jamie are both artists who have set aside their art for personal reasons. Do you have a talent or interest that you're currently not pursuing? What's standing in your way? How important is it that we use whatever special abilities we may have?

6. Jamie doesn't think he could have PTSD since he isn't in the military. Do you agree with him? Have you or someone you love experienced PTSD?

7. Jamie's therapist suggests he write letters to the people he believes he has hurt as part of processing his feelings. Have you ever written not-to-be-delivered letters or used journaling to work through something? How is this helpful? What is hard or challenging about it?

8. Jamie and Emma both know, intellectually, that God forgives sin when we repent and ask for his forgiveness (see 1 John 1:8-9). Why do both of them struggle with accepting God's forgiveness and moving beyond their feelings of guilt? How have you seen this struggle play out in your own life or the life of someone you care about? Why do our emotions sometimes contradict what we know to be true?

9. If overthinking was an Olympic sport, Emma says she'd have more gold medals than Michael Phelps. Is overthinking an issue for you? What kinds of things set it off, and how have you learned to deal with it? Or if you don't experience this yourself, what advice would you give someone who does?

10. Emma's father-in-law tells her, "It's awful hard to lose someone you love. But moving on is a natural part of life. Doesn't mean you forget the person you loved. Doesn't even mean you stop loving them. Just means you stay among the living." Do you agree with his advice? What are some of the things that make it hard to move on after a significant loss? What might make it easier?

11. Were you surprised when you found out what it was that Emma felt so guilty about? Can you relate to her fear of the consequences of her actions, even after God has forgiven her? How does Emma finally break free from her guilt and shame?

12. At the end of the story, Jamie has decided to relocate to Nantucket, and Emma believes they have a real chance at being happy. What changes and growth do you see in both of them that support this hope? What challenges will they still have to face as time passes? Did this feel like a satisfying ending for the book?

# ABOUT THE AUTHOR

COURTNEY WALSH is a *New York Times* and *USA Today* bestselling author. She writes small-town romance and women's fiction while juggling the performing arts studio and youth theatre she owns and runs with her husband. Courtney is a Carol Award winner and Christy Award finalist who has also written two craft books and several full-length musicals. She lives in Illinois with her husband and three children and a sometimes-naughty Bernedoodle named Luna.

Visit her online at courtneywalshwrites.com.

# TYNDALE HOUSE PUBLISHERS IS CRAZY4FICTION!

## Fiction that entertains and inspires

Get to know us! Become a member of the Crazy4Fiction community. Whether you read our blog, like us on Facebook, follow us on Twitter, or receive our e-newsletter, you're sure to get the latest news on the best in Christian fiction. You might even win something along the way!

## JOIN IN THE FUN TODAY.

 crazy4fiction.com

 Crazy4Fiction

 crazy4fiction

 @Crazy4Fiction

By purchasing this book from Tyndale, you have
helped us meet the spiritual and physical needs of
people all around the world.

Tyndale | Trusted. For Life.